1N SEARCH OF THE LOST

SOME THINGS SHOULD NEVER BE FOUND...

THOMAS W PELTIER

This is Ben, the last known living Tasmanian Tiger. According to unverified reports, Ben died in Tasmania at the Hobart Zoo on September 7th, 1936. In Search of the Lost is dedicated to Ben, and all other species of wildlife that have been ill-fated due to mankind. They may be lost, but never forgotten...

Many people have questioned the validity as to whether Ben truly died on that fateful day in September.

Perhaps the contents of this book contain what really happened...

PRESENT DAY
Egypt

THE CAMERA ZOOMED IN ON A MAN STANDING ATOP THE ELEVATED river bank overlooking the Nile River. When the lens hit its mark, he began to speak.

"Welcome to Wild Encounters, I'm Connor Williams." Connor tilted his faded leather Jacaru hat just enough to block the sun from his eyes, casting a heavy shadow across four days of black stubble. A sweaty brown shemagh covered the back of his neck and hung low across his chest.

Forty yards north, along the same bank, the rotting carcass of a bloated hippo baked under the scorching sun, its putrid aroma stagnating everything within the vicinity. Connor could taste the overpowering sour decay but was un-phased. He walked along the bank, paying close attention to every grounded step with cobras thick along this stretch of river.

He placed strategic steps upon rock after crumbling rock. His eyes danced from the ground then back toward the camera. "The Nile monitor is a huge predator reaching lengths of nearly eight feet. They have extremely powerful jaws, serrated teeth for slicing meat and large powerful claws. They're excellent swimmers, usually found around water and they'll dive deep the second they feel any danger. And speaking of danger...this is territory of the Nile crocodile. Nile monitors and the

1

infamous Nile Crocodile share the same waterways, so if I end up in the water with a Nile monitor, I'm in the water with man-eating crocs as well."

Connor slid down the six-foot embankment and stood on the sandy bank at the water's edge. "Nile crocodiles are extremely aggressive and won't hesitate to eat a human. In fact, Nile crocodiles are responsible for over three hundred human fatalities along this river every year. Local villagers rely on this river for drinking water, bathing, fishing, and the kids even play here. If a croc is in the area it'll approach silently, undetectable just under the water's surface, waiting for an opportune moment and just when you least expect it, bam! He comes powering at you full speed and then smash!" Connor slapped his hands together. "He grabs you with his bone splintering jaws and then he'll drag you out there…" He pointed toward the middle of the river. "…into deeper water, never to be seen again." He paused, eyes scanning the water, contemplating the danger. "So that's what we're up against."

The glaring sun reflected off the water, forcing his eyes into a squint. He looked back at the camera, and with a bit of arrogance, dropped his trademark catchphrase. "This *could* be dangerous."

An hour later, the host and crew were aboard their hired vessel and moving upstream. Connor steadied himself on the fiberglass bow of the boat as they patrolled the steep mud banks for the giant lizards. "It's about 10 a.m. and already ninety degrees. We're on the river just north of the Sudan border in Abu Simbel, Egypt. We're gonna cruise the banks by boat, spot the monitors and then catch them…or at least try. The Nile Monitor is most active in the heat of the day. They're cold blooded, so when their body temperature gets too hot, they dip into the water or the shade to cool down. So they're fairly predictable. They like to climb these rocky bluffs and eat basically anything they can find, usually eggs, baby birds or baby crocs…anything they can overpower."

A sudden bit of movement in the camera's viewfinder caught the attention of George, Connor's longtime cameraman. Utilizing their uncanny ability to communicate without words, he alerted Connor with a slight head nod in its direction.

Connor spotted the monitor high atop the sun hardened river bank and within seconds the boat captain was throttling toward it.

"Keep about fifty feet from the bank…we don't wanna spook 'em," Connor said as he scanned the river's surface for nearby crocs.

The boat careened to a stop, then anchored. Connor placed his right foot on the side wall then looked back at George. "Keep both eyes open."

George nodded, sensing a bit of reluctance in Connor's voice, at the same time the boat captain was shaking his head in disapproval, knowing that giant man-eating reptiles frequently snacked on the local villagers. It was a very bad idea for anyone to be in the river at this location.

Connor lowered himself over the side of the boat and was up to his neck in the tannin-stained water.

The boat captain mumbled in disapproval, still shaking his head, and trying to rationalize the situation in thought. *Almost daily, somewhere along the river, a villager is snatched up and eaten by the crocs and here is an American jumping right in with them. If he dies, I still get paid.*

"Does he have any idea what lives in this river?" The captain peered at George.

"Yup."

"Well what in bloody hell is he thinking getting in the water?" he scolded in his British tinged South African dialect.

"It's what he does."

Connor treaded through the thick brown water in silence, making his way to the bank.

The monitor was barely visible from his position at the water's edge; its long muscular tail was all that could be seen as its body writhed around in a crevice, twenty feet above the waterline, marauding a nest of unlucky egret chicks.

Connor maneuvered his way up the crumbling bank and positioned himself just under the lizard. He started reaching for the monitor when —*hisssssssssss*—coiled within one of the darkened crannies, a Banded Egyptian Cobra flattened its hood and struck at his arm. He jerked away just in time as the snake lunged. Connor grinned. The snake struck again, this time at his face. He dodged the strike but in doing so, lost his footing on the crumbling bank and slid down a couple feet. He looked up and found the pissy snake staring back at him, slithering closer.

"Nice try." He grinned in admiration of its territorial aggression.

Aggravated, the cobra raised its head, and struck down again, but this

3

time Connor was fast. He grabbed the cobra mid-body and with ease, flung it into the water below.

"Sorry about that," he said as the snake smacked the water's surface. It swam back to the bank and slithered off, vanishing into a patch of dry-rotted vegetation.

Connor maneuvered his way back up and centered himself under the lizard still writhing in the crevice. He steadied, positioning himself for the capture, and then lunged at the partially hidden reptile, grabbing its tail just behind the rear legs with his right hand. The lizard panicked and tried to flee but found itself locked in Connor's unbreakable grip. He pulled the startled reptile off the bluff and as he did, it lunged with mouth wide open. Connor managed to dodge the lizard's muscled jaws, but in doing so caused the hardened bank to crumble beneath his feet, forcing him to lose his balance. His feet skidded down the steep bank and he ended up falling backwards into the murky river.

At barely an idle, the captain guided the boat toward Connor. George held the camera in place and scanned the water with his eyes, nervous for the man who had just created a major commotion in the crocodile infested water.

Just as Connor regained his footing on the sandy river bottom, he felt a sharp pain and agonizing pressure on his left wrist. The frustrated lizard had found an opportunity and bit down.

Connor looked up at the camera, now a little more than twenty feet away. "As you can see, these monitors can be a little challenging. He's latched onto my wrist and won't let go. In fact, the more I move or struggle, the harder he clamps down." Connor's faced cringed as the monitor bit down even harder, serrated teeth slicing into his soft flesh. A trail of blood streamed down his forearm toward the elbow.

Connor started wading toward the boat.

George spotted what appeared to be a huge tree trunk about forty feet upstream from their host. "Don't move," he said. George was serious by nature, but now his voice was a little too serious.

"Jesus Christ," the boat captain whispered in despair.

Connor froze. Judging by the tone of George's voice, he knew something deadly was in his direct vicinity.

"Where?" Connor muttered without moving a muscle. He wanted to scan the water for the croc but knew he couldn't move. Connor knew crocodiles were attracted to movement and with one being so close any sudden movement would trigger an explosive ambush attack. He also knew firsthand crocs were drawn to hurt or dying prey splashing around in the water. Right now, he was bleeding and had created quite a ruckus. He was in a very bad situation: in the water with a croc, and another huge lizard's teeth embedded in his arm. At any given moment the lizard could start flailing and thrashing, which would trigger an immediate attack from the croc.

George was emotionless and calculating, conveying coordinates to a machine… "Eighteen-footer, thirty feet down and drifting."

George, a wildlife videographer for over twenty-five years, had developed an adept knowledge of wildlife. It wasn't until he was paired up with Connor Williams, that he began being placed in some very hairy situations. He didn't talk much but when he did it was usually for good reason. George and Connor, together for more than five years, had learned how to *read* each other. George always knew what Connor was thinking and had an uncanny ability to anticipate his next move.

Connor couldn't shrug off the feeling of impending doom rushing over him. The monitor lizard was his first concern, he knew if it started thrashing, which was probable, the situation would turn tragic. With extreme caution he lowered his arm with the lizard still attached, into and under the brown murky water. If it decided to flail about, the water would muffle it to some degree.

"He's getting closer, ten feet," George said, his voice apparently un-phased by the grim situation. He knew it was extremely dangerous but then again, he knew the man in the water wasn't any ordinary human. It was Connor Williams, the man who had been charged by a twelve-hundred-pound Alaskan Kodiak bear while they were filming in Alaska. George filmed the entire showdown. Connor held his ground, unflinching.

This bear could have decapitated him with one swipe of its massive claws, but Connor didn't budge. Instead, he yelled and growled right back at the enormous beast. His vocal attack was so primal and intense that even George found himself unhinged and ready to run. The bear halted its attack and retreated with his head hung low in defeat.

George eyed the croc, watching its massive head glide like an arrow toward its target. "Six feet, Connor." George was nervous, an emotional state almost alien to him.

Connor turned his head toward the massive croc riding the current toward him. He raised his only free hand to the top of his head and lifted off his hat, then looked up at George who was still committed to the camera.

George pulled his head away from the viewfinder and their eyes met. Connor gave a slow nod and winked.

Had Connor just gestured his final goodbye? Or maybe he had some sort of plan? George didn't know what to expect. Instantly his mind created a vision of later that night: sitting together drinking beer and laughing about the entire ordeal. Then he created another; he saw himself explaining to the producers, the only other people close to Connor, that their pride and joy had been ripped apart and eaten by a Nile crocodile.

Connor looked away from George and back at the croc as it closed the gap.

With all the force he could muster, he threw his hat to the side of the crocodile's armored head. The water-soaked leather slammed into the water's surface, causing a splash that triggered the croc's feeding response. The huge gaping jaws that regularly take down adult wildebeests and zebras, snapped violently at the hat, creating a fury of gushing water that cascaded in all directions.

As George filmed the croc's aggressive attack on the hat, he realized Connor was gone. He kept the camera on the croc while his eyes panned over the water. George's head twisted from left to right repeatedly, in a desperate attempt to find his friend. The water became silent and the croc disappeared beneath the surface.

"Don't move the boat," George ordered.

Frustrated, the captain steadied their position. "I didn't sign up for this shit."

Silence hovered and then *WOOSH!* The river erupted into another cascade of water that showered the boat.

George could see the croc's back and tail breaching the surface as it thrashed violently, spinning and jerking. His worst fear was confirmed when the tea colored water swirled with a mixture of red maroon. George didn't know how to react. He just witnessed his friend of five years die by crocodile.

"Oh, God," the captain mumbled.

The spinning swirls of red were undeniable. George set his camera on the deck of the boat and dropped into one of the swiveling seats. He couldn't look at the water, didn't want to see Connor's body being ripped apart and eaten by the croc. Instead he stared at the deck of the boat, listless. George ran his fingers over his thick, grey beard, stroking. "Not this time, Connor, not this time."

"Bloody hell," the captain whispered.

"What do you mean not this time?" A familiar voice came from the outside of the boat.

Baffled, George and the captain looked at each other.

The voice struggled. "Could you give me a hand here?"

George looked toward the back of the boat just in time to see an arm swing over the stern with a huge monitor lizard still attached to it.

"It's really difficult climbing into a boat with one of these damned things."

Speechless, George grabbed Connor's free arm, heaving him over the side and into the boat. George's early years as an army medic kicked in; scanning Connor's body for gashes, rips, tears, missing appendages, or any other life-threatening wounds. George noticed Connor's free hand was covered with dozens of bleeding but superficial lacerations. He knew that wasn't the source of all the blood in the water. *But where the hell had all the blood came from?*

Then George's second instinct took over; he grabbed the camera, pointed it at Connor and gave a nod.

With the lizard still attached to his arm and blood dripping from his hand, Connor looked directly at the camera, smiled, and said, "That was pretty dangerous."

THE BEGINNING OF THE END

Tasmania - August 12th 1931

Emergency Town Meeting,
Theatre Royal, Hobart Tasmania
8 p.m.

CLUSTERS OF PEOPLE WERE STILL PACKING INTO THE DIMLY LIT AND already filled theatre. The smoky auditorium was crammed and alive with overlapping conversations speculating the motive for an emergency meeting. The undecipherable ramblings were silenced by the force of a heavy wooden gavel repeatedly slamming into the walnut podium.

"Alright, alright, would everyone please come to order?" Earl Lincoln, the tall and seemingly well postured lawman called out.

Earl was the town's sheriff, at heart a devoted lawman, but the sheriff in Hobart, Tasmania, under Joe McPherson's rule was nothing more than a well-played chess piece. As a young child, Earl was drawn to the law; the idea of protecting people resonated within him, but with sixteen years badged in Hobart, his faith in the very system he had loved was gone.

At his sworn inception, the good-hearted deputy wanted to take down the known corruption firsthand, but as years passed, pressure hit, and money flashed, it ended up sucking him in. Instead of becoming the proud lawman he strived to be since childhood, Earl became a simple pawn to the powerful. During the first few years, he was resistant and saw himself as the one person that would bring order to Hobart, but instead he became a voiceless contributor to its lawlessness. He was lost to the bottle for the latter part of his early years, but as more and more time passed, the remnant memories of his childhood surfaced. Earl decided to reclaim his dignity and work the law as best he could rather than succumb to the forced dishonesty.

"I'm sure some of you know why this meeting has been called…those of you who don't you'll be filled in soon enough. Mr. McPherson called this meeting together on account of a sudden tragedy."

The theatre erupted in a pandemonium of whispers.

Earl gave the crowd a few seconds to revel in their disgruntled speculations then hammered his gavel. "Order, ORDER!" he called out. "I hereby turn this over to Governor Robinson."

Like most politicians, Governor Robinson was a puppet to the rich, a simple extension of the main contributor to his office, Joe McPherson. He was a great marionette, giving the illusion of decisive control, while behind the curtains those with the real power pulled his strings.

Robinson's spindly body hustled toward Earl. As he took the podium he gave the sheriff an unbalanced smile that shone of something amiss. Earl stepped back and turned over the podium.

"G'day folks…sorry for the short notice, but there seems to be a serious situation that needs immediate tending. I'm sure everyone's been speculating as to what's transpired so now I'll quell the beast. Joe McPherson's prize show horse, Winston, was savagely attacked."

The crowd erupted in a frenzy of heightened chatter. Everyone in town knew of Winston, McPherson's trophy show-horse of royal lineage.

"The tigers were the culprit. I won't get into details, I wasn't there. I'm going to turn this over to Mr. McPherson. Once he speaks I'll conclude and give the state's resolution."

Tasmania; Australia's island state had the façade of a growing land of opportunity, but its core was riddled with corruption and unscrupulous privateers. Disconnected from the mainland, Tasmania's government was able to run amuck, covertly operating with individual interests at the forefront. Hobart was the epicenter, the capital city and heart of it all.

Governor Robinson looked over at Joe McPherson, who was sitting out of view in the left wing of the stage. He nodded to the portly man. "It's all yours, Joe."

Joe Macpherson almost crawled to the podium. His round head hung low, perhaps still in mourning for his show horse, perhaps a ploy to woo the audience. His years of strong-arming, shady business dealings, and profit whoring had honed within him a profound ability to manipulate others into submission with slick word service.

McPherson leaned on the podium and went through exaggerated motions of trying to compose himself. He looked deep into the crowd then took an extended pause. "I've been farming for years, and throughout these years I've always dealt with predators trying to attack my animals." McPherson paused and scanned over the crowd, his beady eyes peering through half swollen alcoholic eyelids. "It started with me chickens…an easy snatch and grab." More than convincing as a speaker, his line deliveries were piercing with bursts of strategic aggression.

Joe McPherson, the wealthiest, most successful, and most feared rancher in Tasmania, would burn children if it meant a bigger profit or instilled to him more control over the island. Being the main supplier of meat and wool, Mighty Joe was the head puppet master pulling the strings of all Hobart's reigning politicians.

Years ago, Joe decided upon hating the Tasmanian tiger for the simple fact that it was a top predator. Top predators can be a threat to livestock, picking off the weakest, youngest or oldest animals. Mighty Joe had a deep seated, irrational fear that sooner or later his farm would come under attack by the savage beasts, chomping down his profits. His ranch had been well established for over twelve years with only a chicken or two gone missing on occasion, which could have been the work of any number of animals.

Three days prior, Joe heard a commotion in his horse barn. One of his most expensive and prized show horses, Winston, had been savagely attacked by what he claimed to be a pack of Tasmanian tigers. Winston's stunning aesthetics coupled with his abilities in the ring gave Joe the impressive façade of being a fine equestrian.

MacPherson never witnessed the attack that night nor did he see any of the attackers, but with a drunkard's rage and ignorance as his fuel, he stormed his politicians, dictated orders, and set forth a chain of events that forever altered the fate of those connected to his wrath.

MacPherson leaned forward on the podium, placing his elbows on the chiseled edge. His fingers ran through the grey and thinning hair that clustered at the back of his balding head. He took a long, deep breath, his face anxious and heavy with distraught, conveying the look of a man who had just lost his best mate. "This went on for the first few years as any farmer would expect, a chicken here…a chicken there. But after the first years these marauding beasts decided a chicken wasn't enough and started eating my sheep!" He threw his infecting words deep into the souls of his audience.

With mashed teeth, his fist pounded the podium. "I've seen with my own eyes the evil and destructive nature of these blood thirsty beasts!" McPherson clenched his fist and slammed it again into the podium. "They ain't even hungry…they just enjoy killing…and as soon as one animal is down they move on to the next. What creature of God could be so bloody evil? The god damned Tasmanian tiger!" he yelled and slammed his fist again into the podium, pausing while the audience erupted into festering cackle of voices. Then Joe interrupted. "Three nights back these bastards broke through me border fences and smashed into my stables." The hatred in his words became contagious, infecting the psyche of the crowd. "They attacked me Winston."

"They ripped at his legs…they ripped and ripped until poor Winston could no longer hold himself up!" The crowd gasped. McPherson looked down at the podium. "My poor Winston lay on the floor, screaming in pain…agony…struggling and kicking, and those bloody bastards…"

He paused and then whimpered. "They began…" He choked up. "…they began to eat him alive." Sobbing as he inhaled, he made a fiery change of tone. "Then me dog gave chase…he ran into the stable and chased 'em straight out into the open pasture. I followed with my rifle, but three or four of them tigers had already turned on him and tore 'em up real bad. I had to shoot me best dog.

"He was ripped apart; I had to put a god-damn bullet in me best dog's head! That dog was my faithful…been with me more than eight years. I had to kill me dog." He sobbed. "So then I ran back to the stable, to my Winston, and I felt so god-damned helpless. He just lay there, gasping for air. I didn't wanna do it, but I had to. I lowered my rifle to his head. I killed my Winston." Joe cried. He looked out into the crowd then paused, holding his expression, giving them a brief but still portrait of anguish with reddened eyes.

McPherson punched his fist into the podium, startling everyone within the theatre. "Death to the god-damned tigers!" He slammed his fist even harder into the podium, stunning the crowd and breaking the skin over his knuckles. A slow trail of blood streamed down his fingers and onto the sloped mahogany.

"These blood thirsty beasts need to be shot on sight. They need to be actively pursued and destroyed. Kill 'em before they bleed your horses, kill 'em before they slaughter your cattle, kill 'em before they run off with your children!" he raged, sending the crowd into a hiss.

"Tigers are worthless vermin!" he yelled over the crowds heated bantering. "They serve no good purpose…cold blooded murderers is what they are. I am proposing a bounty to all those who bring 'em in dead. Five shillings a head."

The crowd erupted into a frenzy. Five shillings was an unheard of amount and at that price, it was an easy opportunity for most to afford a better living. The crowd's mutterings escalated as they carried on. The energy within the room changed; the mourning was over, and opportunity was knocking.

MacPherson looked into the stage wing and nodded at Governor Robinson. The crooked faced politician walked back to the podium, almost apprehensive.

BAM, BAM, BAM. The heavy wooden gavel silenced the crowd. Governor Robinson placed his hands in his pockets, looked down at the podium then back at Joe, who gave an affirming nod as to some unseen backroom agreement.

"The state has agreed to enact a shoot to kill ordinance on all Tigers. We will award two shillings per head on top of MacPherson's five shillings." The theatre rumbled with exploding voices, all ready to start killing. "Order! Order!" the governor yelled. "All kill evidence is to be brought to the police quarters out on Yula road. Earl's deputies will be in charge of tallying and distributing payouts. Only the head will be accepted as a kill, no exceptions. All State-owned land is now open for hunting by any means necessary until further notice. Payouts will start next Tuesday and every day thereafter until the kill has been lifted."

FULL FEATURE

Present Day - Denver, Colorado

THE MAJESTIC SNOWCAPPED PEAKS OF THE ROCKIES REFLECTED OFF the exterior glass windows of the eight-story Natural Productions corporate office. It all started with a few passionate film students and some generous contributions for their initial films. Established in 1992, Natural Productions exploded with growth after the worldwide success of their first three documentaries. Within their first ten years they seized control and dominated the documentary segment of cable television. Natural Productions had their own syndicated channel, over one hundred and eighty full time employees and an eight-story corporate headquarters with dozens of producers working on dozens of projects at all times.

Connor ducked into the third-story coffee bar to grab a pre-meeting pick-me-up, but the wind of him being there blew through like a cyclone. It wasn't often that he was in the building, and when he was, nearly every office turned ravenous, sending lucky spies out to spot the elusive Mr. Williams. He ended up being surrounded by a flood of women office workers and a gay intern that converged on him like a pack of wolves on a spring rabbit. His celebrity status was legend around the globe, and unfortunately for him, the office as well. Connor fought his way out of the pack, but not before leaving his always charming impression, never too busy to flirt it up with his fans.

He made his way into the extravagant producer's wing on the fifth floor and shouldered his way through the colossal, hand carved double wooden doors reminiscent of the entrance to Jurassic Park.

Ben and Sheila were seated on the east side of the oversized mahogany table and George at the other. The husband and wife duo, Sheila specifically, would normally spend a few moments gawking at the elevated, mountainous view but today they didn't even take notice. Connor smiled at the group, noticing a bit of anticipation in Sheila's grin, and sped to his usual spot at the head.

"Sorry, there was a mob in the coffee bar." Connor winked at Ben and Sheila, his head producer and co-producer husband.

"I wouldn't expect anything less." Sheila winked, fighting back a smile.

Ben spoke out before Connor was totally seated. "We've got some exciting news." His face beamed. "We've been cleared to start a new project. We've been given the go ahead by the CEO himself."

Sheila cut in. "And this next project is going to be bigger than the series. This is going to be a full feature, guys." She bantered with childlike excitement.

Sheila's father began acquiring real estate in the early seventies and by the mid-eighties he owned an empire. He was one of a select few that worked his way into the honorary billionaires' club. Her parents both died in the mid-eighties willing to her a corporately governed legacy of revolving wealth that required minimal contact.

Ben and Sheila had been together for eleven years before the inheritance. Months after, they became world travelers, finding their true calling on a trip to Kenya. It was there that they were first exposed to the plight of wildlife on the planet. While in the bush, their safari guide explained how poaching, habitat destruction and human pollution were destroying fragile ecosystems around the globe. Although it was an eye-opening lecture, it's what happened next that transformed them; the critically wounded elephant they happened upon.

The five-ton bull elephant was lying on its side, wailing in agony, and struggling to stand. The horror of it sickened Ben and Sheila both; all they could do was watch as the helpless animal bled from a single gunshot wound in the center of its ribcage. Its tusks were gone, one was cut clean and the other was splintered and broken at its remaining short nub. Sheila cried, begging for the guide to do something, and he did. She couldn't bear to watch as he emptied three rounds from his rifle into the weeping animal's head. Neither of them could sleep as their minds were haunted by the elephant's human-like cry. They were scarred emotionally, but it gave them new purpose. They became obsessed with protecting African Wildlife and thus began their crusade.

At a later wildlife conservation conference, she met with Bill Walters, who was the Chief Executive Officer of Natural Productions. Shortly thereafter she began making large monetary contributions to the company. Bill quickly put this upbeat and motivated team of wildlife saviors in charge of producing a new wildlife series.

"Okay, where are we headed?" Connor asked.

George sat without much expression, normal for these meetings. Nearing sixty years of age, he's seen his share of death. Being a war videographer took its toll on the giant's friendly, outgoing demeanor. He started as a field medic in the army then turned in his med kit, swapping it out for a camera. From the Middle East to Northern Korea, he saw what no man should ever see in a lifetime.

In 1976, on assignment in Colombia, South America, he was captured by guerilla rebels only to escape into the jungle, where he survived for seventeen days until his self-made rescue. Despite his coarse demeanor, Ben and Sheila were drawn to his intimidating presence and quiet, bold character. His resume was more than adequate, and he was willing to travel without bounds, placing himself in beyond dangerous situations in order to get the shot. He was a shoo-in and quickly snatched up by Ben and Sheila as videographer for the new series.

"Well, that's up for discussion," Ben said.

"We've been given the opportunity to make a full feature documentary and the CEO is leaving it up to you," Sheila said.

"You're a star, Connor. Everyone all over the globe loves your series, and everyone here trusts you and your decision making," Ben said.

Connor released his trademark smile then looked down at the table.

"I'm flattered, but let's not forget, I'm not the only one making it happen. This series couldn't have been done without my right-hand man. He goes where no videographer would or should go. He does what no videographer would do. Don't give me kudos without giving him his fair share."

"And boy do we know it." Sheila shook her head, sighing. "George, you're the best of the best and we're more than honored to have you. You're the gear that keeps this whole thing turning."

George acknowledged with a subtle nod and nothing more. He was there to do his job and that was it. He didn't let anyone, or anything get to him. He didn't care about kudos.

"So what are the execs looking for?" Connor asked.

"They've given us total control over this project. They trust us, more so, they trust you. Everything you touch turns to gold. Your fans would watch if you were doing a feature on third world toilet paper. Because you're *you*, we could get away with virtually anything," Ben said.

"I appreciate the flattery," Connor laughed.

"Any ideas?" Sheila asked.

Connor stared through the window at the unobstructed view of the snowcapped mountain tops, and then it hit him. He'd been drawn to an animal that has captured his attention for as long as he can remember. It was a case of love at first sight, and first sight being a children's book of recently extinct animals. He would sift through the pages, reveling in the sadness as he turned, staring at animals that would never again be seen alive, and their demise mostly due to the ever-increasing hand of man.

At ten years old, Connor remembered turning the page, and the haunting feeling that came over him as he first examined the black and white photograph, the last known photograph ever taken of the Thylacine. The photo was taken in the mid 1930's from within the wired confines of its quarters. It had the embodiment of a wolf, striped like a tiger, a thick long tail, and haunting, saddened eyes. He kept that book, only to flip the pages and stare at the magnificently striped beast, time and time again, year after year. His final college thesis proposed the Thylacine, an extinct animal, could still be alive. His research concluded that with physical evidence, multiple yearly eye witness reports and an abundance of unreachable areas of vast wilderness in the Australian outback, there was a good chance this animal could still be alive.

Over the years, Connor developed an obsession for the tiger and began collecting every suspect photograph, video, and eyewitness report of the mysterious marsupial. The very thought of the animal still being alive ate away at his soul. As a biologist, he knew that if the tiger was alive, and wasn't discovered soon, the species would surely die out due to such a declined population.

He couldn't remember the last time goose-bumps covered his body, but here they were. It seemed his obsession would now become a reality.

"As a matter of fact, I do. The Thylacine," Connor said, now focusing on the blue above the white capped mountains.

Ben narrowed his eyebrows. "What's a Thylacine?"

"The Tasmanian tiger, Ben."

"Um, are we talking Tasmania?" Sheila asked.

"Yes and no." Connor said, eyes still lost and locked above the Rockies.

"Okay, let's hear it," Sheila leaned forward in anticipation.

Connor inhaled deep then released slowly. After a ten second pause, he turned his gaze to the table. "The Thylacine was a large wolf-like, predatory marsupial, very, very secretive in nature."

"Marsupial, like a Kangaroo?" Sheila asked.

"Yeah, well, kinda. More like a wolf with a pouch. It had these incredible black tiger-like stripes on its back. They evolved to fill the niche in Australia that wolves and other large predators fill on the other continents. They were once abundant all over Australia, but the fossil records show they went extinct from the mainland about twelve thousand years ago. The Thylacine *was* however thriving on the Island of Tasmania until fairly recently, that is until the arrival of European settlers.

In the early 1900's a massive onslaught was launched against the tigers, initiated by the state to calm the farmers threatened by their presence. They were annihilated, and the last known living Thylacine died in captivity in the nineteen thirties at the Hobart Zoo in Tasmania. There's a bit of controversy that surrounds the eradication. Tasmania had a major feral dog problem in the early nineteen hundreds, and rumor has it that the Thylacine was a victim due to mistaken identity."

Ben tapped his pen a few times on the table then interjected. "It's one heck of a story, but I'm not sure where you're going with this. We're in the business of filming wildlife, the story is intriguing, but if they're extinct then we haven't got much of a feature."

Connor raised his finger to Ben. "This is the good part. There have been numerous eye witness reports, some sketchy photos and even a few videos being reported and documented over the past fifty years, some credible, some not so credible. Two years ago, a video was captured that really baffled me. It depicts an animal, dog-like, dragging a carcass through a tall grass patch bordering a thick patch of trees. There are two brief moments in the video that really caught me off guard. One is when the creature peers up, almost as if it acknowledges the person filming. You can see its eyes and the majority of its head and ears. It gives me the chills just thinking about it. In those few frames it looks most definitely like the Thylacine.

"The second moment is when it's tugging the carcass backwards, possibly a kangaroo, into the forest. As its rear heaves up, you can see three distinct stripes running vertically down its back and flank. I don't know what else it could've been." Connor shook his head in angst, with no other feasible explanation.

Connor paused, took a couple breaths, and then started in again. "The crazy thing is this. They've been extinct on the mainland for almost two thousand years and they've been extinct on the island of Tasmania for less than a hundred years, but all of the sightings and reports have been on the Mainland. And for the most part they're all stemming from the far northwest, areas that are virtually untouched and unapproachable."

"What exactly are you proposing, Mr. Williams?" Ben asked with the most curious of tones. Sheila looked at Ben with an expectational smile. She knew this was going to be good.

Sheila has learned to put total faith into Connor and his ideas. She and Ben lacked the experience and expertise most producers in the industry possessed. Instead, they bought their way into the business. Rather than utilizing what little production abilities they had, they turned to the one man that sent them straight to the top of wildlife filmmaking. Not only had *Connor William's Wildlife Encounters* series remained the number one bread-maker for Natural Productions, but it had also become the biggest primetime draw for their cable TV network. Connor personally selected the content and strategically planned every segment, which was a third of the reason for its success; the other two-thirds were presumably due to his addicting personality and ruggedly good looks. They trusted his decision-making abilities without question.

Connor leaned into the black leather swivel recliner and stared at the ceiling. What were only seconds to those in the room were minutes to Connor in his mind.

His thoughts raced, and a puzzle of images started fluttering, landing upon a vision board deep seated in the depths of his mind. The pieces were coming together organized, and a plan was being conceived.

He leaned forward, placing his cupped hands together on the antique mahogany meeting table. "Okay, here's my proposal…"

Ben and Sheila scrambled for their notebooks, aware that Connor spoke fast and didn't slow down with one of his self-inspired ideas. George cracked his lips that were barely visible behind his grey beard and mustache, releasing the dim essence of a smile.

Connor stared off into the Rockies and then turned to the group. "Tasmania…we start in Tasmania and showcase the Thylacine. We'll cover its origins, natural history, habitat, lifestyle etc. Then we'll really go into its persecution and its extinction at the hand of man. Was it a true killer or was it unjustly persecuted? Then the feature really begins, we go after the Thylacine. Next, we present the viewers with the years of gathered evidence that strongly suggests it may still be living in mainland Australia. That's where the fun starts. We'll take a full crew with us, additional support, an Aboriginal guide…we'll give it the appeal of a major expedition. We'll film our adventure, reality style, documenting every step along the way, capturing all the drama, thrills and chills that the inhospitable outback Australia has to offer."

Ben and Sheila continued writing feverishly, jotting notes, and trying to keep pace with Connor's rant.

"We start at the airport, move to our first location, secure our supplies, load up our Land Rovers and start our journey. We drive until we can drive no more, then we foot it. Camping, climbing, surviving… experiencing everything the wild outback can throw at us, it's definitely not going to be a walk in the park. The show will be great whether we find the Thylacine or not. The alluring effect of a reality-based show will pull the viewers in. We conclude the show by revealing what we've come to find about the Thylacine and whether it is in fact living, or we take the other route by sadly announcing that another wonderful species has been completely eradicated due to the unrelenting ways of mankind. Either conclusion works; granted it would be an award-winning feature and one of the most significant wildlife discoveries ever made if we can provide documented proof that the Thylacine is alive."

Connor paused, taking a moment to gauge his producers' expressions. Sheila was still scribbling with her pen and Ben was grinning. Connor turned to George, who gave a subtle nod of approval.

Ben and Sheila gauged each other's expression, and then Sheila dropped her pen to the table. Unspoken, they have already accepted Connor's proposal.

"Any ideas for a title?" Sheila asked.

Connor stared out into the Rockies, "In Search of the Lost."

FROM THE QUARRY

Tasmania - June 1932

A YOUNG BOY WITH SUN-BLEACHED HAIR AND CUT-OFF DUNGAREES watched from behind the weathered, split pine fence as his father's banged up 1924 Oldsmobile motorcar bounced around and kicked up a steady cloud of dust on the dirt road to his home. Petey's dad was one of only a few on the island of Tasmania to own an Oldsmobile. His dad's estranged father left it to him on his passing, along with their sprawling ranch with over a hundred head of cattle.

Petey's father, Greg McKinley, never knew his own mother. She died when he was two years old, forcing his dad to take on all the responsibility of raising a small child. Overwhelmed with the burden, little Greggie was dumped on his grandparents in Australia, while his dad took off to Tasmania.

Greg never had a great relationship with his grandparents. They raised him with more resentment than love, struggling to feed an extra mouth they didn't want in the first place. Growing up, Greg always felt like an unwanted outsider. He kept to himself and worked for his stay, all the while never having a true sense of family. He stayed with his grandparents until he was hired by a state work camp at the age of fourteen. He packed what little belongings he had and started clearing land and building roads for the progress of Eastern Australia.

22

Up until about three months ago, little Petey would wait by the weathered fence with Chewie; a serene fifty-two-pound Kelpie. Normally Kelpies are considered hectic herding dogs whose obsessive-compulsive personalities guide entire herds of livestock without any human direction or guidance. But Chewie was different, always calm, and inquisitive, watching rather than running.

Greg had rescued the young pup from certain death when a desperate, middle-aged local woman was trying to give away a litter of six. She stood in front of the local feed store with the entire brood in a rickety wooden chicken crate. She whined that if the pups weren't taken, they'd be done in and drowned by her husband which was the commonplace for unwanted dogs. When Greg arrived, there was only one pup that hadn't been taken, and it was listless and uninteresting. The other puppies had sold themselves with their awkward alertness and puppy antics. As he entered the feed store, he gave the pathetic pooch a friendly scratch then went about his business. Upon leaving, he passed the little pup without giving it a second look. He sat back in the Oldsmobile and mashed the push-button ignition. Just after he put the car in reverse, his conscience kicked in, pondering the gruesome fate of an unwanted listless pup sitting alone in the box.

Petey was four years old when his dad brought the pup home. Within the first hour he found a piece of old gum that had been unknowingly kicked under Petey's bed.

He gave it a curious sniff then tried to eat it, chewing, and chewing until it softened up so much that it stuck to all his teeth. He kept chewing and chewing in a futile attempt to spit it out, while his new family laughed hysterically. Chewie only seemed appropriate.

Chewie grew out of being a placid runt and into a member of the family, spending his days roaming about the property with Petey, patrolling and protecting his home; he was never more than an earshot away.

Most dogs in Tasmania were never allowed inside and were seldom fed. Ranch dogs would come and go for the most part, some never to return, joining in with the packs or being killed by them. The dogs of Tasmania were more or less vagrants, always coming and going, scavenging for food and forming packs. Breeding freely, the wild dog populations were ever growing, and the packs were reverting back to their genetic instincts of predatory wolf behavior.

Chewie had it made. Every night at about the same time Petey's mother, Millie, would open the front door and let Chewie run out and do his business. Within one or two minutes he would run back up to the door and give a single bark, signaling Millie, who would then let him back in. He would then run straight to Petey's room and curl up at the foot of his bed. Three months earlier, Chewie was out doing his final nighttime business as he had always done before, but this time he never gave a returning bark. Millie called and called, but Chewie was nowhere to be found. Petey cried himself to sleep that night; it was the first time in three years he had slept alone. Day after day, week after week, Petey would walk his property calling for Chewie, but he was gone.

Greg busted his bare knuckles day in and day out, slinging rock at the quarry. The crew out at the Cradle Mountain Quarry made their wages by smashing rock, extracting iron ore, and cutting granite slabs. It was a tough man's work. These guys were toting rock and packing dynamite.

Petey's dad was physically as tough as the rock he worked, yet soft at heart. Greg didn't need the job at the quarry, the ranch alone supported the family with ease, but the extra money would help expedite their relocation from Tasmania back to the mainland.

Petey waited until the Oldsmobile entered the driveway and then darted over the fence, running to his dad's door. "Hi, Dad." Petey tried to lean in through the open window. "Find any goodies today?" Greg would always bring Petey unusual pieces of crystal, rock and fossils from the mine and today was no different.

"I did, in fact I found something a little special today."

"Special? Lemme see."

Greg tugged the metal handle and his door popped open. Petey could see that his father was supporting with care something in his arms. With all the curiosity of a seven-year-old boy, Petey forced his way in between his dad and the car door.

The boy's jaw dropped, and he inhaled. "Ooh! A puppy! Is she mine?" Petey yelled, awe struck.

Greg studied his son's face; to him there was nothing better than seeing his son smile. "It's no puppy, Petey, it's a Tazzie tiger, and she is a he."

"Daddy, daddy, can I keep him?" He reached for the small bundle of fur curled into a ball in his father's arms.

"We have to keep him real quiet, or he'll be good as gone."

The front porch door creaked open. "Aye, Greggie, now what have you brought home?" Petey's mom called out, smiling.

"Come see, Millie." Greg tried to keep his voice low.

"Mom, Mom! You gotta see this!" Petey yelled.

Millie smiled as she approached, but then she noticed the unmistakable black tiger striping along the animal's mid-back and flank, her face became pained.

"Careful, Petey," Greg whispered as he handed the young pup to his son.

"Oh, Greggie. How could you bring home a tiger? He's as good as dead. You know how hard it'll be keeping it quiet?"

Petey nuzzled his face against the pup's head but it was frightened by the whole experience. It gave a slow semi-playful nibble at the boy's hand as he rubbed its belly then buried its head.

Greg watched his son and then sighed. "Look Millie, I had no choice. John went scouting about with his rifle during lunch and shot its mother. Then a few minutes later he finds four pups rustling around in the bushes. He was nice enough to split the pups among us, so we could each collect a bounty. They killed 'em all right there on spot. It sickened me, having to hear 'em get done in like that. Those bastards just slammed 'em to the ground."

"That's so horrible," Millie cried out.

Greg was unique. For a man growing up in Southern Australia, compassion for animals wasn't a common trait. During his entire life, Greg had been surrounded by those calloused toward anything other than human life. Somehow despite all the unsympathetic, he maintained compassion toward all living things; a trait his wife cherished and loved most.

"And then convincing them not to kill this lil' guy was a real doozie. John wants me to get the bounty for the family. So I obliged and took the pup, however I told him I wanted to show you guys what a live tiger looked like. I thanked him, but I was thinking to myself there's no way I'm killing this lil' fella. It just ain't right, and I'm not sure John believes *I'll even collect* the bounty, he's been seeing me bring home all sorts of critters over the years and they tease me as a softie."

"Oh, Greggie, what are we gonna do with him?"

"Can he sleep with me, Dad?" Petey asked, cradling the tiger in his arms. The tiger had grown tired, exhausted from its event filled day, and fell asleep against Petey's chest.

"Not sure your mother wants to be cleaning tiger dung off your sheets mate."

"I'll take her out, please, Dad?"

"She's not a dog, Petey. We don't know if she's even gonna act like a dog, I think she's related to kangaroos," Millie said.

"She's a he," Greg corrected Millie. "And he *is* related to kangaroos."

"Please, please, please can he stay with me?"

"I dunno, Petey," Greg said.

"Greg, you can't let Petey get attached to him, before you know it someone's gonna find out, they'll see him out on the ranch and they'll kill 'em for sure."

"You don't think I haven't thought about that? We can't just set him free, he's a defenseless pup, has no mother, he wouldn't last a day on his own, and even if he did survive, sooner or later he'd get caught in a trap or shot."

They both turned, and together they watched their young son with his back against the dusty tire, slowly stroking the tiger while it slept.

Greg and Millie knew the risks but had no choice; not just for their son who recently lost his beloved dog, but for the innocence asleep in his arms. There were evils stalking Tasmania. The rumor throughout Tasmania pegged the tiger as a vicious killer. The tales of tigers slaughtering entire herds overnight, leaving the carcasses uneaten were plentiful. Tigers had the reputation of being an animal that killed without reason, making it every rancher's number one enemy. There was evil stalking the island, but not of the tiger kind.

MEET THE TEAM

Denver, Colorado - Natural Productions headquarters - Present day

THREE MONTHS AFTER THE CONCEPTION OF THEIR NEW documentary, *In Search of the Lost*, Ben and Sheila put together what they believed to be a unique crew. Through their affiliations with other syndicated producers, they located, and recruited a second videographer, an Australian Aborigine tracker, a wildlife biologist, and a wildlife biologist intern.

As usual Connor and George were late.

Everyone was seated and mingling when the double doors swung open.

"Howdy, folks," Connor said as he entered the room with George trailing just behind him.

"Whiskey sours?" Sheila questioned.

"Guinness, actually," Connor grinned. It was typical for Connor and George to have a few drinks before any afternoon meeting. He noted two young women and a man seated across from his producers.

Connor placed himself at the head of the table. Ben and Sheila as usual sat to his left and the three new team members to his right. George seated himself beside Ben and Sheila.

Connor assumed control of the meeting. "I guess everybody's been briefed?" He took a quick survey of the group, sizing up their abilities and

27

weaknesses with a three second glance around the room. His eyes stopped on Carl; something just didn't feel right.

"I figured we could let our new crew introduce themselves." Ben glanced at Connor for approval.

Connor nodded. "Great idea."

"Why don't we start with you, Carl?" Ben said.

Caught off guard, Carl fidgeted around for a moment while gathering his thoughts; the creepy bone structure of his narrow face was hauntingly visible through his thin skin. "Hi, everyone, my name is Carl, Carl Phillips. I've been in the industry for sixteen years. I started out as a photographer then moved into professional sound and lighting. I usually do studio work. I saw the opportunity to get some great outdoor experience so here I am. Why they chose me out of all the other guys with experience, I don't know. I'm just glad to be here."

Connor noticed a subtle left eye twitch as Carl spoke.

Sheila cut in. "Carl, we chose you because we felt you were a unique individual, we weren't necessarily looking for experience. Remember, this is going to be more of a reality-based documentary. We wanted characters rather than simple positions and we think you're a perfect fit."

"Glad you feel I'm unique." Carl's tone was mildly sarcastic and a little too hard to decipher.

"How about you, Lisa? Tell us about yourself," Ben said.

Lisa was obviously the youngest on the team. She looked more like a cheerleader than a wildlife biologist. She laid both palms flat on the table and took a deep breath, nervousness showing.

"My name's Lisa Cortez. I'm about to graduate from Arizona State with a masters in wildlife biology. I did my senior thesis on the Gray Wolf and its effects on the hoof-stock populations in Yellowstone. I've been working on my internship here with Natural Productions for the past five months. I just want to say I am so excited to be here and thank you so much for this once in a lifetime opportunity. I feel so privileged!"

"Welcome, Lisa, we're very happy to have you. It's clear that you're going to be an asset to the team," Sheila said.

Kate nodded at Lisa and took a quick breath. She hated formal introductions. "I guess it's my turn."

"We all know you, Kate, but why don't you introduce yourself to Carl and Lisa," Ben said.

"Hey guys, I'm Kate Stanton, I'm a senior wildlife biologist here at Natural Productions. You may recognize me. A few years ago, I hosted a few televised documentaries on the plight of Africa's *Big Five* by prize game hunters, aka the *Tear Jerker* series," she joked, throwing a fake grin as a few gruesome scenes flashed in her head. "I had no idea how heartbreaking it was going to be..." She pushed the memory away and continued. "Anyway, I'm from south Florida and I've been with Natural for about four years. I look forward to being out in the field. That's where my heart is. Sure, a lot can be done behind a desk or in the lab, but hands on field research is what I love. Ben and Sheila approached me directly about the expedition. How could I say no?"

Her smile caught Connor off guard, forcing him into a subtle stare. He'd met Kate a few times at special events and conferences, but never paid much attention; he was always too obsessed with his career. But today, her smile was gripping; he found himself admiring features normally trivial to him, her glistening sandy-blonde hair, the way it blanketed her sun-bronzed shoulders and the allure of purity in her childlike smile. He broke his gaze before it became obvious and forced her out of his head. Time to get back to business.

"Thanks, Kate, and welcome aboard," Sheila said. "It's a pleasure to have you with us."

Kate smiled, and Connor found his eyes being pulled back to her allure, odd. This time he found himself noting the perfection of her teeth.

Ben nodded then spoke up. "There *is* one more addition to our team that couldn't be here. His name is Mac and he's an Australian Aborigine. He'll be our guide, not that Connor couldn't handle it on his own. We'll meet up with him in Darwin, Australia. It's a pleasure to have each of you with us. We feel we've really assembled the perfect team to explore the Australian outback in search of our Tasmanian tiger. As you all know this is going to be a reality-based feature documentary. So instead of just filming and documenting the search for the Thylacine, we will be filming the daily struggles of the crew as well. When finalized, we'll be presenting the final project, *In Search of the Lost* as a reality based full feature documentary."

"Let me add this," Connor cut in. "I want everyone to know that this will not in any way take away from our main theme which is searching for my Thylacine. My, I mean, *our* main goal is to find the tiger. I'll admit, I've been obsessed with the tiger for years and all I want to do is find it. Let's bring them back to life."

Kate grinned, barely. She thought it cute and mildly obsessive that he referred to the tiger as *his*, but none-the-less admired his passion.

"By filming the entire journey along the way, I feel we'll capture the true essence of a major expedition." Connor continued. "Not many people have even heard of the Tasmanian tiger, but a whole lot of people love the drama of human interactions. So, traditionally, if we went about our journey and didn't find the tiger, it could potentially be a boring feature. However, if we film the entire expedition with all its trials and tribulations, struggles, adventures or even misadventures, and then never find the tiger, the show will still potentially be a hit. This way everyone wins." Connor paused and scanned the group. "But we're gonna find it."

"I love it, Connor. Ben and I really think you're onto something with this one."

"I've got a really strong feeling the tiger is alive, and I'm…" Connor corrected himself. "*We're* going to be the ones to show the world."

"We can't wait to get it underway!" Sheila said.

Ben stood. "And on that note, we have an announcement to make."

Connor's eyes squinted. *Ben's making an announcement,* he thought. *The budget was already huge, they had assembled their team, and they had already planned the trip. What could the announcement be?*

Sheila blurted. "Ben and I are going on the expedition with you!"

LIFE WITH BENJAMIN
Tasmania - February 1935

"You know, Greg, we really should work on getting Petey enrolled in the public school." Millie scraped some chicken scraps from her plate into a metal bowl then tossed it in the sink.

"Let's give it another year, we'll be out of Tasmania by then and—"

Trying to speak through a mouth full of boiled chicken, Petey interrupted. "I don't wanna go to public school."

"It's best for ya, Petey." Millie plucked the remaining chicken bones from the large metal pot and dropped them into Ben's metal bowl.

"The kids are all bullies. You can't make me!" Petey raised his voice.

Petey had already been enrolled in the Hobart Grammar school, but after three weeks of constant bullying they decided to pull him out. Realizing her efforts were in vain, she decided upon home schooling. The children of Hobart, for the most part, had absorbed the callous, non-nurturing nature of their parents. Hobart had one private school reserved only to those willing to pay its high tuition. This forced the impoverished underclass into its public school, grouping together bands of dysfunctional misfit children that packed together like the wild dogs of the island.

Millie would never allow her son to be terrified by the unrelenting and uncontrollable vagrant children of Hobart. Millie had visited the school and spoke with Petey's teacher, but the bullying continued. Realizing her efforts were in vain, she decided upon home schooling. Millie spent her days tending the ranch with Petey. He would lend a hand and she would teach him in between chores.

Petey grew very comfortable with his new routine and the very thought of returning to public school frightened him. She knew this wasn't a proper education but focused on their relocation to mainland Australia. Once there, Petey would be re-enrolled in a much better public school system.

"Don't take that tongue with your mother, Petey. She means the best for ya."

"I can't wait to get outta here, Greggie. I hate Tasmania." Millie scoffed. "I really hate it here."

"I know, sweetheart, but it's not like we can ship our herd to the mainland. I'm just thankful Paul even left them to me." Greg referred to his father as Paul, he had only seen him a couple dozen times in his early life and they were usually brief two or three day stints.

Paul left his parents' ranch on the mainland when Greg was just a toddler to pursue ranching opportunities in newly developing Tasmania. Paul would make random unannounced visits to his parents' place, usually to borrow money. As the years passed they started seeing less and less of him, mainly due to the growth of his Tasmanian ranch.

After several years, Paul's ranch was self-supportive, and that's when the problems started. Seeing Paul's ranch as competition, Joe McPherson offered to buy him out, but Paul wouldn't sell. Joe didn't like the fact that his competition was on the rise and refusing his offers. Paul started getting strong-armed by McPherson's crew; subtle threats and intimidation by his henchmen, trying to sway him into selling. Fearing he was becoming too entangled with McPherson, Paul deeded the ranch over to his son. One night, Paul's entire herd became spooked and trampled through a corral fence, killing him as he tried to stop them. At least that's what the police report had legally documented.

"Well the sooner the better. This place is crooked," Millie said.

"Wilkins already said he'll buy the entire lot next January," Greg said.

"Yeah, but is he committed or is he just talking?"

"I'll see if I can get him to write up a contract. Will that make you feel better?"

"Just get 'em sold, Greggie. I don't care how you do it."

Petey wiped the chicken grease from his chin. "I'm done, Mom."

"Go ahead and scrape your plate. Benjamin's waiting for his supper," Millie said.

"Can he have a dumpling too?" Petey begged.

"Our Benjamin can have all he wants," Millie said.

Petey grabbed Ben's metal bowl and slopped a few soggy white dumplings on top of his chicken scraps and bones. Millie prepared meals for the entire family, of which Benjamin had become a large part.

"Here, Ben." Petey placed the bowl under the table right next to the eighty-pound beast lying at his feet.

Benjamin raised his head, sniffed the bowl, and looked up at Petey. "Go ahead, Ben," Petey said. Ben looked up as if to say *thank you*, then began eating. Unlike a typical dog, he ate slow and selectively until the bowl was clean. Ben was massive, his formidable white teeth shone amid its gaping jaws, slicing bone without effort.

Beside Ben's bowl was Petey's first stuffed animal; a tattered Koala bear with an oversized head. As a child it had been his favorite toy, carrying it everywhere. Petey didn't hesitate when he gave it to Ben, who then took pride in ownership. As Petey had done, Ben began carrying the toy everywhere but only within the house, leaving it at the door when going out. Ben could have shredded the Koala, but never released more than a few gentle chews upon its soft wooly body.

"Alright, Petey, go run your bath," Millie said.

Petey started toward the bathroom and without hesitation, as if it were his sworn duty, Benjamin got up and followed. Everywhere Petey went Benjamin was either already there or close behind. He clung to Petey as though tethered by some unseen force. There wasn't anywhere Petey went that Ben wouldn't follow, even when sitting on the pot, Ben would curl at his feet. They were inseparable. Whenever Petey would ride into town, Ben would be lost, curling up at the foot of Petey's bed with the stuffed Koala, shivering as though Petey would never return. But when he did, Benjamin would run in circles, celebrating his return by releasing a fury of beautifully harmonic chirps and whistles.

"Bath's ready, Petey," Millie called.

"Coming, Mom." Petey ran into the bathroom with Ben jogging beside him. Millie poured water from the whistling kettle into two cups. "Careful, it's nice and hot." She handed Greg his steaming tin cup. They sipped their nightly ritual of eucalyptus tea with honey at the large kitchen table.

It was a nice ranch, larger than they needed, but Greg's father had purchased it from Bill Wilkins just as it stood. Bill Wilkins was under pressure from McPherson to sell off his stock, but he incessantly refused. Bill then started receiving subtle threats from local thugs. Angered by McPherson's bullying, he teamed with Greg's father and they combined their herd. They agreed to stand up to the bullying and never let McPherson buy them out. They built an additional living quarters for Paul and he became a permanent resident. Paul, along with Bill, his wife, her parents, and their three children had lived on the ranch for a little more than six years, but the repeated threats from the McPherson gang began to take their toll. Rather than risk harm, Bill sold his share off to Paul and then fled back to the mainland, leaving the large ranch house behind.

"What about Ben?" Millie asked.

"What do you mean?" Greg sipped from his cup.

"How the heck are we gonna get to the mainland with a tiger?"

"I've tossed it around a bit. When the time comes we'll figure it out."

"*We'll figure it out?* It's not like we can stick 'em in a box," Millie said.

"Ben's a big boy, I know. Maybe we could put him in the back of the car and cover 'em up."

"What if he gets restless? If anyone see's 'em it'll be a bad scene," Millie said.

"I don't even wanna think about it. All I know is that Ben is part of the family and he's coming with us. We'll figure it out. If anything, maybe I could just pay his way. You know, have people turn their heads. We'll have plenty of cash and God knows the shitty people in this town will do anything for a bit of money."

Millie sighed, thinking back to the day Greg had brought him home. "Geez, whoever would have thought a tiger could settle in like this?"

"Come on, Ben." Petey walked out of the bathroom, pulling up his pajama bottoms. He walked past his parents and led Ben out the front door, a nightly routine. He walked on to the porch while Ben ran off into the darkness to do his business. Petey felt that as long as he stayed on the porch and waited, Ben wouldn't disappear like Chewie.

———

Three days later, under the glaring midday sun, Petey and Ben headed down the hill that bottomed out at the narrow creek in the middle of the cow pasture. "Last one in is a rotten egg!" Petey started running down the hill. Benjamin snapped. He broke out of his protective sentry role and kicked it into high gear, zipping past Petey. Ben was free, gliding, almost floating as his legs dashed at full potential. The beauty of a creature so magnificent, so skilled in its weightless gallop was at full bloom as he floated across the terrain. He neared the creek at full speed and then leapt from the two-foot-high grassy bank, soared through the air, and landed in the cool water. Ben froze, snapped back into sentry mode, and then focused on Petey, scanning the landscape and twisting ears.

"You always beat me!" Petey whined as he jumped into the knee-deep water.

Ben climbed the opposite bank and shook off. He dropped his nose to the ground while keeping his rear to the air, froze, and then exploded into a rampage of play; darting and weaving in circles as though he were evading a predator, then suddenly he dropped into the green grass and rolled onto his back.

"I'll get ya!" Petey started running toward him. He skidded down the slight embankment, and then trudged through the shallow creek. Ben sprung back to his feet and kept his head level with the grass. He eyed Petey as though he were prey. As soon as Petey was within about five feet of him, he spun around and leapt into a full getaway sprint with the boy giving chase. They would take turns, Petey would stop and run the other direction and Ben would reverse his role and chase him down, grabbing Petey's britches and tugging 'til he fell. This 'give and go' pursuit lasted for hours in between catching lizards, crayfish, and snakes along the creek. The sun was relentless, and it wasn't long before Petey became parched.

"I need a drink." Petey walked down to the clear, streaming water and drank from his cupped hands. Benjamin stretched out on the bank watching Petey's every move. Petey went from rock to rock, catching crayfish. He would hold each one up so Ben could have a look too and then toss them back on the pebble bottom.

Petey grew restless with the abundance of crayfish, so he decided he'd snoop around a dead gum tree. Many years ago, this sprawling tree was struck by lightning, sentencing it to a slow death. When rotted roots could no longer support the incredible weight, it fell over and now lay lifeless along the creek bank. Remnants of its once mighty branches, now crumbled and withered, lay in brittle pieces among the ground. The trunk's holes and crannies made perfect homes for skinks, snakes, birds, and mice; allowing them to forage then make short retreats back to safety. Petey loved the addictive challenge of trying to catch the speedy lizards, tearing away the bark and rotted innards, sometimes spending hours without a single capture.

He crept along the sides of the downed tree, hitting all the common holes where he normally caught skinks. He made several passes up and down the tree, but he couldn't find any trace of life. Today it was just too hot; not even the lizards were basking. They kept to the cool musky retreats within the softened wood.

Petey walked back into the water and started wading toward Ben on the other bank. Ben's head rose up on *high alert;* he spotted something, a potential threat. Ben stood and released a series of high pitched, melodic chirps, almost birdlike in nature. Petey knew something was wrong.

Ben's vocalizations were frighteningly similar to the time that Petey had been nearly trampled by a disgruntled bull. About a year ago, Petey was crossing the field by himself when a bull decided to charge him. Ben scrambled from the front porch chirping, whistling, and speeding toward Petey. Greg ran, and Millie watched in horror as the bull drew dangerously close to their son. Ben rocketed past the boy and went head-on with the marauding bovine, trying to divert its attention. The two thousand pounds of unstoppable muscle paid no mind to the tiger and started closing the gap on Petey. Greg and Millie were screaming in terror for Petey to run. Seconds before it would have trampled him, Benjamin's jaws snapped onto the bull's front left leg, shattering the bone, and sending it toppling over in a cloud of dust. They never looked at Ben the same after that.

Petey spun around, expecting to see a charging bull. *No bulls*, he thought. "What is it, Ben?"

Ben leapt from the bank and charged across the water, springing over it rather than through it. Petey looked ahead of Ben and saw a six-foot copperhead streaking toward him. Petey froze. The Tasmanian copperhead has a reputation for being ill tempered and quick to bite. Ben pounced, landing behind the snake. He bit down on its tail and with a quick whip of his head the snake went hurtling through the air. The agitated reptile then slid off in a more agreeable direction.

"Good job, Ben!" Petey hugged his four-legged friend, tight.

Ben gave Petey a long slow lick across his cheek. "I've gotta tell Mom and Dad about this one." Petey kneeled down and rubbed Ben's jowls, looking him in the eye. "I love you, Ben."

Petey ran; he couldn't wait to tell his mom how Ben saved him from the fangs of a deadly copperhead. He ran as fast as his feet would carry him while Ben trotted slowly behind. They only had a hundred yards to go when the distant crack of a rifle sounded, followed by a wad of dirt exploding inches from Ben's side. Petey stopped and started looking for the shooter but realized that a sitting target was an easy shot; he started sprinting toward the house and gave Ben the signal to run.

Millie heard the shot from inside the kitchen and realized it had to have been from somewhere on their property. She grabbed Greg's rifle and kicked the front door open, chambering a round as she ran. The distant rifle fired again, this time exploding dirt directly underneath Ben's front paws. Millie scanned the tree-line outside of their fence and saw two men; one short and rounded and the other tall and skinny. Millie could only assume the hunters thought the tiger was chasing the boy. She waved her arms in the air, trying to signal the hunters.

"Mom, they're shootin' at Ben!" Petey screamed as he reached his mother. "C'mon Ben, run!" Petey passed his mom and ran through the front door, knowing Ben wouldn't slow down until he followed him inside.

The hunter's rifle cracked again. This time the fiery round ripped through Ben's right ear and splintered a chunk of wood from one of the front porch rails. Unaffected by the wound, Ben leapt over the porch steps and ran through the front door.

"What in God's name are you idiots doing?" Millie screamed, watching the two men climb over her fence nearly a hundred yards away. Millie was outraged but couldn't help thinking they were probably trying to protect her son from the chasing tiger. Regardless, she knew she had to keep her cool; there was a large bounty on tigers and these men just watched one run through her front door.

How the hell am I going to explain this? Her mind started racing as the men approached. She could see they were both carrying rifles and the skinny guy had a large sack slung over his shoulder. She knew what it contained, and it sickened her. These men were tiger hunters.

Petey popped his head through the front door and cried, "Mom, they shot Ben's ear. He's bleeding pretty bad."

"Ben's gonna be fine, now get inside and don't come out 'til I come and get you," she ordered in a tone that made Petey disappear. Millie tried to steady her shaking hands. The type of men that made a living killing tigers weren't the kindest of folk and judging by the looks of these two, they were the worst.

The two men were about twenty yards from Millie when the fat one spoke. "G'day, ma'am."

"That's far enough." Millie snapped. Her grip tightened on Greg's rifle.

"We's just checkin' on ya, no reason to get burned up." The fat man put his hand across the skinny man's chest, forcing him to stop.

"Checkin' on me? You idiots nearly shot my son and…" Millie cut herself off.

"And what?" the fat man probed.

"You nearly killed my dog. I don't see any reason for you to be here so go ahead and get off my property." Millie said.

"Why so rude? We thought your *dog* was a tiger, and we thought it was going after ya boy. You should be thankin' us," the fat man said.

"Thanking you, for what? Nearly killing my boy and his dog?"

"Well your dog looks *and* runs a lot like a tiger," the fat man insisted.

Millie took offense at his accusatory tone and it scared the hell out of her. She knew they saw a tiger. "Get the hell off my ranch. You can go straight down our drive and be back on the main road." Millie pointed toward the driveway leading to the road.

"Oh, we know the area *reeeeeaaaaal* well," the fat man bolstered. "By the way, where's *Mr.* McKinley?"

"Never mind where my husband is. Now get off my property." Millie motioned her rifle toward the road.

The two men started walking and as they passed, the fat one got uncomfortably close to her. Their eyes met, and the fat man sniffed in her scent.

"Never did get your name," he said, looking back.

"Never mind my name." Millie snapped.

"Well sorry for not introducing ourselves. My name is Smitty and this here is Tanner." The fat man patted his skinny's shoulder. "We'll be seeing ya."

WELCOME TO DARWIN

Darwin, Australia - Present day

THE TEAM ARRIVED TOGETHER IN AUSTRALIA, LANDING AT THE Darwin International Airport. George and Carl had already begun simultaneously filming their trip. As instructed, they were to film each other as well as the team to ensure everyone would be a part of the production.

Ben and Sheila secured the temporary rental cars for the group and from there they headed to Expedition Outfitters Unlimited to pick up their reserved Land Rover expedition vehicles. The team was led through the retail area of the store to a small office hidden at the rear. Connor sat down and signed paperwork while the rest of the team trembled with excitement, studying the wall of photographs from previous expeditions. There were all sorts of pictures of off road vehicles, some upside-down, atop boulders, partially submerged, and on fire.

The store manager handed Connor a large, bulging yellow envelope filled with paperwork and keys then winked at him.

"Any questions about the vehicles?" the manager grinned, speaking with a heavy Northern Australian accent.

"Nope." Connor returned the grin. "I guess you're gonna ask that every time, huh?"

"Alrightie, follow me." The manager led the team through the door at the rear of the store that opened into an open warehouse. As they each passed through the door, their eyes were pulled toward four savage looking expedition vehicles arranged in a semi-circle.

Ben and Sheila were a bit subdued. They weren't used to being on camera and the experience was surreal. Over the years they had rented a few expedition vehicles for their semi-soft safari adventures, but now, they stood in awe of four Land Rovers that were at their least, intimidating.

These weren't just any Land Rovers. These were the newest Land Rover Discoveries decked out with everything any adventure seeking individual would need. At first glance they looked like something out of Jurassic Park, but ten times meaner. Bright yellow with jet black trim, they sat high enough off the ground anyone with a fear of heights would have reconsidered climbing in. They were raised four inches higher than factory Rovers and had an upgraded suspension system. The transmissions were all-time four-wheel drive with an optional four-wheel low for climbing or descending steep grades.

The fronts of the vehicles were armored with oversized brush guards which made them look like something out of Mad Max. Each had a super heavy-duty winch attached to the front bumper that could pull a vehicle out of anything. The roof was covered entirely by a heavy gauge steel rack that could carry a near infinite amount of supplies. One of the most interesting features of the vehicle was the large plastic snorkel that protruded from the hood and rose well above the driver's side window. Instead of a standard air intake which is normally at hood level, this one was at the level of the roof of the vehicle. The snorkel allowed for driving through the deepest of water, preventing it from entering the air intake and destroying the engine.

Kate dangled her set of keys in front of Lisa. "It's all yours."

"Oh, my God...I can drive?" Lisa screamed. She ran to her designated Rover, admired its ferocious architecture and strange sexual prowess, and then climbed into the driver's seat. The key slid into the ignition and with a simple twist, the Rover sprung from its slumber with the roar of a thousand lions. The hair on her arms shot up as she signaled the start of their epic journey. The lions calmed to a rumbling idle, waiting for their next command.

With vehicles secured, the team separated into them and proceeded south west toward base camp in Batchelor, Australia. There they would discuss permanent vehicle assignments and meet up with Mac, their Aborigine guide. The base camp, an old primitive campground near Fitzroy Crossing, was located just outside of the Great Sandy Desert. Fitzroy Crossing was a hub for those preparing to take the harrowing journey through the sandy hell. There was a fueling station and an expedition outfitters camp providing supplies needed to cross the desert. It was the final bit of civilization before entering the desert.

The team's journey through the desert wasn't needed; a much shorter trip could have been planned, but Connor decided on a longer and more challenging route which would take the team through the Great Sandy Desert and then the Hamersley Mountain range. Connor planned the trip strategically, knowing it would present its own challenges and stressors to the crew as well as opportunities to film some of the beautiful Australian interior.

The Rovers thundered one after another down the weather beaten, sun cracked dirt road; every little bump rattled the contents and passengers alike due to the stiff suspension. After a two hour drive they pulled into the base camp. It looked like an old Indian village with one supply building and a few canvas tents used for shelter from the intense mid-day sun. The day time temperatures normally reached well into the low hundreds and the night time temps dropped faster than a lead weight in a fish pond. As soon as the sun disappeared the chill set in, dipping down into the low thirties.

Each one of the Rovers pulled in to form a stylish semi-circle around what was to be their initial camp. Everyone exited the vehicles, stretched, and then converged in front of the Rovers.

A wooden door creaked then slammed shut, causing the team to spin around. A frizzy haired Aborigine walked from the supply house toward them. "G'day fellas. Glad you made it by before the vampires come out," he joked. His friendly voice didn't quite match his rugged appearance.

"Ha, ha," Connor laughed. "We have about an hour 'til sundown... You must be Mac."

"In the flesh."

Sheila couldn't help but stare at his odd appearance; the full bushy black beard and large afro full of curly dark hair with white sun-bleached tips.

Lisa smiled after she read his t-shirt. *Don't Feed the Aborigines*, depicting an Aborigine with a slashed circle over him.

"It's so nice to finally meet you, Mac!" Sheila said.

"Wow, I totally love your hair," Lisa said.

"I'll let you touch it if you let me touch yours," Mac teased, non-threatening and playful. Everyone chuckled.

With the addition of Mac, the entire team was finally assembled.

Lisa and Kate had already decided they were sharing a tent. Ben and Sheila were sharing a tent. Connor and George were paired together as usual, so that left Mac and Carl paired up. They also decided they would travel in the same groups as the tent arrangement.

Ben and Sheila were still trying to erect their tent while everyone else was finishing theirs. Because of their extreme wealth, they really hadn't spent any un-chaperoned time in the wilderness. Every trip they had taken into the wild was catered with guides and laborers who handled every aspect of the outing. They never had any real expedition experience, so they felt this trip would be a perfect way to get their feet wet but had no idea what was in store for them.

Connor and George had set their tent hundreds of times, and being the first to finish, they walked over to lend a hand to their well-intentioned, but bumbling producers. Within sixty seconds Ben and Sheila's tent was complete.

Dinner that night was easy. With the help of a caterer, Mac had prepared a small celebratory feast consisting of lobster and prime rib at the producers' order and expense. Everyone ate in near silence, exhausted from the day's travels. After dinner, everyone, with the exception of George, changed into warmer clothes. The temperature had dropped from ninety degrees to fifty-five in less than an hour.

One by one, everyone migrated to the fire and sat on the large log sections. Ben and Sheila huddled next to each other as the temperatures continued to drop.

"So tell us about yourself, Mac. Where are you from? How did you learn the outback?" Ben asked.

"Okie, dokie. I'm a Pitjantjatjara. I'll say it again for all you slow folk, pee-jan-ja-jara, that's a group of Aborigine from Uluru. My family is from Uluru, home of the red sand mountain and I grew up there as well. It's basically the south western portion of the desert. When you grow up in Uluru you learn the land. There's really no choice. It's a dry, challenging place to live. Now I live in Darwin working as guide for people like you that wanna see the outback. I gotta tell ya it makes me feel kinda special. People pay me a good bit of money just to see where I grew up."

"Well, it's a fascinating place," Sheila said.

"Indeed. So why you looking for the old tiger anyway?" Mac asked.

"I think they're still around," Connor said. "New sightings keep popping up year after year. There's gotta be something to it."

Shelia cut in. "It would make great TV as well."

"Dingos are all over the outback. Maybe that's what they've been seeing out there," Mac said.

"Believe me, that's a very strong possibility and I'm sure that a percentage of the sightings are, but there's a piece of footage that in my opinion rules out the Dingo. The video shows a large dog-like animal dragging a carcass through some foliage and at one point in the video you can see vertical stripes on its rear flanks. I just don't know what else it could be," Connor said.

"The video *is* very intriguing, Mac," Kate added.

"Well, I've never seen a Dingo with stripes so maybe you're onto something. Either way you've got one heck of journey ahead a ya. Not sure why you wanted to cross the desert. You could have just flown to the west coast and taken public road for most of the trip."

Connor grinned. "What? And miss all the fun? If I'm bringing a film crew and expedition team to the Australian outback, we're gonna see the Australian outback."

"Well you got the outback, mate. You just wait," Mac said.

They talked for another hour before settling into their tents. Lisa and Kate melted into the warmth of their sleeping bags while they chit chatted, and girly gossiped about the other team members. When they ran out of conversation and a silence hovered, Lisa took a stab in the dark.

"Ever thought about hooking up with Connor?"

"Hooking up?" Kate laughed.

"Yeah, you two seem like a perfect fit."

"How do you figure?" Kate already knew the answer. She had heard it from so many people, so many times before.

"From what I can see, Kate, you're both intelligent, both great to look at, and share the same passions."

"Thanks for the compliment, Lisa, but I don't think it would ever work. He's so driven and busy with his productions. And believe me, what woman hasn't thought about being with him? He's a total package."

"Well, ya never know 'til you try and if you wait too long someone else will end up stealing him away," Lisa teased.

"Like who, maybe you?" Kate asked with a tinge of playful jealousy.

"Nah, not me. Don't get me wrong, I adore him."

"So, no hooking up with Connor?" Kate asked with a tidbit of possession, laughing.

"Nah, he's got your name all over him."

———

Next morning Connor was the first up. While everyone slept he was busy preparing his signature breakfast, eggs with bacon and pancakes fried in the leftover bacon grease. Connor loved to cook in the great outdoors. Cooking over an open fire gave him the nostalgic feeling of camping with his late father. On camping trips, it was always tradition for his father to wake first and prepare breakfast. As a child, Connor's favorite was pancakes cooked in bacon grease. The smoky smell of bacon, the pancakes crispy from cooking in bacon fat, and the sweet and salty flavor was delectable.

Camping with his dad was pretty much the only time his father could spend any quality time with him. Connor's father was a high school science teacher always too busy during the school year to focus on his son. During the summer months, his father's responsibilities of being a teacher lessened, and they would go on weeklong camping trips. On these trips his father would make up for lost time, by teaching Connor to fish, predict weather patterns, start a fire, set up a tent and how to be an appreciative outdoorsman. The most vivid memories of his father were from these trips, and it was from them that he grew to love and truly bond with him. The pancakes fried in bacon grease stuck with him. By taking his father's ritual and making it his own, he kept the fondest memories of his father alive.

Carl was the first out of his tent, camera in hand and filming. The smell of bacon grease filled the chilled air and permeated through the tents. The strong smell of crispy fried pork fat was a tantalizing alarm. His greedy eyes scanned the towering mound of pancakes, eggs, and bacon. "Wow, catering by the host. Is that for us?" Drool pooled under his tongue so he spat it out, just missing the table.

"Indeed, it is my friend. Help yourself." Connor was a little put off by the spit but let it go.

Mac walked from the patch of woods holding up a stringer full of large carp. He hollered to Connor. "Thought I'd be making the breakfast mate?"

Ben and Sheila slid out of their tent just in time to see Mac approaching with his catch. Sheila was intrigued by the dark-skinned Aborigine, walking from the woods, fish in hand with a compound bow strapped across his back. She couldn't help but stare, studying his rustic embodiment of Australia.

Connor flipped a crunchy-edged pancake with the old aluminum spatula. He tilted his father's well-aged and over-sized iron skillet so not to cause a grease splatter as it landed.

"Sorry, Mac, I'm the breakfast guy on this trip. Throw those fish in the fridge." He nodded toward Ben and Sheila's Land Rover. "We can have 'em for lunch." He then laid the pan flat causing the bacon grease to flood the pancake, crackling. The pan and spatula were his father's and they were both his most guarded personal possessions. Connor toted these on nearly every trip, keeping his father close.

Ben and Sheila's Land Rover was equipped with a rear refrigerator-freezer for cold storage. They spared no expense when it came to food, bringing along enough eggs, bacon, and dry pancake mix to feed a small army for a month, per Connor's request. Each member also had their own wilderness pack loaded with enough sealed and rationed food, water, and survival gear to last three weeks; the trip was scheduled for two.

That afternoon, everyone took it easy, resting up for their long trip across the Great Sandy Desert. While they slumbered around, a group of foot travelling, nomadic Aborigines entered the camp. It was common to have traveling Aboriginal families or groups make their way into Fitzroy Crossing, a popular *Aboriginal* camp long before becoming the supply hub for trekker's wishing to cross the desert. This particular group of Aborigines was a family complex composed of six male elders, two females and four teenage boys. Family complexes of Aborigines held onto their culture by handing down ancestral knowledge and practicing traditions taught to them by preceding generations. This knowledge gave the Aborigines a superior edge when living in the wilds of the Outback, however with the encroachment of *progress,* the knowledge and functioning family complexes of aborigines was succumbing.

Connor welcomed the group and insisted they join them that evening by the fire for an evening of food and drink. The final night before the expedition was to be a night of fun.

The sun crept its way past the horizon leaving in its place total darkness and a sudden chill. Sheila wanted to be a helpful part of the group so she took the initiative by trying to start the fire. Guided by the light of a battery driven camp lantern, she started by stacking heavy pieces of quartered logs on top of the last few smoldering embers.

George couldn't just watch any longer. "Nice try, but it won't catch like that."

"Well get over here and teach me big guy."

George positioned his camera atop one of the Rover's bumpers, angling it toward the fire pit and then walked over to Sheila. "You've got hot embers underneath these heavy logs. It's just gonna smother 'em out. Grab some small kindling and some dried leaves." He pointed toward the patch of forest.

George pulled Sheila's logs off the smoldering embers and set them aside. Moments later she handed him an armful of dried leaves and small sticks. He dropped it all to the ground then selected a small handful of leaves, placing them directly on the embers.

"Now what you wanna do is get some air moving over the embers, they'll heat up and catch the leaves." George blew, and the embers turned from grey to glowing red. "See how they turn red? That's when you touch a few leaves to 'em and keep blowing. Why don't you give it a shot?"

"Doesn't look too tough." Sheila crouched down and began to blow.

The embers turned red, so she pushed a pile of leaves on them and after a few seconds they began to smoke.

Lisa and Kate were walking toward the fire circle when they noticed Sheila kneeling on the ground blowing into the fire. "All right, Sheila, get that fire started!" Kate cheered. Kate was impressed to see her producer on her hands and knees starting the fire.

The leaves began to catch and started billowing with smoke. Sheila let out a victorious laugh.

"Blow a little harder," George said, smirking at his unintentional innuendo.

Sheila took a deep breath and started blowing harder on the fire. The more it smoked, the more she kept blowing. George turned his attention to Lisa and Kate, exchanging gestures as Sheila kept puffing. "Whoa... George, I...don't feel so..." Sheila toppled over sideways just missing the pit of embers.

"Oh, my God!" Lisa yelled and ran to Sheila.

"Oh, boy," George said, unconcerned. "You're not supposed to inhale the smoke."

Kate dragged her unconscious producer further away from the smoking embers. "Sheila, are you ok?"

She was unresponsive.

Connor saw the commotion from across the camp and realized what had happened. "She'll be fine," he said, walking toward the group. This wasn't the first time he saw someone pass out from starting a fire. All too often the inexperienced unknowingly inhale too much smoke while blowing, causing them to pass out.

"Whoops," George said.

Kate shook Sheila's shoulder and tapped her cheek. "Sheila...yoo-hoo."

"Oh, my God, we need to get her to a hospital!" Lisa whined, panicked.

Connor raised an eyebrow. "Whoa whoa whoa, slow down, Lisa. She'll be fine. Just give her a minute." Connor walked over to Sheila and sat her up. "Welcome back to earth, sweetheart."

Sheila's eyes opened and began blinking, taking a moment to gather her thoughts.

"G e e e e o o o or r r r g e!" Sheila snapped back to reality and scolded. "What did you do to me?"

"Sorry, boss." George tried his hardest not to grin but couldn't maintain.

"Next time maybe you should just start the fire, George," Kate laughed.

An hour later everyone was sitting by the fire. The Aborigines accepted their invitation and joined the team. They were drinking Matilda Bay Premium pilsner, George's beer of choice when in Oz. Ben and Sheila ordered in several cases for the expedition. Connor was a firm believer in drinking on the job, but only when filming was complete, and danger wasn't eminent.

The fire pit was roaring. Mac had created a spit to roast the large carp he had harvested that morning. The meaty fish sat well above the flame, but at the perfect height to slow roast. The aromas of wild lemon grass and ginger drifted around the camp as the stuffed fish began to cook.

The four teenage Aborigines carried a couple of homemade drums and two didgeridoos. They took their seats by the fire and started their music. The drums kept a slow, primal rhythm while the didgeridoos came to life. These young natives were making an ancient music with nothing more than the instruments the earth had given them. There were no plastics, no fabrication, no molds, and no metals, only the simplest of our world's natural gifts. Everyone sat silent, listening to the raw native sounds played by Australia's first and only native people.

After a few songs one of the Elders spoke out. His English perfect, with a thick Aussie dialect. "So why all you people wanna cross old Sandy anyway?"

From across the fire the smoke blended with his long curly grey hair and beard. He wore a leather head band that struggled to keep his untamable hair pressed back and away from his face. Connor admired his adornments; necklaces rimmed with teeth and claws, clay beads and braided leather wrist wraps that announced his tribal status as chief. In his left hand he clung to a five-foot-long walking stick etched and painted with various lines, circles, and hieroglyphic animals.

As eager as everyone was to answer, they left this one up to Connor. After all it was his show and he was, without question, the *head honcho*.

"We're filming a documentary and we want to show everyone how treacherous and full of life a desert can be," Connor said.

"Ah." The elder smiled. "It's not so terrible if you know what you're doing. Lots of sand and heat, some snakes, maybe a camel or two."

"And then we're headed to the Hamersley Mountain range in search of the Tasmanian tiger," Connor said.

The elder stopped grinning, his face more serious. "The tiger, why would you go and do a thing like that?"

Everyone noticed the elder's immediate change in tone and Connor responded. "I believe they still exist. And if they do, we'd like to show the world, get it protected and ensure its survival."

The other elders began shaking their heads and murmuring to each other in their native language. One elder pulled out a mortar and pestle and started crushing and grinding some wild herbs and berries gathered from their walkabout.

"The tiger is alive and well. They're hidden and with good reason. They don't want to be found. They are at peace. Don't muck wit' 'em," the elder scoffed.

"Are you saying you know they exist?" Connor grinned, but then straightened his face, serious.

The chief elder leaned in and scanned the eyes of each team member, more agitated. "Listen, they don't want to be found. Leave 'em alone."

Another elder spoke up. "If there were no tigers, there would be no hope for man."

"Not sure I follow you," Connor said.

"The tiger is the last journey for the soul of man. If they die out, then man will walk the earth forever. You people wanna put 'em on the television and exploit 'em. You white men exploit everything. You don't give a damn about the balance of nature," the elder snapped.

Connor sighed. "Look, I didn't mean to—"

Mac cut in, speaking in his native language to the angry elder. The drums stopped, and then the didgeridoo's tapered into silence as Mac's voice grew more aggressive. He argued with short bits of rebuttal from the disgruntled native. The elder finally shouted in his native tongue, throwing his hands toward Connor in universal disgust. The team sat motionless, almost breathless. The quarrel grew louder until it seemed a physical confrontation was eminent.

The chief elder laughed and cut in, addressing everyone. "Sorry for Mikey's abrasiveness. He's very strong in his beliefs. He carries a bit of a grudge toward outsiders."

Mac shook his head in disbelief and turned away from the disgruntled elder.

"Why is he so upset?" Lisa asked.

Sheila spoke up. "I wanna know why in the world he holds a grudge toward us?"

George's deep voice answered. "White man arrived, white man conquered."

"Oh…" Sheila put the puzzle together.

"Listen," the elder said. "We have an old story that tells of the tiger. It's a very special story that's been a part of our culture for thousands of years."

Mac tilted his head toward the disgruntled elder. "Yeah, but it's just a story. This guy here is losing his cool over a fairy tale."

"A story it is, but it's very special to us. You should know this yourself," the chief elder said to Mac.

"It's one thing to know the story and it's another thing to take it literally and curse others for doing something to help the damned tiger."

"Let me tell you all why the tiger is so special to us," the elder said.

Connor looked at George who was already adjusting his camera.

The chief elder slid his hand across the ground, cupping a small handful of dirt and pebbles. As he brought his hands together he may have mixed the dirt with something unseen. "There's a lot more to the tiger than meets the eye." With a quick flick of the wrist he tossed the dirt into the fire, causing the flames to erupt viciously and then settle. Everyone in the team jumped in reaction to the sudden flare up.

The elder rubbed his fingers across a four-legged striped figure that had been etched into his walking stick, tracing its white outline.

"Our people…" the elder nodded at Mac, "regard the tiger as a sacred animal and with good reason. We honor the tiger and must protect its spirit. You see, in the beginning, God was all there was. And after a good long while, God decided to break himself into pieces and create life.

Don't ask me why, 'cus I dunno. I reckon he was bored. Anyway, we have many, many lives, we are the pieces of God. Look around, life is dying all around us every day, but there's a constant supply of new life joining us. We all live and we all die and then we come back to this world again, over and over. We are *all* little pieces of God gradually working our way back together. And while we live this physical life, we are constantly evolving, trying to better ourselves. Life after life after life we keep evolving to higher levels of living."

The elder raised his walking stick high overhead and aimed toward the stars. "Eventually every life will reach the highest level, just under God, that is the tiger and through the tiger is the only way a life can reunite with God. God made the tiger and marked it so all would know that it was sacred. He gave it piercing eyes and a massive head, intelligence and cunning, and a very special ability to communicate with all life, then he painted it. He gave the tiger magnificent stripes like no other, for all to see. The tiger is the final vessel for a life, its final physical journey. When a tiger dies, the life is finally rejoined with God." The elder laid the walking stick in his lap, his fingers traced the engraving of the tiger. "That is why the tigers are in hiding and that is why you should reconsider your journey."

"That was quite intriguing," Connor said.

"Beautiful," Ben said.

"Wow, so according to your story, if the tigers *were* truly extinct, then all life would keep coming back and never make it to God?" Sheila asked.

"Righto," Mac said, "but it's just a story."

The elder shook his head, irritated with Mac's nonchalance.

The team reveled over the story for a few minutes until the chief elder called everyone's attention. "Come on, everyone, we have a treat for ya." The elder walked to every person in the group and handed them each a small, soft but firm, grey clay-like ball about the size of a marble. No one knew quite what to do with it so they sat quietly waiting for instructions.

Connor saw the grey balls being handed out. "Oh boy," he mumbled. He knew exactly what they were.

The elder finished handing out the balls then sat back down. "Put it in your mouth and chew. Swallow your spit, but don't swallow the ball," the chief elder said.

"Um…can you at least tell us what it is first? No offense, but I have no idea what this is, and I've got this thing about putting unknown objects in my mouth," Lisa said.

"Don't worry, Lisa. It's kinda like chewing tobacco," Connor said.

"Oh, tobacco, how bad can that be?" She grunted.

George and Connor were the first to start chewing the pituri ball.

"I'll pass," Carl said.

"It's really not so bad, Carl," Connor fibbed, he was aware of what lay ahead.

"Nah, I'm sitting this one out."

Sheila rolled the gob around in her mouth, cheek to cheek. "Oh! That's horrible!" Sheila cried, plucking it out with her fingers.

"C'mon, babe, it's not that bad. It tastes kinda like burnt plastic with a hint of sweetness," Ben said.

She tossed it back in. "I can't do it, honey." Sheila pulled it from her mouth again.

Lisa and Kate fought to keep from gagging, their faces contorting.

The elder laughed. "Give it a minute and the nasty will go away as it numbs your tasters."

Connor grinned. "It is pretty damned pungent, and should my tongue feel this numb?" Connor prided himself on being able to eat some of the nastiest foodstuffs from across the globe, but he couldn't help but cringe at the nasty goo ball rolling around in his mouth. He knew *of* the pituri balls, but never had one. Now, he knew, they were something he would never forget.

The elder tapped his stick on Connor's leg then smiled at his lack of reflex. "That means its working mate. It'll open you up and let you walk between worlds. My people have been making this stuff for generations, but we all make it a little different. Ya never know what to expect with this stuff. Fairly safe though. I've never seen anyone die while using it, at least not 'til the next day." The elder winked at Kate and Lisa.

Mac passed on the pituri. Irked by the elder, he made his retreat. He felt judged by the group, as though he had abandoned his culture. "I'll see ya in the morning. We have a big day ahead of us." By the time Mac made it to his tent the pituri was already taking effect on the team.

A strong but pleasant numbing sensation overcame Connor's entire body. It was quite euphoric, as though an invisible envelop of electric cotton padded his entire body. Inhibitions were fading, this was the freest he had ever felt. The rest of the team was getting hit with the same feeling. Carl however became an observer. He sat back and watched as the group became quiet, disappearing within themselves. They were aware, in touch with every cell within their body, every electrical pulse, every movement. Every thought, feeling and physical sensation was amplified and slowed beyond perception. They continued their induction as the didgeridoo's hummed along in the background.

One of the young Aborigines began drumming a primeval rhythm; it captured Lisa with its slow tempo. She moved like an ocean's waves, up and down, making her way to the fire. With no fear, worries or even the slightest of inhibitions, her body swayed, illuminated by the orange glow of the flames. The warmth touched her skin and she embraced it, almost to orgasm as her heightened and amplified senses took over.

Carl gawked as though he had never seen a woman before, incessant. His eyes were fixated on her ass, rhythmically swaying to the slow drumming. A couple of the Aborigines noticed Carl's infatuation, laughing it off.

George laid down beside the log he was seated on and stared at the stars, lost in his own introverted world.

Ben and Sheila tried to describe their current state of ecstasy to one another but were ineffective. Their faculties of communication were rendered temporarily out of service. They would look at each other and spout the occasional murmur of gibberish. Word forming didn't work but they didn't know.

Kate fought the overwhelming urge that pulled her toward Lisa. Kate wasn't a dancer, not even close to one, and always felt insecure and uncoordinated whenever she tried. Kate had been a shy and reserved child, awkward and uninterested in being a girl. During her teen years she metamorphosed, transforming into a more than beautiful woman. She remained a dedicated tom girl, growing up catching anything that slithered or crawled. Even though she grew up outdoors, she held strongly to her newfound feminine persona, never presenting as a tom-boy; but more like a beautiful woman infatuated with the natural world. Dancing wasn't a skill she ever mastered. There were times she tried to dance only to be heckled. She became insecure, vowing never to dance, at least in front of anyone. Finally, the years of insecurity were gone. The pituri had released all inhibitions. She moved like a burning flame with a slow flicker toward Lisa. The slow pounding drum echoed as the two female bodies started writhing closer together. Kate was dancing, an unstoppable force of exuding sex. The chief elder grinned. Kate's body writhed and danced like it never had before.

Connor broke from the inner euphoria then trained his eyes on her, absorbing. He couldn't believe what he was seeing; her pure sexual beauty flowing in front of him, writhing. It was overpowering, he wanted her, now, every bit of her, uncontrollable.

Over the years, Connor had been pushed toward Kate by a few producers only to come up with excuses for not pursuing the lead. The fixation on his career ruled him and now he was beyond successful. There was never time for relationships or extracurricular activities, but now things were different. As an established, and respected household name, perhaps it was time to focus on something other than his career.

George sat up, crossed his legs, and watched on. His mouth transformed into a slow, mildly expressive grin as he studied the two girls. They were dancing in a snake-like fashion, twisting and swirling around the fire. George and Connor looked at each other. They both grinned, but their movements and expressions were slowed to almost nonexistent.

Ben and Sheila appeared to be watching, but their faces were expressionless. There was no judgment, they were blank.

Lisa snaked her way in front of Kate. Face to face and eye to eye they now moved with the slow pounding of the native drum. Without touching, their bodies moved up and down, swaying within inches. Eyes fixed and locked into the others lustful gaze, they inched closer until warm breath on warm breath. Lisa and Kate were lost in a primeval dance of seduction.

Ben and Sheila melted into their camp chairs. Every muscle went limp and their eyes closed as they slipped into a temporary coma lost in their own subconscious.

Carl peeked out of his tent to see what was going on. The way the two young women danced together was so erotic he couldn't keep his eyes off them. He stared for a few seconds before he grabbed his camera and started filming. There was no harm in him making a little tape for himself was there? No one would know. He had been too good at keeping his personal fetish to himself all these years.

His camera continued to record as the dancing slowed and the two women took one another's hand. Carl panned to the Aborigines who grinned as the girls disappeared into the darkness together. He retrained his camera on the girls as Lisa and Kate sped off to the confines of their tent.

———

The Aborigines covered both George and Connor with heavy wool blankets before they left the fire. Connor continued to lay motionless beside the smoldering logs until he was jarred back to consciousness, almost panicked. He sat up, brushing the dirt from his face.

Two glowing eyes appeared out of the darkness on the opposite side of the defunct fire. Connor squinted, struggling to decipher the movement emerging from the blackened tree line. The eyes drew closer and closer until the body attached to them began to illuminate. Connor could feel every thud of his heart, this was his moment. It continued to approach, nearing the still glowing red embers. He could now see it; a massive Thylacine was staring at him with menacing black eyes. He found himself paralyzed, perhaps a wave of the pituri? Connor knew the pituri still had a grip on him, he insisted. How else could he rationalize the telepathic communication he could somehow feel with the beast? In what sounded like a haunting chorus of echoed whispers, *"Please…leave us alone,"* rumbled throughout Connor's soul. His trembling became near seizures, terrified.

Another figure then emerged from the tree line, a young teenage Aborigine girl. She walked to the tiger's flank and knelt beside it, crying. The tiger nuzzled the girl with affection then without notice, bared its elongated fanglike canine's. The Thylacine's gaping jaws seized the girl's throat. Connor's heart pounded from the inescapable terror. He was still paralyzed and unable to turn his head away. With an effortless shake of its head, the tiger ripped the young girl's throat apart. Then with a flick of its head, the large bloody chunk of throat landed at Connor's feet.

Panicked, he managed to break free of the pituri's grip, falling backwards unto the cold hardened earth. He found himself awake, surrounded by the chill of the early morning darkness, snoring George, and nothing more, relieved. Still under the influence of the pituri, he passed back out.

Seven a.m. and the sun threw its red orange hue over the camp. Kate opened her eyes and was face to face with Lisa. *A little close,* she thought. Confusion set in. *How did I get here?* she wondered. Kate lifted her sleeping bag and discovered she and Lisa were both naked. "What the hell?" she whispered. Lisa stirred a bit after hearing Kate's commotion and then opened her eyes.

"Morning," Lisa groaned.

"Um…good morning?" Kate replied, still confused but catching on.

"What's for breakfast?" Lisa slurred, trying to doze back off.

"Forget breakfast! I wanna know what we had for dinner." Kate got a little louder. "Lisa, do you have any idea as to why you're in my sleeping bag and, uh…why we're naked?"

"What?" Lisa said, half asleep.

"Oh, my God," Kate gasped.

Lisa's eyes sprung open followed by a gasp. She covered her mouth with the realization she was truly naked and in Kate's sleeping bag.

"The pituri! I don't remember anything. It was that nasty ball of clay," Kate whispered.

"Jesus! I can't remember a damned thing either," Lisa whispered back.

"I think this needs to stay between us," Kate asserted with a mischievous smile.

"Aw, c'mon, you don't want to tell everyone that we woke up in the same sleeping bag wearing nothing more than our birthday suits, and that neither one of us has a clue as to how we got here?"

"Do you think we, um?" Kate raised her eyebrows. "Uh, oh my God, never mind."

———

Over breakfast the team barely spoke. Kate and Lisa would randomly glance at one another and grin. Everyone ate as though it was their last meal, scouring down eggs, bacon, hash browns and coffee. The only thing missing was Connor's pancakes. He just wasn't himself. Visions of his dream continued to haunt him.

"You ok, Connor?" Sheila asked then sipped from her coffee.

"Yeah, yeah, just a little shaken from a dream last night."

"Wanna share?"

"Nah, I just need to get it out of my head. It was so real."

"Best way to get it out is to talk it out," Sheila said, warming her cold hands on the hot cup.

"Really, I'm fine."

"Oh, come on, macho man," she prodded.

"Ok. It's not that big of a deal. It just freaked me out. To be blunt, I had a Thylacine tell me to leave it alone and then it ripped a young girl's throat apart. Normally, I would just shrug it off, but it seemed so real."

"Oh, my, I wasn't expecting that, but it was just a dream and I'm sure it's because of all the mumbo jumbo the cranky old Aborigine was saying last night."

"Believe me, I know. Sounds crazy but it felt like the tigers were sending a message not to continue on the expedition. I'm sure it's a product of my imagination and the pituri. I just need to get it out of my head."

Ben spoke up, enthused. "Well, shake it off 'cus we're about to cross the desert!"

"I'm good, let's get packed up. It's time to play in the sand box."

OFF TO HOBART

Tasmania - 1935

GREG SAT ON THE FLOOR NEXT TO PETEY AND EXAMINED BEN'S EAR, giving him a gentle scratch under his neck. The bullet had ripped through the tip, leaving a small, blood encrusted hole. "He'll be fine, son." Greg stood up, gave Petey's head a rub then sat at the kitchen table.

Millie sunk into her chair at the table. "I was scared, Greg. I don't ever wanna feel that way again."

"I'm so sorry, Mil."

"They were reckless, shooting toward the house," Millie spouted.

"So they know about Ben?"

"I think so. I told 'em he was our dog, but I don't think they bought it."

"Maybe it'll pass, like it never happened."

"They were really disturbing. The fat one said he knew the area *really well*, and then he asked where *Mr. McKinley* was. He was trying to scare me, and it worked. Then he sniffed at me as he walked by."

Greg slammed his forearm into the table. "We need to get the hell outta this place."

"What if they had killed Ben? I'd a killed them myself." Millie's eyes watered, and a single tear trickled down her face.

"I'm gonna quit the quarry. I've got to be here in case they come back."

"I don't want you to quit if it'll get us out of here quicker," Millie whined.

"What if they come back when I'm not here?" Greg's voice strained.

"Let's go to the sheriff," Millie said.

"Earl can't do anything without a name."

"Smitty and Tanner."

———

Greg drove out to the quarry the next morning to let the crew know he had some business to handle in town.

Downtown, Hobart had a fresh ocean breeze that supplied the town with salt air. Today was warm and blue, not a cloud in the sky. The ports were lined with trade ships, bringing supplies to and from the mainland. The Sheriff station was on Main Street, three blocks from the docks.

Greg and Petey peered through the glass and twisted the handle. "It's locked."

"No one's in?" Millie asked.

"Apparently not," Greg said, aggravated.

"Maybe they're out making…"

"Can I help you folks?" A voice came from across the street.

Greg recognized the sheriff. "Yeah, we've had a bit of trouble out on our property."

"McKinley?"

"Yeah," Greg said.

"I thought that was you. Greg, right?" Earl said as he trotted across the street.

Greg eyed Earl's dull and slightly corroded silver sheriff's badge as he neared.

"Yep, it's been a while, Earl."

"Indeed, it has. Hey, I was just headed out for some breakfast, wanna tag along?"

"Nah, we've had a problem at our ranch. We're here on business," Greg said.

"Well there's no law saying we can't do business over breakfast. Come on, it's on me."

Greg looked at Millie for approval.

Earl looked down at Petey. "What's this monster's name?"

"Petey." He couldn't stop staring at the sheriff's holstered gun.

"Well Petey, how's about some hot griddle-cakes with berries, my treat?"

"Dad, can we?" Petey begged, smiling.

"I reckon so. I don't see any harm in it."

They all walked a few blocks down to *Norma's Café* that overlooked the harbor. The diner was built nearly thirty years ago and was the first one in town. Now there was an eatery on nearly every street. From the sidewalk Norma's looked a little lopsided; it was built on the slope of the hill that descended to the marina. Inside, the floors were made of various remnants of solid wood deck planks, most likely from an old dismantled ship. The rustic looking pieces fit like a puzzle and creaked with every step. Earl chose the largest table situated in front of the café's main window, providing an unobstructed view of the docked ships.

"So what's the problem?" Earl asked.

"Well…when I was working at the quarry yesterday, some hunters came on to my ranch and started shooting at my dog, they nearly shot my son. Millie was home. She heard the shots, grabbed the rifle and ran outside. One of their bullets just missed her. It ripped through the front porch tearing out a chunk of wood."

Petey knew he was supposed to stay quiet when adults talk but he couldn't hold back. "They shot Ben's ear."

"They shot your dog?" Earl asked.

"Yeah, they shot a hole right through his ear," Petey answered.

"Do you know who they were?" Earl asked.

Millie spoke up. "The fat guy said their names were Smitty and Tanner. That Smitty bastard got close and sniffed me like a dog."

Earl dropped his fork.

"You ok, mate?" Greg asked.

The sheriff grabbed the white table linen from his lap and wiped his mouth. "I'm fine."

"You went pale, you sure you're all right?" Greg asked.

"Yeah, yeah, my stomach went tipsy on me."

"Maybe you should lay off the eggs," Greg smiled.

"So is there anything you can do about those hunters?" Millie asked. She was more concerned with her family's safety than the sheriff's queasiness.

"Chances are they won't be back," Earl said.

"You know of 'em?" Greg asked.

Earl was reluctant to answer. He knew the pair well, too well. "I think they work for McPherson." Earl forced a soggy bite of toast dripping with runny egg yolk into his mouth. He didn't want to lie, not to good people.

"Think they'll be a problem?" Greg asked.

"Nah, I'll stop by McPherson's ranch, see if I can track 'em down. You wanna press charges?" Greg looked at Millie. Earl knew that even if they did press charges nothing would come of it.

"I don't wanna start trouble," Millie said. "I just don't want those guys anywhere near me or my family again."

"Well, I'll find 'em and give 'em a lil' scare." Earl was ashamed. He knew his words were meaningless and that there was nothing he could do to Joe's goons. It sickened him.

"We'd appreciate that, Earl," Greg said.

"How 'bout I have the doc take a look at your dog's ear?" The guilt was ripping away at his conscience. He didn't become sheriff to lie and give false hope to those who needed it most.

"Ben's not a dog," Petey blurted. Greg cut Petey off and Millie faked a few nervous laughs.

"Petey hates it when we call Ben a dog…he'd rather think of Ben as a person rather than an animal," Greg added.

Petey realized his slip of tongue and followed his parents' lead. "He's more than a dog, he's my best friend."

"Well he's a lucky dog to have a friend like you, Petey."

Earl insisted on paying for breakfast. Greg gave a little resistance but gave in to the sheriff's assertiveness.

Their meeting with Earl left Greg and Millie feeling secure. Greg was confident he could return to work at the quarry without having to worry about his family being threatened. They made a day out of being in town; walked around the docks and visited the shops that lined the cobble stone streets. Midafternoon they climbed back into the Oldsmobile and started their journey home, or at least that's what Petey thought. His eyes opened wide and he grinned ear to ear when they pulled into their next destination. Greg and Millie had kept their plan a secret from Petey.

Greeting them was an oversized bamboo entrance gate with massive bamboo fence boards on each side. Above the gate was a massive slab of Karri tree that had been chiseled into the words *Hobart Zoo*. It was a fine piece of craftsmanship; every hand scraped chisel mark stood out, giving an aged rustic look. The zoo itself wasn't impressive by any means, with its unnatural caging, concrete floor and prison bar enclosures, chicken wire wrapped around cheap wood frames, and a couple of inexperienced and underpaid animal keepers who spent more time drinking and playing cards in the supply house rather than tending the zoo.

The zoo wasn't one of Hobart's priorities. Although Hobart was nearly recession proof, the stock market crash of 1929 affected the zoo's main government contributors. The zoo had taken a backseat and was temporarily shut down until McPherson saw it as a way to grab the public's interest. McPherson bought the zoo from the City of Hobart in 1932. He invested just enough to keep the doors open and its inhabitants alive. The animals were condemned, forced to live in unnatural prison-like enclosures until their end. Depression for the animals was eminent. There was no enrichment or interaction; days would go by without a single visitor to the zoo. The current worldwide depression was not limited to mankind. The zoo was once vibrant but now, its life was fading.

Greg drove through the open gate and parked in the empty lot. Petey took notice and sprung to attention. "Are we going in?"

"You bet ya." Greg smiled.

"It's been about five years, do you remember coming, Petey?" Millie asked as she opened her door.

"Of course I remember, this is my favorite place." Petey jumped out of the backseat and onto the gravel parking grounds.

"Come on, come on!" Petey said.

One of the keepers had been out in the park throwing some damp hay into the elephant enclosure. He noticed the unexpected guests walking through the entrance. He scurried to the gate, snatched their small admission fee without a word and then disappeared into the supply building.

They walked to the first exhibit, an elephant, swaying from side to side on a circular concrete slab surrounded by a six-foot wall of rusted steel prison bars. There was no roof or protection from the elements, the cage was bare other than a watering trough, a pile of hay and several large dung piles. The corners of the elephant's eyes were stained with tear trails streaming past its lower jaw. Petey ran to the small wooden fence that kept visitors from getting too close.

Millie stared into the elephant's depressed eyes. "Greg."

"I know," he said.

"This is horrible," Millie whispered.

Petey stood in awe of the elephant's massive size, but even he could sense something wasn't right.

"Maybe he's just old?" Greg said.

"It doesn't matter how old he is. He's absolutely miserable," Millie whispered, concealing her distraught from Petey.

"Not much we can do."

"We can give an earful to the Governor," Millie said.

"Like he cares…"

Petey stared at the elephant, puzzled as to why it kept swaying back and forth. "Mom, I think he's sad."

"I know, Petey."

Moving from enclosure to enclosure, they witnessed misery and horrid conditions at every stop. Greg and Millie decided they had seen enough and refused to continue. They were headed toward the exit when Petey noticed an enclosure somewhat hidden behind the wombat cage. Greg and Millie resisted, but Petey insisted on taking a look, darting away from his parents. Petey passed the wombat enclosure and spotted something very familiar. It was lying within the confines of the dilapidated old enclosure.

Petey ran to the wire cage. "He looks like Ben!"

"Not too loud, Petey," Greg hushed.

It was curled up, sleeping in the only patch of sunlight that somehow found its way through a hole in the wood-scrap roof.

"Sorry, Dad." Petey made kissing sounds, reaching his fingers through the squares of the wire fence.

"Careful, Petey, that's not Benjamin," Greg whispered. The tiger raised its head and peered up through squinted eyes.

"Oh Greg, he looks sick," Millie winced.

Petey made a few more kissing sounds to call the sluggish tiger over. As he did, another tiger came pushing though a plywood door that led from a small three by three shelter box at the rear of the enclosure.

"Mom, look!" Petey said.

"Get your fingers out, Petey," Greg said as the tiger staggered toward them.

"He can barely walk," Mille cried. The tiger wobbled its way to them, wavering like a drunkard, with ribs and hips showing through its loose hide.

"This is criminal," Greg said as the tiger sniffed where Petey's fingers had been. Greg kneeled and held the back of his hand to the cage. The tiger sniffed Greg's fingers through the small squares in the wire then leaned against it. Greg scratched the tiger's dusty coat and it seemed to enjoy the attention, raising its head as Greg scratched harder. The other tiger wanted in and struggled to its feet, swaying as it walked toward the strangers.

"These guys are pretty tame," Greg said. The second tiger leaned against the wire expecting a rub.

"Can I, Dad?"

"Let your mom have a go first."

Millie's fingers went through the fence and began scratching its back. "He seems friendly enough, you can give 'em a scratch," Millie said.

Raspy and angered, a voice blurted from behind them. "Watch it! They'll rip your fingers off!" Mille and Petey jerked their fingers from the wire and spun around.

"Jus' muckin' wit ya," the man laughed.

Greg continued to stroke the tiger's flank. "Why are these guys so tame?"

Petey couldn't help but stare at the old man's brown leather eye patch. Coupled with his gnarly silver beard, he was the epitome of a pirate working in a zoo. "They been here since pups, five or six years I'd say. They're used to people."

"Why are they so skinny and weak?" Millie scolded.

"No one wants to see tigers, they're a nuisance, hell they're lucky they ain't been killed and turned in fer the bounties. McPherson was gonna kill these two himself, but for some reason or another he didn't. Probably jus' forgot about 'em." His voice rattled as he tucked the smoldering cigarette between his dry, cracked lips.

"So you haven't been feeding them?" Millie scorned.

The keeper coughed a few times, fingered his cig, then heaved up a mouthful of putrid brown and blood tinged phlegm, spatting it to his side. "We been feedin' 'em. Jus' not as much."

"That's no way to care for an animal." Greg stood and faced the keeper.

"Can only feed 'em when we got tucker, mate," the keeper said.

"Why don't you set 'em..." Millie started to ask, but stopped herself short, realizing they would be shot on site if released.

"Set 'em free? Hell, I'd kill 'em and get the bounties me self before I'd do something stupid like that," he bolstered.

"You should be ashamed of yourself," Millie scoffed.

"Look, lady, if I had more food I'd toss it to 'em, but I don't."

They drove home, distraught from their day at the zoo. Every inhabitant suffered from some sort of neglect, but the tigers were starving to death, probably under order of McPherson. Greg and Millie felt helpless, but what could they do? The city wasn't willing to assist a privately-owned zoo and the current owner had a devout hatred of tigers.

———

Two weeks later, McPherson was irate. Who in their right mind would give a rat's ass about the tigers? They were cold blooded murdering sons of bitches, but somewhere, someone was upset about the conditions of the tigers at his zoo. Someone had been complaining to all the big wigs around town who in turn started putting a little pressure on McPherson to fix the problem.

Tonight, McPherson was in his twelve-stable barn, going over some business with Smitty. His lavish barn was more or a less a live-in country club, complete with a two-story living suite, outfitted with a full bar and poker table. He designed it as a getaway from his much younger second wife who had left him four years prior. Divorce was taboo and practically unheard of, but McPherson had already done so twice. It's no coincidence that both wives had fled Tasmania to the mainland in an effort to escape the wrath of *Mighty Joe*. McPherson had the ability to make the life of anyone living in Tasmania less than tolerable.

Smitty took a swig of his watered-down gin. "Got anything for us?"

McPherson squinted at Smitty, swigged his iced vodka then puffed on his oversized spit-soaked cigar. "Nuttin' much right now." His glass clanked as he hammered it onto the granite bar topper. "Where's your skinny?"

Smitty could tell something was bothering Joe, his normally shitty demeanor was shittier than usual. "Tanner's fishin' in your pond trying to fetch up some grub. Something buggin' ya?"

"Ah, it ain't shit, just some townsfolk bitchin' about the zoo, complaining about skinny tigers and shit."

"Doesn't seem like much of a problem. Just get rid of the tigers," Smitty said.

"Ah, they're gonna cause a big fuss if they just disappear. They been bringing 'em food for the past couple weeks, making me look bad."

"Why don't ya just have your keepers feed 'em more?" Smitty asked.

"I ain't giving them murdering beasts shit. They're killers." McPherson bit down on his cigar.

"Maybe you could get some new ones."

"There ya go, you and yer skinny get me some new tigers. Then we can toss out the old." McPherson fumbled to spit out a few shreds of tobacco clinging to his tongue.

"I know just the spot for one. It's living on a ranch with a family. We nearly got it a few weeks ago. It's a big fat one."

"You talking about the McKinley's place?"

"Yeah, you know about it?" Smitty asked.

"Earl came out here a couple weeks ago and said the McKinley's were complaining about you two idiots shooting at their dog."

"They ain't got no dog, they got a damned tiger out there. It was following their boy around. We tried to shoot it, but it…"

"What in the hell are those idiots doing keeping a beast like that."

"You want us to grab it and stick in the zoo?"

"I'd rather you kill the damned thing but go ahead and get it. Switch it out with one of those skinny fuckers at the zoo."

"Earl wants you to stay clear of 'em, but it ain't up to me what you fella's do on yer own damned time."

"So how much we get for bringin' in a live tiger?" Smitty asked.

"Triple."

ENTER THE DESERT

Present day

THE CONVOY OF LAND ROVERS THUNDERED ACROSS THE SUN cracked dirt road. Thirty miles later the road dissipated, covered by large areas of blown sand. As the expedition continued south, scenery slowly became red, tinged by the high iron content within the sand.

Connor was driving the lead vehicle accompanied by George who hadn't spoken since they left the outpost. "Do you remember anything about last night?"

George sat up and sighed. "Sure, I remember sitting by the fire, chewing on that little chunk of dirt and then waking up beside the fire this morning."

"Damn it, that stuff was potent. I feel like I need to remember something. I just can't."

"I don't remember a damned thing. It's gone. If it comes to me, great, if not, oh well," George said.

"I wish I was as laid-back as you, but it's driving me crazy. The girls... Lisa and Kate...they did something, it's right there, but I just can't remember. Those Aborigine's know what went down, did you see them? They were grinning from ear to ear."

Mac jerked the wheel to avoid a large desert skink basking in the Rover's path. Carl's camera tumbled out of his hands and he juggled to keep it from falling. His beady eyes glared at Mac, irritated. Mac took notice.

"There was a lizard," he pleaded.

Carl shook his head, irritated. He pressed a few buttons on his camera then put his eye to the viewfinder. Several minutes had passed and Mac broke the silence.

"Anything good?"

"Just reviewing some footage," Carl said.

"No sound?"

"I have it off."

"Turn it on, I'd love to take a listen."

Carl turned his gaze toward Mac and looked him in the eyes. "No."

"Crabs in ya pants, mate? Or maybe you don't wanna jinx the footage or something?"

"Something like that." Carl's voice was void of emotion.

"Good stuff at least?"

Carl pressed his eye back to the viewfinder. "You could say that."

———

Ben was driving but barely, he had become a living zombie with lifeless eyes fixed on the vehicle ahead. Sheila was silent. Her mind was off meandering in the endless desert, somewhere between daydream and sleep.

———

Lisa looked over at Kate as she slept against the passenger window. She took advantage of the moment and used it to gawk. She took in Kate's splendor, all of it. Hidden behind her outdoorsy façade was a woman with an incomparable natural beauty. Kate's blonde hair blanketed her cheek, accenting bronze sun-kissed skin. Lisa was lost in admiration of Kate's splendor until her mind was jarred back to reality by the thundering impact of her vehicle slamming into the back of Mac and Carl's Rover.

"Shit!" she screamed as her Rover came to a smashing halt.

Kate sprung up, panicked by the crash "What happened?" Her heart raced, confused.

"I don't know…I looked away for a second and then bam!" Lisa said, unbuckling her lap and shoulder belt.

All vehicles in the procession had stopped on Connor's lead, with the exception of Lisa, whose Rover had smashed into the back of Mac and Carl's. Mac darted from his passenger door and ran over to Lisa as she climbed out in disbelief, holding her head. He saw the front end of Lisa's vehicle embedded in the back of his bumper and rear hatch.

"You guys ok?" he asked.

"We're fine. I'm so sorry. I looked away for a second…I'm so sorry. Are you guys ok?"

"No worries here, just glad you're ok."

Everyone climbed out of their vehicles to investigate the commotion at the rear of the convoy.

"Is everyone ok?" Sheila asked.

Carl was the last, grimacing as he stumbled from the Rover, rubbing his neck and filming. "You gave me whiplash."

Mac's face went crooked. "Well, judging by the impact I'd say you're gonna live."

"I'm so sorry, Carl," Lisa said.

"Well you should have been paying attention," Carl snapped. He continued to rub his neck while trying to record the damage to the Rovers.

"I only looked away for a second." *Or maybe a little more* she thought to herself. Carl made her nervous with his video camera. He swayed it toward her each time she spoke, as though he was trying to catch evidence for an unseen accident attorney.

"Well, you shouldn't have, and now you've destroyed two vehicles and you probably gave me whiplash!"

"Whoa, whoa, whoa," Ben interrupted. "That's why we have insurance, the damage is minimal, and accidents happen. No need to get heated and beat Lisa up over it."

"Well, I'd prefer not to have her driving behind me from now on," Carl insisted.

"Fine," Ben said. "Sheila and I will follow your vehicle from now on."

Connor took note of Carl's pompous attitude. Rather than inject, he studied. Connor crawled underneath Lisa's Rover to investigate.

"Only problem I see is a small radiator leak. There's a small crack in the housing with a slow drip."

"Can it be fixed?" Kate asked.

Connor shimmied from under the Rover. "Nope, at least not out here with the tools we have," Connor said, brushing the sand and dirt from his pants.

"Will it drive?" Lisa asked.

"Should run fine, but we'll have to keep a constant check on the radiator fluid. It should make the trip as long as we keep up on the coolant level."

"I'm so sorry guys!" Lisa whined.

Sheila put her arm around Lisa and squeezed. "It's ok. It happens, sweetheart. It's really not that bad."

The Rovers fired back up and the convoy headed south west across the desert. Lisa's vehicle was now in front of Carl and Mac's, with Sheila and Ben trailing. One hundred and twenty miles into the desert and all sight of structure was lost. Their six-hundred-mile trek across the Great Sandy Desert had officially begun. Every direction was flat as far as the eye could see, with the occasional burst of thorny succulents. The road was gone after two hundred twenty miles, and they were then guided by GPS alone. The vehicles were slowed to thirty miles an hour due to the uneven and lumpy terrain; any faster would be damned near unbearable.

George was on drive duty, with two hours of light before sunset. Connor scanned the landscape from his passenger seat searching for a suitable camp. "What do you think about Carl?"

"I don't like 'em. I don't trust 'em and he's a whiner."

Connor grinned. "Had a feeling you'd say something like that."

"Call 'em like I see 'em."

"Maybe it's nothing, but do me a favor, keep your eyes on him will ya? I'm not sure if I trust him either."

They drove another thirty minutes before spotting a rocky outcrop to the east. Connor followed his instinct and changed bearings toward the gathering of rocks and the row of trailing vehicles followed. Proceeding, smooth red rock replaced sand. Connor parked his vehicle next to the largest boulder nearly the size of a small home. He exited the vehicle and gazed at the immense free-standing rock. The rest of the team staggered out of their Rovers and approached.

Connor patted the reddish stone. "This should give us some cover in case we get hit by a sand storm. Let's set up camp."

Everyone was slow to function with the exception of Mac. Fatigue and jet lag had set in.

With the camp established, the team sat around two folding tables with collapsible camp chairs. They were all tired, and all agreed against starting a fire. Instead they ate prepackaged meals while the sun set. The cold chill of night hit them about five minutes after the sun had settled. Worn out and tired, silence was the conversation of choice.

"I'm gonna scout around for a few minutes," Connor said.

"Go for it, young man. I'm going to bed," Sheila grabbed Ben's hand and pulled.

"I'm with ya, honey," Ben said.

"Mind if I tag along?" Mac asked.

Ben raised an eyebrow and Sheila's jaw dropped into a quasi-smile.

"With Connor," Mac winked at the couple.

"Let's go, Mac," Connor said, oblivious to Mac's joke.

"You guys don't need to bother filming tonight. Just hit the sack," Connor instructed George and Carl.

Within seconds Carl was headed off to his tent. "You don't have to tell *me* twice."

The rest of the team disappeared into their tents as soon as Connor and Mac walked off. The sun had vanished, but the moon immediately took over, illuminating the red rock and sand, giving plenty of light. They walked about a hundred yards to another large rock, almost as big as the one they parked against. Connor noticed an inconspicuous four foot by four foot dark rounded opening in the rock.

"Wanna check it out?" he said, shining his ultra-bright LED flashlight in and around the dark hole.

"You bet," Mac said.

Connor crouched and made his way into the dark opening. Mac followed. The cave walls were encrusted with sparkling mineral deposits that reflected the flashlights beams. Once well inside the entrance, it opened up into a slightly larger pocket about seven feet in diameter and four feet high. While examining the cave walls, Mac noticed another small opening in the rock. "This one's a bit smaller, Connor."

"Looks like it's gonna be a tight squeeze. Sure you're up for it, Mac?"

"Let's see, I could be lying in a tent, sleeping next to Carl or I could be crawling through a dark hole with you. I love all these options," Mac joked.

Connor lay on his belly and started wiggling head first through the narrowing rocky tunnel.

———

Lisa and Kate each slid into their own twenty-degree chill rated sleeping bags. They inch-wormed toward each other in an attempt to share body heat but the bags were just too thick. "You really should've gone along with them," Lisa said as she tucked her chin into the sleeping bag.

Kate laughed. "I knew you were going to say that."

"Well, why didn't you? He was just as tired as the rest of us. The only reason he even offered was because he wanted you to join him."

"No way! You really think so?"

"Uh, yes! Its late, he's tired, and he offers up to anyone to tag along for a little walk."

"Oh, wow, maybe you're right, now that you put it like that. Ugh! I can be so dense sometimes."

"It could have been the perfect opportunity for you two to *really* get to know each other." Lisa raised her eyebrows a few times, insinuating.

"Sure, me, Connor and Mac. That's just how I like it."

"Mac only went because he didn't want Connor to go alone. If you went, I guarantee Mac would have stayed. Jesus, Kate, anyone can tell you two belong together. What the hell are you waiting for? You should get out there right now. Put your clothes back on and go find them."

"Ok. It could be fun." Kate grabbed the khaki cargo pants from her pack and wrestled them on from inside the sleeping bag.

"Go get 'em tiger."

———

"It's a real tight squeeze." Connor grunted, wedging his way forward. He transitioned from hands and knees to belly crawling.

"Need a pushy on the tushy?"

"Hang on…almost there…looks like it gets bigger." Connor struggled through the narrowing hole. The air changed as they ventured deeper into the rock. It went from absolute dryness to warm, muggy, and musky, reminiscent of a damp basement.

Connor broke free of the fissure's grasp and slid belly first downward into the next cavity, which was much larger than the last, about the size of a small outdoor shed. He shined the light around the floor, and then noticed something that stood out, a pile of bones. Connor could almost stand, but the overhead of smooth rock was very uneven.

"Come on down, Mac." His voice cast a bit of urgency. "We've got human bones." His eyes focused on a human skull. Connor knew they had stumbled upon something special, they had found the needle in the haystack.

"I've got this thing about bones and dark caves," Mac grunted as he squirmed his way down and through the constricted opening.

"You're not afraid of bones, are ya?"

"Depends on the ghost attached to 'em." Mac entered the opening and kneeled beside Connor.

Connor studied their positions, noting their closeness. Then he carefully lifted a skull and examined its teeth.

Mac shook his head in disbelief. "I'll be damned, Connor." He whispered. "It's a tiger."

"I know, it's fascinating, but this is what's even more incredible, it looks like it died curled up next to the human."

"It's a child huh?"

"Yea, it's a boy." Connor studied the skeleton with his flashlight. "I don't see any broken bones, looks like everything is intact. I'm not sure what to make of this, Mac. It's our first bit of proof the tigers are or were still here on mainland Australia until fairly recently. Supposedly they went extinct from here two thousand years ago."

Mac squinted and shook his head. "But why the heck is it curled up in a cave with a boy?"

"That's the million dollar question."

———

Kate's breath swirled, barely lit from the flashlight. She walked the camp perimeter searching for clues as to where Connor and Mac headed. She scanned the ground, but the hard, red rock prevented tracks. She was determined …

———

"Wow, get a look at this, mate." Mac shined his flashlight upon the cave wall to his right. Connor's beam met Mac's, illuminating a cluster of subtle rustic hieroglyphs drawn onto the sparkling surface.

"Good eye, Mac." Connor moved to the wall for a closer look. Just as he did they both heard an odd grunting sound echoing around the cave. They looked at each other and silenced their breathing.

"You heard that right?" Mac whispered.

Connor nodded, listening.

"What the hell was it?" The sound of faint rustling echoed around the cave and then stopped. They looked at each other, bewildered.

"What ya think?" Mac whispered.

"I have no idea." Connor did a mental run-through of every possible desert dwelling animal that could make that sort of noise and there were none.

Mac shifted closer to Connor. "We've got all sorts of big bugs and small goanna's. As far as I know none of 'em moan like that." The rustling started again. Together they held their breath, listening, and then it stopped again.

"H e e e e e l p M e e e," a young voice with a raspy Australian dialect echoed around the cave.

Connor and Mac turned their gaze upon one another; Mac's eyes were about to pop from his head. "For fuck's sake, did you hear that, mate?" Mac couldn't stop his hands from shaking.

Connor didn't speak. His eyes squinted, focusing and he gave a slow nod.

"Help me!" The voice echoed around the cave, but this time it was much louder and more distinct.

"I don't know about you, but I think it's time to go," Mac whispered.

"Come on, Mac, relax, after all it sounds female. What's the worst that can happen?"

"I sure as hell don't wanna find out." Mac hunched his way toward the entrance and stopped just in front of the holed entrance. Something grabbed his left calf and squeezed. He opened his mouth to scream, but nothing came out. He gasped when whatever was clutching his calf shook at his leg, then managed to gulp just enough air to release the loudest, ear piercing scream Connor had ever heard.

Panicked and terrified, Mac broke free of the ghostly grip and ran without consideration of the uneven rocky overhead. Connor spun around directing his flashlight just in time to see Mac strike his head on the rock ceiling and drop to the floor, unconscious.

————

Carl focused the camera on Mac's face. "I think he's coming to."

Lisa gently tapped the side of his face. "Come on Mac, wakey wakey."

Mac was lying on the ground with a pillow beneath his head. After a few more seconds he slowly opened his eyes and stared up at the star filled sky.

"I'm dead ain't I?"

"Um, not quite Bushman, you're very much alive," Connor laughed.

"I got me lights turned off?" Mac whimpered.

"Yep," Connor said.

"Oh Mac, it's such a relief to have you back. Are you ok?" Sheila asked.

Mac looked around, puzzled. "I reckon. What happened?"

"You don't remember at all?" Connor asked, trying to gauge the severity of Mac's concussion. He knew the slight amnesia was normal, however, the severity of the amnesia coupled with the amount of Mac's downtime could alert him to how severe the actual concussive brain injury was.

Mac eased into a sitting position and used his arms to tripod behind him. "Well, I remember being in the cave. I remember finding the bones. Oh, yeah, and then we heard that rustling and some creepy ghost lady was bugging me out. Awe crikey, don't tell me I fainted?" Mac paused to reflect. "That'd be embarrassing."

Kate's face twisted, writhing between pity and laughter. "I'm so sorry, Mac."

"No worries, Katey. It's not your fault."

"This is gonna be interesting," Ben whispered to his wife.

"Mac, I'm so sorry." Kate struggled to contain her undecipherable grin. She was plagued with guilt yet couldn't hide the smile.

"Girlie, it's not like *you*..."

Kate put her hands on Mac's shoulder and interrupted. "Mac, I couldn't sleep, so I went looking for you guys. I found your foot prints by that huge rock so I crawled in and followed your voices. I thought it would be funny to scare you both a bit. I could see the light from your flashlights so I turned mine off and made my way through. I grabbed your leg."

Mac rubbed his head. "I...I thought you were the ghost of them bones in the cave. I about wet me self when you grabbed me."

"I'm so sorry, Mac. I was only playing around."

"Guess I punched out, fainted like one a them funny lil' goats."

"No Mac, you took off like a bat out of hell and slammed your head into the rock ceiling." Connor handed Mac a fresh icepack, then gestured to the center of his own forehead.

Mac felt around 'til his fingers crossed the enlarged knot protruding from his forehead. "Well that explains the throbbing."

"I really am truly sorry, Mac, you're such a nice guy," Kate pleaded.

"I had no idea what was going on." Connor grinned. "I heard you gasp and it sent me spinning around with my light just in time to see you get dropped like a sack of bricks. She scared the hell out of me too. I didn't expect to see a woman lying on the floor of the cave. She triggered your fight or flight response. You obviously chose flight but were flying blind my man. She and I had to go back to camp and grab some rope.

We felt bad leaving you there, but you were out cold, and we couldn't drag you through that hole. We made a harness and pulled you out."

Mac sat up and rubbed the sore knot on his head again. "Well at least I didn't have to crawl back through that tiny little hole. I made you blokes do all the work."

"I love that about you, Mac, always looking on the bright side," Sheila said.

Everyone scattered to their tents and once again settled in for the night. It was clear and cold with a slow steady breeze.

Kate sighed as she slid into her sleeping bag. "Oh, my God, I can't believe I caused all that." She zipped the bag all the way up to her chin.

"I've gotta hand it to ya, you sure know how stir things up," Lisa said.

"I just wanted to give 'em a little scare, not a concussion!"

"Now you'll have to look for another chance to get your hunk alone."

"Uhhhhhhgggg," Kate grunted in play agony.

––––––––

Sun-up and the smoky aroma of bacon was drifting around the camp, making its way into everyone's tent. One by one everyone started emerging into the cool morning air, as if a dinner bell had been rung. They were all caught by the allure of hot and crispy, pan-fried pork fat. Carl was the first to grab a spot at the table.

"Wow," Carl said. He couldn't chew fast enough, his beady eyes darted back and forth between the bacon on his plate and Mac's forehead as the Aborigine approached. "Nice goose egg."

Mac sat down at the table. "It's really that bad? It's sore as hell."

"Whoa," George's burly voice gave a slow mumble. He couldn't help staring at the baseball sized bulge on Mac's forehead. Even the worst Hollywood special effects studios wouldn't have believed it.

Sheila's eyes widened as she neared the table. She tripped over the camps stuffed trash bag, managing to right herself, still staring at Mac's swollen forehead. "Oh, my. Maybe we should get him to a doctor."

"I'm digging the attention, but is it really that bad?"

"It looks like you've got a softball protruding from your skull," Ben said.

"It sure does," Connor agreed.

Sheila turned to Connor. "What do you think? Should he see a doctor?"

"I'm fine and even if I went to a doctor, what are they gonna do? Nothing, they'd tell me to take it easy for a day or two. So, if you guys want me to take it easy then feel free to collapse my tent and pack up the truck. I won't argue with that," Mac laughed.

"He's right," Connor said as he used the last bit of bread to mop up the remaining egg yolk, now cold from the brisk morning air. "Even if he has a concussion, there isn't anything that can be done, just make sure you *don't* hit your head again." Connor knew the dangers of a secondary injury to an already concussed brain. Not good.

Sheila shook her head, discontented. "You need to take it easy, Mac."

"Righto," Mac said and winked at her. "Looks like Carl will be taking on my share of the labor."

Carl peered at Mac, unamused.

"Ya know, Mac, we never had a chance to check out the hieroglyphs you spotted on the cave wall."

"And I'm perfectly content with never going back in," Mac said.

"I'm sure, but I've gotta go back and take some photos. We've also gotta report the skeleton."

"We're gonna have to call the police?" Sheila asked. "How long do you think it's been in there?"

"If I had to guess, I'd say anywhere from thirty to a hundred years. And yeah, we need to get it reported."

"How the heck are the police gonna find it? Will we have to wait for them to get here?" Ben worried about production time but then realized, this was good stuff, perfect for their reality film.

"I'll mark it with GPS, give them the coordinates and then let them know who we are and what we're doing out here. It shouldn't be a problem," Connor said.

Sheila nodded. "Great thinking."

Connor swallowed his last tidbit of cold bacon. "I'm gonna get some footage with the digi-cam. George and Carl, you guys can stay behind and get your gear packed. I'm off to the cave."

Lisa kicked Kate's leg under the table.

Kate struggled to keep her composure but managed to speak with confidence. "I know that cave pretty well. After all, I made it through crawling on my belly without a light. I'm up for it."

"Great, anyone else want to go?" Connor shoved a proverbial needle right into Kate's heart shaped balloon, bursting it.

She wanted to be alone with him, but then he threw out an open invite. She was crushed that he didn't care the slightest about being alone with her. She now knew his only concern was his work. He was the same old Connor; too obsessed with work to care about a woman. *To hell with him*, she thought. *I give up.*

It sounded adventurous and intriguing to Ben and Sheila, but neither accepted.

"Looks like it's just us, Kate."

In an instant Kate felt better, no one else volunteered to go, but then again it didn't really matter; Connor had blinders on as usual.

The rest of the team started breaking down the camp while Connor and Kate ventured off. Connor led the way into the cave with Kate following a few feet behind. Kate felt hopeless, let down, and really would've preferred to curl up in the tent with a half-gallon of Ben and Jerry's finest, but right now that wasn't an option. Instead, she kept her chin up and went through the motions of being a professional wildlife biologist.

They snaked their way through each narrow opening until finally reaching the cavity containing the bones and hieroglyphs. Connor aimed his flashlight. "Kate, you've gotta check this out."

Kate's flashlight panned over the pile of bones. "Human bones, they're so small next to the Thylacine's."

"Yeah. A young boy is what I'm guessing." Connor removed his backpack and pulled out a camcorder. "I want to record everything exactly the way we found it."

"Do you think it's a crime scene, Connor?"

"I don't think so, but who knows? The hieroglyphs may shed some light on what happened, but then again maybe they were here long before this kid died."

The camcorder's spotlight lit the entire room. Kate was intrigued by the pile of bones and leaned in to get a better look. "What the heck went on down here? It's not like the Thylacine ate the boy, his bones are perfect."

"I know, the tiger definitely didn't eat this kid. Maybe they're unrelated and came to rest apart from each other."

"That's possible, but this is such an obscure place out here in the middle of nowhere."

"Yeah, it looks like we found a couple of needles in the haystack," Connor said. "What the hell brought a child and a Tasmanian tiger to this cave? I just don't get it."

Kate started scanning the floor for any other clues. As she made her way across the cave, her head struck a low hanging cluster of jagged rock. "Oww." She moaned, rubbing her forehead.

Connor rushed over. "You just pull a Mac?"

"Yeah, but at least I'm still conscious."

"Lemme take a look." Connor placed his right hand on the side of Kate's face and tilted her head down toward the reflected light. "You've got a nice scrape."

Kate stared up and into his eyes with a melting softness in her gaze. She found herself lost in them, although they were focused on her injury. She was unable to speak.

Connor's gaze shifted from the wound down to her eyes. It happened, his focus shattered.

She was looking at him and *he* was looking at her.

———

His world froze from the sudden shock of her femininity. He was enslaved, pulled in and locked by the allure held in his very hands. *Where did this woman come from?* He pulled her closer and she surrendered to his embrace.

He caressed her cheekbones with his thumbs, studying her face for the first time.

"You're so beautiful," he whispered. Looking down, drawn to her parted lips, he pulled her mouth to his until their lips touched.

"You guys in there?" Carl's voice echoed around the cave walls. Connor broke away from Kate, jolted.

Damn it. Kate cursed within as she closed her eyes and exhaled, unmoving. She was aggravated, but excited. She knew a fire had been lit, finally, and this was just the beginning.

Slapped back to reality, Connor took a few steps from Kate and answered. "Yeah, we're in here." They looked at each other, locked gazes...until...

Carl pushed his way into the room and took quick note that Connor and Kate seemed a little apprehensive. Their gaze broke and they both pretended to scan the walls. Carl knew they were putting on a show. "I figured I should come in with the H.D Cam and film whatever you guys found down here."

"Good thing," Connor mumbled, grinning from the impeccable timing.

Carl picked up on the hidden sarcasm. "Did I interrupt anything?" Carl raised an insinuating eyebrow at Kate.

"Not at all, Carl, not at all," Kate snapped.

"Well if you two need some alone time I can just leave the camera here and you guys can film everything yourselves."

"Whoa buddy, you're a little quick to assume," Connor said.

"Look, I really didn't feel like hauling my camera through this shit-hole in a rock, but I did and when I get here lil' sassafras over there has an attitude about me being here."

Kate gasped, laughing in disbelief. "Did you just call me little Sassafras? What the heck is that supposed to mean?"

"You didn't interrupt anything, and I think you rattled Kate a bit with your assumptions," Connor said. "So now that you're here, this is what we'll do, take a prolonged panning shot of the hieroglyphs maybe a minute and a half to two minutes and then cut. And for the bones let's do the same thing."

EXIT THE DESERT

Present day

THIRD VEHICLE BACK IN THE PROCESSION, LISA HELD THE WHEEL while Kate peered out of the window with an unbreakable grin.

"Okay, Kate, what happened? Let's hear it! That ridiculous grin is driving me insane."

Kate looked over at Lisa and smiled ear to ear. Her face was glowing like a child's on Christmas morning.

Lisa's jaw dropped, she took a huge gulp of air and then she smiled. "I knew it!"

———

The expedition vehicles thundered for hours along the varying mounds of wavy sand. Connor was used to the ocean of small two-foot, snake-like sand waves. This forced the Rovers to travel at fifteen mph for much of the trek, any faster and they would be airborne. The smaller waves were followed by growing regions of massive dunes, some as high as ninety feet. The larger dunes were intimidating but no match for the rovers.

After the first dune, Sheila refused to let Ben drive the rover over the remainder of hills before them. Arms crossed and unflinching, she insisted he and Connor temporarily swap. Connor accepted. He knew

Sheila had a hard time trusting the monstrous machines, feeling as though the vehicle would flip due to the extreme angles of the climb and descent. When traversing upwards, Sheila's back pressed hard against the seat-back. He remembered being terrified at the unnatural transfer of weight from his legs and buttocks to his back the first time he had done it, but the surreal view of the sky through the windshield made it all worthwhile. Going down wasn't any better for her because she had to rely on the seatbelts to keep her from falling forward. With each dune conquered, he could see Sheila become more confident and there was even a little sadness on her face at leaving the last of the large ones behind.

They reached the next checkpoint two hours ahead of schedule. Connor tallied, and everyone agreed to continue forward. The team decided to drive until they reached the outskirts of the desert rather than spend another day in the middle of Old Sandy.

Carl drove and was at the rear of the procession, leaving George on camera duty. Carl and Mac barely spoke. Neither of the men knew each other, nor had any interest in trying. Carl's pompous dryness combined with Mac's zest created a quiet mismatch, at best.

Connor gripped the wheel and led the caravan. He focused on the flatness of the horizon, lost in thought. His mind couldn't escape the brief but jarring moment with Kate. *A woman would get in the way,* he thought. He had been programmed since youth by his father that a woman would hinder a man's goals and aspirations.

When Connor was eight years old his parents divorced. His mother wasn't content being married to a mundane school teacher. Sure, it was great in the beginning, but as life went on, it became too routine, too boring. The divorce was unexpected and swift in its execution. It wouldn't have been so bad had Connor's dad not been blindsided. He loved the woman he married, but had no clue of her discontentment, nor did he realize that she was in bed with a fast talking, money wielding accident attorney. Connor's parents fell into the boring trap of monotony, a pitfall that ended relationships.

The day that ruined him was a Wednesday. As usual, he wrapped up his teacher duties as school let out, then picked his son up from aftercare just after four o'clock. Driving home was like any other day, but as he pulled into the driveway something was different, he could sense it. Her car was gone, but that was typical. She was always out buying groceries or shopping for something trivial. Today he sensed something amiss, and it wasn't until he walked through the front door and into the living room that he realized what it was. Her self-made paintings were gone from the walls. Connor was still outside.

He chased a colossal grasshopper that had been sitting on the front porch, oblivious to the panic his father was now battling. From room to room he rushed, darting in for seconds, finding clue after clue that she was gone. Tears fell but he didn't cry, not in front of Connor. He didn't bother calling her, her note said it all. The broken man fell to his knees, he covered his face with his palms until Connor's hand touched his shoulder.

That's when the tears stopped, and the repression began. His father flipped a switch, the mourning was over, and the hate had begun. He had to explain to his boy how his mother had walked out on them. He had to hold his son as he repressed the pain, embedding the hate deeper within him. She did this. Their relationship did this. Connor cried and cried.

Connor's father hid the pain, embedding its torment deep into his psyche. Instead of letting go, he held on to the plague of negative emotion, year after year, burying it deep. It wasn't long after that his health started failing.

Over the years, Connor's father scorned and warned, preached, and bitched about never getting close to a woman. She told him the truth; that she fell out of love with him, that he had a dead-end career and that she wanted more. This added to the hate and resentment. He saw her as the reason for his mundane lifestyle, she held him back.

He instilled thoughts within his son that relationships are a hindrance to success and that his wife was the reason why he was never able to be anything more than a school teacher. Connor's father had dreams, but he let them go. He traded them for the fear of failure, and the need to earn a safe income to sustain a wife and son. He blamed her for stealing his dreams and leaving him at an age where he believed in the false notion that attaining them was impossible. Connor, even as a child, had above average common sense, he understood his father's resentment. But the years of pessimism toward relationships began to manifest within him. Not in the same way his father managed to sustain, but in other ways. Connor had to accept the pain of having a mother walk out on him. A mother that had been good to him, nurtured him and loved him, then disappeared from his life. This, combined with the barrage of brainwashing put forth by his father, rooted some deep-seated attachment issues within him.

His father clung to the hate, carrying it with him in death.

Connor never had the urge to commit. He loved women and became friends with many but would never allow a serious relationship to form. He toyed with them, and as a gentleman, had sex with them, however if a woman started getting too close emotionally, he would withdraw or initiate a break up. While in college, his focus was strictly upon studies. Many women were drawn to his allure and there was sex, but that's as far as it went. He was charming and always considerate, but in the end, there was no attachment.

When hired by Natural Productions, the only focus was on his newfound career. He concentrated on work and was determined to make a name for himself. Connor was a natural, somehow crafted to perfection with what he did. With ease he glided to the top in his field. Connor landed directly under the limelight of syndicated TV and was given the title of most eligible, but unobtainable bachelor.

"Make heads or tails of those cave paintings?" George asked.

Connor's mind broke from the memories as he turned his attention to George. "Um, ugh…not yet, I haven't really had a chance to look. I think Mac needs to be the one to examine them." Connor paused. "George, can I ask you something?"

"You've never had to ask before."

"Good point. What do you think about Kate?"

"You mean what do I think about you and Kate?" George grinned a bit.

He looked over at George. "Damn, it's that obvious?"

"Not at all. No one would have any idea if it weren't for Carl."

"Carl? What's he spreading around?"

"When you guys came back from filming in the cave, he made his rounds and made sure everyone knew he caught you and Kate."

Connor interrupted. "Caught us doing what?"

"He said he caught you two making out. I think the skinny boy was trying to get Ben and Sheila rattled."

"And what was their reaction?"

"They loved it. Sheila went on about how it was long overdue, that you two need to get together."

"Ya gotta love that woman."

"She makes it easy. But hey, on another note, I don't like Carl."

"This is just a temporary assignment for him."

"Good. As for your question, I'm with Ben and Sheila. I think it's about time. You're both great people."

"There's no *Kate and I* just yet. We did have a moment in the—"

"Whoa, sandstorm!" George threw his arm in the direction of the dark swirling horizon ahead. Connor hammered the brakes and skidded to a stop causing all the vehicles behind him to do the same. They all managed to stop about thirty feet from each other.

Connor stepped out of the vehicle, his eyes never straying from the dark mass, maybe a mile away and coming at them.

"It's massive." The sky ahead was black, and the horizon was gone. As far as the eye could see, nothing but dark striations of swirling sand raged toward them. George looked at the storm and then back at Connor for direction. Connor was speechless, momentarily. He was busy surveying the monstrosity heading straight toward them.

Sheila climbed out of the passenger seat eying the swirling mass that enveloped everything ahead. "Wow, what is that? A storm?"

"Oh, gosh," Ben said, exiting the vehicle.

Lisa and Kate were already running toward the lead vehicle. "Holy shit," Lisa said as she neared Connor.

Mac walked slowly, staring in awe. "Great googa mooga."

Walking with Mac, Carl loaded a fresh battery then powered up his camera. "Is that what I think it is?"

Mac's walk became a run. He yelled to the group. "We're gonna need to take cover, fast."

Everyone stood behind Connor and watched the storm approach.

They stood in awe, peering at the shifting walls of swirling dirt, like vacationing beach-goers ogling over an approaching tsunami. Most of them clueless to the ensuing havoc.

"What's the plan?" Mac asked with frightened urgency.

Connor tore his gaze away and looked back at the row of vehicles. "Everyone head back to your Rovers, get out your mess kits and take out the large heavy-duty Ziploc bag. Grab the tape from your med-kit. Put the Ziploc over the snorkel on your Rover then secure it in place with the tape."

"What's going on, Connor?" Sheila asked, fearful.

"Listen up," Connor spoke loudly and commanded everyone's attention. "Sheila, Ben, Kate, Lisa, Carl, that's a massive sandstorm, by far the largest I've ever seen. I've seen storms tiny compared to this one completely erase dunes and create massive new ones. This storm has the potential to bury us. We need to get the snorkels covered up or the wind's gonna force sand into the air intake and clog our filters. We need to get the intakes covered a.s.a.p. Once your intake is covered, get into your vehicle, and stay there. We can't out run this storm on this terrain. If we try to drive, we will kill our engines. We will weather this out. It's gonna get dark, real dark. If one or more of the vehicles get buried, don't panic, those remaining uncovered will dig you out as soon as the storm passes. You'll know the storm is passing when you can see light again. *Do not panic* if you get covered. If you panic, you'll use up all the remaining oxygen and you'll suffocate. *If you don't want to die, don't panic.* It's that simple. Any questions?"

Mac gave a nod. "Well done."

Sheila was confused and didn't understand, she hadn't prepared for eminent danger. "You're scaring me, Connor."

"Good, now turn your fear into action and get your vehicle secured."

"What do you mean suffocate?"

Ben grabbed Sheila just above her left elbow and led her away. "Come on, honey, we signed up for this."

Following Connor's direction, everyone rushed back to their vehicles and began covering their intakes.

George pulled the tape tight, sealing off the air intake on his vehicle. "This looks bad."

"I know. This thing is big."

"Sheila's gonna panic if she gets buried."

"I know. Ben's pretty confident though. I think he'll keep her on track, he has to."

An eerie calm fell over the area. Connor studied the storm as it churned its way closer. It was approaching fast but appeared to be moving in slow motion due to its immensity. It looked as though an atom bomb had exploded, sending its mushroom cloud outward at ground level. It spread across the horizon for as far as the eye could see. To anyone that didn't know better, it would have been deemed a mountainous wall of smoke caused by some horrific explosion, but it wasn't. It was the mother of all sandstorms.

The sun was blocked, and an eerie orange glow enveloped the area. There was no wind, none, only silence as the storm drew closer.

Connor ran to the rear of the convoy to make one final check on his team. He opened Carl's door. "You guys good?"

"Looking forward to the blizzard, mate," Mac joked.

Carl glared at Connor with a crooked face. "Were you serious about being buried? Why can't we just turn around and head back the other direction?"

"I was being serious so get ready. The rear vehicle has the greatest chance of being covered up." Connor winked at Mac as he shut Carl's door and headed to the next vehicle.

Connor opened Kate's door. "Ladies, I do hope you're enjoying your stay here in the Great Sandy Desert." The girls grinned, but it was obvious to Connor they were nervous.

"We've got this." Lisa grasped the wheel and gave it a shake, taking reassurance with its immobility.

Connor looked at Kate. "Everything's gonna be fine, trust me."

"I do," she whispered. Connor leaned in and kissed her cheek. She was caught off guard and pleasantly overwhelmed by the unexpected gesture. He nodded at Lisa, shut Kate's door, and headed to the next vehicle.

Connor tugged at the door handle. *Tap tap tap.* "Why is your door locked?"

Sheila paused, and then pressed a button on the console. Connor opened the door and leaned in. "Sheila, what if your Rover gets buried? We will lose time by trying to break your windows because your door was locked, time that could have left you with a bit more air."

"I'm sorry, I'm just nervous."

"And besides, the locks aren't gonna keep the sand out."

"I don't think I've ever been scared like this, Connor."

Ben rubbed her leg. "Oh, babe, come on. This is all part of the adventure."

"That's right, a little danger is part of it. You guys are fine. Now settle in, relax and enjoy your flight." Connor felt a sudden gust cool the side of his face and fling his hair. It was brief, but a sign it was upon them. Connor closed Sheila's door.

The temperature plummeted from ninety-two degrees to sixty-six in less than a few minutes. Connor jogged toward his Rover, leaning into the sporadic gusts.

George was standing at the rear of his vehicle, steadfast and filming the approaching storm, his large frame immovable by the gusts. Connor had to tuck his head and cover his eyes with a forearm; the wind started throwing sand.

"This should be fun," Connor shouted over the howling gusts.

George nodded, silent. He panned the camera across the black mass, stopping to his direct left, on Connor.

Squinting, Connor leaned in close to the camera. "It doesn't get any less scripted than this." Sand was stinging his exposed neck. He huddled in front of the lens. "We've run into a storm, and not the kind that brings a little thunder and rain, but the kind that brings hellacious winds and flesh ripping sand. I've been through a few sand storms, but this by far is the largest I've ever seen." Connor turned his head, grimacing as a blast of sand whipped his cheek. "This sand can strip paint from a vehicle or skin from a body. It's no joke. We've got everyone secured in their vehicles and we're prepared for the worst. We're gonna hunker down and see what kind of hell this thing brings."

In an instant the wind began raging and sand was whipping in all directions. Connor and George stood beside the Rover for a few more seconds, but the stinging granules were too much. Through squinted eyes, they both pried their doors open against the wind and slid in.

Connor's face was gleaming, in love with the rush of sudden change. "The storm is still approaching and it's already scouring the paint."

In a slow shape-shifting wave, the orange glow surrounding the vehicles dissipated into a smoky grey-brown apocalyptic darkness. It was three in the afternoon, but the air was a shade of midnight. The chaotic border of the storm was over them, bringing with it the howls of hell; screaming winds, moaning in agony, haunting, screaming.

George spotted a shadowy silhouetted commotion in his side-view mirror. "What the hell are they doing?" He whipped the camera around and started shooting through a section of the rear hatch window that wasn't cluttered with supplies. Connor spun and could make out the figures of Sheila and Ben shuffling around outside their vehicle.

"Shit, it's Sheila." Connor put his sunglasses on and snatched the shemagh from the rearview. He looped it around his neck and head, covering his ears and the open border around his glasses.

He held a special attachment to this shemagh. He bought it off a poor merchant child in Kabul a few years back. The ten-year-old parentless child had captured his heart, the victim of a suicide bomber. The boy, Rafiulla, Rafi for short, lived on the streets, selling handmade clothing and touristy trinkets from the native clay. Connor and his film team were there shooting a segment on venomous arachnids and snakes of Afghanistan. They were running dry, unable to locate any creatures, and that's when Connor enlisted the boy, and it paid off.

The boy had a universal love for creatures that most in the area feared. He had been catching these religiously persecuted animals for most of his young life and knew exactly where they hid. Connor paid the boy a salary more than a year's worth of street slinging would have brought in. During their week together, Connor and the boy became buds. In parting, Rafi gave Connor his late father's shemagh. It was tan with dark brown embroidery, made with heavy cotton, and no matter how sweaty or submerged it became, the shemagh magically held its aroma of sandalwood incense. In an instant Connor treasured the gift and developed an immediate affinity for it. The shemagh became a trademark fixture for Connor. It fit him well.

He forced the door open, struggling against the increasing wind.

Once outside, he released the door and it slammed shut. He could barely see through the tinted lenses, feeling his way toward their location.

Ben grabbed Sheila's arm and pulled. "Get back in the god-damned car!" He yelled as the winds howled against him. He held her with one arm while the other covered his eyes. The sand was already filling his nose, ears, and the cracks around his lips.

"I'm not getting buried alive!" Sheila screamed, terrified with panic and crunching bits of sand. Her inability to cope with the danger manifested into irrational terror. She tried to jerk free of Ben's grip but was unsuccessful. Covering her eyes, she forced her head against the hood of the vehicle to shield her face from the stinging sand.

Connor, like a knight shrouded in armor was almost unaffected by the piercing sand. His improvised head dress, emanating the essence of sandalwood, provided a homelike calm. The adornment protected his important parts as he walked through the shredding sand. His khaki cargo pants and long sleeve shirt shielded the rest.

Connor grabbed Sheila's arm. "Sheila, get back in your vehicle." He spoke through the shemagh. Sheila's breathing was erratic, gasping for air but taking in too much sand.

Sheila cried through her arms. "I can't breathe."

Connor noticed Mac to his immediate left wearing a similar set up with sunglasses and a make-shift head dress.

Mac leaned in to her ear. "Sheila, sweetheart, it's not a good time to take a walkie. Time to get back in the Rover." Mac's voice soothed her, she trusted him. Her muscles loosened, and she spun, burying her face against Mac's chest.

"Can I help?" an unexpected female voice shouted.

Connor twisted his head. Kate was wearing the same set up as Connor and Mac. Within seconds the storm grew irritated with those who dared to stand amongst it. The wind lashed out, worsening.

Mac held Sheila tight, using all his weight upon her as leverage to the wind. "Alright, Sheila, the party's over. It's time to get inside."

Sheila's nails clawed through Mac's shirt, digging into his skin. "Stay with me!"

Mac looked at Connor for approval. Connor nodded, gesturing them both to get in the vehicle. He opened the passenger door and a fight ensued. He wrestled to hold it open against the invisible rage. Mac guided Sheila into the passenger seat and Connor eased the door until it whipped out of his hands and slammed shut. Mac opened the rear passenger door and pushed a pile of supplies to the other side of the seat, then climbed in.

Connor and Kate each took one of Ben's arms and led him around the vehicle to the driver's seat. Ben didn't speak, he couldn't. He was blinded and had both arms covering his face as he struggled to breathe through the sand. Connor used brute strength once again to open the door and keep it from slamming out of control. Kate shoved Ben into the vehicle and Connor let the wind take the door, slamming it shut. Connor turned to Kate, both balancing against the wind.

"Your turn," he yelled. He wrapped his left arm around her shoulders and started toward her Rover. The wind was pulling both of their head dresses away from their sunglasses and allowing sand to enter and sting the skin around their eyes. They walked slow then fast, lurching with the unpredictable gusts until they reached Kate's Rover. Connor popped the door latch and the wind sprung it open, so forceful it bent the hinge mounts. He waited until Kate was safely inside and then pushed against it, marching it forward like a Clydesdale against the wind, until it was closed. Connor turned to head back to his vehicle but then he heard a loud tapping coming from Kate's vehicle. The tapping didn't stop, and he could tell by its incessant intensity that something was wrong. Connor grabbed the door handle as an anchor and tried to look through Kate's window. There was too much sand swirling around his eyes and his glasses were just too dark. He forced the door open about a quarter of the way.

"Lisa's gone!" Kate yelled.

"Gonna check each vehicle. I'll be back so stay put."

Connor trudged his way to the last vehicle in the line. His steps were heavy, like waltzing through invisible mud. Mac and Carl's Rover was just behind Kate's. He forced open the driver's side door. "You seen Lisa?"

"Yeah, she went out right after Kate did. I saw George grab her."

"George?"

"Yeah, I saw him lead her to your truck."

"Great." Connor was relieved, one less loose end needing to be tied.

"Now listen, Mac's with Ben and Sheila. She freaked out and he's making sure she keeps it together. Kate's alone so I'm heading back to her vehicle," he shouted over the howling winds.

"Well that works out for you, doesn't it?" Carl snorted. "So I have to stay here by myself?"

"Yeah, can you handle it? Or would you rather me sit here with you and leave Kate alone?" Connor let go of the door and the wind slammed it shut.

Connor leapt into the passenger seat of Kate's Rover, pulled the shemagh from his face and inhaled, finally the air was sand-free. He finished unwrapping the shemagh from his head and took off the sunglasses. Sand fell everywhere.

Kate pushed the ceiling panel, and a dim yellow light barely illuminated the cab. She looked at Connor and sighed behind a barely detectable grin. The grin disappeared when she asked, "What about Lisa?"

"Don't worry, she's safe. Evidently, she went out just after you did. She was blinded but George came to her rescue. Carl said he saw George head back to our Rover with her."

"What a mess," Kate sighed.

"Nah, this is what it's all about."

"Does anything ever get to you?"

"Maybe, Carl, but other than that, not really."

"I'm so glad I'm not the only—"

Loud enough to be mistaken for a gunshot, a golf ball sized stone pummeled the metal hood of the Rover, leaving an equal dent in its place. Kate screamed.

"Glad we opted for the premium insurance." Connor kept brushing sand from his face.

Kate tried to conceal her optimism. "Looks like we're gonna be here for a while, huh?"

"Yeah, I'd say half hour, maybe an hour." Connor looked down at his shirt now covered in sand.

"You're covered." Kate reached over the center console and brushed his closest shoulder.

"Sorry about the mess."

Kate became an opportunist and saw a small window of opportunity in front of her. Rather than let the clock tick, she took action. She leaned across him and tried to wipe the sand from his furthest shoulder. In a sudden act of aggressive courage, she straddled him, and continued to brush his shoulders and hair.

"Don't worry about it," she whispered. Her soft, sensual tone resonated within him. He leaned back, sinking into the Rover's leather seat, and gazed up at her.

She brushed a few bits of sand away from his lips and then leaned in, placing a small kiss. She pulled away and looked into his eyes. Connor pushed her hair back and tucked it behind her ear. He leaned in and she met him half way.

They kissed, and Kate popped each of Connor's shirt buttons open, one after another, craving his chest. She spread the shirt open to reveal his muscled and lightly haired chest. She pushed the shirt back, over his shoulders, and he slid his chiseled arms out of the sleeves. Connor pulled Kate's sweater over her head, unveiling a succulent pair of soft white breasts. She pushed her chest against his.

The wind raged outside; the storm was now in full force. The vehicles all swayed from side to side from the equal bursts of violent air. The absence of sun caused the temperature to drop into the low sixties and there was less than three feet of visibility in all directions.

Connor kissed Kate's neck, one slow kiss after another. As he did he noticed something was different. With each kiss, he felt an unfamiliar warmth deep within his being, repressed emotions dissipating within him. He touched her skin with his tongue and savored the taste, wanting more.

She reached down and unfastened the weathered leather belt on his cargo pants. Then she worked open the button, his zipper went down. She closed her eyes while Connor unbuttoned her jeans and worked them off. Kate forced her pelvis into his. Connor grabbed himself and pulled Kate's underwear aside. He held her close, unlike anyone, ever before. They were lost within each other, oblivious to the raging storm. She gave herself to him.

Sheila had a death grip on the overhead grab bar. She knew the Rover was going to topple over with any one of these ever-increasing gusts. "Oh, God!" she screamed as the Rover shimmied.

Mac rearranged the rear seat clutter and placed himself in the middle, just behind the front seat center console. "Don't worry, pretty lady, it's just a little shake shake."

"Oh, God," Sheila cried out again.

Ben grabbed at her free hand, but it was clenched to the seat. "Just breathe, sweetie. Use your Khundalini. Surely that stuff has to be good for something. Think yoga, breathing and calming of the mind."

———

Kate sensed Connor was near climax. He grabbed her around the waist and thrust deeper. They looked into each other's eyes.

Twelve minutes later the sun appeared, and the storm had passed.

Tap! Tap! Tap! An obnoxious heavy tapping came from outside the driver's side window. Startled by the intrusive knocking, they both scrambled back to reality. In a flash, Kate was dressed but disheveled. She popped the door open and sand poured from the weather stripping along the door's seal. Carl aimed his camera directly at them.

"I didn't interrupt anything did I?" Carl spoke with antagonizing sarcasm.

"No, Carl, that's twice you didn't interrupt anything." Connor matched Carl's sarcasm.

"Looks like the storm's over, time to get up lovebirds."

"Ya know, Carl, it's really not safe yet. There's a pretty good chance there's gonna be some flooding through this channel. You should get back to your Rover."

"Flooding?" Carl rolled his eyes. "It's the middle of the desert."

"Look, Carl, I'm not asking you, I'm telling you. Get back to your vehicle," Connor commanded.

"Oh, I see, you two want more alone time. I'll go see how everyone else is doing."

"Really Carl, it's not safe, perhaps if—"

Carl closed the door on him mid-sentence and walked off toward the next vehicle in the procession.

————

Carl walked to Ben and Sheila's vehicle and knocked on the window. Ben opened the door. "You guys gonna stay in there all day? The wind is gone, and the sun is about to come out," Carl said. Then he noticed his feet were wet. He looked down and could make out a steady stream of water about four inches deep flowing around his shoes. "Damn it, now my feet are soaked."

"Your feet are soaked?" Sheila said in disbelief. "We're in the desert, why would your feet be wet?"

Mac opened his door and looked down. The emerging light mirrored off the shallow stream of water flowing underneath the rover. "Head to your vehicle now, mate, or you'll be swimming back to it."

"Loosen up," Carl wined.

"Carl!" Connor's voice yelled from behind. He spun around to see Connor standing beside his Rover pulling off the bag attached to the snorkel. "Get back to your vehicle now!"

Pissed, Carl threw his arms into the air and headed to his vehicle. More and more light was emerging as the storm wafted away.

Mac grinned at Ben who was seated in the driver's position. "Mind if we change seats?"

Ben removed his hands from the wheel and gestured. "By all means."

Mac jumped out of the Rover and ran to the snorkel, quickly tearing off the bag that had sealed it from the sandstorm. Mac noticed George doing the same thing to his own vehicle with his free hand, camera in the other.

Carl felt a cold chill wash upon his legs. He looked down to see water racing around his calves. The road-like ravine they had traversed was now a shallow rapid river.

Connor and Kate slid their bodies through the Rover's open front windows. "Run, Carl!" Connor snapped.

Carl froze. He didn't know whether to run to his vehicle or look back toward the source of the charging water. He couldn't help it; his curious urge to look won, camera following.

"Oh, God," he muttered to himself. A five-foot wall of churning water came raging toward the vehicles. He stood there, unable to move, frozen in disbelief.

"Damn it," Connor said as he began kicking his boots off. "Kate, you're gonna have to take the wheel just in case." Connor knew his boots would be unnecessary anchor weights if he had to swim.

"Got it." Kate saw the shallow stream of water below the Rovers but didn't see the cascade of turbulence ahead of the vehicles.

Carl was immobilized by fear, frozen in his last step, unable to move. He was halfway between Ben and Sheila's, and Connor's Rover.

Connor grabbed a one-hundred-foot coil of rope from the rappelling bag in the back seat and strung it over his shoulder. He slid out of the window and into the cold water, yelling an order. "Carl, snap out of it!"

He maneuvered through the rising turbulent water to the front of the vehicle and tied one end of the rope to the brush guard, then looped the other end around his waist. Carl tried to turn toward Connor but couldn't.

The rampaging surge of water slammed into the front of George and Lisa's vehicle but stalemated with the Rover as George stomped on the gas and powered through it. The revving engine roared, pushing them forward, almost floating, causing it to sway from side to side.

Connor leapt through the water as he made his way toward Carl.

"Come on, Carl! Help me out!" he yelled, pleading.

The rushing wall of water then slammed Mac's vehicle, sending water up and over the hood.

"Aaahhhhhhhhh, God help us!" Sheila screamed in terror.

"I think God's sitting this one out." Mac gritted his teeth as he fought the steering wheel. He powered the engine and fought the flow of water that was forcing them backwards.

The wave of water then slammed into Carl full force. He fell backwards and was carried, overcome by its power. Rather than struggle, his helpless, ratty head bobbed just above the surface as he went with the current; his hand still clenched on the now worthless camera. Carl was floating past Connor, fast.

"Take the rope!" Connor yelled, now struggling to keep his own head above water. Connor waved the rope to get his attention, but it was futile. Carl's mind wasn't there.

Carl had a choice. He didn't choose fight, he didn't choose flight. He gave up, apparently lacking any sort or hypothetical backbone.

Kate watched in horror as Connor disappeared below the surface.

"Connor!" she screamed. She knew what he was doing. He was going to tether Carl to the rope; he wouldn't let him drown no matter how pathetic of a person he was.

Mac's eyes opened even wider. "Oh shit, hold on!" A five-foot wall of water smashed their Rover. He couldn't keep the vehicle moving forward; instead it started floating backwards on a direct collision course with Kate's vehicle. Sheila was hyperventilating and on the verge of passing out. Her fingernails were embedded into the vinyl covering of the *Oh Shit* bars mounted along the ceiling. The Rover swayed from side to side, damned near full floating and warring its way through the flood.

Kate stared at the churning surface behind her Rover scanning, trying to find any glimpse of Connor. She noticed the front end of Carl's Rover was sinking and the rear bumper was rising. Kate's head twisted faster; *he's been under for too long.* Her heart was racing, terrified as she scanned the surface, and then a thundering impact jarred her Rover. The impact sent her falling through the door window, but she was quick. She managed to snag the door frame with her left hand, preventing her from toppling out.

Mac's Rover was taken backwards by the raging water. It gained speed as it floated and then pummeled the front of Kate's. The steel on steel cracked and groaned, denting, and bending as the turbulent water forced them together.

Kate struck her chest against the door frame. Her vehicle lost its grounding and began drifting backwards toward Carl who somehow seemed to be maintaining his position, about thirty feet behind Kate's Rover. Kate tried to power her vehicle forward, but the force from Mac's impact and the raging water prevented any gain. Kate was headed directly toward Carl's half sunken Rover with Carl in between them. Kate jerked the steering wheel, turning it from side to side, stomping the gas pedal, and trying to steer, braking, and then gassing in a futile attempt to alter her course, otherwise Carl would be crushed. The gap between Carl and the two vehicles was closing fast. Carl somehow kept his head above water, bobbing and oblivious to Kate's Rover.

Kate's vehicle gained momentum as it drifted. She knew it was too late; she couldn't prevent crushing the spindly man against his half sunken Rover.

"Oh, God, no!" she screamed as the impact with his soft body was eminent and then *BAM,* the smashing and grinding of metal on metal sounded. A second unseen massive impact caused Kate to slam her head against the driver's side window rail, lacerating her left eyebrow. Blood poured into her eye as she struggled to maintain consciousness.

George had managed to maneuver his vehicle out of the flooded gully and onto a higher bank. He and Lisa were watching from the high ground when he realized Carl was about to be crushed. George hammered the accelerator and charged his vehicle back into the raging water with enough force to knock Kate's Rover off its course. The impact left her dazed for a few seconds, and then she returned, focused. The jarring shift in position allowed Kate to resume some control over the vehicle. She stomped on the accelerator and powered her Rover onto an elevated slab of rock. Her eye burned from the hot blood seeping into it. She twisted her body and looked over her shoulder. She saw Carl still bobbing around in the water but now closer to her position…maybe attached to a rope, possibly pulled by her Rover. *Connor must have tethered him at some point but when?* She threw her head in all directions but found no sign of him.

Mac's vehicle continued its backwards momentum until it collided into the front of Carl's half sunken Rover. Carl had been inadvertently pulled to safety by Kate as she managed to power her four-wheel drive onto higher ground. The sunken Rover was just deep enough to allow Mac's rear wheels to rest up on the front bumper.

The force of the rushing water continued to push Mac's Rover onto the top of the mostly submerged Rover. Mac stopped trying to work the accelerator in fear of toppling the Rover over, for it was now resting on the roll-bar enforced roof of the submerged vehicle. From inside the vehicle, it felt as though death by drowning was inescapable. They were helpless. The Rover was being carried away in slow motion which made it all the more terrifying to its helpless, caged occupants.

The grinding of metal on metal wailed as though the Rovers were in agony and dying painful, slow, torturous deaths. The amplified howls of battle were haunting to those within the beast's belly, unable to escape their cries.

George gunned his Rover through the shallows and drove onto the same elevated slab of rock Kate had stopped on. The water level was dropping, almost as fast as it had appeared.

Kate jumped from her vehicle and looked downstream, frantic, and panicked, her head and eyes darting. George and Lisa climbed out and walked down into the ankle-deep water, observing the aftermath.

Kate's panicked eyes jerked from left to right as she scanned the area.

"Connor!" Kate called. "He went in to help Carl and went under. I never saw him come back up. Connor!" she called out again, her calls turning to mixed cries.

Kate saw Carl untying the rope that Connor had fastened to his waist. She started walking in his direction, picking up speed until she broke into a full-blown sprint. She came to a halt then pummeled his chest with her palms, knocking him off his feet and causing him to land on his back.

"You mutherfucker!" she screamed. "Why did you just fucking stand there when he was trying to help you? If he's hurt, I'll—"

George grabbed Kate's shoulders and held her back. "Hold on, Kate."

"You better get that psycho away from me," Carl said as he stood back up. "If she touches me again I'll sue her fucking ass."

"Carl," George paused and stared down at the spindly man, "if you make it back."

Carl peered back at George but said not a word.

The flat sand covered path they had been following became an uneven gulley of smooth, rounded red rock. The raging water had moved the sand downstream, uncovering the bottom of an ancient river bed.

Carl's Rover had sunk up to its door handles in a massive natural fissure that was part of the ancient river bottom. Ben and Sheila's vehicle was on top of it, crisscrossed upon its roof. Mac was the first to climb out. He stepped onto the partially sunken Rover's roof, slipped on the wet windshield, and ended up sliding off the hood and into the few inches of water remaining in the gulley. There was too much tension among the others to even notice. Ben and Sheila sat and slid down one by one on their butts. From the ground, Sheila looked back up at the pile of Rovers she had just climbed out of; it was an odd sight indeed.

Mac headed toward the rest of the group. "Do I know how to park a Landie or what?" He grinned but it was cut short.

"We can't find Connor," Lisa said, panicked.

Sheila gasped. "What do you mean you can't find Connor?"

"If I know Connor, he's around here somewhere," George said with confidence.

Ben twisted his head back and forth, eyeing the gulley. "Well, where is he?"

Kate had already turned and was climbing the four-foot rocky embankment just behind them. She hop-stepped to the top and then scanned the water's path.

"He went in after Carl," she snapped as she panned over the scene. "Connor told him to get out of the god-damn water, but he just stood there, like an idiot! He had plenty of time to get out of the water, but he just stood there! Connor grabbed one of the rappelling ropes, tied it off to the bumper and tried to hand it off to Carl. He nearly drowned trying to get that bastard to grab the rope, but he wouldn't take it. He just bobbed around like a mindless idiot. Connor went under and tied it around Carl's waist."

"That was the last time I saw him." Kate's voice cracked. "Oh, God, no," she cried with the sudden realization that she had witnessed Connor's last living moments.

"Hold on, Kate, I'm sure he's around here somewhere," Ben said.

"Let's find him," Mac said, walking back into the washed-out gulley.

George twisted his head in the direction from which the flood came. "It's safe to say he wouldn't be up there."

Mac looked upstream and nodded. "Right on. I say we start from here and work our way downstream."

Downstream of their position became a washed-out gully of smooth river rock riddled with fissures, some large enough to swallow a Rover. The gully stretched on for as far as the eye could see, tapering off into the horizon.

Lisa stepped down into the gully. "He probably got carried downstream. How far would the water travel?"

Mac started walking downstream. "Well, it depends. It could flow for dozens of miles or it could be channeled into a narrow gulley which would force it to travel even further, or it could hit a big depression a mile from here and create a temporary little lake. There's just no way of knowing. All we can do is follow the trail."

George stepped down and toward the sunken Rover. "Let's form a line and work our way down stream."

Without hesitation, everyone began lining up across the gully, placing themselves about ten feet apart.

Carl sat himself in the passenger seat of Kate's Rover; he left the door open, leaned back and closed his eyes. Lisa looked back at him.

"Carl," she shouted. "You're not going to help?"

"I almost drowned if you didn't notice," he snubbed, pompous.

"Yeah but you didn't," George ended his argument.

"Look, I was just tied to the back of a truck and dragged all around in freezing water."

"What a way to repay the man that just saved your ass." Mac shook his head. "You're seriously not gonna help?"

Carl ignored Mac, leaned back against the head rest, and closed his eyes.

The team started the search, stepping slow and scanning the sand and rock for any sign of Connor. They made their way around the peculiar vehicle stack.

Ben was on the raised outer edge of the gulley, giving a vantage point that allowed sight beyond the sporadic raised rock in the distance. Something caught his eye. He ran back to the partially buried Rover and ripped the binoculars from the velcro attached to the dashboard. He darted back onto the raised side of the gully, held the viewfinder to his eyes and focused in.

"I...I think I see him." Ben spotted what looked like a person lying on the ground, but he wasn't sure.

George rushed over to Ben, took the binoculars and focused them to his eyes. "It's him."

George ran back to Kate's Rover, grabbed Carl by the arm tossing him out of the vehicle, sending the skinny man to the ground. Carl was about to spout off but stopped himself. George forced the driver's seat back to accommodate his extra-large size and then climbed in. He twisted the key and the sleeping beast roared to life.

George slammed the shifter in gear and hammered the accelerator. The Rover spun its wheels and sped down the small embankment. It hit the bottom of the gully head on, jerking him violently within. He twisted the wheel then hammered the accelerator again, kicking heavy wet sand and rock behind it.

George mashed the brakes and slid on approach to the group. "Let's go!" he shouted through the window. Mac jumped in the passenger seat and Kate jumped in the back seat behind Mac.

George stomped on the accelerator. "Grab the med kit and the AED from the back."

Kate leaned over the rear seat into the cargo area, rummaged around for a second and then spun back around with the AED and med kit in hand.

As the Rover approached, George could see that Connor's leg was wedged between two rocks, which would have kept his head below water level. As they neared his motionless body Kate began trembling. She was thrown against the back of the front seat as the vehicle slid to a stop. George and Mac jumped out of the Rover simultaneously and ran to Connor. George grabbed him around the torso, just under his arms and lifted him, while Mac pulled his leg from the split in the rock. George reverted back to his Army field medic mentality as he laid Connor on his back and felt for a pulse.

"Shit, no pulse." George rolled Connor onto his side and a large amount of water poured from his mouth. He laid him back down and ripped open his shirt.

Kate couldn't help but think, sickened and surreal, that just moments ago she had unbuttoned that very shirt.

"Mac start CPR. Kate give me the AED," George ordered with a calm yet direct sense of urgency.

Kate handed George the Automated External Defibrillator. He opened the small, one foot by one-foot, heavy yellow rubberized box, pulled out a pair of large, sticky electrode pads and attached them to Connor, one under his left ribcage and the other over his sternum.

Kate stood back, behind Mac who set a strong tempo with his chest compressions. She watched on with hope and horror as they worked. The man she had just fallen in love with was dead.

George pushed the large yellow power button on the AED and a computerized male voice took control. "*Analyzing rhythm, please do not touch the patient,*" the robotic voice commanded. Mac stopped CPR and lifted his hands off Connor's chest. After a few seconds the robotic voice spoke again. "*Shock advised, please clear patient and press the charge button.*" George pressed the big red charge button and a loud elevating tone began sounding. "*Press green button to deliver shock.*" George hit the green button and Connor's entire body contracted then went lifeless. George felt for a pulse. "*Resume CPR.*"

"Nothing," he said. George leaned over and gave Connor three breaths of air and began CPR himself.

Lost in focus, they didn't see the rest of the team pull up. Sheila put her arm around Kate and held her tight. Ben crouched down beside Mac. "What can I do?"

"We need epinephrine," George said as he continued to pound on Connor's chest.

"Oh! I…I have an epi-pen…It's epinephrine!" Sheila yelled, realizing she packed a few extra for the trip.

Sheila was highly allergic to bee and wasp stings. If stung, she would experience anaphylactic shock, develop hives over her entire body and her throat and tongue would swell shut, causing a severe life-threatening situation.

Sheila scrambled toward the Rover George had slid in on then stopped just short of the passenger door. "Shit! They're in the other Rover! Lisa, help me get them," she yelled. Lisa jumped in the driver's seat and floored the accelerator.

Another minute had passed, George stopped CPR and pressed the red button on the AED. "*Analyzing rhythm, please do not touch the patient.*" After a few seconds the AED spoke. "*No shock advised, resume CPR.*"

"Shit!" George yelled. He knew that *no shock advised*, was a bad thing. Connor's heart rhythm had changed from shockable to non-shockable, which meant his heart had settled into a less savable condition. "CPR Mac, hard and fast."

He heard the squeal of tires as Lisa jammed on the brakes and skidded on the smooth rock. It took a few seconds before he heard Sheila yell, "Got 'em."

Less than a minute later Lisa slammed the brakes again, sliding to a stop beside the team.

Sheila sprung from the passenger seat. "Here are my epi-pens!" She shoved the three pen shaped auto injectors into George's hand.

He popped off one of the caps and grabbed Connor's limp arm. George was searching for the largest vein he could find. In the field, George would have used an I.V. to give medications, but now that luxury wasn't available. An epi-pen was designed to dose medicine into muscle, not a vein, but a dose of epi into muscle during cardiac arrest is about as useful as water in a gas tank. George was familiar with the auto injectors and knew if he found the largest, most visible vein, he could most likely get it punctured with the epi-pen and in turn get the medicine circulating to Connor's heart.

George found the massive pipeline of a vein on the inside of Connor's forearm, just below the elbow. He centered the injector over the bulge and pressed it until it was firm against his skin, then he pressed the release button. Nothing happened. Not even a click. George looked at Connor's vein for any sign of penetration. Nothing. Mac continued CPR, about twenty to thirty chest compressions, stopping and then giving two or three breaths of air then resuming the compressions. Mac had broken into a heavy sweat but was diehard.

"Damn it," George said under his breath. He reached down and grabbed another epi-pen. "How old are these things?" he said while popping off the cap.

"She's had those things for years," Ben said reluctantly. "She's never needed 'em."

Sheila didn't know what to say. She had been carrying around medicine that could save her life, yet they were all light-years beyond expiration.

George placed the second epi-pen directly over the vein and applied pressure. He placed his thumb on the button and pushed. Nothing happened. "Dammit!" George snapped. This time it was serious.

George tossed the broken epi-pen to the ground and snatched up the last one. He placed it over the vein and applied pressure, his thumb pressed the button and he heard a faint click. He held the pen in place for a couple seconds to ensure all the medicine dispersed, and then pulled it away to verify that it had infiltrated the vein. He scanned Connor's arm for blood, a dot, a speck, any sign of puncture, nothing.

"Son of a bitch!" George snapped. His mind raced. He snatched up one of the epi-pens and examined it closely; a circumferential line ran around the center of the pen. Had it been screwed together he thought? He twisted at the pen and it didn't budge. He bore down, putting all his might into it until there was a loud crack and then it began to unscrew. The threads had been sealed with glue as part of the manufacturing process. George broke the seal and opened the pen. He slid out the small glass vial of epinephrine that had a tiny needle attached to the bottom of the cylinder. The top of the vial had a rubber stopper that was supposed to be depressed when the spring was released. The springs were dead; years of being loaded in the *ready* position caused them to lose their coil. Even the springiest of steel cannot hold a compressed coil forever; gradually it loses compression until there is no compression left.

George was relieved to see the epi-pens infrastructure. He knew what to do. He lined the small needle up with Connor's large vein and slid it in. "I need something thin, like a pencil."

Ben reached into his pocket. "I've got a pair of tweezers in my utility knife." Ben whipped the knife out and fumbled it, trying to get them out. George reached out with one hand while the other held the needle embedded in Connor's vein.

Using one hand, George bent the flimsy tweezers in half to create a long metal pin. He placed one end of the straightened tweezers against the rubber stopper in the vial and pushed the medicine into Connor's vein.

"It's in," George rattled. "Ben, take over CPR."

Ben jumped right in and began compressions.

George wiped the heavy sweat from his brow. "Hard and fast with the compressions, we need to get the epi to his heart."

Kate paced a four-foot line, back and forth. "God-damn it, Connor, wake up! No, no, no, no, no, this isn't happening," she cried as she broke away from the group.

George raised his hand to Ben's shoulder. "Hold on."

Ben stopped, sweat beads covered his forehead.

George leaned in and placed two fingers over Connor's carotid artery, just under his chin along his neck. He waited a few seconds. "Nothing. CPR."

Ben leaned back over Connor and started pumping again.

George grabbed the next vial of epi and slammed it into the same vein. "Keep it hard and fast. This has to get to his heart." George tossed the spent vial of epinephrine. Blood was running down Connor's forearm from the injection site, a sign that Ben's CPR was good enough to promote circulation.

————

Carl was walking toward the group and was about midway when Kate spotted him. They both stopped walking. She clenched her fists and gnashed her teeth thoughts of rage and hatred saturated every ounce of her being. She wanted to maim, torture, and then kill the worthless shell of a man whose cowardice had cost the life of her new love. She fought an immense internal struggle, instead of attacking, she gave a stare that stripped him of all dignity and for that moment, he felt it. She turned and walked back to Sheila's side, crying.

And in that moment, Carl reflected. He realized his actions were the reason Connor was now lifeless. He knew if he had reacted when Connor called upon him, this never would have happened. He felt bad, but then his mind justified his actions. *He shouldn't have jumped in, I didn't ask him to help me.*

George grabbed the last epi and slammed it into Connor's vein. "Come on, Connor, wake the fuck up."

Kate gripped the handle of the six-inch knife pouched on her belt, focusing her hatred upon the ground, trembling. "Sheila, please, get him out of here. I'll kill him." She spoke with a clarity that made Sheila move.

"Carl, I don't know exactly what happened." Sheila fought back her tears. "But right now, I think it's best if you get back to the truck."

"I didn't do anything," Carl whimpered, playing innocent.

"Get the fuck out of here!" Kate screamed.

"Stop CPR," George said. He reached in and felt for a pulse on the carotid artery. Everyone held their breath waiting for George to speak. He readjusted his fingers and kept feeling for a pulse. He squinted his eyes. "I've got a pulse."

Kate dropped to her knees and started crying. Sheila got down with her and put her forehead against hers, and then Lisa dropped to her knees and hugged them both as they cried together.

Mac saw Connor's chest rise and fall on its own for the first time since they found him. He kept watching and it did it again. "He's breathing, for fucks' sake. You did it, bloke."

"He's not out of the woods yet," George cautioned, knowing the risks of brain damage were high from being down so long. "Where's the satellite phone? We need to get him flown out of here."

"Isn't it in your vehicle?" Ben inferred.

"I'll get it." Lisa kissed the top of Kate's head and then darted toward George's Rover. Within a minute she had scoured the Rover in its entirety. "It's not in there," she hollered, then went from one vehicle to the next vehicle, searching every nook and cranny for the phone, but it just wasn't there. She ran back to George. "There's no phone in any of the Rovers."

George looked around, then came to the realization there was no satellite phone, but he would deal with that issue later. "We need to set up camp. Go ahead and set up the large field tent for Connor. Mac, you stay with me and help keep an eye on him."

George stood; Kate broke her embrace with Sheila and ran straight into his arms, crying hysterically. George wrapped his grizzly bear arms around the tiny girl that wouldn't let him go.

———

Three hours later, Connor was on a cot in the large twelve by sixteen research tent showing no signs of waking. He was covered with two wool blankets and his head upon a pillow. Everyone in the tent was illuminated by the sullen orange glow of the battery-operated LED faux kerosene lamp. Kate sat at the head of the cot, gently stroking her fingers through Connor's hair, while everyone else sat at the collapsible plastic table. She stared at his face, watching, and waiting for any sign of life.

George sipped his black coffee. "We'll take off at first light and head to the closest town. Two trucks are out of commission so we're gonna double up. It's gonna be a tight fit, Connor is gonna be stretched out on the cot."

Mac nodded. "We can stack more gear up on top, just tie it down."

Kate kissed Connor on the forehead and joined the group at the table. "I think we should leave now."

"I agree," Sheila said as she leaned into Ben for warmth.

George shifted his eyes toward Kate and placed his tin cup on the table, still steaming. "I've thought about it, but I think we need to play it safe. Even if we leave now, the nearest town with a phone is about an eight-hour drive. At this point there is nothing a hospital can do for him other than supportive care. I think the smartest thing to do would be to get some rest and take off at first light."

———

Carl was detached from the group. No one spoke to him directly, and he hadn't spoken to anyone either. He sat at the table staring into nothing, shifting his gaze on occasion but that was all.

———

The brisk night air settled in. Kate and George stayed within the tent to keep an eye on Connor and agreed on a two-hour watch duty. George sat first, and it came and went without incident; no changes, no movement, nothing notable. Kate couldn't sleep during George's watch; she couldn't stop the plaguing thoughts. The entire event kept replaying over and over in her mind.

Two hours later, George laid down in the other cot on the opposite side of the tent and was asleep in less than five minutes. Kate moved her chair next to Connor's head. She whispered in his ear. "Come back to me, Connor," and kissed his forehead. She slid back into the chair and wrapped herself in a heavy wool blanket. She stared at him, alone with her thoughts, blinking occasionally. Her blinking slowed until her eyes closed and didn't reopen.

The sun's light broke the horizon, illuminating the desert with its picturesque orange radiance. An aroma was in the air, one that permeated Kate's dreams, throwing her into an unexpected state of tranquility. She began to stir. Her back was stiff from the three hours spent in the less than comfortable folding chair. Kate wanted to open her eyes, but she knew the lucid tranquility of her dream would be gone. Her eyes cracked, something was wrong.

She shoved the blankets to the ground, sprang out of the chair and spun around. George was snoring in the other cot. She fought to unzip the tent door, but just couldn't move fast enough to keep up with her racing mind. She jumped through the open flap and scanned over the camp. She panicked in the sudden shock of disbelief...

Kate's eyes were fixed, she couldn't speak. *I'm dreaming,* she thought. In a stupor, she walked toward the man who was busy cooking. He set the spatula down and faced her with an almost invisible grin. When she was within ten feet of him, she ran into his arms. He squeezed her, but she squeezed harder—much harder. She held onto him, knowing that in this moment she could never lose him.

Connor came back from the dead, made his signature breakfast, and enjoyed it with the team. Kate sat beside him, but it wasn't close enough.

———

Sheila shook her head, once again in disbelief, staring at the pancakes upon her plate. "I really think we need to call off the trip and get you to a hospital, young man. Seriously, Connor, you died. Your heart stopped for several minutes."

"Listen everyone, I appreciate all the concern but I'm fine. I feel great. Actually, I feel better than great. I don't need the hospital. I'm not sick."

Ben could see they had already lost the battle as Connor was inherently in charge. "So, what's the afterlife like?"

"You wouldn't believe me if I told you."

Mac raised his hand. "Was Elvis Presley there?"

Sheila poked at one of the pancakes then set her fork down. "C'mon, Connor, what was it like? Did you know what happened? Were you aware at all? What can you remember about yesterday? I think we all really wanna know, if you don't mind telling."

"Okay, okay." Connor smiled. "This is how it went down; I remember tethering Carl, then getting pommeled by a surge of water floating downstream and realizing the current was totally overpowering me. I tried to swim toward the higher shoulder, but something caught my leg. I tried to swim back against the current to free myself, but it was impossible. The water kept getting faster and deeper until it was over my head."

"Oh, my God, that's horrible." Sheila winced.

Kate teared up, having to relive Connor's drowning.

"So I took the biggest breath I could and went under. I tried to jerk my foot free, but it was impossible. This is the craziest thing. I knew I was going to die and I was completely at peace with it. Only one thing bothered me. The thought of you guys having to watch me die and deal with my death. In that moment, I had no fear of death, none what so ever. But the thought of you guys having to deal with my death is what truly bothered me. I held onto that breath for as long as I could, but I had to breathe, my body needed air.

I tried and tried to free my leg, but then finally I couldn't hold my breath any longer. I had to breathe in. I felt the cold water enter my throat and lungs and then whoosh! It happened. I couldn't feel a thing. No more struggling. No more anxiety about anything. I left the water. I floated up and right out of it. I could see everything from an aerial perspective."

Lisa rubbed her forearm with the palm of her hand. "Oh, my God, I'm getting the chills."

"I was in control, watching from above. I saw Carl clinging to the rope and trying to keep his head above water. I saw Ben and Sheila's Rover slam into the other and slide on top of it. I watched George slam his Rover into Kate's."

Sheila covered her mouth and whispered to Ben, "Oh, my God, he really saw everything happen."

"I did see everything." Connor heard Sheila's whisper. "I realized I was still in control, still alive; but free. I was flying. I…willed my way over to you guys, I tried to speak but you couldn't hear me, my voice was a thought, a projection of my thoughts. I know it all sounds crazy, but I knew what had happened. I knew I was dead but still alive…but I wasn't dead at all, and I was so curious. I started to move across the desert until I had this feeling… I just felt I was being called by something. I can't really explain it, but I just knew someone was trying to communicate with me, and as soon as I opened up to it, they appeared." Connor paused, and everyone waited, anxious.

Lisa couldn't tolerate the silence. "Who appeared? Who appeared?"

"This is gonna sound weird and mildly cliché, but it was my father." Connor looked down and took a second to breathe.

"He hugged me," he said with a calm while fighting the tears begging to escape. He took a few more quick breaths. "It was so surreal. He didn't speak, but I understood everything he conveyed. It's so strange and I know how crazy it sounds, but it was like we were using telepathy. I'll spare you the details, but I received some much needed closure from him." Connor looked at Kate and an odd silence hovered for a few seconds.

"Absolutely phenomenal." Ben spoke up. "I've heard of this sort of thing. You were given a glimpse of something the rest will only see at our end."

Connor shook his head. "I dunno, the largest part of me believes it was real, but the analytical side of me is shrugging it off as some sort of near-death dream or hallucinations."

Mac squeezed his beard. "I dunno, mate. Sounds like you were walking in spirit to me. You described exactly what happened during the flood. You saw us, mate. How else could you have known?"

Connor looked at Mac, serious. "Is that really how it played out?"

"You were dead-on, no pun intended, but it's incredible. You were floatin' around out there." Mac gestured to the air with his hands. "Who else did you see? You said *they appeared.*"

Connor nodded. "This is where it gets a little weird, and it's why I'm siding with dreams. The next to appear were a young girl and a large Thylacine. They gave me a feeling of love and wisdom. I couldn't see them very well and it's hard to explain. They were fuzzy, as though they were on a different level than that of my father. It was so much more difficult to communicate with them. They gave a warning that we needed to halt our expedition, or we would suffer gravely. It felt like a warning, not a threat. Then all of a sudden, they were gone. That's all I remember."

Sheila inhaled deep and shook her head slow, from side to side. "How many signs do you need? It's time to call off the expedition."

"No way, for all I know it was a hallucination or a dream."

"I don't know, I think you were on the other side," Sheila said. "And besides that, you need to see a doctor."

"Sorry, boss, I'm fine and we can't call everything off based on that. We've come too far."

Sheila frowned. "Must you be so stubborn?"

"Listen, I understand and appreciate everyone's concerns, but we're moving forward. We've come a long way and there's no way I'm turning back now. Let's take the day off. Get some R and R, and then shove off in the morning. Oh, yeah, one more thing..." Connor turned his head to the stacked Rovers. "Does anyone have *any* idea how we can get that thing down?"

George cracked one of his barely detectable grins. "Glad to have you back."

SEIZED

Tasmania - 1935

GREG HUGGED PETEY AND THEN GAVE MILLIE A PECK ON THE LIPS. "Love you guys, see you this evening." He walked off the porch and climbed into the Olds, waving as he fired up the engine. Ben heard the engine and ran outside, pushing the front door open with his snout and situating himself between Petey and Millie, the stuffed Koala still hanging from his jaws.

"You too, Ben!" Greg hollered as the wheels started forward.

They watched as Greg drove off, disappearing over the first rolling hill as he headed to the quarry.

It was Friday, which on the farm meant trough cleaning time. Millie would pull the drain plugs on the six-hundred-gallon aluminum watering troughs that gave the cattle a supply of fresh water, and then Petey would scrub them out and refill. It didn't take long for the tubs to turn green with algae, about ten days, and although harmless, Millie didn't like the idea of her cattle drinking green water. It would normally take Petey about an hour to clean all five of them; using a bristled brush, he would scrub them free of the green ick so quick to bloom on the metal walls. This was Petey's biggest chore around the ranch, and in return for his help, dinner was Petey's choice. This was the Friday ritual.

Ben laid in the shade of the barn and kept a watchful eye. In just under an hour, Petey threw the green-tinged brush into the soap bucket. He looked over at Ben who was looking right back at him, anticipating. "Come on, Ben." He sprung up and followed Petey toward the house.

Millie almost buckled on the porch steps, carrying a fifty-pound sack of feed over her shoulder. She carried it off the porch, then toppled it into the wheelbarrow.

Petey walked past with Ben trailing. "All done, Mom, need help?"

"Nah, this is the last one. That was fast, little boy. Did ya scrub 'em clean?"

Petey rolled his eyes. "Come on, Mom."

"There's some sweet tea on the table for ya."

Petey ran into the house. He loved it when his mom made sweet tea for the weekend. She loaded it with eucalyptus, lemon, and so much honey the tea thickened a bit.

Mille struggled with the worn-out wheelbarrow. It was so lopsided under the weight of the feed. She made her way through to the back of the barn then dumped the bags next to the feeder. The veins in her chiseled arms bulged as she heaved each bag three feet off the ground onto the rim of the circular feeder. A bead of sweat ran across her forehead then into the corner of her eye. She raised her forearm to rub it out.

"Lemmee give ya a hand wit dat?" A voice spoke from behind her.

Her stomach sank, heart raced, and she recognized the voice.

Millie's fingers dug into the coarse burlap sack and she allowed the grain to finish emptying into the feeder. She dropped the empty sack to the ground and picked up the next, unscathed. Using all her strength, she threw the final sack onto the edge of the feeder and slit it open with her razor-sharp folding knife. The grain poured into the feeder like blood from an open vein. "There's no business here for the likes of you, so you best be on your way." She forced her focus on the pouring grain.

"Some hospitality would be nice. We been out all day looking for tigers," Smitty said, staring at Millie's curves. Smitty was holding a coiled rope with a sliding noose on one end. He and Tanner were positioned side by side, boxing Millie in at the end of the barn. The rear gates in front of her that opened into the pasture were latched shut; there was only one way out and it was blocked.

"Well, there's no tigers around here so get on your way." Millie stared into the funneling grain. She could feel her hands trembling.

"Ya know tigers are foul creatures, they give off an odor. You always know when you're getting close to 'em cus you can smell 'em."

"Get the hell off my property." Millie tried to conceal her shaking hands under the grain bag.

"It's so odd." Smitty sniffed the air. "Cus I really think there's a tiger round here. I can smell it."

"All you smell is cow shit," Millie snapped.

"Oh, I don't know 'bout that, ain't no mistakin' the stench of a tiger." Smitty eyed Millie from head to toe.

"This is the last time I'm tellin ya, get the hell off my property." The grain bag emptied, and Millie folded it over her hands, concealing the small blade.

"Damn, you're good lookin'," Tanner finally spoke, then smiled, revealing his rotted brown teeth.

"My husband's gonna be home any second, and he's gonna put holes in each of you."

"Now that's no way to talk to a couple blokes trying to do you a favor. We know your husband's at the quarry. We got plenty a time."

"Get outta my barn and off my property," she shouted. Millie came to the realization she was in an inescapable situation. No longer was her mind filled with thoughts of self-preservation, now it was filled with thoughts of protecting Petey. She knew the house was too far away, he wouldn't be able to hear her call out.

"Well, we're gonna have a look around first," Smitty said.

"Like hell you are!" Millie snapped.

Tanner grabbed his crotch and started rubbing. "I say we check *her* out first."

"Come near me, I fucking dare ya!" Millie taunted.

"Calm down, we just want the tiger," Smitty said.

"I told you we don't have a god-damn tiger around here!" Mille yelled.

"We're gonna take a look in your house, hope you don't mind." Smitty smiled.

"You go anywhere near my house and I'll kill you!" Millie roared. She envisioned these men entering their home and killing Ben in front of her son. She wasn't going to let that happen.

"Where's that boy of yours? He knows where the tiger's at," Tanner said.

"He's not here, he's at the public school," Millie lied.

"Mmm, that means we're all alone." Tanner started rubbing his crotch again. "I say we get to know each other a lil' betta." Tanner started toward Millie.

"Just don't beat 'er up too bad," Smitty said.

Millie's entire world collapsed around her. Suddenly she was in a tunnel and all she could see was the approaching man.

Tanner stopped in front of her, sniffed her cheek as she trembled, and inhaled the sweetness of her skin. He grabbed her button-down shirt and ripped it apart, exposing her bare breasts.

"Hot damn!" He was so impressed that he looked back at Smitty for agreement.

He spun back around and grabbed at Millie's breasts, aggressively squeezing, and manhandling them until they smeared with blood.

He was confused; he hadn't been that rough. Then he noticed the blood running down his arm. He froze and looked into Millie's unwavering eyes.

Tanner followed the trail of blood up his arm and then grabbed his neck with his right hand. "Oh fuck, she's killed me," he cried.

When he had briefly looked back at Smitty, she struck like a snake, slicing his neck just under the jawbone with her blade.

Tanner held his neck, stumbling backwards in disbelief.

Smitty grabbed at his friend's neck and examined the wound. "You idiot. She got ya good but missed your pipes. You'll be fine."

Tanner realized he wasn't gonna die and retaliated. "Fuckin' bitch!" He stomped toward Millie. "I'll fuckin' kill you."

Millie took a defensive position and held the knife outward, taking small jabs at Tanner. He rushed in and Millie swung the blade, slicing Tanner's right forearm. He picked her up in a giant bear-hug then threw her to the ground. The impact dazed her, almost knocked her unconscious and the knife went spinning out of reach.

"You stupid fuckin' whore!" Tanner kicked her in the ribs with his heavy tattered leather boots.

Smitty, from several feet away shook his head and looked her in the eyes and she stared back at him. "Shouldn't a cut him." He turned and started walking out of the barn. "I'm headin' up to the house."

"Nooooo," Millie cried in between gasps for air, but fractured ribs were robbing it from her.

Tanner ripped at Millie's shirt, pulling it off. "I'll be fuckin' this bitch." He tied it around his bleeding neck.

Millie stood and charged Smitty. Tanner kicked her feet from under her, sending her crashing face-first to the hard dirt floor.

Tanner walked up behind Millie and stomped on her lower back. "That's what you get fer cutting me, bitch." Tanner sat on Millie's hamstrings and started jerking her dungarees down. Tears flooded her eyes as she helplessly watched Smitty walk up the hill toward her home. She wrestled and fought but couldn't move; his weight was too much and she could barely breathe.

Smitty made his way onto the front porch then peered through the window. He saw little Petey napping on the couch and no sign of the tiger. He pulled the squeaky screen door open and then pushed on the heavy wooden door, letting it swing all the way in. Smitty stood in the threshold scanning the room, then froze. His eyes were locked with the tiger at the end of the hallway, staring him down with teeth fully flared.

Before Smitty could react, the Thylacine was in full stride. Smitty jumped back onto the porch and slammed the screen door. As he did, the tiger went airborne and launched through the screen. Smitty used the coil of rope as a shield and Ben mashed his teeth into it then landed on all fours. Ben started snarling and shaking the rope. Smitty held the coil with one hand and worked the lasso around Ben's neck with the other. He tightened the noose around Ben's throat then held it high so that the tiger's front feet were lifted. Ben's teeth were snapping and clanking, trying to get at the fat man holding the rope.

Smitty looked over his shoulder toward the barn and saw Tanner pulling up his pants. "Hurry the fuck up!" Smitty yelled, exhausted.

Petey was awakened by the scuffle. He made his way to the door and saw Ben flailing around with his front feet off the ground, the fat man holding the rope.

"Ben!" Petey screamed. "Get off of 'em! You're hurting 'em!"

Petey ran up to the fat man and unleashed everything he had, but his flurry of kicks and punches amounted to nothing more than a slight distraction for Smitty.

The fat man caught Petey with a jarring elbow to the head that sent him falling backwards. Blood gushed from his forehead.

"Hurry the fuck up!" Smitty yelled. He was running out of breath and the tiger's teeth were getting closer and closer.

Petey picked himself up and disappeared into the house.

Tanner made it to the front of the house, reached into the firewood pile and selected a large club of a log.

Petey reappeared holding his father's rifle, just in time to see Tanner crack Ben over the head with the heavy slab of wood. Ben fell to the ground, motionless. "Bennnnnnnnnnnnnnnnnn!" Petey screamed in horror. He raised the rifle sight to his eye. Smitty and Tanner paused as the boy aimed. Petey squeezed the trigger. *Click.* Nothing happened.

Smitty grinned at the boy. "Helps to load it first, ya lil' bastard." Petey disappeared back into the house.

They hog tied Ben to a five-foot post and started toward the road. Ben's head hung limp with his neck arched back and blood dripping from his mouth.

"Shoulda parked a little closer. This guy's heavy as shit," Smitty bitched.

Tanner kept pressing on the shirt tied over his wound. "I gots ta get this stitched up, its bleeding bad," he whined. Seconds later a rifle cracked, sending a patch of dirt flying up in front of Smitty. Tanner ducked, startled, but Smitty didn't flinch.

Smitty looked back up the long driveway; he could see the boy on the porch with his eye to the rifle. "Bloody hell! That kid's persistent."

INTO THE MOUNTAINS

Present day

EVERYONE FELT GREAT LEAVING THE DESERT BEHIND. THE TREK made for some great footage, but it was time for the next phase of the trip. As they made their way out of the desert, they entered the rocky foothills of the Hamersley Mountain range. The sandy desert terrain had gradually dissipated, and a more hilled and rocky topography took over. As they continued west, the new landscape was of raised rock full of cracks and gorges with a slight increase in plant life. Cactus and succulents were being replaced with wild bush grasses that sprouted from the pockets of dirt trapped between the rocks.

As they progressed, the exposed rocky outcroppings took on a purplish red tone due to heavier concentrations of iron. The low-lying areas, gulleys, and flattened pathways were the darkest maroon from the rain washout. Iron's metallic odor was faint, nauseating Sheila as they trekked. This strange new landscape was a sign they were venturing deep. The path was scattered and in large spans, nonexistent. The Rovers marched through the new uneven terrain with ease; they couldn't be stopped, at least not yet.

Connor and Mac led the procession, followed by Kate and Lisa, then Ben and Sheila and finally Carl and Mac drove the heavily damaged Rover that had been half sunken in sand.

Mac's Rover looked as though it was used in a crash-up motor derby. The entire front end of the vehicle was damaged; from the bent brush guard to the crushed quarter panels and hood, the spider webbed windshield to the partially collapsed roof. It looked as though it would have been better served in a salvage yard, but it roared forward. Mac had no qualms about driving it. If the engine ran, its purpose was served. Carl on the other hand was put off by the thought of traveling in such a destroyed vehicle. Every time the brakes were applied, even the slightest, it would screech and scream with metal on metal. Filming wildlife within half a mile of this vehicle was damn near pointless.

Connor wrestled the wheel as he maneuvered up and over a large cluster of stair staggered rock. "I love this stuff," he said as he pressed the accelerator, forcing the Rover to climb again.

George tried to steady his camera. He clung to the *Oh Shit* bar with his free hand as the vehicle slow jerked and snapped over the rocks.

———

As Lisa tried to climb the same four-foot wall of rocks a tad faster, her Rover jolted with severe aggression from side to side.

Kate leaned forward and put both hands on the dashboard. "Oh, geez! It feels like we're gonna flip." Their bodies jerked around as the Rover scaled the uneven rocks.

"Nice work, Lisa!" Kate said as they cleared the obstacle.

Lisa couldn't stop grinning. "Thanks. I definitely have to get one of these when we get back home."

"Having fun, huh?"

"I love it."

"Wonder when we'll be setting up camp?" Kate said.

"I was just thinking the same thing. Sure hope it's soon. I'm beat."

"So are you bunking with Connor?"

"Ha ha, real funny, Lisa." Kate smiled.

"Oh, come on, you know you want to."

"Connor hasn't shown much interest since the accident."

"Really?" Lisa fought the steering wheel.

"It's probably nothing. He just hasn't really said anything to me, or even made that warm eye contact. To be honest, I felt kinda awkward around him."

"Well, I'm sure everything's fine. He went through a lot."

"Yeah, it's probably just me." Kate sighed. "I just thought he would have given a more personal goodnight yesterday. Instead he just said good night to everyone and disappeared into his tent."

"That does seem a little odd, but he was probably just beat. Give it a little time."

Kate stared at Lisa, contemplating.

"Yeeeessssss?"

"Can I tell you a secret, Lisa?"

"Of course."

"You cannot tell a—"

"Enough already! What is it, Kate?"

"Connor and I made love."

"What! When? Are you serious?" Lisa screamed.

"During the sandstorm."

"Oh, my God!"

"It was the most passionate and intense moment I've ever experienced in my life."

"Oh, my God, let's hear some details."

———

The team drove another hour before being forced to stop at the top of the flattened ridge of a massive canyon. At some point in history, ten or twenty million years ago, it had been a massive river with prehistoric flora lining the banks. Now the ancient waterway was as dry as a two-million-year-old bone. Connor knew this would be difficult to cross. First, they would descend into the canyon over a hundred and fifty feet down with jagged rocky steps and loose, crumbling rock. The second step was easy; crossing the bottom of the ravine which was fairly flat. To get out however, they would have to ascend the opposite bank, another hundred and fifty-foot climb up the same crumbly terrain. At first glance it seemed impossible, and for the most it was.

The group set camp on the flat rock top of the canyon, just feet from the edge. A mild chill settled in, but nowhere near the freezing temperatures after dark in the desert. In the far distance, beyond the ravine, lay a small mountain range with scattered treetops glowing by the light of a near full moon. Connor took a moment away from the group and stood upon the edge, overlooking all that lay ahead. The vastness of the earth before him was put in perspective; it carried on in every direction and in varying landscapes. From atop the ridge he could see distant valleys, tree laden mountains, and barren fields of rock. It was immense, but he knew the tigers were out there somewhere.

————

Ben, Sheila and Carl had already turned in for the night.

Mac poked at the fire with a hardened stick, trying to entice the flame. "Carl's probably cursing me right about now. You shoulda seen the look on his face when we were climbing about the bumpies earlier."

Kate smirked. She snuggled into her chair, wearing sweatpants and sweatshirt, knees pulled up to her chest. She wasn't feeling talkative and was hoping Connor would sit beside her. He didn't.

Connor yawned. "We should all get a good night's sleep tonight. Tomorrow we're doing some serious climbing. We're crossing this ravine and then we're going over that big hill." He pointed at the illuminated mountain glistening in the distance, a few miles away.

"I can't wait. It's gonna be intense," Lisa said.

Mac looked at Lisa. "Intense?" He laughed. "You'll be screaming before we're done. It's a monster."

"You've been over it before?" Kate asked.

"Not me personally, but I've heard its falling apart. They call it McKinley's bluff. All the off-road guys trek out here just to smash their trucks on it."

"Oh, my God, I can't wait. This is gonna be so much fun," Lisa said.

"Once we clear this ravine and the first mountain, there's a nice valley of rainforest. It sits pretty low between the mountains and there should be a shallow river we get to cross," Connor said.

"Haven't you had enough water by now?" Mac joked.

"You'd think."

Kate grumbled something inaudible under her breath. The mere thought of a joke being made about what had transpired during the flood wasn't funny to her, not at all.

"Wassamatta, Katie?" Mac pecked.

"I just don't understand how you guys can joke about what happened."

"Ya know she was pretty upset when you went all out-of-body on us." Mac looked at Connor.

"Yeah?" Connor looked at Kate, but her gaze was down and into the fire.

"Aw, man, she came unglued on the skinny, thought she was gonna rip Carl's head off with her bare hands."

Kate didn't know what to say. She sat in the chair, chin on knees, her gaze never leaving the fire. Connor looked over at Kate for a reaction and got none; she appeared lost in her own thoughts. But Kate wasn't lost. She heard every word, focused.

"Anyway, I'm off to beddie," Mac said.

Lisa stood on cue. "Great idea." Her exaggeration was obvious.

Kate placed her feet on the ground. "I'm right behind you." She felt used; sex and then no follow up, nothing. Kate walked away from the fire, following Lisa toward their tent. As she leaned in, a hand grabbed her right arm, and pulled her out.

Connor pulled her face to face with him and whispered, "I've missed you." He stared into her eyes.

She crumbled, finally. "I've missed you too, but where have you been?"

"I thought we were trying to keep this low profile?"

"News flash, Connor. The cat's out of the bag."

"What do you mean?"

"When we couldn't find you after the flood, I went ballistic on Carl. I thought he killed you, well…he did kill you, and I couldn't hold back, I was hysterical. It was obvious to everyone that there was more to *us*."

"I had no idea. I thought we were trying to keep this quiet. Ya know there really isn't any reason to."

"Right?" She pondered agreement with a childlike enthusiasm.

"Okay, it's settled then. But let's keep it tame when around the group. After all, this is a *business* trip." Connor winked.

"Hardly," Kate said.

Connor grabbed Kate's shoulders. "Listen, go get some sleep. We're all going to need it for tomorrow." Connor tucked Kate's hair behind her ear and gave the softest of kisses upon her lips. Her stomach filled and fluttered with velvet winged insects of epic proportions, bringing with a calming sense of relief. She kissed his cheek, then slipped into the tent.

FOUR-WHEEL LOW

Present day

As usual, the team awoke to the tantalizing aroma of bacon sizzling to perfection. The distant tree laden mountain tops were the first lit by sunrise. The first bit of sun heated the rock surrounding the team, bringing out the earthy aroma of the prehistoric sediment. They wolfed down the early morning buffet of coffee, pancakes, eggs and bacon and then broke camp. Once the vehicles were loaded and ready to go, Connor gathered everyone and asked for attention.

"Alright everyone, this is where it gets a little dangerous. Seatbelts are to be worn at all times, no exceptions. We're going down one Rover at a time. The rocks on this hill are loose like cookie crumbs and can break away at any time, and just because they held together for the truck in front of you, it doesn't mean they'll hold for you. Listen up as this is important. Make sure you put the small shifter lever into four-wheel low before you start moving. This will keep the Rover moving at a controlled, slow snail's pace even if you stomp the accelerator. While descending, if for some reason you start sliding, *do not* jam on the brakes, steer yourself into the slide. If your Rover goes sideways, brace yourself 'cus it's probably gonna roll all the way down. Keep your arms and head away from the window or else you'll lose 'em. This is going to be a slow descent. These vehicles were made for this." Connor patted the driver's door of the Rover. "This is why we paid so much for the insurance on 'em." Connor walked about thirty feet to the lip of the ravine and everyone followed.

Sheila clutched onto Ben's arm, frightened by the height as she looked down into the ravine.

Connor pointed down along the near vertical rock wall below their feet. "See the skinny little pathway that weaves in and out along the wall?" Two feet below the lip of the cliff was another seventy to eighty-degree angular slab of rock just wide enough for a vehicle. "That's what we'll be driving on. You'll want to hug the wall as much as you can, stay away from the edge or you'll be going down a lot quicker than you should. It's very steep, so once you start, there is no turning back. Is everybody ready?"

Lisa backed away from the edge. "Um… I was before this little pep talk. Now I'm scared."

Mac threw his arm around Lisa. "Come on, girly, it's just a little hill."

"I'm a bit nervous too," Sheila said.

Ben stood up, confident. "I can do this, babe. This is one of those defining moments. We'll be talking about it for years."

"George and I are descending first, followed by Lisa and Kate, Ben and Sheila then Carl and Mac." Connor paused. "Oh, yeah, hey Carl…"

Carl looked over at Connor.

"Try not to break this camera." Connor winked at Kate.

Carl laughed, analyzed the sarcasm then mumbled under his breath.

Connor shifted his Rover into four-wheel low and pressed the accelerator, forcing it to a slow crawl over the lip of the ravine. George filmed from the passenger seat, capturing the angular degree of the descent by leaning out of the window and panning.

The team stood at the edge, watching as the rock crumbled and dry dust went airborne from the slow-crawling, rock-grinding vehicle. Connor followed the steep angular path that had been used by other off-road vehicles. He guided his Rover to the bottom without incident.

Once at the bottom, he drove into the flat ravine, climbed out and looked up at the group. "Okay, it was easier than I thought it'd be!" he shouted up. "It's your turn, Ben, come on down!"

Ben gave a hefty thumbs-up and then climbed in.

Sheila was already holding the *Oh Shit* bar.

"Let's get this show on the road," Ben said as he shifted into drive.

"Please be careful, Benjamin," Sheila said.

He idled his way to the raised bumpy lip which was just high enough to stop the Rover. He pressed the accelerator to inch over, but it was too late; he hadn't put the second shifter in four-wheel low drive. The Rover lurched forward. Ben mashed the brakes, but it had already sped off the ledge and beyond the rock trail.

The Rover slipped over the second ledge of the path and was angled almost vertical. Its metal undercarriage grinded on the rock as it slid slow, tires screeching in intermittent bursts as it slid down the near vertical sheet of rock until it was caught by a protruding ledge.

Ben and Sheila found themselves hanging against their shoulder restraints. The Rover was fixed upon the ledge; its front tires were over the lip with the metal undercarriage caught on it. If it slid forward any further, a hundred and twenty-foot freefall to the bottom of the ravine would be inevitable. Sheila's screaming was indescribable.

Mac had already tied a rope to his Rover's brush guard and started sliding down the ledge after them, using his feet to slow his descent. He made it to the Rover within seconds. Its position was nearly vertical with its front end aimed down. Connor was climbing up from the bottom.

Mac made it to the small ledge that stopped the Rover and looked through the open rear passenger window to see Sheila hyperventilating.

"Calm down, Sheila, you'll only make it worse." They were seated and hanging against their seatbelts.

"Listen, I'm gonna lean out and open your door. Don't do anything." Mac leaned out, holding onto the rope that he had tethered to his Rover's brush guard, and then popped the latch on Sheila's door, causing it to fall open against gravity.

The Rover rocked back and forth, pivoting on its undercarriage, the pivotal point being just between the passenger and rear doors. "Now, when I lean out and say *pop it*, you're gonna hit the button on your seat belt and I'm gonna grab you. I want you to wrap your arms around me and squeeze like I'm your hubby, then you're gonna heave up onto that ledge. Alrighty?"

Sheila gasped and acknowledged with a series of uncontrollable trembling nods. Mac dropped down against the opened door with the rope fastened around his waist. "Pop it."

Sheila mashed the seatbelt harness button and fell onto him. He held onto the rope and fell back against the ravine wall. Sheila reached up and out, snagging the ledge as soon as it was within reach, at chest level. She pulled at the tattered rock while Mac pushed her bottom up and onto the ledge.

She cried, speechless and trembling, seated and pushing herself backwards until her back was against the wall of the four-foot ledge.

Mac gave a quick nod to Sheila. "Alright, hubbie's turn." At that very moment, the rock under Ben's vehicle broke away, causing it to slide forward until it hung on the rear axle. Mac pulled himself onto the ledge, then darted to the driver's side. "Ben, I'm gonna throw this rope to you. Try to slowly open your door."

"Mac, please help me," Ben spoke slowly, barely audible.

"I need you to do exactly as I say." Mac's voice frightened Ben, it was too serious. "Now slowly open your door. Don't let it fall open."

Ben popped the door handle and lowered it, hanging from the seatbelt harness, stretching himself out until it stopped in its fully open position.

"Get ready for the rope. Are you ready, Ben?"

"I... I think so." Ben grunted as he hung against the harness.

"Here it comes." Mac tossed the rope and it landed perfectly on his door. "Now tie it around your waist."

Mac, with his peripheral vision, saw Connor pull himself onto the ledge with Sheila. "Wanna take over?"

Connor shook his head. "You've got this." Connor backed against the wall and put his arm around Sheila.

Ben was struggling to get the rope around his waist while hanging against the harness. His movements became erratic. "It's kinda hard tying a damned rope when I'm upside down like this." Frustrated, Ben pressed the button on his seatbelt causing him to fall against the steering wheel. The Rover's axle started ripping through the rock.

"For fucks sake, tie the god-damned rope," Mac yelled.

Connor sprung to his feet. "Shit, it's going over." The Rover's axle started breaking free of the crumbling rock. Connor spiraled a section of the rope around his right forearm and gripped it tight with the palm of his hand. He dropped off the ledge with the rope tightened around his arm and dropped down onto the open door. "Grab onto me!" he shouted as the vehicle slid, grinding.

Ben awkwardly kicked his way out of the front seat and threw his arms around Connor just as the door dropped below him. The Rover plummeted to the bottom. The rope twisted tighter around Connor's arm from Ben's extra weight. He grunted, straining and in pain as they dropped several feet below the ledge. His veins were swollen with blood, screaming for more oxygen as he clung to the lifeline.

Mac kept a steady tension on the rope, wanting to pull harder, but resisting, knowing Connor could lose his grip. Hand over hand, Connor pulled himself and Ben up the rope. His back and arms were ready to explode. When Mac saw that Connor was close enough, he grabbed Ben's arm and pulled him up and off his savior. Mac turned around to help Connor, but he was already sitting on the edge, looking down at the pile of smashed Rover, smoking and in flames.

Mac placed his hand on Connor's shoulder, noting the rope burns and blood on his forearm. "You alright, mate?"

"Yeah, I'm fine. Just wondering what our insurance deductible is."

———

Lisa, Kate, and Carl watched the entire scene play out from above.

Lisa looked at Kate. "How's it feel to be dating Superman?"

Kate smiled, rolled her eyes, and released an extended sigh of relief.

Connor climbed back up to the top of the ravine and sat on a small boulder. Kate looked over at him with an unbreakable stare, lost in infatuated admiration.

Ben and Sheila sat silent in their harnesses as they were hoisted up by Kate, Lisa, and Carl. Ben peeked at Sheila, afraid to look any longer in fear that it would trigger retaliation. He could tell by the way she was staring blankly at the cliff wall that she was pissed. Ben did the right thing and kept his mouth shut. He knew that with time, she would get over it, but right now would be a bad time to get her started.

I guess I'm not the swashbuckling adventurer I thought I was. His pride was stripped as he sat helplessly in his harness, being pulled to the top by two girls and Carl. Ben climbed into the backseat of Lisa's Rover next to his wife, only to have her instantly exit and get in Mac's vehicle. The other two vehicles made it to the bottom without incident.

———

Connor pulled whatever was salvageable from Ben and Sheila's upside down, smashed pile of smoldering Rover. The fridge and freezer containing the bacon, beer and other luxury foods was destroyed and unreachable due to the collapsed roof. Ben and Sheila's pre-furnished hiking packs were both thrown from the wreckage as it tumbled, rolling over and over. Each pack contained a tent, sleeping bag, miscellaneous camp gear like matches, coffee, water sterilizing tablets and enough freeze-dried food and water rations for two weeks.

Connor could see the resentment in Sheila's eyes so he insisted she ride with him while Ben tagged along with Mac and Carl.

The team explored the ancient river bed on foot for a couple hours, examining the millions of mollusk fossils embedded in the lower half of the ravine's limestone walls. Lisa and Kate chiseled a few souvenirs from the wall. They all loaded into their vehicles and were ready to make their ascent out of the ravine when Mac spotted something peculiar in the side view mirror.

What the heck is that? He shrugged it off and fired up the Rover. He was waiting for the next vehicle to start rolling but couldn't help thinking the odd symmetry of what he could see was most likely not a product of the desert. He turned off the ignition and hopped out.

Connor saw Mac get out of his Rover so he stuck his head out of the window. "What ya got, Mac?" he yelled back to him.

"Dunno, it's something, maybe an old car," Mac said as he walked toward the deep curve in the ravine wall less than fifty yards away. Everyone else got out of their vehicles and followed.

Connor was a few feet behind Mac and as they neared it was obvious. "How the heck did that get here?"

"Beats me," Mac said as he grabbed the door handle and tried to pull it open. He gave it a hard jerk and the handle ripped away from the door.

Connor gave the rusted pile of a car a quick once over. Its paint had been eaten by the sun, leaving bare steel to fight the elements. The entire body harbored blotchy rust, giving the car a crusty burnt orange look. Its tires were hardened into black cracked and crumbling circles. The windshield was caked in thick dust that would not wipe away.

Ben's face lit up as he neared. "Holy macaroni! It's an Oldsmobile!" Ben was very passionate about early automobiles, so much so that he completely restored his own 1915 Finley Robertson Porter, a true piece of automotive history.

Mac tossed the broken handle through the open side window into the front seat. "This thing's been here for decades."

"Uh, more like a century," Ben said.

"Any idea what year it is?" Connor asked.

Ben scratched his head. "Well, if I had to guess, I'd say between 1915 and 1930."

Connor climbed through the driver's side window and sat on the rusted seat springs. "Incredible." He started searching for any clues to its prior life. The interior was just as bad if not worse than the exterior; dust blanketed every nook and cranny, the leather-bound seats were reduced to a pile of rusted springs, seat backing was nonexistent, however the wooden dash trim had held up remarkably well. "I wonder why they were hiding."

"Hiding?" Sheila spoke for the first time since her incident with Ben.

"Why *else* would it be backed into this hole in the wall?" Mac said as he leaned in through the window opposite Connor. He pulled himself halfway into the rear compartment that used to be a small back seat. He tugged on the floorboard latch, popping it open to reveal a small one foot by one foot square storage area. "Looks like I found a dolly. I can't reach it from here. Can you grab it mate?"

Connor turned around, stretched, and blindly reached into the compartment, pulling out the doll.

"Check it out!" Lisa said, leaning in to the window.

Kate recognized the shape. "It looks like a Koala."

Connor studied the object. "That compartment really protected it from the elements."

Mac reached out from the back and gave it a squeeze. "It's made of goatskin, that's tough stuff."

Connor handed it off to Lisa so they could play *show and tell* with the antique teddy bear. It was about eight inches tall with an abnormally oversized head, just as dirty as the day it was placed into the compartment. One by one, they passed it around, taking pleasure in its authentic purity and simplicity.

Mac forced himself even further through the window, far enough to thrust his hand into the compartment to retrieve a small piece of paper. He pushed his way out of the window and back onto his feet. "You guys gotta see this." Mac's tone became serious. He stared at what turned out to be a black and white photograph.

Connor looked through the window at Mac. "Why? What ya got?"

Mac reached through the window and handed it off to Connor. He looked at it for a second then pulled his head back, then pulled it closer, verifying what his eyes had seen. He stared at the picture in disbelief.

"Earth to Connor," Kate said. "What is it?"

"It's a picture," he said.

"Of?"

"Of the Thylacine enclosure at the Hobart Zoo in Tasmania," Connor said.

"Oh, my God. Talk about coincidence," Kate said. "What are the chances?"

"I'd say next to impossible." Connor handed the photo to her.

Kate realized it was too much of a coincidence. "This is just too much."

Connor cupped a hand to his chin and felt around on the stubble, thinking. "I know. Mac, any input?"

"Well, the way I see it is its either one hell of a coincidence, or..." Mac paused.

Connor looked up at Mac. "Or?"

"Or we were supposed to find it."

Connor stared at the bear as the girls shared it.

Ben looked over Kate's shoulder at the picture. "What are the chances? This is either one hell of a coincidence or there's something strange going on. If we had driven just a few feet off, we would've missed it."

Kate looked at Connor. "If we had driven off our current course by just a foot we never would have made this find. It's not like we're following a path or a road. That's one ridiculously outrageous coincidence. I don't buy it."

Connor and Mac searched every rusted-out pocket within the vehicle for any other clues but found nothing. Though dumbfounded by the coincidence, they could do nothing more than move on.

OVER THE MOUNTAIN

Present day

Connor popped the latch on Sheila's door. "That wasn't so bad now was it?" He teased as he guided her out. She'd kept her eyes sealed for the entire ascent up the ravine.

Once her feet were on solid ground she cracked her eyes. "Wow." She looked up at the massive mountain sitting at her feet. She could first smell a more fragrant air. Dark green pines were numerous and scattered about the smooth rocky incline, bursts of tall, red grasses with fluffy seed feathers clustered in the small soil pockets and a light foggy haze hid its upper elevations. A choir of songbirds could be heard in the distance.

"She's a real beauty, aye?" Mac asked. The entire team stood in appreciation.

Ben placed himself beside Sheila. "It's incredible. The desert is right behind us and a gorgeous wooded mountain range right here."

Sheila was so damned angry at Ben, but she wanted to share this moment with him. She looked at him with angry eyes and he looked back apologetically. She gave in. "Get over here, Benjamin." He stood behind her and wrapped her in his arms. Kate and Lisa smiled at each other in adoration of Ben and Sheila's cuteness.

"This is nature at its finest," Kate said.

Connor stood close beside Kate. "And it shouldn't be too difficult to cross."

"The trees aren't too thick and its relatively smooth terrain," Mac said.

Connor looked at the position of the sun. "We've got a few hours left. Let's go ahead and cross it. There's a shallow river on the other side that flows along the mountain. It should be a great place to make camp."

The Rovers crept up the mountain like tortoises climbing a sand hill. Once they neared the summit, fog prevented them from driving straight through. It was stop and go every twenty feet or so as they had to exit the vehicles on foot and walk ahead to ensure a safe route. Connor would walk thirty or forty feet in front of his vehicle to ensure there were no drop-offs or potentially dangerous terrain. Due to the unpredicted lack of visibility, it set them back a couple of hours. Rather than camp on the mountain in the heavy dampness of the fog, they pushed on. The fog broke midway through the descent which allowed them to speed up just enough to reach the bottom before midnight.

INTO THE JUNGLE

Present day

THE SUN SEEMED LATE TO RISE. THE MOUNTAIN HAD SHIELDED THE sunrise, allowing for a few extra hours of dusky sleep. Even Connor slept until almost nine, which was quite a stretch from his regular six a.m. breakfast preparation. Connor and Mac hobbled out of their tents at the same time.

Mac scratched at his scalp through the thick matted locks of black and blond hair. "Those frogs made quite a racket, didn't they?"

"They do, but I didn't even hear 'em. I passed out," Connor said.

The tree frogs' piercing loud barks and chirps echoed all through the night until first light, then stopped abruptly. This was a natural sign the team was getting close to the river and away from the dry, skin cracking desert region. The mountain they crossed was a natural barrier between the flat desert like arid zone and the more humid and warmer jungle, which lay ahead of them.

Sheila poked her head out of the tent. "Morning, boys."

"Morning, Sheila. Ready for some more off-roading?" Mac joked.

"Watch it, Mac. She can be deadly in the morning," Connor said.

"Actually, I had a wonderful night's sleep and I look forward to our day of adventure."

Connor and Mac looked at each other, baffled.

"That's refreshing," Mac said. "I bet your hubbie will be glad to hear that."

"Give a woman a good night's sleep and all worries disappear." Connor laughed.

"Who said we were sleeping?" Sheila grinned and winked.

Mac was distracted by Lisa. He couldn't help but notice her climbing out of the tent wearing form fitting, long john pajamas that accentuated her well curved body.

"Turkey's done," Mac joked as Lisa stretched her arms to the sky.

"Turkey?" Lisa asked. Connor laughed under his breath.

"Yeah, your timers have popped up." It took her a second, but she caught on that her nipples were abruptly protruding through her pajama top. She crossed her arms and threw a playful evil-eye at Mac.

With the exception of George, who was out exploring the area, the team talked over coffee, reminiscing about the ups and downs they had already experienced on the trip. Connor emphasized to the group that even though they had lost a vehicle, it made for great footage and would be a great contribution to the final product. Luckily, all of the footage was well protected in a weather and fireproof box stored in the rear compartment of Connor's vehicle.

While everyone was chatting at the table, George walked out of the jungle. "I hope everyone's got their walking shoes. The jungle across the river is thick, the trucks aren't getting us much further."

"How far off is the river, George?" Connor said.

"Less than a mile and it's really shallow, more like a stream, maybe six inches at most."

"I take it we don't need the Rovers to get across?" Connor said.

"Nope," George said.

Connor looked around at their camp. "That settles it then. This is gonna be our base camp. From here on out we're going on foot. Everyone needs to get your compass out and check your headings. If anyone gets lost, you'll need to find your way back to the vehicles." Connor pointed toward the river. "That's the direction we're heading, look at your compass, if you get lost, go the complete opposite direction of what your compass is showing now. We're heading west, so if you get lost, head east. It's pretty simple. Does everyone understand?"

Mac eyed Sheila as she fumbled around with her compass. "Couldn't they just look for the big hill and walk back to it?" he joked, pointing at the enormous mountain behind them.

Connor rolled his eyes. "Or, you could do that too."

At the expense of Natural Productions, everyone carried their own fully-stocked individual hiking pack and they all sported new Timberland hiking boots and Gore-Tex all weather jackets.

The river was just as George described; shallow and small, flowing gently over the glistening bed of rounded pebble. Everyone crossed with ease. Forty yards further west of the river, vegetation abounded, thick and green with a more subtropical appeal.

Connor led the group in single file. He carried a heavy bladed black machete, cutting back as much vegetation as possible while maintaining a steady pace through the jungle. His objective was to create a noticeable path, one they could retrace on their way out.

The mid-day sun was shielded by the heavy canopy of evergreens and spindly palms, keeping the interior warm and humid, but not overbearingly hot. The ground was covered with various bush palms and ivy vines, creating a thick and secretive habitat for insects, arachnids, reptiles, and small mammals.

Connor stopped abruptly and faced the line behind him. "Oh yeah, watch where you step."

"And what exactly are we watching for?" Sheila asked.

"Creepy crawlies," Mac said.

"That's right, but the creepy crawlies out here can kill you," Connor said.

"Maybe you shouldn't have told us," Ben laughed.

"Just watch out for snakes and spiders. Most are harmless, but there are a few widow makers out here," Connor said.

Ben squinted his eyes at Sheila and joked, "Widow makers, huh?"

"That's funny. I was thinking the same thing." Sheila squinted her eyes right back at him.

Lisa peered into the jungle. "What's that crunching sound?"

Connor put his finger to his lips. "Ssshh." Everyone stopped moving and listened in.

Crunch...Crunch... The sound was getting closer.

"Sounds like a cassie-kicker," Mac whispered.

"What's a cassie-kicker?" Carl asked.

Connor looked at Mac. "A cassowary?"

"Well, that's what it sounds like to me," Mac said.

"Shit," Connor said. He had forgotten about them, and the threat they posed.

"What do you mean *shit*?" Carl's face stiffened.

Connor waved his arms to get everyone's attention. "Listen up everyone, take off your hiking packs, hold them in front of you and get back to back with everybody else." Everyone wrestled off their packs and huddled together, forming a tight circle, holding their packs as though they were expecting an NFL linebacker to come charging.

Connor and Mac stood apart from the circle, holding their packs like a shield, trying to spot the kicker bird.

Ben couldn't wait and had to ask, "What exactly is a cassowary?"

"Think Jurassic Park raptors but smaller," Connor whispered. "Cassowaries are giant flightless birds, up to about a hundred and thirty pounds. They're not even known to be here so that may not be what it is. They have a rep for being extremely aggressive, kicking with their razor-sharp claws, slashing the stomach, and disemboweling anything in its way."

Mac turned to Ben. "You don't muck around with these birds." The group wasn't used to seeing Mac so serious, and it frightened them.

"Shhh." Connor listened in.

Everyone listened but heard nothing.

"Maybe it's gone?" Carl said as he panned his camera.

Connor looked at Carl and shushed him directly. "Shhhh."

Carl grunted and looked the other direction. He spotted some movement through his camera's viewfinder and zoomed in. "Oh, I see it. It's just a kangaroo." Carl pointed at the red kangaroo chewing on some sort of fruit, forty yards behind them.

Connor faced Carl and mouthed the words, *Shut up*.

Connor and Mac both glanced at the kangaroo; their common sense told them it wasn't the source of the crunching; it was too far off.

Carl laughed out loud. "Ha, ha. All this huddling for a kangaroo."

Connor jerked his head toward Carl in disapproval and put a finger across his lips.

Suddenly the slow crunching became a steady gallop and from out of the jungle brush came a massive, prehistoric looking, blue bird with a horn-like crest protruding from the center of its head. It was charging directly at the source of the voice. Carl, being a seasoned videographer, held his ground, at least for the moment. The kicker bird stopped about thirty feet from the odd-looking huddle of people.

The cassowary started making some god-awful hacking noise, like a first-time drinker trying to expel two bottles of Mad Dog 20/20 from the pit of an aching and unsettled pre-collegiate stomach. Then it started dancing, lunging in a few steps, and then backing up, raising its silly, stumpy little wings in some sort of threat display, then lunging in and backing up and barking, all over again. This bird put on one hell of a show.

It kept getting closer and closer to the group with each forward lunge. And with each lunge, Carl's fear of being disemboweled grew and grew. He could now see the massive dinosaurian recurved talons and as the bird danced closer it got the best of him. On its next lunge, he bolted.

Carl dropped the camera strapped to his neck and darted toward Connor and Mac. The dinosaur bird gave chase; it was locked onto Carl. Just as he was about to pass Connor and Mac, Connor kicked his feet out from under him, sending him face first to the ground with the psycho bird leaping over him with its gnarly claws extended, missing its toppled target.

Instead of turning its aggression toward Connor or Mac, which is what Connor had expected it to do; it went back for Carl, who was now belly down and looking up. The flightless monstrosity sprung off the ground and extended its claws; this time it was focused on Carl's back. As it was about to penetrate its target, an extra heavy-duty hiking pack slammed across the bird's body, toppling it over backwards. The bird scrambled to its feet and gazed at Connor with an expressive look of confusion. The bird realized it had met its match and ran off into the jungle.

Silence hovered over the group for a few seconds, and then Kate lashed out. "What the fuck, Carl? How the hell did you make it this far in life?"

Carl stood up and brushed himself off, completely ignoring Kate's verbal lashing.

———

Following Connor in a single file line as he hacked away at the dense overgrowth, they pushed on. Every sound produced by the forest frightened Carl to the bone, he was now on edge and obsessive, his shifty little eyes scanned in every direction, fearful of what might lay just beyond the ferns and palms.

Sheila swatted a large, shiny, black and green bug off her vest. "Is anyone else being bombarded with bugs?" She swung at the mosquito's constantly buzzing around her head.

"Not really," Lisa said.

Connor grinned as he swung the machete. "It's your perfume."

Sheila knew she was busted. Connor had told her not to wear anything fragrant while on the expedition. Unable to shower, she felt a little splash would freshen things up a bit. "I only used a dash."

"That little dash is like wearing the nectar of ten thousand flowers. It's an insect attractant."

"Lesson learned." Sheila swung at another large bug that tried to land on her face.

They continued for two more hours, stopping when they entered a flat, open area in the jungle. Connor kicked a few dead branches out of the clearing. "This should be a good spot, let's call it a day."

Carl slung the pack off his shoulders and dropped it to the ground. "Thank God."

Connor pulled Sheila's pack from her back. "Let's get your tent up first. You need a break from these bugs." He laughed as he dodged the swarming mass of insects orbiting around her head.

———

Mac blew gently on the glowing ember, trying to get the dried forest litter to catch. As the ember glowed brighter, smoke started billowing from the pile of dead leaves and twigs, until a single flame transformed the pile into a blazing fire. The darkness was now hued with soft orange overtones, giving everyone a warm, fiery glow. The crackles of the fire were inviting, and it wasn't long before everyone surrounded it. With the darkness came mosquitos, lots of 'em, and the smoke seemed to keep them at a tolerable distance. The darkness awakened all sorts of unseen nocturnal creatures, filling the night with chirps, barks, screeching and croaking.

Connor opened his chair and set it next to Kate. "How is everyone feeling?"

Mac pulled the small twig from between his teeth. "I'm great. Love being out here in the bush. Only thing that'd make it better'd be a few beers." He grinned at Ben in regards to his cliff diving incident.

"Yeah, yeah, yeah," Ben said. "Even if we salvaged them, they'd be a little too warm."

"Glad to see you can laugh about it now, Ben," Connor said.

"But it could have been far worse," Sheila cut in. "I'm so thankful to have you guys. You saved our lives."

"Well the way I see it, I had to save ya—you're signing my paycheck," Mac said.

"You're so funny and such a pleasure to be around. I'm, really gonna miss you when this trip's over. Why don't you come back to the states with us?" Sheila asked.

"Aw, you've got me feelin' all warm 'n fuzzy inside. I've always thought about hittin' the states, but this is my home."

Ben reached over and put his hand on Mac's shoulder. "Just remember, my friend, you'll always have a place to stay across the ocean."

Mac nodded and cracked a crooked grin. He wasn't used to this much attention and it made him feel a little awkward.

"You've always got this carefree happy-go-lucky spirit about you, how do you do it?" Lisa asked.

"For all I know, we're only given one chance at this life. Make the best out of every minute, because you'll never get this minute back; once it passes, it's gone forever. Live in the moment, don't let troubles consume you, love everyone, even if they don't love you."

"Beautiful," Kate said.

"Have you always been like this?" Ben asked.

"Nah, it's taken years of Chinese food and fortune cookies to get to this level of enlightenment," Mac said.

Everyone laughed except for Carl. He spit the small, mashed toothpick he had been gnawing onto the ground. "Sounds great but some people choose to live in the real world."

Kate was about to unleash on the spindly man but felt Connor's gentle touch to her shoulder. She looked at him.

He shook his head. "It's not worth it."

———

Connor and Kate waited. It couldn't have been any slower as time ticked by. All they wanted was to be alone, but the conversing continued for more than an hour. Connor and Kate sat waiting, grinning, and smiling until everyone eventually disappeared into their tents. The fire transformed into a smoldering bed of red embers, projecting a romantic red glow.

Kate pulled Connor's arm over her. "It's getting chilly."

"Yeah, it's colder than I thought it would be."

Kate reached for a small piece of wood and threw it on the coals. They both watched as it started smoking, and then ignited. Kate warmed her hands over the toasty flame, but it died out a minute later. "I'll grab a few more pieces of wood."

"Okay, let's go."

Kate put her hand on his chest and pushed him against the seat. "No, no, no, sit back and relax."

Connor sunk into the chair and crossed his arms. "If you insist…"

"I'll be right back." Kate smiled. She walked just outside the light of the glowing embers and into the underbrush, feeling around for dead limbs that had fallen from the canopy. Finding nothing she walked a few steps further into the darkness. *Here's a good one.* Kate pulled a large, broken branch hanging from above her. Searching for more, something reflective shining in the distance caught her eye. She squinted, trying to focus in on the gleaming. A spine-tingling chill shot through her body and every hair stood on end; she was being watched. The biologist in her, told her to remain calm and analyze. *It's some sort of nocturnal animal, but it's big, must be a kangaroo, wait, can't be a kangaroo, their eyes don't reflect light. Maybe it's a tree kangaroo? No, tree kangaroo eyes glow red, these are greenish. What the hell is that?*

Connor listened but he could no longer hear the crunching underneath her footsteps. "Kate?" he called, raising his voice just enough to not disturb the others. He walked over to the edge of the woods. "Kate!"

Inside the tent, Carl's shifty eyes opened. He slid into his boots, taking care not to disturb Mac who was sound asleep. Carl grabbed his camera and crept out of the tent without making a sound.

Kate's heart skipped when another set of eyes appeared just beside the larger set. She hunched down and watched.

Connor called a little louder with a bit of concern in his voice. "Kate!"

It caught her attention and she spun around, whispering, "Connor, get over here." She turned back toward the glowing eyes, but they were gone.

Connor stepped through the thick undergrowth, stopping behind Kate. "Did you see something?"

Kate scanned the darkness. "I was picking up this branch when I noticed a large set of green eyes staring at me. I can't figure out what they were. Then a second set appeared. What the heck could it have been?"

"Well, kangaroos are the first that come to mind, but their eyes don't reflect at night. Maybe they were crocodiles?" Connor joked.

"Real funny, Connor, what were they though?"

"Wish I could tell you."

Kate hesitated. "I think they were Thylacines."

"That's a pretty bold claim. I'd have to label them as mutant dingoes before I could even begin to say that word. Let's check out the area in the morning and see what we find. Maybe we'll find some feces or tracks."

"Great idea, I can't wait." Kate stared into the darkness with Connor behind her.

Connor leaned in, placing his mouth against her ear. "There's something else that can't wait," he whispered, and then nuzzled her ear lobe. His warm breath filled her ear canal, sending warm shivers throughout her entire body. She dropped the sticks that were so firmly placed under her arm.

She turned around and he grabbed her shoulders, pushing her back against the smooth bark of the massive ficus tree. The tree that had been so generous as to supply them with a near limitless supply of kindling. Its smooth, curvy bark cooled her spine as she pressed against it. He moved from her ear to the side of her neck, tasting the sweetness of her skin. One by one, he popped the buttons on her flannel shirt, exposing her breasts. His fingers slid down to her belly, then popped the button on her jeans. The sound of her zipper forced her heart into a gallop. He pushed himself against her and they joined.

From forty yards away, a camera focused in. Carl watched in silence through the green tinted luminescence of the viewfinder.

———

No longer would the team be awakened by aromatic bacon permeating the morning air. Regrettably, all the eggs and bacon were left to rot in the fridge that had been entombed within Ben's Rover. The jungle birds would now provide the wake-up calls. The morning wake-up call was obscene. One or two Cockatoos at close range could nearly make ears bleed; now the forest was full of them, and not just Cockatoos, but dozens of other bird species, large and small, all screaming the first hour before dawn and the three hours after.

Ben crawled out of his tent and noticed that the others were already packed away. "Good grief." He stood up and stared into the canopy in disbelief. He was the last up; everyone else overcome by the noise had already broken down the camp.

Connor gathered just enough saliva to swallow a dried up piece of wheat bread pulled from his M.R.E's. M.R.E's, meals ready to eat, are vacuum packed meals designed to last for many years, are utilized by the military, expeditioners or anyone else needing a shitty meal edible for eternity. "You want the good news or the bad news?"

"I always take the good news first." Ben spoke loud enough to overcome the birds.

"Good news is that this is probably the last day we'll have to hear this."

"That's certainly good news, how about the bad?"

"Bad news is that this is gonna last for about two more hours."

Everyone forced their pre-packaged breakfasts down. George however enjoyed it, savoring every last bit down to the instant coffee which he drank at room temp.

Connor cinched the straps tight on his backpack, securing the rolled tent. "Kate, Lisa and I are gonna check something out in the woods. Kate saw something unidentifiable last night and it's got us stumped. We're gonna look for some clues as to what it may have been. We'll be back in a few minutes and will head out when we get back."

Carl mumbled under his breath, "Going back for a ménage trois."

Connor raised an eyebrow. "What was that, Carl?"

"Oh nothing, just thinking out loud."

"Back in a bit." Connor led the girls into the forest.

They searched high and low for anything that could yield a clue but found nothing.

After a few hours of trekking, the team made it to a large grass clearing in the forest. A river divided the clearing in half. It was considerably larger than the first river they had traversed, but small and shallow enough to easily cross.

Lisa aimed her face at the sky and sighed. "Geez, it feels great to get into the sun."

Mac dropped his pack and eyed the river. "Lobster anyone?"

Connor shrugged the pack off his shoulders. "I'm game, let's break here. Who wants to catch lunch with us?"

"Lobster?" Lisa asked.

George dropped his pack to the ground. "Crawdads."

Lisa's face lit up. "Oh wow, this will be just like the creeks back home!"

Ben was addicted. One after another he plucked the feisty crustaceans from the water, fascinated with the thought of catching his own food.

Kate and Lisa were just frolicking around in the water, splashing each other and screaming, romping like a couple of Labradors set loose on a lake. George, Connor, Mac and Ben were focused on the task at hand, turning every rock, grabbing at every skittish little delicacy. Ben was the only one getting pinched, but he slowly learned how *not* to grab the crustaceans. One after another, they tossed them into the pot until it was filled. Carl agreed to film as long as he was dealt a fair portion of the catch.

Sheila bathed in the river, without soap. She scrubbed until her neck and wrists were red, trying to eliminate all traces of the sweet perfume she had regrettably doused.

Mac had the afternoon fire crackling before anyone even knew he had started one. In less than five minutes their catch had boiled to red perfection. The entire group sat in the mid-day sun, enjoying its mild warmth and eating little red lobsters.

The river-romp was memorable, but it was time to move on. Everything was perfect and danger free; a beautiful setting along a pristine river, great new friends, great food, and the serenity of the wilderness.

————

As they made their way across the shallow flowing water, their reluctance to leave was obvious. They didn't walk with their normal pep—no one wanted to leave. They looked like heartbroken children forced to leave a carnival.

Sheila looked back toward the bank. "Oh, Honey, I forgot my wet clothes." Sheila trudged back toward the bank, sloshing along the way. She'd hung them from a low branch with the hopes they would be dry before putting them into her pack.

Everyone waited in the water for Sheila to get back in formation.

Seconds after reaching the bank, Sheila screamed in terror. Everyone spun around to see what the commotion was about. Sheila was kicking her feet and walking backwards. Mac was at the rear and the closest to her. He started in her direction to assist. She fell over backwards and continued kicking and screaming. Mac leaped up the bank and saw a massive, six-foot black snake attached to her left shin.

"Fuck'n A," Mac said under his breath. He realized the situation was bad, really bad. He made it to Sheila within seconds. The snake was still attached to her shin, chewing and gnawing. He grabbed the snake just behind its head and tried to pull it off, but Sheila's kicking was too much.

Connor appeared at Sheila's side. "Calm down, Sheila."

"Get it off me! Get it off me!" she continued screaming and kicking her legs.

Mac grabbed Sheila's ankle with his free hand and tried to pin it to the ground. "Hold still, lady, I can't get it off you unless you stop kicking!"

Connor threw his torso over Sheila's thighs and his weight slowed her flailing.

"Got it," Mac said as he pried the snake's mouth off Sheila's leg. He secured the snake's body with his free hand then backed away from Sheila.

Sheila was crying and attempting to kick. Connor grabbed Sheila by the shoulders and gave a firm shake. "Listen! If you don't calm down it's gonna get worse."

Sheila looked at Connor. "But it hurts so bad!"

Connor started looking around in all directions. His mind raced as he tried to gain control over the situation. Everyone gathered around Sheila.

"What kind of snake is it?" Ben asked.

"Tiger," Mac said, holding the snake.

"Is it poisonous?" Ben asked.

"Uh, deadly," Mac whispered so that Sheila couldn't hear.

Ben's mouth dropped open in disbelief. "Wha…wha…what do you mean deadly?" His voice trembled, and he struggled to catch his breath.

"Give me a shirt," Connor barked. Kate threw him the damp shirt Sheila had dropped. He snatched it out of the air, wrapped it tight around her leg, directly on top of the wound.

"The antivenom was in the god-damned fridge," Connor said.

"Well go get it!" Sheila cried.

Connor shook his head. "Damn it!" he yelled. "By the time we get there and back it'll be too late. You need it within the first few hours for it to work."

Kate stroked Sheila's head in an effort to calm her. "It's ok, Sheila, breathe."

Connor stood up and kicked his pack. "Damn it!" He yelled even louder. "No phone, no fucking antivenom! Think people, think!"

George raised an eyebrow. He had never seen Connor lose control or yell at anyone, ever.

"I can make a fixer, but it ain't guaranteed," Mac said.

Connor looked down at Mac who was standing back, away from Sheila, still holding the thick black snake. "We're out of options Mac, do whatever you can. Anyone else? I'm open to ideas."

Mac disappeared into the forest with the snake.

"Can we carry her back to the Rover?" Ben said.

"It's pointless, this venom is very fast acting, it gets in and does its job in minutes. It would take us a day and a half to get back there, and the antivenom would be totally useless then."

Lisa looked up at Connor. "Well, we could at least drive her to a hospital, couldn't we?"

Connor shook his head. "We're about a three days drive to the nearest hospital. The venom would be out of her system by then."

In hearing that, Ben felt a little relieved to know that in three days the venom would have run its course. "So in a few days the venom will be out of her system and she'll be fine?"

Connor looked directly into Ben's eyes. "If she lives, Ben."

"What do you mean, if she lives?" Ben was appalled.

"Ben, listen to me, your wife was bitten by a tiger snake, one of the deadliest snakes on the planet. With antivenom she'd probably survive, without it, it's not good."

Ben started shaking his head in disagreement. "We didn't sign up for this, Connor."

"I didn't either, Ben."

"We thought this was going to be an adventure, fly to Australia, and do some hiking, some exploring, you'd keep us safe, but NO!" Ben grew irate. "You've nearly killed us! This is bullshit!"

Connor looked at Sheila to see if she was listening, but she was too consumed by the pain, so he looked back at Ben. "I know you're upset but control yourself. You and Sheila signed yourself up for this trip. I warned you."

"I regret coming on this god-damed cluster fuck of a trip."

"I'd love to argue with you, but right now we need to focus on your wife."

George stroked Sheila's hair. "Slow your breathing, honey. If you keep hyperventilating you're gonna get cramps all over your body."

Sheila squeezed Kate's hand so hard that a few finger joints popped. "I don't care! It fucking hurts!"

Mac appeared from the woods with his hands full of leaves, bark, and some round, bulbous, root looking thing. "Someone grab me a pot and get a fire going," he yelled as he hustled to the water.

Lisa ripped the pot from her backpack and rushed it over to Mac.

"Grab a big strong stick or a round rock. I need to mash this into a pulp," Mac said. He lowered the pot into the river, added two inches of water and then the mixture of leaves.

"Fire's started!" Kate yelled. She managed to ignite a small pile of kindling on the dead embers from their earlier fire.

Mac handed the pot off to Kate. "Great, get this boiling." He then handed Kate a piece of smooth grey bark. "Put this bark in the fire 'til it holds a flame, and then bring it to me." Mac scanned the ground. "I need another pot!"

"Oh, God, please help me! I can't take the pain," Sheila cried.

"Working on it, sweetheart," Mac said.

Lisa held out an oblong, two-pound, rounded river rock. "Will this work?"

Mac grabbed the rock. "Perfect." He dropped the bulbous root into the pot and started grinding it with the rock. After two minutes of smashing, it was decimated to a creamy grey paste. "The bark burning yet?"

"Right here." Kate passed the flaming, foot long piece of bark to Mac. He held it for a moment, ensuring the flame was scorching deep into the wood, then blew it out. He snapped off the burnt end and tossed it into the pot, then began smashing once again.

Mac looked over at Kate. "How's the tea coming along?" He kept grinding the darkening paste.

"It's boiling," Kate said.

"Bring it to me when it turns red," Mac said as he continued pounding his concoction.

Kate tilted the pot so that Mac could see the tea. "How's this?"

Mac eyed the bubbling and thickened liquid. "Perfect, can I borrow your shirt?"

Kate untied the flannel shirt from around her waist and handed it over. Mac covered the tea pot with Kate's shirt and strained it into the creamy brown mixture he had mashed. He mixed them together, creating a dark purple, pungent and thick liquid.

"It's done," he said, kneeling next to Sheila. "Undo the tourniquet."

Connor untied the damp shirt he had tied over the bite. Mac spread a small amount of the thick purple liquid over the swollen and oozing wound.

"Okay, Sheila, now for the hard part. You need to drink this down," Mac said.

"Just give it to me already!" she cried, grabbing at the pot. She put it to her lips and started chugging. She heaved two or three times but managed to drink the entire lot. Her pain disappeared and was gone within ten seconds. She tried to thank Mac, but the words came out in a drunken slur. She looked up at her husband with a clumsy, cross-eyed confusion; in the fourteen years they had been married, he had never seen her this way.

Everyone watched as Sheila kept trying to speak. She looked up at Ben and gave an undecipherable expression, half a second later, her eyes rolled back, and she passed out.

SHEILA'S TRIP

Present Day

I MUST BE DEAD, SHEILA THOUGHT. *WHERE IS EVERYONE?* SHE FOUND herself alone in a dark, mist covered forest, reminiscent of a cheap Hollywood horror movie set. It was terrifying yet beautiful, silent and haunting.

"Ben?" she called but heard no reply. *Oh, my God, I am dead.*

"You're very much alive." An unseen raspy male aristocratic voice echoed throughout the forest. Sheila spun around, looking for the origin of the mysterious voice. It reminded her of Uncle Bob; a fifty-five-year smoker whose voice rattled with coarseness and ancient wisdom.

"Over here," the voice called out, almost British.

Sheila spun back around and couldn't believe her eyes. She took an extended blink and then re-opened her eyes, only to find the same image. The voice came from the direction of an enormous tree. Embedded within the aged and gnarly old bark was the face of a grumpy looking old man; his features looked as if they had been carved with wood chisels. His exaggerated eyebrows raised and then lowered.

Its wooden mouth moved as it spoke. "I know, I know, a talking tree. I get that all the time."

"Am I dead?" Sheila asked.

The tree laughed a series of deep bellows that sent a few of its dried leaves spinning toward the ground. "You're not dead. Do the dead talk to trees? Most likely not, so please don't ask again."

"Well, where am I?"

"Same place you've always been. Right here."

"But where is here?" Sheila begged, confused. She watched as the tree yawned.

While its mouth was agape, a black raven flew into it, disappearing. "You're in your own reality, outside of your physical body. Don't over-think it."

"I don't understand. How do I get back? And you're not real!"

The tree laughed, and its bare branches shook, dropping a few more dried leaves. "I am very real and don't worry about getting back. Enjoy your time here, it's very limited."

"So, if this is my reality, then who are you?"

"It doesn't matter who I am, just get ready for your message." The tree opened its mouth and a radiant white raven emerged from within and perched upon his lower lip. Its pure white feathers contrasted with the surrounding darkness. It gave a single caw and then flew off.

"A bird just flew out of your mouth! And my message?"

"You don't stop with the questions, do ya? The ravens are special. We exchange attributes, wisdom, knowledge, mischief…anyway, you're here to receive a message, so just relax and you'll be back before ya know it."

"I don't understand any of this."

"You will." The tree's eyes shifted to the far left, peering into the endless darkness. "Aaaahhh, here they are now."

I must be dreaming. Am I dreaming? Am I about to meet a supernatural being? She knew this was unlike any dream she had ever had. She must have died, and this was the afterlife. Suddenly a terrorizing sense of fear overcame her.

"Don't be afraid," a young boy's voice came from behind her. She spun around to see a handsome little boy, maybe ten years old, shirtless, and wearing worn-out brown pants, golden brown sun kissed skin and piercing green eyes. "My name's Petey."

The boy's soft Aussie dialect and innocent presence stripped her of any fear. "Hi, Petey. I'm so confused, are you a product of my imagination?"

"Nope, I'm as real as you. I know this is a bit weird, but right now you're stuck on the other side."

"Stuck?"

"This is your home." Petey gestured with his hands. "But for the moment, you're still living in the physical world."

"Well, how did I get here?"

"You were sent here. We need to give you a message. Sorry about the snake, it was the only way we could do it."

"Oh, my God, you caused the snake to bite me? How?"

"Well, not me personally, we both had a hand in guiding it."

"We? What do you mean by *we*?"

"Benjamin was the agitator. I just gave him the idea."

"Benjamin? My husband? Agitator?"

"No, not your husband, that's just a coincidence. Ben steered the snake toward you, which put you here with us." Petey spoke with a calming maturity that didn't quite fit his young image.

"I could have been killed."

"Nope, no chance of that, we knew the outcome before it happened."

"This is just too crazy for me. And where is this Benjamin?"

"He's right here, but he doesn't want to frighten you."

"Should I be frightened?"

"No way, he's my best friend."

"Well, tell him to come out."

"I don't have to. He can see *and* hear you."

Seconds later, from out of the darkness a huge Thylacine slowly emerged. It was massive, standing almost four feet high, its head and neck were thick and muscled; its eyes a beautifully marbled walnut brown and its stripes, bold and defining. It walked through the dense, eerie mist that covered the forest floor then stopped at Petey's side.

Sheila wanted to be afraid but wasn't. Instead, she felt a sense of calm by the presence of the massive Thylacine. "You're so beautiful," she said, captured not only by the majestic beauty of the beast, but more so by the energy emanating from it.

"Benjamin says *thank you*," Petey said. "If you were completely free of your physical body, you could hear him yourself, so for now I'll just translate."

"I guess this is my message?"

"Yea, we tried to connect with Connor, but he didn't take it seriously, he thought it was a dream."

"This is all so overwhelming. This is just a dream."

"Benjamin wants you to know that even though things may not seem like they are going to work out, *they will*. We want you to know that you are our last hope."

"What do you mean?"

"You must stop your expedition."

"Stop? Why?"

"Because if you find what you're seeking, all will be lost."

"We *just* want to find the Tasmanian tiger. We want to help them. We want to show the world they still exist."

"We know you do, but they cannot be found. Our message is simple; please leave 'em alone."

"But we've put so much time and money and energy into this expedition, we have expectations."

"We know you will do the right thing."

"Benjamin wants to know if money holds more value than life."

"No, of course it doesn't."

"Benjamin says to never forget that."

"How do I know if any of this is even real? You could be a figment of my imagination for all I know. This is all just some vividly weird dream."

"We knew you would say that and we understand. That's why we have everyone else here to see you." Petey pointed behind Sheila.

"Everyone else?"

"I've missed you *Gum Drop*." A hauntingly familiar male voice came from directly behind her.

"Daddy?" She spun around and leapt into his arms, crying with joy. "I love you, Daddy!"

"I love you too, Gum Drop, and I've missed you more than you know. We don't have much time. Tell your mother I'm fine and that *yes*, I'm the one who blows out the damned candle. She'll understand, trust me."

"I'll tell her. Dad. You look so good!" Sheila hugged him again, refusing to let go. She knew as long as she held him tightly they couldn't be separated.

"You really should say hi to your grandparents," he whispered into her ear.

Sheila raised her head from his chest and looked into his eyes.

After the glee filled family reunion, her father once again came face to face with her. He looked into her eyes and spoke with a serious sincerity. "Petey and Benjamin really need your help, sweetheart. As crazy as it sounds, all humanity depends upon it."

"All humanity, Daddy?"

"There's a path that every spark of life follows, and what you seek is a very important part of that path. The tigers are purposely lost and must remain that way. It sounds crazy, hell it is crazy by all standards, but there is so much more to life; there are balances, and balances must be kept, when the balance is lost, everything topples. A balance on earth is beginning to topple. Man has been reckless. The expedition must stop. There is a bigger picture here, much bigger."

"I believe you, Dad. The expedition is over."

"I love you, Sheila. I wish I could stay, but I have to go now. You'll always be my Gum Drop…"

Sheila tried to hold on, but he drifted out of her clutching arms. "Don't go, Daddy! Daddy, no!" Sheila cried as he drifted backwards toward the forest. "I don't wanna lose you again!" She reached for him.

"I'll never leave you Gum Drop…" He faded away into the forest and Sheila dropped to her knees crying.

"Benjamin wants me to tell you not to cry, your father is always with you," Petey said.

Sheila gazed up at Petey. "I know. I've always known." Sheila stood and stared at Benjamin, paused, thinking before she spoke. "Who are you, Petey? And why are you with Benjamin?"

"We thank you, Sheila. It's time to go back."

———

Three tin cups were nearing empty, randomly scattered upon the folding camp table. Connor, Ben, and Mac sat and sipped within the large tent, watching over Sheila, waiting. Just after guzzling Mac's special jungle brew, she passed out and had been sleeping ever since.

Ben dozed with his head against crossed forearms as Connor and Mac's conversation teetered him in between. "How's she looking?" he slurred. His eyes blood shot from the obvious.

"Actually, much better than I had expected," Connor said. "Let's see." Connor looked at his watch. "It's 10:00 a.m. She's been sleeping for seventeen hours. She's survived the worst of it."

"But she's gotta deal with the hangover from the *nasty* I made her drink," Mac said.

"Her leg was swollen, and I feared it would go necrotic, but that was last night. Somehow it looks fine today. I can't explain that one," Connor said. "When tissue gets hit with venom like that, it's dead, but now it's nearly normal. What was in that concoction, Mac? It's pretty damned impressive."

Mac shrugged his shoulders. "I'll sell you the recipe." He cracked a subtle grin. "Ben, why don't you stretch your legs, mate. Go walkabout for a bit."

Connor stretched his arms overhead. "Great idea, why don't we go look for some fruit in the forest?"

Ben sat back in his chair. "Ya know, that doesn't sound like a bad idea."

Carl and George were catching crayfish in the river, while Lisa and Kate sat in their collapsible camp chairs, sipping tea in the cool morning air pondering the fate of the expedition.

Connor, Mac, and Ben exited the tent and walked toward the girls. "Who's up for a fruit trip?"

Carl and George made their way to the group.

"Mmm, sounds like a great idea," Kate said.

"Count me in," Lisa said.

Ben's face was a little uneasy. "Ya know, guys, I don't feel right leaving my wife. I'm gonna stay with her."

Connor put his hand on Ben's shoulder. "Understandable."

"You should at least put your feet up and get a little shut eye," Mac said.

"What if she wakes up or something goes wrong?"

"I'll stay," Carl said. "I don't feel like going anyway."

Connor nodded, accepting Carl's decision to stay behind. "Well, I guess that settles it. Ben, go get some sleep. Carl, keep an eye on Sheila. We'll be back in an hour or two."

As the team headed off into the forest, Carl and Ben went back into the tent with Sheila. They sat at the table and had a moment of silence until Carl spoke up. "Why don't you try to get some shut eye?"

Ben's exhaustion was gaining momentum. "Maybe just for a few minutes." He knew he needed to sleep and would be useless otherwise.

Carl unzipped his camera bag and pulled out a tiny bottle of lens cleaner and a felt cloth. "I'll stay in here, clean my camera, review some footage and watch over Sheila. Go lay down. If she so much as moves a muscle, I'll run and get you."

"You won't leave her?"

"Of course not." Carl used his peripheral vision as Ben exited through the screened tent door. He kept his beady eyes on him until he disappeared into his own tent. Carl sat at the table, going through the motions of cleaning his camera while maintaining a constant glare at Ben's tent for any sign of movement. After twenty minutes of fidgeting with his camera, he left Sheila's side, crept over to Ben's tent, peered in through the screen door and confirmed that he was sleeping. Carl walked back into the tent with Sheila, leaving the door behind him unzipped. He went to her bedside and eyed her from head to toe, then walked back to the door, poked his head out and looked around, then made his way back to her unconscious body.

Carl looked nervously back at the tent door and then back at Sheila. "Pssst, Sheila." He lightly tapped her face and received no response.

"Sheila, can you hear me?" he said a little louder. He pulled the blanket off her torso and placed his hand on her belly. He started rubbing her gently, and then gave another shake. "Sheila?" She didn't respond. He knew his time was limited, so he started popping the buttons on her shirt, starting from the top and stopping mid-abdomen. He reached in with one hand and fondled her breasts. It wasn't enough; he then slid his hand under her bra and started rubbing her nipples. He leaned over her in an attempt to taste—

"What the fuck are you doing?"

Carl sprung back against his chair and looked over his shoulder. He saw Mac standing just outside the screen tent door, holding the door open. "She a…um, ah…she was burning up, so I opened her shirt." Carl fumbled his words.

Mac shoved his way through the door and placed his hand on Sheila's forehead. "She sure as hell doesn't look hot to me, she's not even sweating, and it looks like you're getting your jollies on," Mac snapped.

Carl jumped to his feet, put his hands up in front of his chest and backed away from Sheila. "Aw, c'mon, man, she started moving around and mumbling that she was on fire, you must be crazy to insinuate that I'd touch her inappropriately."

"I call 'em like I see 'em, and if I see you anywhere near her again, I'll cut your god-damn nuts off." Mac stared into his eyes, unflinching.

"Don't threaten me you, Neanderthal," Carl fired back.

Mac walked toward Carl who retreated, stepping backwards. "At least we Neanderthals don't have to get our jollies off on unconscious women."

Ben poked his head through the tent flap. "Is everything ok? What's going on? I could hear you guys from my tent, is Sheila ok?"

Carl answered as fast as he could. "Yeah Ben, she's fine, she moved around a bit and started mumbling she was on fire, I tried to cool her down a bit, but Mac insisted my intentions were other than pure."

Ben looked at Mac.

Mac shook his head in disgust. "Just watch out for this guy, I don't trust him." Mac's shoulder collided with Carl's as he marched out of the tent.

Ben looked at Carl, who then raised his hands and shook his head in disbelief. Then turned toward Mac who was just outside the tent pacing back and forth. "Where is everyone else?"

Mac stood in the doorway, blocking it. "I came back to fetch another pot, we found a few trees full of fruit." Mac grinded his teeth and shook his head from side to side in anger. "Don't let that man get anywhere near your wife. I don't trust him."

———

Six hours later and Sheila still showed no sign of consciousness. Connor feared she may have slipped into a coma, but he avoided using that dreadful word in front of the group. He decided they would carry her out in the morning using a stretcher crafted from tree branches and sheets. It would be a long, slow, back breaking hike, but no other option existed. With less than an hour of sunlight, they ate from personal rations and discussed the morning extrication plan.

Carl became uncharacteristically more visible to the group, he didn't want to appear guilty, and so by making himself more *available*, he felt it would quell everyone's suspicions. Everyone except for Mac, who kept a watchful eye on every move the spindly man made. Mac didn't further mention anything to the group about the incident with Carl. Instead, he decided on keeping a very close eye on him.

They all sat by the small fire just outside Sheila's tent, and finished their rations.

Mac poked a long stick into the fire until its tip glowed red then circled it in the air making a slow, hovering trail of smoke. "The forest is so damned thick, someone's gonna have to do some serious chopping if we're carrying a stretcher."

Connor sipped his coffee. "I'm thinking Carl can film, George will take lead and work the machete, and you, me, Lisa and Kate on the stretcher. George can cut the hell out of some jungle."

"What about me?" Ben said.

"We can alternate on the stretcher with you, Ben, that way we can each get a break, but continue hiking," Connor said.

"How long do you think it's gonna take to get back to the trucks?" Kate said.

"Realistically? Probably four days," Connor said.

"She's gonna need some water. She's gotta be dehydrated," Lisa said.

Connor thought about George's medic experience and looked at him for insight. "I've thought about that, maybe we could—"

"Ben?" Sheila's voice called out from the tent. "Ben?" Everyone paused, looked at Ben, then sprang from their chairs and ran into the tent.

Ben was the first in. "Right here, sweetie, right here," he said as he grabbed her hand. She was squinting and trying to focus.

Everyone surrounded her except Carl. He hid his face behind the camera and kept an odd distance. Mac picked up on it right away.

"How do you feel?" Lisa whispered in a soothing tone.

"I feel…" Sheila bent her arms and turned her head from side to side. "I feel fine, a little groggy, but fine."

Ben wrapped his arms around her and squeezed. He put his mouth to her ear. "You scared the hell out of me, sweetheart."

"Sorry, honey," she whispered back.

Connor pulled the blanket off her legs. "No pain in your leg?" Sheila stretched her toes out and then in, bent her knee and then straightened it back out.

"None, I feel fine."

Mac ran his fingers over the puncture site on her leg. "Remarkable!" He was puzzled the deadly neurotoxin and hemotoxic venom left her leg with nothing more than two miniscule fang marks, no bruising, no necrosis. It was unexplainable. He couldn't believe it was the work of his concoction.

"Indeed," Connor said. "Indeed."

"How long have I been out?" she asked.

Mac looked into her eyes and paused with seriousness. "Three months."

Sheila's jaw dropped open as she gasped. "Oh, my God! Three months?"

Connor grinned at her. "No, no, only two days."

Sheila squinted at Mac. "I'll ring your neck, Mister."

"I'd be happy."

"Do you feel like trying to stand?" Connor asked.

"How about I sit up first, I feel a little stiff."

"You ok, sweetie?" Ben guided her into a sitting position.

"I'm fine, really, just thirsty. Can I get some water?" Kate handed Sheila her canteen. As Sheila drank, water ran down each corner of her mouth, soaking her shirt. She kept chugging 'til it was empty.

"I guess you were thirsty," Kate said.

"Oh, my God, I just remembered something," Sheila said.

Carl became stricken with fear and thought she had somehow remembered what he had done to her.

"We have to stop the expedition."

"That's fine," Connor said. "You were bitten by a deadly tiger snake and you've been unconscious for two days, I think that's grounds for dismissal."

"No, Connor. This isn't about me. I'm fine really." Sheila placed her feet on the ground and stood up. She squatted up and down and stretched her arms. "See, I'm fine."

"So if you're fine, why do you want to stop the expedition?" Ben asked.

"Because of my dream."

"Your dream?" Ben laughed.

"I know it's going to sound crazy, but I had a serious experience."

"Care to share?" Connor asked.

"Well, first there was this talking tree, but he was real…and then this little boy…" She struggled to recall his name. "*Petey! Petey* was his name! And he was friends with a giant Thylacine named *Benjamin*. They said we had to stop the expedition. They said if we didn't, bad things would happen, not to us, but to the entire planet. We have to stop the expedition."

Ben looked around at the group to sum up their expressions. "That's one heck of a dream, sweetie."

"It wasn't a dream. I thought it was at first, but it wasn't. I asked them to prove to me that it wasn't. My father was there, my aunt and uncles, my grandparents, it wasn't a dream."

"Sheila, I hate to say it, but sounds like you overdosed on Mac's potion," Connor said.

"Listen guys, it was real."

"I believe it was real to you," Ben said. "But it was just a dream."

Sheila sat back down. "God-damn it, guys, I'm serious about this. They said the fate of the world hinged on our cancellation of the expedition."

"Mac, can you talk to her," Ben said. "Tell her she was just hallucinating because of that stuff you made."

"I gave you a cocktail of different medicines from the bush, and a large part of that cocktail was a hallucinogen that's supposed to open your mind, it's part of our traditional medicine, and we've been using it for hundreds of years, maybe longer. The best part of it is listening to all the crazy stories people tell after taking it. It makes for some very vivid hallucinations, but that's all they are, figments of your imagination."

"But they were so real, so nice, so caring, I could feel their love. My dad even called me Gum Drop." Sheila's passion was fading.

"I understand, I really do, but all that stuff was already in your memory," Mac said.

"None of it was real?" Sheila whimpered.

"I'm afraid not," Connor said.

"But my dad." A single tear fell from her left eye.

"I'm sorry," Mac said.

"But they said the fate of the world depended upon our cancelling the expedition."

"Are you listening to yourself, sweetheart?" Ben said with a soft certainty.

"It sounds crazy doesn't it?" Sheila said.

"It's only because of the stuff I gave you." Mac mimicked Ben's tone.

"But they were so real."

"They *were* real, Sheila, they were *real* to you," Connor said.

They all sat by the fire and chatted about Sheila's miraculous recovery. Connor and Kate were dumbfounded; any bite from a tiger snake would have left the victim's bitten appendage grotesquely deformed, rotted, and black. Intrigued by Mac's elixir, they insisted he gather the identical ingredients at first light, so they could save them for analysis back home.

Everyone bid a warm goodnight to Sheila then disappeared into their tents. Although Mac explained the probable cause of her experience, she wasn't totally convinced. She settled down into her sleeping bag, and oddly enough she was tired even after two days of sleep. She closed her eyes, but visions of the otherworldly experience flooded her mind. "Ben, I'm not comfortable continuing."

Ben opened his eyes. "Continuing with what?"

"The expedition, I really think we need to go back."

"I thought we already went over this."

"I know, but I feel really strongly about it, Ben."

"So you want to convince everyone to quit?"

"No. I just don't want to be a part of it any longer."

"All because of your dream? Mac told you that everyone who's had that concoction has crazy dreams, just like the one you had."

"I know what he said, I heard him. I'm sorry, honey, but my mind is made up."

"Come on sweetie, just sleep on it since we've come this far."

"Ben, I'm hiking back to the trucks tomorrow, with or without you."

———

The next morning Ben crawled out of his tent to the sound of avian chaos. He found a couple of silent love birds snuggled up by the fire.

Ben walked up behind Connor and Kate. Her head was nestled against his chest with a wool blanket covering her body. "It's great to see you two have gotten so close."

Kate turned toward Ben and her face broke into a smile. "Morning, Ben."

Ben put a hand on Connor's shoulder and one on Kate's. "You're glowing, Kate."

She smiled and tried to hide her blushing by leaning onto Connor's chest.

Ben sat in his damp camp chair and let out a large sigh, looking at Connor. "I need to talk to you for a minute before everyone else wakes up."

"What's wrong?" Connor said.

"It's Sheila."

"Is she ok?" Kate said.

"She's fine, hell, she's more than fine. She is just set in her ways."

"How so?" Connor asked.

"She's made her mind up. She and I are heading back to the Rovers."

"I had a feeling this might happen," Connor said.

"She doesn't want it to be an issue, she wants you guys to proceed, just don't try to talk her out of it. I tried last night and it's futile. She's pretty emotional about it."

"I'm not sure about you two going back on your own," Connor said.

"We can handle it, the trail is easy to follow, and you can still barely see the mountain from here."

"Yeah, but what about psychotic killer birds and snakes?" Connor said.

"We'll be fine, and besides, you don't have a choice."

"I don't have a choice?" Connor was stunned by Ben's definitive tone.

"No, you work for us." Ben laughed.

"I don't know about this. I don't like the idea of you two being alone out there."

"We won't be alone, we have each other, and besides, you don't have a say in this. We are heading back, and you are proceeding."

"Just let me run a few things by Sheila first," Connor said.

"That's the very reason she sent me out here by myself. She knew you would try to talk her out of it, but we've made our decision and we're sticking to it."

"Ben, if that's your decision I'll respect it, I don't necessarily agree with it, but you're grown adults."

"Thanks, Connor, we're gonna leave the same time you guys do. Can you please let everyone know not to bug her about it?"

"I'll do my best."

———

Connor briefed the rest of the team about the sudden change in plans. Their only concern was that Ben and Sheila make it safely back to the vehicles. It was obvious that Ben and Sheila weren't the most capable of outdoorsman, but rather than pestering them to stay with the group, they offered tips and advice for anything they could potentially encounter. Mac gave them a twenty-minute crash course on the basics of bush survival. He threw out all trivial bullshit and fed them pure meat and potatoes, graduating them with a large side of reluctance on his part.

After a few final goodbyes, Ben and Sheila turned away from the group and started back toward the mountain.

LEAVING TASMANIA

Tasmania - February 1935

THE REAR WHEELS ON GREG'S CAR SPUN AS HE ACCELERATED UP HIS long, narrow driveway. It was unusually dark for this time of evening. He couldn't remember the last time it had rained like this. The wipers squeaked in bursts, barely working and at times it seemed as though he could see better without them. He didn't expect his family to be waiting on the porch for him; the moaning wind was blowing the rain sideways. He grabbed his thermos, cracked open the door and made a dash for the house. As he jumped the three steps to the porch, he noticed the front door was wide open. He walked through the threshold and his feet sloshed in a massive puddle of rain pooled on the inside floor. Right away he knew something was wrong.

"Millie," Greg called out. He looked around the living room and spotted a box of spilled rifle ammunition scattered about the floor. He glanced up at the rifle rack and confirmed his fear, his gun was gone. "Petey?" Greg's voice trembled with worried concern. Greg became frantic as he ran through the house, dipping his head into each room, searching for his family.

Greg ran onto the front porch and stared down at the barn. A single lamp dimly lit its interior. Leaping from the porch, he ran through the rain, slipping and nearly falling in the soft mud. He ran through the barn's open double door entrance and stopped just out of the rain.

His eyes focused then his breath left him. His gut began random contractions, contorting and uncontrollable. On the floor of the barn Millie was lying face down, her body was pale and lifeless, and her head was unnaturally twisted to the side, her pants down around her knees. He knew immediately that her neck was broken.

Petey was curled up next to his mother. His head nuzzled up next to her head with one hand clutching Greg's rifle. Greg was horrified, and he gasped but couldn't breathe, tears flooded his eyes and face, diluting with the rain dripping from his hair. He wanted to hold his family, but couldn't, he was paralyzed with agony, the burden of viewing his dead family was too much to bear. He dropped to his knees and began to gasp. The gasps turned into heaving sobs.

"Nooo!" Greg screamed. "Whhyy! Oh, God, no!" Greg's gut heaved in and out. He fell forward, slamming his forearms on the muddy floor.

"Dad…"

Greg silenced himself when he heard what sounded like his son's voice. He struggled to raise his head and squinted through rain-soaked hair.

"Dad!" Petey screamed, released the rifle, and ran to his father.

Greg forced himself to his knees and caught his son as he dove into his arms. Petey cried and clung to him, burying himself deep within the safety of his arms. Greg pressed Petey's head against his chest. Suddenly a thought entered his mind. *Where is Ben?* Greg scanned the barn expecting to see Ben's dead body but found nothing. Petey's cries grew louder. "It's ok, son, I've got you."

Petey's cries were muffled against Greg's body.

Greg cradled his son's face and raised him to eye level. "Petey." Greg fought to control his sobbing. "I need you…I need you to tell me what happened. Ca…ca…can you do that for Daddy?" Greg's tears were falling uncontrollably.

Petey gasped between sobs. "The men…they took Ben…and, and…they…killed mama."

Greg forced his son's head against his chest. He sobered by switching his agony to malevolent hatred. He wiped a forearm across his eyes. "I need you to tell me, son. Do you know who they were?" He already knew but wanted confirmation.

"The...the men that..." Petey cried. "...that tried to shoot Ben."

They killed my wife; they killed Ben, all for a fuckin' bounty, he thought.

Greg stroked Petey's head and stared blankly across the barn. Cries were sobered, and pain was replaced. *McPherson and his henchmen are dying tonight.*

Greg held Petey until he cried himself to sleep, and then carried his boy through the rain and into the house. Greg laid Petey on his bed and covered him. He stood in the doorway and looked back at his son sleeping—without Ben. He remembered the heartache Petey had suffered from the loss of Chewie, and now he'd lost Ben as well. Greg was drowning with rage.

He walked off the porch and back into the cold rain. The deafening thunder rumbled as he entered the barn. He knelt beside Millie and stared into her hair, forcing himself not to look into her opened and lifeless eyes. His voice cracked in between quieting sobs. "I loved you yesterday, today, and tomorrow. I'm so sorry, love. We were so damned close, so close to leaving this god-damned place." He wanted to touch her but couldn't. "Please understand, I have to do this." He covered her with the wool horse blanket. "Goodbye, Millie."

Greg walked out of the barn, through the rain and back into the house. He looked in on Petey, still fast asleep. Greg gritted his teeth at the thought of Petey waking, only to remember he was now motherless and his best friend was gone. Greg walked into his bedroom, pulled the top drawer from his dresser, and tossed it onto the bed. He rummaged through clusters of unorganized papers, then pulled out a packet and tucked it under his arm. He walked with calm into the living room, grabbed the box of rifle ammunition and then went back out into the rain.

Greg made a final trip to the barn, this time his crying was replaced with silent focus. He stood upon a flipped water trough, reached atop an overhead wooden cross beam, and felt around blindly until his fingers brushed along dust covered steel. He wrapped them around the bone handle and as he pulled, a vicious twelve-inch Bowie knife emerged. He wiped the dusty blade along his wet pants, revealing a cold shine. Greg snatched the rifle from the muddy floor and headed toward the door. Just before he exited the barn he stopped and looked back at his wife's covered body. He paused, blew a soft kiss, and then disappeared into the rain. *McPherson and his henchmen are dying tonight.*

EXIT THE JUNGLE

Present day

THE DENSE OVERGROWTH, INITIALLY ALMOST IMPASSABLE, WAS finally thinning out. The upper canopy that had been completely interwoven with vines and air ferns was opening up, allowing larger patches of sunlight to touch the forest floor. Even the bird songs were dying out as the team pushed further west.

Kate could tell Connor's mind was occupied, he hadn't said more than a few words in the two and a-half hours they had been hiking.

"So how do you think Ben and Sheila are making out?" Kate asked as she followed his steps.

"Honestly?" Connor said as he marched.

"Of course."

"Part of me thinks they'll be fine, while another part of me thinks they'll be eaten alive."

"Eaten alive?"

"By the jungle itself, bugs, snakes, getting lost, hunger, thirst, killer birds."

"They only have a day and a half hike, and then they'll have the safety of the vehicles."

"I know, and maybe I'm just a little over protective, but I believe in preventing the preventable."

"Preventing the preventable?"

"Yeah, everything is preventable. If they get ripped apart by a cassowary, it could have been prevented. I could have prevented it by insisting they stay with us."

"You could come up with a million different scenarios of what *could* happen, but that doesn't mean they will happen," Kate said. She took note of his protective nature, part of it worried her, but for the most part she liked the idea of having such a successful and protective man at her side.

"I just don't feel right about it, knowing them and knowing the jungle, they don't belong out here. They've never been alone in the wilderness before. This isn't the best place to *go it alone* for the first time. I'll feel responsible if something happens."

"It was their choice Connor, you tried to stop them, but their minds were set."

———

As they progressed, the jungle continued to change. The dense, fully flourishing rain forest that was full of life, transitioned into a thinned out evergreen forest with the occasional flurry of scattered under-brush. Large boulders appeared from time to time and increased in frequency the farther west they travelled. The tall spindly pines looked as though they had been starved since seedlings, struggling to survive in an environment lacking nutrients as the soil gave way to rock.

Connor looked up and noticed more sky than canopy. "We're running out of shade, let's break here." As if on cue, everyone slung their packs to the ground and sat on the nearest seat-level boulders scattered about.

Lisa sighed as she wiggled backwards onto the thigh-level rock. "Much better."

Kate copied and arched her back beside Lisa. "Tell me about it."

Mac looked ahead squinting and could see a yellow and red rock canyon in the distance. "Looks like we've got some big rock to cross."

"Yeah, I don't think we'll be in the rocks long though, a day, maybe two tops," Connor said.

That night everyone was out of conversation, tired from a long day of hiking. George, Carl, and Lisa turned in while Connor, Kate and Mac hung out by the fire.

Kate could feel the need for sleep adding weight to her eyelids. "Okay, I'm hitting the sack."

Mac couldn't resist. "I'll be there in a bit, sweetheart." He looked at Connor for a response, but he sat unmoved, staring into the fire.

Kate placed a hand on his shoulder. "You okay?" Kate's touch combined with her words snapped him out his trance-like state.

"I'm fine, I'm fine. I'll be there in a few."

"Well, I'll keep the bed warm for ya." Kate leaned in and kissed Connor on his forehead then disappeared into her tent, leaving the two men fireside.

Mac kept quiet, giving Connor a chance to strike up some conversation, but after a few minutes of silence, he could wait no longer. "What's buggin' ya, mate?"

Connor continued to stare into the glowing bed of red embers. "I'm fine, just thinking a bit."

"You wanna talk about it?"

"Don't think I need to, nothing that can really be done about it anyway."

"Well, you've been mulling it over for a good while, want a second opinion?"

"You don't miss a thing, do you?"

"Not hard to miss when its right in front of me face." Mac grinned.

"It's probably nothing."

"Let's hear it then."

"It's just something that Sheila said after she woke up. When she was telling us all that stuff about the little boy and the big Thylacine. Do you think there's any possibility any of it could have been real?"

"Sure I do, I believe it was all real."

"You do? Well, why don't we stop the expedition?"

"Because I believe it was real for her, it had to do with her journey, not ours."

"But she said that she was told *we* needed to halt the search."

"She stopped *her* search; she did what they told her, that's the way it was supposed to work out, because that's what happened."

"How can you tell if the message was meant for all of us or just her?"

"Because we didn't get any messages, at least not yet."

"In my opinion we did receive a message. It was from Sheila."

"Well, when you look at it that way, you could be right, but who's to say what she saw wasn't a total figment of her imagination?"

"That's the hard part, but what's been haunting me is something else." Connor paused.

"And what might that be?"

"Sheila said something that didn't click until earlier today. She said they tried to give me a message."

"Well, did you get one?"

Connor paused and looked directly at Mac. "I believe I did."

"Don't hold back, let's hear it." He sat up and waited.

"Remember those clay balls we had at Fitzroy Crossing?"

"Ah! The pituri, how could I forget? That's some crazy stuff."

"That's when I think I received the message. It was terrifying. I saw a large Thylacine rip a girl's throat out. It was so surreal, felt so unlike any dream I'd ever had."

Mac shrugged it off. "Doesn't sound like much to me, and besides, you were under the influence of a nasty hallucinogenic."

"I thought you'd have been more receptive to these messages, but it seems like you don't put much faith in them."

"Well, I've seen a lot of people have lots of crazy visions after taking lots of crazy bush drugs, and if any of 'em were real, we'd be in a load of trouble."

"So you don't believe in the other side?"

"Oh, I do, but I also believe that our crazy bush drugs distort reality, allowing our minds to go bizarro."

"So you don't see any correlation between my dream and Sheila's?"

"I can see a correlation, but I'd say it's expected."

"Expected?"

"Yeah, you're both on an expedition, crossing some unexplored territory in search of an animal killed off by man. I'd think that would make all your dreams a lot alike."

"Good point. So you don't buy into the other side trying to warn us?"

"Nope."

"I think I feel better."

Mac's arms stiffened, and he started shaking in his chair. He bent his head back and opened his mouth, contorting. Connor was ready to lay him down. From his perspective Mac was having a seizure.

Mac suddenly stopped all movement and then turned to Connor. "I just had a vision and they gave me a message for ya." Mac's breathing was erratic.

Connor's eyes opened wide, confused.

"They told me to tell you…to…stay off…the piiitttuuurriii," Mac did his best ghost voice.

Connor laughed and shook his head. "Good night, Mac. I've got a preheated sleeping bag waiting for me."

JAGGED ROCK

Present day

CONNOR AWOKE AT THE CRACK OF DAWN, FEELING REFRESHED, AND his worry was gone. He shifted himself against Kate's back, into her warmth.

"Morning," he whispered in her ear.

She rolled over. "Good morning, handsome."

"Sorry if I've been a little pre-occupied."

"Given the circumstances, it was expected. You carry a lot of weight as the ring leader."

Connor smiled. "You ready to climb some rock?"

"Just don't let me fall," she whispered, staring into his eyes.

Connor put his mouth against her ear. "I'd never let you fall."

———

Breakfast was served right out of sealed plastic MRE pouches: scrambled ham and eggs that tasted like salty Jell-O with the occasional chewy bit of leathery ham and instant coffee. George loved the salty Jell-O and was delighted to finish both Lisa and Kate's, being sure to scrape out every mushy morsel from the bag with his plastic fork.

After the quasi-black coffee was forced down, they packed up and made the short march to the edge of the canyon. They could see down the ravine and into a maze of weathered and broken jagged rock, steep drop offs and thinning ledges. The cliff stretched on for miles in either direction with no sign of an ending. Across the treacherous gorge was another forest, their main destination. But to get there, they first had to cross the mile-wide canyon.

They all stood at the foot of the cliff and stared at the monstrosity that lay before them.

"Oh, my God, we're crossing that?" Lisa was overwhelmed.

"Looks pretty formidable, huh?" Connor said.

"Um, it looks like a death trap," Lisa said as she scanned the gnarly rock.

"Don't let it intimidate you. Climbing is a mental thing; just know you can beat it," George said.

Connor stomped on the rock under his feet. "This actually looks like a great spot to anchor." He leaned out and looked over the edge then looked behind the group. He spotted a large boulder almost twelve feet from the edge that would make a good rope anchor.

"What happens if someone slips?" Lisa said.

Kate threw her arm around Lisa's shoulder. "Don't worry, girl, we got this. The first step-off is the worst, everyone tends to freeze up, but once you do it a few times it's a piece of cake."

"I think Lisa needs a quickie crash course," Mac said.

"How about just a quickie course, minus the crash?" Lisa joked.

Connor flipped his hiking pack over and unzipped its largest pouch, revealing coils of rope and various rappelling hardware. "Everyone gather around, let's go over the basics before we get started." Connor looked at each person and labeled them, experienced, or not experienced. "Kate, I've seen you rappel on your last documentary. Are you good to go?"

"I'm good, I love rappelling." Kate was shocked and flattered that Connor had actually watched her show.

Connor waved Lisa over to him. "I know you've never done it so I'm gonna give you a quick lesson. How about you, Carl? Any experience?"

"Been climbing and rappelling since the eighties."

"Great, so everyone's confident except Lisa."

Connor went over the basics of rappelling with her, while everyone else just listened in. "It's a fairly simple concept, a harness around your waist and thighs, a figure eight belay attached to the front of the harness, rappelling rope and gloves. Let's start with your harness. Go ahead and get it out of your pack." Everyone had their own harness and hardware in their hiking packs.

Kate had an unexpected streak of jealousy as she watched Connor get behind Lisa and wrap his arms around her. He tugged away at her harness in an attempt to tighten it. She couldn't help but imagine him wanting her tight younger body. *Is he attracted to her? Does he want her body? She's beautiful.* Then he released the embrace and moved on to attaching the rope; she could see it was strictly platonic. The jealousy was gone.

Connor stressed the importance of gloves. Bulky and somewhat cumbersome, they protect their hands from unexpected injury, usually rope burns. He also demonstrated how to attach the rope to the figure eight, and then had Lisa repeat it, over and over, until she could flawlessly secure it herself. Connor wouldn't let anyone climb unless they could secure and attach their own equipment. So after a few more rope loops and equipment checks, she felt as though she was ready to start rappelling.

Connor secured the rope to a large, sturdy boulder perfectly situated to serve as an anchor. He wrapped the rope three times around the base and then secured it with a carabineer. He threw the remaining two-hundred-foot section of rope over the cliff, everyone watched it fall and fall.

"'At's a nice drop," Mac said watching the rope barely touch the bottom.

George grabbed the rope without hesitation and strung it through his figure eight. George was a veteran to rappelling and climbing and decided to film from the bottom. "I'll go first."

Connor tugged on George's harness, making sure it was secured, only to make the burly man laugh. George was a better climber than anyone on the expedition. "Sounds good, we'll lower all the gear to you. Carl, you go last and shoot from up here."

"You got it, boss," Carl said, with a slight tinge of sarcasm, barely noticeable.

George fastened the rope to his harness, picked up his camera and backed toward the edge. "First step's a doozie." He winked at Lisa then jumped backwards over the vertical ledge and was gone.

Lisa laughed out loud. "Oh, my God, that looks so fun." She ran to the edge and leaned over, watching George kick off the wall and swing out while dropping.

"It's such a rush," Kate said.

Once George was grounded, Connor pulled the entire length of rope back up from the bottom then attached all the hiking packs to it then lowered them down to George.

Mac stepped up to the rope. "Mind if I have a go?"

"Go for it," Connor said.

Mac walked to the edge, secured the rope to his harness, then looked down. He took a step back then tried to lean out. He stopped, cracked an awkward grin, and looked down again.

"I thought you were good," Connor said.

Mac eyes focused on George at the bottom. "I am, well, I can do it, I just don't like it." He backed over the edge and with bumbling grace, descended. As soon as he reached the bottom he gave a big thumbs up. "Piece of cake!"

"Kate, why don't you go ahead of Lisa?" Connor said.

Kate couldn't have grabbed the rope any faster. "Don't have to ask me twice," she said as she secured herself to the rope. Connor gave her a quick peck on the lips just before she leapt backwards off the ledge. She showed off by kicking out from the ledge and descending as fast as she could fall.

"Ready, Lisa?" Connor asked.

"My stomach's full of butterflies," she said as she watched Kate reach the bottom.

Connor watched closely as she secured the rope to her harness.

"How's that?"

"Perfect. Just remember, hold the rope behind you to stop, bring it forward slowly to descend, you control the speed with your gloved hand, just open your hand slowly to pick up speed, close it to stop. Got it?"

"Yeah." Lisa's hands started clamming up as she backed to the edge.

"This is the hardest part," Connor said. "Just know you can do it. Once you're over the edge its child's play."

Lisa's face cringed as she tried to lean back. "I'm scared." She tried to smile it off.

Connor grabbed the rope and demonstrated. "Just lean back, let the rope hold you up, and walk slowly backwards."

Lisa leaned back but couldn't get her feet to move. Her mind was saying walk, but her body was saying no. "Oh, geez, I don't think I can do it," she said, looking over her shoulder and down at the others.

"Sure you can. It's easy once you get over the ledge, and this is where every first timer gets stuck."

"I'm serious. I really don't think I can do it."

"I know you can, it's just a mental block, tell yourself it's easy and that you are in total control."

Lisa kept trying to force herself over the ledge, failed attempt after failed attempt. The frustration got the better of her and she started to cry. She didn't want to burden the group, but knew she wasn't going down that cliff.

"Let's take a breather," Connor said.

"I can't do it. I just can't do it. I'm sorry," Lisa cried.

"It's ok, kiddo. Don't let it get to ya. This happens all the time. Why don't you take a breather and relax for a bit?"

Lisa unstrung the rope from the figure eight and dropped it on the ground. "I really don't think I can do it."

"Just give it a minute and we'll try again."

Everyone at the bottom knew exactly what was going on; Lisa was experiencing what nearly every first time rappeller experienced, fear of death. Connor leaned over the ledge and yelled, "Give us a few minutes."

Connor sat on the boulder right beside Lisa. "This really is just a mental block and it happens to everyone on their first time."

"I know, I see how easy it was for everyone else, but I just can't bring myself to do it. I can't take the first step over."

"Don't look down, that's what gets ya, it's a shock to the system."

"I'm afraid of falling."

"As long as you keep your hand on the rope, you won't fall. You know lots of people do this as a hobby because it's so much fun. I'm willing to bet you fall in love with it."

"I want to do it, I really do, I just have a really bad feeling about it."

"Listen, when you're ready to try again, we're gonna do something different. I want you to close your eyes and listen to my guidance, are you willing to do that?"

She nodded, but not wholeheartedly. "I…I guess so."

"I'll walk you through the entire descent. All you have to do is follow my instructions."

"That sounds easy enough."

"Just say when and I'll get you to the bottom."

Lisa took a deep breath. "Okay, just give me a few more seconds." Lisa tried to avert her mind from the task at hand. After another minute of deep breath procrastination, she stood up and clapped her hands together. "Okay, I'm ready."

"Go ahead and secure yourself to the rope." Lisa grabbed the rope and strung it through the figure eight perfectly, as if she had done it a thousand times before.

"Beautifully done. Now go ahead and get in position." Lisa turned her back to the ledge and pulled the slack out of the rope. "Remember, you're going to do everything I tell you, no more, no less."

Lisa closed her eyes. "Got it."

"Perfect. Now lean back and let the rope's tension hold you up." Lisa leaned back, and the tension held her upright. "Perfect. Now with every step, I want you to let the rope slide though your gloved hand. Now step back with your left foot." Lisa stepped back as ordered. Connor stood beside her at the ledge. "Now step back with your right foot." Once again, she followed perfectly. "Step back again with your left foot, perfect, now step back with your right."

She did exactly as he commanded, eyes squeezed shut.

"Now it's gonna change a bit. I want you to keep leaning back and place your left foot on the rounded ledge, then do the same with your right." Lisa did exactly as commanded. "Now bend your knees a bit and lean back even further. This is where we transition over the lip."

Lisa started bending her knees then opened her eyes. She instantly became stricken with fear.

"Oh, God, I can't do it,"

"Remember the plan, Lisa? Close your eyes, I'm in control," Connor said, calming.

"I don't think I can do it."

"Stop thinking and just follow my direction. I'm not gonna get you hurt."

"I'll try, I'm just so scared."

"Forget all your emotions; just let me have total control."

"Okay, okay." Lisa closed her eyes and once again surrendered to Connor's control.

"Now bend your knees and lean back, put tension on the rope." Lisa bent her knees and leaned out over the ledge. "Perfect. Slide your left foot down about a foot and keep leaning back. Excellent, now the right." Lisa was now completely parallel with the ledge. Connor could see the rope trembling from her uncontrollable shaking. "You're doing great. Just relax and breathe. It's a piece of cake." Connor had a feeling she was about to lose it. "There's a small protrusion beneath your feet, so you're going to step onto it, slide your left foot back until your heel hits it, then place your foot directly on it."

Lisa placed her left foot on the rocky protrusion. "I'm feeling better. It's not as bad as I thought it would be."

"I knew you'd do fine. Go ahead and place your right foot on the protrusion." Lisa slid her right foot back a little quicker; and the rope slid through her gloved hand. She was becoming more confident with each backwards step. "Let's see you take a couple small steps back."

"Is there anything below me?"

"Not really."

Lisa kept her eyes closed and took two small steps backwards, carefully placing each foot while releasing just enough rope to descend.

"You're doing such a great job."

"Should I open my eyes?"

"You can, just don't look down."

Lisa opened her eyes, looked up and was amazed that Connor and Carl were almost ten feet above her.

"Oh, my God! I'm really doing it!"

"Indeed, you are. Try a few wall kicks." Lisa toyed with the idea then bent her knees and kicked off the yellow rock wall, swinging out about a foot and right back in. "The harder you kick, the further you'll swing."

"This is actually fun." Lisa bent her knees and kicked out even harder, swinging out about three feet and then right back in again.

"If you release a little rope when you kick out like that, you can descend."

Lisa kicked out and released just enough rope to descend about four feet, then slowed herself to a stop.

"You're looking like a pro already."

"Looking good, girl!" Kate yelled from the bottom.

Lisa let go of the rope with her free hand to give Kate a thumbs up. The shift in weight caused a small bit of the rock wall beneath her feet to break away. Her feet slid off the wall, sending the rest of her body into the cliff. Her chest and face slammed the jagged wall.

"Connor!" she shrieked.

"Relax, Lisa, are you ok?"

"I think I broke my nose," she screamed as her eyes flooded with tears.

Connor could see her white tank top swirling in crimson as blood poured from her nose.

"Listen, everything's fine."

Lisa hung from the rope with her body dangling against the cliff. "I can't hold the rope like this. It's hurting my arm." Lisa was having a difficult time keeping the rope behind her back with her face and body pressed against the cliff.

"Bring your knees to your chest and get your feet back under you."

Lisa struggled to get her knees up, but the sharp rock wall kept snagging her jeans, making it almost impossible.

"I can't!" she cried, gasping and panicked. "Connor, help!" Lisa started kicking in a frantic attempt to get off the wall, one after another her knees kept smashing into the unforgiving rock. She was breathing erratically, hyperventilating. Her sympathetic nervous system was taking over, supplying her heart with adrenalin and brain with endorphins which masked any pain she would be feeling otherwise.

"Stop kicking!" Connor yelled, but with a controlled calm. Connor knew that panic was what got people killed. Connor watched as her knees kept pummeling the jagged rock wall. In her thrashing, she started to rotate on the rope until she was completely upside down.

Lisa was lost. In her mind thoughts were running out of control and she was flailing in every direction.

Connor realized that if he didn't act fast that she would soon pass out from hyperventilating and plummet to her death. *Shit. I don't have any more goddamn rope up here! How the hell am I gonna get to her? Think damn it, think.* Connor started looking around, scanning every direction, looking for something, anything he could use. All the hiking packs, including his with the extra rope had already been lowered to the ground. Out of luck and out of resources, he tightened his rappelling harness and forced on his gloves. He clamped his carabineer to the rope with Lisa attached to it, he couldn't attach his figure eight. There was too much tension on the rope. Without the figure eight there was no speed control, he would fall straight to the ground with nothing to control the descent other than his own muscle power.

Connor grabbed the rope with his gloved hands and slid down to the flailing intern, stopping just above her waist. Even with gloves, his hands could feel the heat of friction. Connor's grip on the rope was unbreakable, like eagle talons.

"Lisa, I'm right above you, now calm down or you're gonna kill both of us."

She was oblivious and continued kicking and screaming.

"LISA, STOP IT!" he yelled, but she continued. Connor was reaching for the loose end of the rope that she somehow managed to keep behind her back. Just as his fingers began to clench it, she brought her control arm forward and dropped almost ten feet, jerking to a stop as she unknowingly put her control arm behind her. Connor dropped down to her level and clenched the rope with one hand. With his other hand he tried to reach past her kicking legs and grab the dangling free rope from behind her back. The free rope was attached to Lisa's figure eight, if Connor could secure it, he could control the situation.

Clinging single handedly to the rope, Connor reached down with his free hand, past her legs. *Almost got it*, he thought and then *bam*! She kicked him in the forehead with enough force to split it wide open. "LISA, STOP IT, GODDAMN IT!" he yelled. Blood was running into his left eye and it burned.

Lisa dropped another twenty feet and once again jolted to a stop.

Connor slid on cue after her. He gave up on words and reached for the free rope dangling from Lisa's hand. His arms and shoulders were reaching the point of failure. *Fuck, I can't let go, we both can't die in front of everyone.* Reaching out and using all the strength he could summon, he made one last attempt to grab the rope. As he did he noticed something calming yet eerily alarming, no more kicking or screaming. He stretched his fingers outward toward the rope, and touched the smooth nylon casing, then contact was lost as Lisa began falling, unconscious.

Connor knew this was it, all or nothing. His muscles were expended, and Lisa was falling. He released his grip on the rope and dropped. Closing in and dropping feet first, his speed of descent was faster than Lisa's. He was free falling. Lisa's rope was looped through the figure eight giving it a bit of slowing friction.

Reaching her but still free-falling, he grabbed onto the back of her shirt and spun her right side up. He positioned himself behind her then wrapped his left arm around her chest. With his other hand he jerked the rope from Lisa's grip, and yanked it behind his back. They jerked to a rapid slowing stop, and then impacted feet first onto the ground. Supporting the majority of Lisa's weight, Connor's knees buckled upon impact slamming his tail bone onto the rock bottom. He lay there and didn't move, staring up at the vertical wall.

The moment they hit the ground, Lisa snapped out of her dazed consciousness. She looked up at the cliff. "Oh, my God," she murmured with a sudden realization.

Connor's eyes shifted toward the bodies rushing toward him, barely noticeable through his blood-spattered face.

Mac put a hand on his shoulder. "Jesus Christ, this is rappelling, mate, not skydiving."

CLINGING TO THE ROPE

MAC KNEELED BESIDE CONNOR, LEANED IN AND EXAMINED THE three-inch gaping laceration on his forehead. "Normal blokes would need a few strings in that."

"Stitches, my God, you need stitches," Kate blurted, examining the wound on his forehead. She eyed Connor from head to toe, trying to calculate the extent of his injuries.

"I'm fine," he mumbled, tired. "Lisa, how about you?"

"I think I'm ok," Lisa mumbled, scanning over her bloodied knees and torn pants.

"You guys look war-torn," George said with the camera aimed at their bloodied faces. Most of Lisa's white tank top was bloodied, her jeans were ripped, and she had numerous superficial abrasions all over her arms and shoulders.

"How the hell do you do it, mate? You're one valiant son of a gun," Mac said.

"Come on, Mac. What choice did I have?"

"Oh, I bet I could have found another choice." He winked at Lisa.

Kate gently rubbed Connor's back. "What do you say we set up camp here for the day?"

"That's fine. Can someone give me a little water?"

Carl slid as fast as the rope would allow then slowed to a smooth, quick stop in front of the group. "Got it all on tape," Carl said as he untethered himself. "That was a pretty ballsy move, man."

Connor tilted his canteen in acknowledgement then started chugging.

Lisa tried to stand but was unsteady. "Kate, can you give me a hand?"

Kate grabbed Lisa by the elbow and pulled her up. Lisa started to walk toward her hiking pack but collapsed back onto her butt. "Oh, my God, my knees."

Connor looked at Lisa's bloodied knees. "I thought that might be a problem, I saw you kicking the hell out of the wall. George, can you check 'em out?"

George set his camera down and knelt beside Lisa, then cupped his hands over both her knees. "Alright, sweetheart, gotta take 'em off."

Without hesitation, Lisa unbuttoned her jeans and tried to wiggle out of them but couldn't. Carl started recording. He tried to appear nonchalant as her waistline became visible, exposing her black underwear.

George carefully maneuvered her jeans down, unveiling her lightly tanned and firmly toned legs. Carl's eyes were fixated on her crotch. He walked behind the rest of the group in order to get a better close up, zooming in on his fixation.

George took a good look at her exposed knees. "Ouch."

"What do ya think, George?" Connor asked.

"Swelling, gonna be soccer balls."

"Figured as much," Connor said.

"Are they bad?" Lisa asked.

"I've seen worse, but only from grenades." George grinned. "Everything's in place, but you've got some serious water building on them. They're gonna be swollen and painful like this for a few days."

Connor sighed. "Looks like we'll be *here* for a few days,"

"I'm so sorry, Connor, it's all my fault. If I had just listened to you, none of this would have happened," Lisa lamented.

"No, no, it's not you, I'm agitated with myself. This is one of those things I could have prevented. I could have prepared you a little more, could have let you practice a little longer. I could have tethered you down."

"Listen, you guys just move on, leave me here. You don't have much further to go, right?"

Connor shook his head in total disagreement. "No way, I'm not leaving someone else behind. Uh, uh."

"I mean seriously, how much further are you guys going?"

"A few miles," Kate said.

"Just start a fire for me and make sure I have plenty of wood."

"No way, it's not happening," Connor said.

"Oh yes, it is. I'm a big girl and can make my own decisions. I'm not gonna let my stupidity slow the expedition."

"It wasn't stupidity, Lisa." Connor shook his head repeatedly. "I put you in an environment you weren't comfortable in. I'm the stupid one. We stay here 'til your swelling goes down."

"I'll be really upset if you don't move on. This is all my fault and I'm not gonna hold up the expedition." Lisa's eyes started tearing.

"You can't even walk." Connor's voice grew louder. "Do you really think I'm gonna just leave you at the bottom of a cliff by yourself?"

"I can walk. Knees just hurt and besides, when you leave in the morning they could be a little better."

"Or a little worse," Connor said.

"Even if they are, all I need is a bottle of ibuprofen, my hiking pack and my tent. I'll be in the shade, in my tent, and I'll be relaxing for a few days. That actually sounds really nice."

Kate sighed. "It kinda does, actually."

"Fine, do whatever the hell you want!" Connor forced himself up, grabbed his hiking pack and limped off.

Everyone watched in silence as he hobbled away until disappearing behind a cluster of large rocks.

"Oh gosh, I didn't mean to upset him," Lisa whispered.

"He's fine, look at what he's gone through on this trip so far," George said.

"I just hope he's not mad at me."

"He's not mad at anyone. He's tired and needs a break," George said.

"He doesn't like the fact that Ben and Sheila are out there alone and now you want to be left alone." Kate sat beside Lisa. "He *thinks* he's losing control of the situation."

George handed his canteen to Lisa. "Connor likes to make sure everything and everyone is perfect. He feels responsible, and when things go wrong he takes it personally. This is new for him. He's not used to being responsible for this many people."

"I can stay back with Lisa, if that'll make him feel any better," Carl said.

Mac looked directly at him and chuckled.

"No offense, Carl, but I'd feel a lot safer without you," Lisa said.

"What's that supposed to mean?"

"You give me the creeps. I've seen the way you stare at Sheila and Kate, it's like you're a damned pervert who's never seen a woman before. I don't trust you."

"I have no idea what you're talking about."

"Aw, c'mon man, it's so obvious, and to be quite honest it freaks me out," Lisa said.

"This is ridiculous. I don't have to take this shit." Carl grabbed his pack and walked off.

Mac winked at Lisa. "Bravo."

———

Connor had walked off from the group, set up his tent and even though it was only four p.m., he went to sleep.

Kate gave him some space by bunking with Lisa just after sunset.

Kate folded her pillow and propped her head up. "Boy, you really told Carl."

"That guy grosses me out." Lisa rolled her eyes. "He's always staring at you and Sheila to the point that it's obsessive. I'm sick of seeing it, it's like he's a serious pervert or something."

"That's funny 'cus I've seen him staring at you too. I don't trust him at all. I get a real bad vibe off him."

"And to think he offered to stay back with me. I don't want that guy anywhere near me."

"Did you see the look Mac gave him when he offered to stay behind with you?"

"No. Why?"

"Mac looked like he was going to rip his head off, Lisa. I could literally hear his teeth grinding."

"I guess Mac sees it too."

"He must. Hey, you don't mind me staying behind, do ya?" Lisa asked as she zipped the sleeping bag up to her neck.

"Not at all, I wish you could come, but given the circumstances, I think it's probably the best option."

"Connor seemed pretty pissed," Lisa said.

"I've never seen him get mad like that, but he is only human."

"I still think he's perfect, and he risked his life to save me."

"If you could've only seen it from my angle, he was basically free falling to catch up to you. We felt so helpless on the ground, just watching you guys dangling around."

"It's like he's Clark Kent and you're Lois Lane."

Kate smiled and closed her eyes. "Tell me about it," she whispered.

———

Daybreak brought a chilly, peaceful morning without the deafening sounds of jungle birds to awaken everyone. The wall of the cliff shielded the sunrise, giving the team a couple extra hours of shade. By 9:00 a.m. everyone was packed and ready to move. Lisa was ever more insistent on staying behind and wouldn't have it any other way; her normally petite knees were swollen to the size of softballs. George helped her out of the tent and sat her in a camp chair in front of the fire. Everyone scouted the ravine, gathering every scrap of wood available.

After a long, slumbering sleep, Connor was refreshed and more accepting of Lisa's decision. He sat on a rock opposite her. "Lisa, why don't we just wait here a few days 'til your knees are better?"

"No way, Superman, you have an expedition to finish. Get outta here." Lisa smiled and gestured with open arms. "This is all I need. This is paradise and I look forward to it."

"Okay, be safe and stay off your feet."

Mac leaned over Lisa from behind and kissed her cheek. "If you need us, just send smoke signals." Everyone chuckled a bit. "What? I'm serious."

INFILTRATION

Tasmania - 1935

THE OLDSMOBILE'S TIRES FLUNG MUD AS THEY SPUN THROUGH THE foot of water rushing across the road. The ground was saturated and minor flooding already started in the lowest areas. Greg hammered on the gas as he sped toward Mr. Wilkins ranch. The Oldsmobile's engine raced, careening through the curves and accelerating on the straight a-ways. In no time at all, he was at his first destination. Greg pulled onto the ranch and noticed a light was on in Mickey Wilkins home. He accelerated on the narrow driveway and slid to a stop, less than two feet from the Wilkins front porch.

Greg grabbed the packet of papers and jumped out, just as the front door opened. The light from the inside silhouetted the six-foot-high and well-rounded figure wearing nothing but a pair of white briefs.

Greg darted through the rain and jumped onto the porch.

"What in the hell are you up to?" Mickey said.

"I'm here to make you an offer you can't refuse."

"You're soaked, mate," Mickey said.

"Mickey, I don't have much time. I need to sell you my ranch."

"You know I'll have the money in a few months. Are you all right?"

"No, well, I will be, I just need to sell you my ranch tonight."

"Tonight? Ha, ha, now I know you're not—"

"Mickey, I'm bloody serious."

Mickey paused and studied Greg. "Why such a hurry? It's ten o'clock, man, I was off to beddie."

"Please, Mickey, we need to do it now."

"Come on, mate, you know I won't have the money 'til season."

"That's why I'm gonna give it to you for half."

"Half? Half of what, Greg?"

"Half of what we agreed on."

"That's not even funny."

"I'm not joking, Mickey. I'll give it to you right now for half of what we agreed on, but we have to do this now."

"Why? What's gone wrong? Are you leaving in a hurry?"

"I'm leaving yesterday."

"Oh, bloody hell. Come on in, we can't be doing business on a porch." Mickey walked in and sat at the table, extending an arm for Greg to do so as well.

"I really need to do this fast, Mickey. No offense, but I can't sit around."

"Ol' Millie's got a hand in this, huh?" Mickey smiled.

Greg looked Mickey square in the eye and didn't respond.

"You sure picked one hell of a night to come by. Annie is with her parents on the other coast. She'd be running ya off at this time of night."

"Sorry, Mickey, I just need you to sign the deed. Let's write up the specifics real quick and make it official. Can you pay me now?"

"I can pay you if you really only want half 'cus that's all I got. I'm not sure I feel right taking it for that amount. The original deal was a fair dinkum, but *half of that*? Are you sure about this?"

"I'm sure."

They wrote up the specifics and signed the deed. Mickey paid Greg in full and the transaction was complete. Mickey tried to pry Greg for some info as to his sudden and unexpected visit but was unsuccessful. Greg took Mickey's hand and shook it with great appreciation, then disappeared back into the storm.

Greg fishtailed as he spun out of Mickey's driveway and onto the dirt road. He drove as fast as he could without losing control on the wet road. He drove dangerously fast, but as soon as he neared the next destination he raised his foot off the pedal, slowing down as he contemplated his mission. Greg knew if he proceeded, there was no turning back and his life would change drastically. But that didn't even matter because in the course of one day his entire life had been rearranged. He thought about turning back, taking the money, and starting a simple life on the Mainland. He thought about the corruption that plagued Tasmania, he thought about his father's so-called accident, a grizzly image of Millie fighting for her life overcame him. Fueled by rage, Greg hammered the accelerator to the floor and sped toward his next destination.

Greg turned off the headlights and slowed his Oldsmobile to a crawl just outside of a long driveway with a closed metal gate. He pulled off the road then killed the engine. The rain was relentless, hammering away on the metal roof of his car. He grabbed his rifle from the passenger seat then paused; he stared through the windshield for a few seconds, thinking, then set the gun back down. Instead, he grabbed the massive Bowie knife that slept in a tattered leather sheath. He tethered it to his belt then stepped out into the rain. He gently pushed his driver's side door closed until he heard it latch. The storm's fury would have drowned out any sound, but Greg wasn't taking any chances. He looked up at the large wooden placard that towered above the driveway entrance, and as the lightning cracked, it illuminated—McPherson's Ranch.

He climbed over the metal gate and made his way up the long incline of the driveway, crouching and moving in spurts. He kept himself out of the open, ducking low along the wooden fence lining the driveway. The weather worked in his favor, the wailing rain and wind covered up any noise while the clouds blanketed the area with total darkness.

Greg darted from the cover of a spindly hedge to the edge of the elongated covered porch. He stepped slowly onto the wooden beam, it creaked, and Greg paused, waiting. Nothing came of it so he then crept to the front door. Greg was too focused to notice the intricacy of the engraved architecture of the porch. Greg noticed the sound of the rain was amplified by the home's metal roofing, which pinged and panged with every drop of falling water, surely working to his advantage.

The outer door was framed with heavy wrought iron, its twists and curves demanded full attention, the detail was intricate with braids, bars, and crescents adorning; but the rage driven man grabbing its handle didn't notice. Using both hands, he twisted the knob ever so slowly until it popped. Pulling outward, the door began to move.

Greg ran his fingers along the beveled ridges that outlined the slab of Karri tree that had been crafted into Joe McPherson's inner front door. The heavy rustic wood grain slid beneath his fingertips until they were stopped by cold brass. Greg gave the knob a subtle twist and it too popped. A heavy push on the massive door cracked it open about four inches. A subtle wave of cologne and cigar smoke entered his nostrils. His prey was near. Greg's head pushed through, he felt the warmer air of the room rush his face and now tasted the pungency of stale cigar smoke, an all too surreal sign of where he was. He turned sideways and slid his body through the gap.

Oil lamps lit the interior with an orange glow. He was now standing in a magnificent foyer covered with polished marble tile. To the right was an oversized large living room with a massive leather sofa and matching leather chairs surrounding an inside bar centered upon the outer wall.

The bar was complete with every liquor available on Tasmania. The bar itself had eight empty barstools that sat along its outside perimeter. To the left of the foyer was the immense kitchen. The countertops were fitted with hunky slabs of black and silver granite, finely crafted solid wood cabinets lined the walls, and the newest appliances filled the kitchen. Straight ahead was a long hallway riddled with doors that led to McPherson's bedroom.

Greg could see a dim orange flickering light emanating from a room at the end of the hall, a candle perhaps.

Did Joe McPherson kill Millie and Ben? No, he didn't pull the trigger or snap Millie's neck, but what he did do was start a chain reaction. His irrational fear and hatred of the Thylacine coupled with his controlling fist, clenched down upon Tasmania unleashed an evil upon the land. Greedy bounty hunters scavenged the country, killing any and every tiger for an inflated bounty, slaughtering entire litters, even the pups were fair game. Decent, reputable men saw the promise of money in hunting the tigers, and so even they began raping the wild for a hefty payment. The children of Tasmania were taught to hate the tigers; if a parent told their children something is bad, dangerous, and evil, then it becomes bad, dangerous, and evil. This nonsensical state of mind swept over Tasmania like a disease, infecting without prejudice. Greg knew Joe McPherson was the source of it all.

Greg leaned against the wall and pulled his boots off one at a time. He left them in the foyer then silently started toward the lighted room like a moth drawn to light. Greg knew McPherson was divorced and lived alone, and if lucky was passed-out drunk.

The flickering was coming from the last door on the right. He tried to peer into the other open doors along the way, but darkness prevented inspection. Greg put his back against the wall and inched himself closer to the lit doorway. As he leaned to peek through the door, the wooden floor board released a short, but audible moan. He froze, listening for any commotion within the room, but the sound of the pinging rain on the metal roof made it impossible. After a few seconds he slid his feet a little closer to the door, trying to shift his weight to a different spot on the floor. Greg started leaning in and once again the floor released a creaking moan. Greg stopped leaning, but his imbalance forced the floor into a stuttering series of moaning croaks. Greg straightened himself out and took a deep breath. He controlled his breathing and listened, waiting, but the rain was just too loud.

Greg leaned in and as his eyes neared the light, the crashing sound of breaking glass came from within the room.

"God-damn it." A man's voice bitched.

Greg recognized the voice—McPherson. *He must have dropped a whiskey glass.* He knew that meant one of two things would probably happen: Joe would get up and get another glass or he would stay in the room and go to sleep.

Greg pressed his back firmly against the wall and wrapped his fingers around five inches of hand carved bone. He pulled, unleashing the hellish blade from its pouch then lifted it to his chest. Greg focused his ears upon the bedroom, a floorboard creaked then the light passing through the door was interrupted by a shadow.

A smoldering cigar released a dying stream of smoke as it died alone in its gold embroidered, black ceramic ash tray. Joe McPherson sat on the edge of his extra tall king size bed staring at the mess he created, and less than willingly he knelt to the floor. He bitched under his breath as he picked up the splintered glass fragments, placing them into the base of the glass that had remained intact. He wiped the watered-down bourbon from the floor with his damp bath towel then started toward the door.

Joe dragged his feet as he walked; the five bourbon and waters were settling in. He shuffled through the door and felt a sharp sting just under his jaw. He dropped the broken glass, sending the shards scattering upon the floor.

When McPherson emerged through the door way, Greg thrust his blade under Joe's chin, sending the blade tip through his soft tissue, stopping just before penetrating his tongue. Joe stopped in his tracks and was confused at the sudden onset of stinging pain. Greg stepped out of the shadows and placed himself in front of McPherson.

"Where are they?" Greg growled. McPherson's first thought was to go for his gun in the nightstand, but he couldn't move.

"You...you...you're a...dead son of bitch," McPherson garbled his words, unaware the blade had penetrated so deeply.

Greg clenched his teeth and spoke slowly. "Where are Smitty and Tanner? I won't be asking you again." Greg thrust the knife a little deeper, piercing the very bottom of Joe's tongue. Joe could feel warm droplets of blood spattering upon his feet. Greg's voice was frightening, cold and empty.

"I...I...I duh duh dunno!" McPherson cried.

"Why did you send 'em out to my ranch?"

"I swa...swa...swear to you...I didn't send 'em." McPherson struggled to speak with the knife nearly piercing his tongue. Greg pushed the steel blade a little further, McPherson could feel the tip under the base of his tongue. Blood ran down the shiny blade then streamed across Greg's clenched fingers, dripping on McPherson's bare feet.

"All, all, all right! All right!" McPherson cried. "They wen wen went...aff aff...after the tiger. Plee, please don't kill me."

"Why?"

"They are go, go, gonna put it in the zoo."

"Why?"

"To re...replace the tigers at Hobart."

"They killed my wife," Greg growled.

"Ah, Jesus...I...I'm so, so sorry." McPherson put on his best show, he didn't give a damn about Greg's wife, and he was trying to save his own skin.

"It's because of *you* that she's dead," Greg whispered, and then twisted the blade a bit.

"AHHH! Come on, mate." McPherson screamed in pain.

"Where are they?"

"I dunno. They…u…u…usually den up at Le…Nora's motel." Joe was finding it more difficult to speak.

"Lenora's Motel," Greg murmured to himself, recalling it as being the most rundown shithole motel in all of Hobart.

"So the tiger is alive?"

"That…was…the plan."

Greg jerked on the knife, forcing Joe to follow. "Come on." He led him down the hall, out the front door and into the pouring rain. Joe stumbled a bit, but managed to keep Greg's pace, following him like a leashed dog, all the way to the barn.

"Wha…Wha…" Joe gurgled a bit, unable to swallow because of the blade. A mouthful of bloody spit ran down his chin. "Wha…what are you go go gonna do?"

Greg looked into McPherson's quivering eyes. "I'm going to kill you."

"Pa…please…I'm so, so sorry…I…"

Greg shoved the blade hard, filleting McPherson's tongue and puncturing his palate, embedding the tip in the roof of his mouth.

"AAAAAGGGGHHHHHHH!" McPherson tried to scream, but the blade robbed his tongue of any movement; all he could produce were wretched vowel sounds as blood bubbled out of his mouth.

Greg eyed a coil rope hanging on the barn wall. He looked back at the hysterical McPherson, and with one quick motion he ripped the knife down and out of Joe's fat chin. Greg swung full force with his right hand and caught the fat man's chin. His body went limp and crashed to the ground unconscious.

He dragged McPherson's body to the closest horse stable and laid him face down under one of the fence rails. Greg tied his arms behind his back and then secured them to the railing. He raised Joe's feet to the railing and tied them together with the rope. Joe was hog-tied to a fence rail. It was only when Greg backed away that he noticed McPherson was naked.

Hobart zoo was another forty-five minutes from Joe's ranch, but Greg knew it would have to be his next stop. Maybe he could catch Smitty and Tanner at the zoo making the switch. The rain began to ease as Greg sped toward Hobart. It was nearly two a.m. and he couldn't stop thinking about Petey waking up alone.

Greg killed his lights as he entered the vacant parking lot of the zoo. He parked in a corner well concealed with a large patch of leafy bamboo. The main entrance gate into the park was closed with a heavy chain and lock securing it; maybe it was to prevent vehicles from driving in, but the four-foot metal fence was an easy obstacle for even the most novice Olympians. The rain had finally tapered off; leaving behind fast moving clouds that kept covering and uncovering the moon. The sudden spurts of darkness gave Greg temporary concealment as he threw himself over the gate. Once inside he relaxed; there was no sign of Smitty and Tanner and he knew that McPherson would never pay a guard to watch over the zoo.

Greg walked toward the Thylacine enclosure, retracing the steps that he and his family had taken just a few short weeks ago. He walked slowly, placing his mind in that day at the zoo; Millie's zest for life, the endless love for her son, her compassion for the tigers, all her smiles, all her personality, everything. It had all been taken away.

The flashlight flickered a bit then fizzled out, Greg tapped it a few times, awakening it from some sort of an electrical slumber. He pointed the beam toward the Thylacine enclosure and saw a pair of eyes gleaming from within. *Is that you, Ben?*

As Greg neared the enclosure another set of eyes emerged from the left rear corner and ran to the front of the cage; it started jumping and running around in circles, chirping and whistling.

In the midst of all his chaos, rage and inner torment, Greg found a peaceful calm. He smiled. "Ben," he whispered, reaching his fingers through the cage. It wasn't his wife, but it was the next best thing, his son's best friend. "Shhhhhhh, I know boy, I know." Greg knelt down, reached through the rusted wire and gave Ben a rejoicing rub. He put his face to the cage and accepted a flurry of licks.

Greg had no control over the tears that flooded his face. He didn't think Ben would be found alive, but there he was. He stood up and panned his light across the cage. "Let's get you outta there."

The flashlight's beam panned across the cage, stopping on a rectangular structure on the back wall. Ben followed as Greg made his way around the outside perimeter of the cage to the rickety door secured with a rusted padlock. The crooked door rattled as Greg shook it, testing its sturdiness. The hinges were barely holding the door to the frame. Greg grabbed the padlock and jiggled it a bit. The lock was pointless, the door was so flimsy anyone could have easily pulled it off the frame; the tigers however were so weak and apathetic they never took notice. Greg put one hand on the door frame and wedged the other between the door *and* the frame, and with one swift jerk the screws securing the padlocked latch popped from the wood and the door swung open.

Ben jumped through the open door and pushed himself against Greg's legs. He chattered a series of distinct whistles, almost as though he was trying to tell Greg about everything that had happened.

"I know, I know, Ben." Greg patted Ben's flank and hugged him tight. "Let's go home."

Greg pushed the door closed and pounded the screws back into their loosened holes. He shined the flashlight into the cage for one last look at the pitiful tigers. The one on the ground was scrambling to his feet. It managed to stand, but was shaky, spreading its legs in order to keep from falling. The other tiger poked its head through the rectangular hole of its plywood shelter; it tried to step over the lip of the rotted-out doghouse but fell forward onto its chest. It situated itself where it fell, unable to get back on its feet.

"I'm so sorry, guys." Greg said. The other tiger started walking over. Greg stood there and watched as it limped over to the door and stared up at him from behind the rusty wire. The flashlight's beam went from one tiger to the other. Greg grabbed the door and ripped it back open; this time it fell to the ground. He stepped inside the cage and scooped up the wobbly tiger. As Greg lifted it the poor thing grunted. He could feel its bare, bony ribs and hips pressing against his body. He carried the tiger straight to his Oldsmobile and laid it on the back seat. Ben followed close. Greg headed back to the cage to retrieve the other tiger. It was standing at the threshold to the door, staring up at Greg with a weak body, but excited eyes. Greg snatched up the other tiger and walked toward the exit. As he did, it stretched its neck and gave him a slow sniff across the cheek.

Greg had been home for more than three hours. He thought about waking Petey but decided to let him sleep. He placed the two weakened tigers in one of the barn stalls then went on to the torturous task of burying Millie. Forcing himself devoid of emotion, he buried her under the largest tree on the property. The ground was softened from the rain and he was able to dig fairly deep in a rather short amount of time. Greg and Millie weren't religious by any means, so no biblical ramblings were needed. When he was done, all that showed of the grave was a rectangular patch of dampened dirt, no crosses, and no makeshift headstones. He started to walk off then turned back toward the grave. He unsheathed the massive knife still attached to his belt and stabbed the tip into the tree. He carved hard and deep, causing the tree's sap to bleed. When he finished, Millie's initials were boldly engraved into the grey leathery bark.

Greg didn't have time to mourn. He didn't have time to wallow in grief. He didn't have time to think about the abstinence of trivial conversation. He didn't have time to think about waking up alone. He was driven. He knew he had ventured past the point of no return and had to act fast.

Greg sizzled up some bacon and hard-fried a couple of eggs for Petey. He wanted to make his son as comfortable as possible.

"Dad…" Petey said as he dragged his feet across the floor, making his way into the kitchen.

Greg looked over at his son and noticed he was holding Ben's Koala. "Hey son, I made ya some breakfast."

Petey's eyes started watering then he burst into tears. Greg grabbed Petey, pressing his head into his chest. "Let it out, son, let it out." Greg wanted to cry with his son but couldn't. He felt bad but could not produce tears. "She's in a better place now, son. She's watching over us."

"Is she still in the barn?" Petey cried.

"No, son." Greg's words were gentle. "I buried her. She's not in that old body anymore, she's free as a bird now."

"I wanna see her," Petey cried.

"We can't see her right now, but we'll all be together again. I promise."

Greg let Petey cry it out until the sobbing slowed then he tried to redirect his attention. "I went out last night while you were sleeping. I brought something home for ya." Petey's sobs transitioned to faint whimpers.

"What, Dad?" Petey wiped his eyes.

"I can't really tell ya, you'll just have to see. Let's take a walk to the barn." Petey's face dropped, he associated the barn with his mother. Greg understood Petey's expression. "It's ok Petey, she's not there. I buried her proper."

Greg took Petey by the hand and led him through the front door. As soon as Petey stepped onto the porch his eyes stretched wide and he screamed. "Bennnnnnnnnnnnnnnn!" Ben was sniffing around at the entrance of the barn. After hearing Petey scream, he turned and broke into a full sprint, so fast that he appeared to be flying. Petey dropped to his knees and opened his arms; within seconds Ben was showering his face with licks. He spun wildly in circles, releasing an uncontrollable barrage of harmonic whistles and chirps.

"You got 'em back!" Petey wrapped his arms tightly around Ben's neck. "You killed those men, Dad?"

"Not ye—" Greg stopped himself. "No, Petey. I didn't. There's something else..." Ben broke away from Petey's grip and ran to the barn. "Let's go see what Ben's up to."

As they entered the barn, Greg eyed his bloody Bowie knife, its tip was embedded deep in a support pole; an unwanted memory tried to pry its way in, but he relinquished it immediately.

Petey noticed some movement from within one of the horse stalls. He ran over to investigate. Petey inhaled with excitement. He saw two bony tigers lying on the floor amongst the thick hay. Both tigers raised their heads and looked at Petey. "Dad, look!"

"Uh huh, I see 'em." Greg looked in at the tigers curled up in the warm hay. It made him feel good to see the tigers away from the shitty zoo. He had done the right thing and was proud.

"Oh, Dad, look at 'em!"

"Now we just need to fatten 'em up. They nearly ate a whole side of beef this morning, I think they're gonna sleep it off."

Greg and Petey sat with the tigers for a while, immersed in the unexpected goodness that came out of a wretchedly horrid situation. They both needed the tigers just as much as the tigers needed them. It was a mutual necessity. The tigers were more than content, rolling on their backs while the two humans stroked their full bellies. Ben flopped down between the tigers and joined the session.

They left the tigers in the barn to sleep off their feast. In the house, Greg and Petey finished off breakfast, cold eggs and bacon seemed to hit the spot. "You go ahead and eat up anything you want out of the fridge, Petey."

Petey's eyes widened and a smirk of disbelief appeared on his face. "I mean it, help yourself. We're leaving Tasmania in a day or so and we need to eat all the perishables."

Petey raised his eyebrows. "Really? We're leaving?" Petey was in disbelief.

"We are, son. We're getting the hell outta this crooked place."

"Don't you have to sell the ranch?"

"I did. It's done, and I've been paid. I've just got to run a few errands in town and I'll be back."

"Can I come?"

"I need you to stay here and watch the place. I'm gonna hide you out in the barn."

"Why you gonna hide me?"

"I just wanna play it safe. No one's coming out here, but just in case they do…"

"What about the tigers, Dad?"

"I'm gonna hide 'em with ya in the loft. If anyone comes along try your best to keep the tigers quiet. Don't worry, I won't be long."

Petey was reluctant, but when he heard that the tigers were gonna be with him he became anxious.

One by one, Greg carried each tiger over his shoulder, up the ladder and into the loft. From down below it looked like a typical open loft, jam packed with various boxes and old furniture, but it had ample space to conceal three tigers and a boy. Before he left, Greg gave the tigers a massive raw slab of beef hind quarter. All three ate until their bellies were rounded then quickly fell asleep. Out of boredom, Petey whittled a few hunks of wood into what looked like turtles but were meant to be tigers. He eventually dozed off alongside Ben on the floor of the loft.

The drive went rather quickly as Greg sorted his thoughts all the way into Hobart; *get lots of dry kibble for the tigers, get plenty of non-perishable food for him and Petey, figure out how to conceal the tigers for the ferry ride to the mainland, locate Smitty and Tanner.*

After stocking up on jerky and canned goods at the Hobart Grocery, Greg made his way to the Feed and Seed. The sweet smell of grain and molasses filled the air of the store. Greg looked around for the owner, Mr. Murphy, but no one was in sight. The place looked lifeless. He grabbed two fifty-pound sacks of dry dog kibble and leaned them against the front counter. Greg knew Mr. Murphy would probably know the where-abouts of Tanner and Smitty. As owner of the Feed and Seed, Mr. Murphy was privy to all the town's gossip.

Greg stood at the counter scanning the aisles for him, but the store was empty; Greg could have walked right out the front door with his kibble if he so desired, no one would have known, but that just wasn't in Greg's character. After a few restless minutes of waiting, Greg's saw a clipboard with a "pickup" list beside the till. He fingered the list and slid it into view.

Pick up list for today

- John Campbell 12 alfalfa bales, 4 sweet feed
- Bill McIntyre 8 Alfalfa bales, 3 sweet feed – collect 25 shillings
- George Flemming 4 Alfalfa bales, 2 salt licks
- Curtis Brinkman 8 Alfalfa bales, 6 sweet feed, 6 wood shavings
- Joe McPherson 18 Alfalfa

Greg knew McPherson wouldn't be picking up the hay; he was a little too tied up today, but then again Joe would have never done the grunt work himself anyway. Greg's thoughts were interrupted when Mr. Murphy's teenage son Eric appeared in the storefront window, laughing it up with an attractive young lady. He peered through the glass and spotted Greg standing at the counter. Greg watched on as Eric shooed the girl off and darted into the store.

Eric rushed behind the counter. "Awe geez, sorry to of kept ya."

"No worries, mate, just picking up some kibble. Sorry to break you away from your lil' lady friend."

Eric tried to conceal his grin as his white complexion reddened.

"Two large kibbles, anything else?"

"That ought a do it," Greg said as he slid a few coins toward Eric. "Been busy?"

"Nah, you're the second person in this morning."

Greg nodded at the clipboard. "Looks like you've got a few big orders on your pad."

"Nah, those are just the regular pickups."

"I see you've got McPherson on there. I was out at Joe's place and he wanted me to let you know that his order needs to be held for a few days. He's got his barn all ripped apart, redoing it and such, he doesn't want to have his lot of hay kept out in the rain."

"So his goons won't be coming in?"

"You talkin' about Smitty and Tanner?"

"I dunno their names, one skinny and one fat bloke. They're always trying to act tough, always braggin' about beating people up."

"Yup, that's them. Sorry, mate, just ignore 'em. You do any hunting?"

"Nah, between my studies and this place, I've got no time."

"Well, if you know anyone interested, the forest between Fisherman's Creek and Old Worter Road is loaded with tigers."

"Ya know, those goons of McPherson's hunt tigers, maybe if I tell 'em when they're here they'll leave me the hell alone."

"You better let 'em know 'cus I saw about six of 'em gnawing on a roo carcass."

"I'll be letting 'em know for sure. It'd be great if it gets 'em off my back and outta the store."

"Just remember, make sure those guys don't deliver to McPherson or he'll get all worked up."

Eric scribbled something on the pad next to McPherson's name. "Got it, I'll hold McPherson's order for a few days."

———

Three hours later, the cowbell hanging from the door of the Feed and Seed sounded as it swung open. Eric looked up from his book to see the pudgy lil' man walking toward the counter with his skinny counterpart just behind him. Smitty leaned over the counter trying to peer into Eric's book.

"What ya readin'?" Smitty barked.

He didn't want to answer but knew it would get worse if he didn't. "I'm studying algebra." Eric knew some predictable, smart-ass response would follow.

"Oh, a college boy, you think you're smart?" Smitty barked.

"What can I do for you, guys?" Eric ignored the comment.

"*Real smart kid* workin' in a feed store," Tanner snipped from behind Smitty.

"Load us up," Smitty ordered.

"Some bloke was in earlier and he said McPherson's order needs to be held for a few days."

Smitty wrinkled his face. "Why the hell does he want his order held?"

"The guy said he just came from McPherson's place and that he was redoing his barn. He had no place for the hay and didn't want it to get wet."

"Well, that's news to me." Smitty squinted at the boy in disbelief.

"He also said the woods between Fisherman's Creek and Old Worter Rd were chock a block with tigers. He said he just came from there and at least ten of 'em were rippin' apart a roo."

"Thought you said he'd just came from McPherson's."

"Either way, it is what it is." Eric snapped back.

"Whoa boy, you getting cocky." Smitty stood up and stared into the kid's eyes.

"Does it make you feel tough trying to intimidate a kid?" Eric asked.

Smitty raised the back of his hand in a bluffed attempt to backslap. "Why I ought a…"

"Look guys, you got a bunch of tigers waiting on ya. I wouldn't waste too much time trying to bully a kid when you could be out snatching some bounties."

"I'll smack you around next time we're in." Smitty reached behind the counter and snatched a bag of chewing tobacco then walked toward the door. "Come on, Skinny, we got some tigers to kill."

———

Greg returned home after the trip to town. He helped the tigers down from the loft and moved them to the house with Petey. Greg was confident that Petey could stay in the house without fear of the men returning. He told Petey he had one more errand to run and that he would be home in a few hours.

Greg left at dusk and the orange evening glow was sinking fast along the tree lined horizon. Greg pulled his Oldsmobile off the road and drove behind some low-lying scrub palms; concealing his vehicle behind the foliage. He walked out of the scrub and looked down the long darkening road and, just as he predicted, the silhouette of an old truck with flatbed trailer was parked a few hundred yards from him. It was one of four vehicles in McPherson's personal fleet. Greg knew Smitty and Tanner were in the woods.

Greg was unarmed, leaving the rifle with Petey. His wife's murderers were in the exact isolated location he had sent them. He didn't think, didn't plan. He simply disappeared into the darkening forest.

VENGEANCE

Tasmania - April 1935

"These god-damned thorns are eating me alive," Tanner bitched as he pushed his way through the dense undergrowth.

"Keep ya bloody voice down," Smitty snapped, forcing himself to whisper. "It's hard enough nowadays without *you* scaring 'em away."

The forest was filled with oddly shaped greenery; scattered patches of knee level ferns, long runs of thorny vines. Overhead, palm fronds opened like umbrellas; every fifty feet or so a massive Karri tree would vanish into the sky above, some with trunks more than fifteen feet in diameter. The silence of night was settling in, blanketing the woodlands as songbirds sank into the safety of their nests.

Smitty found a suitable blind spot situated in a waist level fern patch that would allow him to scan in all directions without being seen. He centered himself within the dark leafy fronds and whistled to Tanner. "Get in here!"

"I ain't gettin' in there 'til ya check fer snakes," Tanner said as he picked at the large gauze bandage taped to his neck.

Tanner was a follower, a true idiot. He never went to public school, never learned to read or write. His father was found dead, at home, when he was twelve years old, a single bullet to his forehead. They never did find the killer. Rumor was Tanner had done it himself, but there were way too many people that wanted his father dead.

Tanner's father was a crooked man, constantly in and out of jail. When he wasn't beating some whore for shitty service he was swindling money, stealing livestock, and reselling them to other ranchers. Tanner never learned to connive *quite* like his father; he resorted to stealing from kids and bullying the weak. Tanner was jailed for an act of pure stupidity, stealing a branded calf, and trying to sell it back to the same ranch. It was during that jail stint that he met Smitty.

"Ain't no damned snakes in here, now move yer bloody feet." Smitty struggled to keep his voice to a whisper.

Tanner poked and prodded around in the ferns with his vintage .22 caliber bolt action rifle, before settling in next to Smitty.

"Ain't been no tigers round here for more than a year," Tanner moaned.

"That kid at the Feed-n-Seed said that fella had seen 'em, I ain't passin' up no free money," Smitty whispered. "And if I have to tell ya to shut ya bloody mouth *again*, I'll shoot ya myself."

The fat man turned his head and hawked a gooey load of brown tobacco spit; his cheek bulging with a large wad from McPherson's personal crop. Smitty had a working relationship with Joe McPherson, the richest and most dangerous man in Tasmania. Smitty was never allowed to publicly socialize with Joe; instead, Smitty would visit his ranch once or twice a week to see if he had any *jobs* for him. Smitty had the reputation around town of being a big mouthed thug, regardless of his short, pudgy and unintimidating size. Because of his confrontational demeanor, the people of Tasmania learned to walk away or turn their heads when they saw him coming. It was common knowledge he kept a ten-inch skinning knife tucked away in his boot, and the thought of it was enough to keep most people at bay. Smitty was hauled off to jail more than a dozen times for battery, disorderly conduct and disturbing the peace only to be released as soon as McPherson caught wind of it. Most thugs were cowards hiding behind big mouths, but Smitty was different, he had a big mouth, and he wasn't a coward. He was dangerous, he feared no one and preferred action over words.

"Pickin's are slim getting', we gonna have ta start rustling again," Tanner whispered.

"There's plenty a tiger out there, we jus' gotta find 'em."

"Once we kill a few, we should go muck around wit' that O'Leary girl while her folks are gone."

"Ya know that ain't such a bad idea. Maybe we—"

"I see one," Tanner blurted. He raised his .22 and aimed at the center of the *now* motionless silhouette.

"Kill the mongrel," Smitty whispered. "This bounty buys the booze."

The .22 fired, toppling the silhouette, fifty yards away.

"Hee, hee! Got the lil' bastard," Tanner blurted.

"Keep it down, you idiot. You're gonna scare the rest of 'em away. Go and fetch your head but be quiet about it."

Tanner fumbled his fingers around his belt line then looked over at Smitty. "I ain't got my knife on me."

"Well how in the hell you gonna cut off its fuckin' head?"

"Gimmee yer knife."

"Ya need to start thinkin' a lil' bit, if yer goin' huntin'. Bring yer goddamned knife," Smitty bitched as he reached into his boot, pulling out the shiny ten-inch blade. "Bring it right back." He couldn't stand giving up his blade. Even when he slept, the blade was always within reaching distance, but the only way they could collect a bounty was with a head, so he handed it off with regret.

Tanner crept off into the darkened forest. He looked back toward Smitty who was now indistinguishable from the fern patch. The darkness had arrived, transforming the forest from the evening purple sun-fire to haunting shades of black.

Tanner made it to the spot where he dropped the beast, looked around for a moment expecting the tiger to have wandered a few feet, but found it in the exact spot. He leaned his rifle against the enormous Karri tree and knelt down in the ferns to examine his kill.

"Shit! This ain't no bloody tiger." Tanner stood up and kicked the dead wallaby. "Ahhh, stinks to fuckin hell." Tanner wasn't the brightest, but even he knew that it took days for a carcass to stink like that.

"Tanner…" a strange voice whispered behind him.

Tanner reached for his rifle, but it was gone.

The stranger forced his words through clenched teeth. "This is for Millie."

He had secured Tanner's rifle and holding it by the barrel, swung with devastating force. The wooden stock of the gun collided with Tanner's mouth and nose, spraying shards of rotted tooth enamel into the back of his throat. The impact knocked him off his feet and sent him crashing on his back behind the Karri tree, unconscious. The stranger swung again, this time shattering and collapsing his skull, again, and then again, until Tanner's face was a bloody pulp of gurgling fluids.

The stranger reached down, and to the music of Tanner's obstructed airway bubbling with blood and teeth, he pried the shiny steel blade out of his clenched hand.

———

Smitty grew restless in the fern patch. "What's takin' that hoon so long?" Smitty spent his entire existence bitching. *Never* was there a truly pleasant moment in his life, in one way or another. Everything attached to Smitty was tarnished and corrupt. Five minutes later, Smitty grew restless and began walking in the direction of his only loyal follower. "God-damned idiot that kid is."

Smitty bitched under his breath as he walked, until a strange voice called out from the darkness. "You like killing tigers?"

Smitty started, spinning his head in every direction, searching for its source.

"Tanner? What in the bloody hell are you doin'?"

"Tanner's dead."

Smitty kept spinning, searching for the origin of the unfamiliar voice.

"Do you have *any* fuckin' idea who yer runnin' off to? I'll fucking kill you ya bloody fucker!" Smitty double checked his rifle, making sure a round was chambered in his six shot 30/30. "Show yerself! I'll fucking end you!" The rifle cracked as he shot blindly into the darkness.

"You can't kill me, Smitty."

"Oh, I can kill you, just show yerself!" Smitty yelled, his temper raging. He cocked the rifle and fired again.

"Big man with a gun, huh, Smitty?" The unfamiliar voice taunted from the darkness.

"To hell with a gun, I don't need no gun to kill you!" Without thinking, blinded by the intensity of his rage, Smitty threw the rifle, sending it spinning out of sight into the forest. "Show yerself, you little bitch."

"You're dying tonight, Smitty."

"So come kill me you bloody chicken shit bastard!" Smitty roared.

The stranger walked out of the darkness and entered the patchy moonlight, ten feet behind the fat man. Smitty was sobered by the cocking of a rifle as it chambered a round directly behind him. He turned to face his adversary, saw him with his own rifle.

Smitty squinted, trying to make out the stranger's face. "Do I know you? Who the hell are you?"

"I'm the man that's killing you tonight." With one arm the stranger raised Smitty's rifle and aimed low.

"Oh, I see, a big fucking man with a gun!" Smitty yelled mocking the stranger's earlier words.

"No, just a man. *You* gave me the gun." The stranger's voice was calm, too calm and Smitty knew it meant trouble.

The rifle cracked. It released a fury of searing lead that entered Smitty's left knee cap, then exploded as it exited the back of his leg, collapsing the fat man.

"Ahh! You've destroyed me leg! You bastard!"

"Does it hurt, Smitty?"

"Fight me like a man you wretched coward. Ahh, me fucking leg! You bloody bastard, come get me!"

The stranger dropped the gun and walked toward Smitty bare handed. "Is this what you want?"

"I'll rip your bloody head off." Smitty lowered his voice to a snarling growl. He ignored the pain and struggled to his feet.

The stranger closed the gap on Smitty, and then swung with his right arm, only to have Smitty deflect it and counter with a left jab that didn't connect. The stranger stomp kicked Smitty's shattered knee with extreme force, hyper extending it. As Smitty fell backwards, he held onto the stranger's shirt and they fell together.

Smitty pulled the stranger tight against him with his right arm and reached into his boot with the left. His knife was gone.

"Is this what you're looking for?" The stranger pushed the shiny blade straight into Smitty's abdomen. It popped through the flesh and entered the slushy cavity until it would go no further. Smitty thrashed for a few seconds trying to break free of the stranger's grip, but as he removed the blade, his energy left him.

"You've killed me," Smitty whispered.

"Not yet. This one's for Benjamin." The stranger pushed the knife once again, this time hard and fast into Smitty's rib cage, puncturing his lung.

"Who...who...the hell...is Be ...Benjamin?" Smitty gasped for air.

"And this one's for Millie." The stranger jerked the blade out and thrust it into his ribs again. This time it went lethal as the tip punctured his heart.

Smitty's grip loosened. His head dropped back to the ground.

"I...I...know...who you...are..." Smitty fought to breathe.

The stranger, still on top of him, leaned in closer and spit in the dying man's face.

"Fuck...fuckin ...kill...kill me already...mate." The stranger's spit stretched across Smitty's lips as he gasped his final words.

The stranger stood up, watching the fat man's futile attempts to inhale. His gasping slowed as his internal organs began shutting down. "Pa...pa...paleeeease kill...me mate..." Smitty gasped.

The stranger stared into the dying man's eyes as his gasping slowed to a dead stop.

BACK TO THE MAINLAND

Tasmania - 1935

GREG ROSE JUST BEFORE DAWN. HE PUT THE TIGERS BACK IN THE barn and started loading the Oldsmobile with suitcases packed with clothes, important paperwork, and a few keepsakes. He woke Petey and told him to stuff his knapsack full of whatever he wanted to bring. The rest would be left behind.

He modified the rear trunk of the Oldsmobile with a make-shift cover to hide the three tigers during their trip. He attached a large four-foot by six-foot plywood sheet on top of the trunk and stacked the luggage on top. Underneath the plywood was the tigers' area; just large enough for all three to fit with little room for movement. He understood it would be near torturous for them. If need be, they would have to urinate and defecate where they lie, unable to move in their cramped quarters.

Greg stopped in the threshold to Petey's room. "You about ready, lil' boy?"

"I think so." Petey was sitting on the floor of his room stuffing his knapsack with his favorite toys and books. "Will our new place have a creek, Dad?"

"I think we can arrange that, wanna give me a hand loading the tigers?"

"Sure." Petey pulled the drawstring on his knapsack and threw it over his back. They walked out onto the front porch and saw a car making its way up the driveway. The sun had already breached the horizon, heating the humid air.

Greg pushed Petey backwards. "Get in the house, Petey." He then pulled the door shut.

Greg's heart started pounding. His first thought was that McPherson had gotten loose and sent some lynch men out after him. As the car drew closer he realized it was the sheriff. *Had they found McPherson? Am I under investigation? Had they found Smitty and Tanner? Did someone see me?* Within seconds, Earl was stepping out of his vehicle and walking toward the porch.

Greg nodded once. "Sheriff."

Earl eyed the suitcases in the back of Greg's car. "G'day, Greg, you headed off somewhere?"

"Actually, we are, heading back to the mainland for a bit."

"Family?"

"You could say that. Don't mean to be rude, Earl, but we were just leaving. Is there anything I can help you with?"

"Well, I was just stopping by to follow up with Millie, see if there's been any more trouble with those vagrants. Can I speak to her?"

"No, no you can't."

"What's with ya, Greg?" Earl could sense something wasn't right. "Hi, Petey." Earl waved at the boy peeking through the front window. Greg looked at Petey with frustration then back at Earl.

"Look, Earl, we're really busy. Could you come back in a day or so?"

Petey poked his head through the door and stepped out onto the porch. "Morning, Sheriff!"

"Good morning to you, Petey. Hey, could you tell your mother to come outside? I just wanna have a lil' talkie."

Petey's expression dropped and his eyes teared up instantly; he started to sniffle, his breathing grew heavy, and he ran back inside. Earl and Greg's eyes met in an awkward extended stare.

"Alright now, something's amiss. You wanna start talking?"

"Look, Sheriff, please just go about your way. Let us be."

"Where's Millie?"

"God-damn it, Earl, please just leave it alone."

"Something's off, I'm not here to stir the muck but I just want some answers, like where's Millie and why did your son get all riled when I asked?"

"She's dead, Earl," Greg snapped. He stared down into the heavy wood grain on one of the pine floorboards of his porch. Earl instinctively placed his hand on top of his revolver.

"Oh, God, man, please tell me you're joking."

"Jesus Christ, Earl." Greg looked into Earl's eyes. "McPherson's men."

"Oh, God, no, mate."

"They came while I was at work; they raped her…then…then they broke her bloody neck," Greg cried, finally.

"Aw, Christ, Greg, I'm so sorry. Those bastards will hang."

Greg squinted at Earl then let out a sarcastic sigh of ill-humor. "There ain't no law in Hobart, Sheriff, this land is corrupt. It's dirty and it's run by *McPherson*. Go hang *that* bastard. He's the one that killed my wife." Greg cracked the door open and gestured for Petey to come out. "Petey saw the whole thing."

"Oh, God, man, that's just horrible."

Petey poked his head back through the door and wiped his red eyes.

"McPherson is as crooked as they come, has been for years and you've never done a god-damned thing about it." Greg clenched his teeth.

"I do what I can, Greg, I have to work within the law." Earl took offense but kept a consoling tone.

"The law? The townsfolk talk. Everyone knows how Hobart law works. McPherson's men are exempt from the law and everyone in this god-damned place knows it. They're free to plunder, pillage, rape, and murder, spend a night in jail then be free the next god-damned day. What kind of law is that?"

"I do what I can with what I'm given. I have to work within the threshold of the law." Earl defended his position, but knew Greg was right. He felt worthless. He was sickened. He had unlawfully released the men who had killed Greg's wife on numerous occasions. He was nauseated by the fact that if he had acted within the law that Greg's wife wouldn't have met her demise.

"Can I ask you something, Earl?" Greg looked deep into Earl's distraught eyes.

"Anything, Greg."

"Did McPherson kill my father?"

"I honestly don't know," Earl spoke softly. "But I've always suspected his men had a hand in it." Earl knew McPherson had taunted Greg's father and even had him bullied around as encouragement to sell his ranch and he wondered if McPherson's goons beat him to death, but he didn't know for sure.

"Was it investigated, Earl?"

"It was, his injuries were consistent with being trampled."

"Or beaten," Greg added.

Earl knew McPherson had Greg's father killed. An awkward silence developed as Earl became lost in his thoughts. He was a failed lawman.

"Let's show the sheriff our dogs," Greg said. He grabbed Petey's hand and the three walked toward the barn.

"I need to get going, Greg. I've gotta find those bastards."

"This will only take a minute."

"You got some nice dogs, Petey?" Earl asked. Petey looked up at his father and didn't speak.

They walked through the threshold and Greg started toward one of the stables. Ben saw Petey and leapt between the railings to meet him.

Earl saw the large tiger leap between the fence railings and jumped backwards. He watched on as the tiger leaned against Petey's legs and gave a gentle lick across the boy's face. Petey returned the affection by wrapping his arms around Ben's neck.

"I'll be damned." Earl muttered.

Greg looked back at Earl. "That's what they were after."

"The tiger?"

"The bounty on its head." Earl's eyes shifted to some movement coming from within the stable.

"How many have you got, Greg?"

"It was just Ben 'til a couple days ago."

"You took these guys from the zoo, didn't you?"

"They were dying."

"So you're the one that busted 'em out."

"You gonna arrest me?"

"I don't arrest people for doing good deeds."

"What do you arrest people for?"

The lack of true justice in Hobart contributed to Millie's death. Earl couldn't escape the haunting reflection that he was partially responsible.

"I never thought they could be so tame." Earl ran his hand back and forth over Ben's back.

"Even the wild ones are somewhat docile. It was no pack of tigers that tore up McPherson's horse. It was a god-damned pack of wild dogs."

"How can you be sure, Greg? These are wild animals."

"I'm telling you it was a bloody pack of dogs. Doesn't even matter. Either way people are gonna kill 'em until there's no more to kill."

"I can talk to the Governor and recommend a ceasefire."

Greg rolled his eyes. "Good luck." He knew the Governor was just as corrupt under McPherson's control.

"So I guess you're taking these guys with you?"

"They'd be dead if we left 'em."

"Well I can pull some strings and see to it that you get 'em to the mainland without any questions."

"That would make things a lot easier, Earl. It'd be appreciated."

"How long you gonna be gone?"

Greg looked into Earl's eyes and shook his head.

"Listen, I'll let the Ferrier know you're taking the tigers across on business. Let's say you're taking them to a zoo on the mainland."

"How soon can you let 'em know?"

"I'll leave now and head straight over."

"Thanks, Sheriff."

"It really is the least I can do."

Just after Earl left, Greg modified the rear bed of the Oldsmobile into an improvised cage utilizing a hog trap. The tigers could now stand and were exposed to fresh air and the luggage was secured atop.

Greg stopped the Oldsmobile at the end of his driveway and looked back at the ranch. He tried to push away the memories, but they kept swarming. Just as he stepped on the accelerator, Petey blurted, "Oh no, Dad! I forgot Ben's Koala."

Greg reached between the seats and tapped on the compartment just behind them.

"No, we didn't." Greg smiled at his son.

"It's in there?"

"You bet ya."

———

The ferry was a massive steel ship, slightly outdated, with forty-five private rooms, a lounge with full bar and a drive on deck that could hold twenty-two automobiles. It was one of only two ferries making the constant loops from Tasmania to the Mainland. The voyage, if on schedule, would take a little more than fourteen hours; departing at 1:00 p.m., it would arrive in Melbourne, Australia, at approximately 3:00 a.m. with unloading beginning at 6:00 a.m. Most boarders emigrating would drive their motorcars directly onto the main deck and retreat to a room for the night, and then exit the ship at 6:00 a.m.

It was a peculiar site for the ferry deckhands and passengers alike to see a motorcar transformed into a rolling cage with three tigers; it stood out like a two-legged horse on a high-wire. Word spread throughout the ship and before long a huge crowd was gathered round the Oldsmobile. Greg fabricated a story of how the tigers were going to be placed in a new zoo being built in the Northern Territory. When the novelty wore off, everyone dispersed back into the bowels of the boat.

Greg and Petey slept on deck beside the car. They spread out their blankets and pillows then nestled in together. The cool night air, coupled with the salty sea breeze made for a much needed, revitalizing night's sleep. Greg's sleep was so deep not even the air horns that sounded at the Melbourne port could wake him; it wasn't until the first hint of sunlight, just before six a.m. that he cracked an eye.

Melbourne wasn't the city Greg had remembered. What used to be a place of opportunity teaming with street vendors, corner musicians, the alluring smell of bakeries and greasy, deep-fried foods, was decimated to a morbid graveyard of a city, riddled with trash, vagrants, panhandlers, and pick pockets, even the air was stale. The great depression swept through the city like a plague, stripping away the vitality of what was once a thriving metropolis.

The hungry street people watched as Greg drove slowly down Main Street, they eyed his spectacle of a motorcar as it passed.

"Where we going?" Petey asked.

Greg glanced at a couple of crooked looking young men standing curbside. It seemed as though they were planning an ambush on the vehicle. "Into the country. As far away from this place as we can get." Greg accelerated away from the conniving onlookers and continued driving northwest until he cleared the city.

Two miles out of Melbourne the paved road became a hardened dirt road. Ten miles outside of Melbourne, they stopped at a nearly run-down petrol station; it was unkempt and haunting, a lone ghostly building under the hot dry sun, and everything was covered with a layer of sandy blonde dust. The attendant was unbecoming. He peered long and hard at the father and son through his excessively thick and nearly opaque glasses from the decrepit wooden chair situated in the shade of the building's dilapidated overhang. He pushed his greasy, thinning black hair out of his eyes, and as he gimped toward the car he turned his head slightly sideways, a thick stream of tobacco spit jettisoned from the blackness of where a tooth once resided. The tooth's absence wasn't all bad; the broken off rotted stump made a perfect spit hole.

Greg unstrapped two ten-gallon gas cans from the roof of the makeshift cage and had them and his Oldsmobile filled.

"Du fawty." The attendant's voice was nearly indistinguishable.

"Oh, two forty?" Greg gave him the exact change, got back in the driver seat, and closed the door. The creepy attendant rested his forearms on Greg's door and leaned in.

"Ware yee eaded?" Greg was nauseated by the stench of death emanating from the attendant's mouth.

"Mildura." Greg held his breath to avoid the stink.

"Takin nem tigaz up daya?" The greasy attendant pulled a wad of mush from the hole in his grin then flicked it to the ground.

"That's right." Greg motioned toward the trio of tigers. "I'd love to stay and chat, but we best be off."

"Wash out fa yee lell buy dare, gad deamed boongs are meekin' a wok a beout…nay all oba da gad damned raud."

"I'm sorry. Did you say to watch out for me boy cus the bongs are all over the road?"

"Yeap. Facking boongs."

"I'm sorry." Greg was puzzled. "What's a Bong?"

"Abbees." The attendant grunted.

"Aborigine?"

"Yeap." Greg wanted to leave, he was readily capable of vomiting from the putrid death rot spewing from the man's oral cavity, but curiosity got the best of him.

"Why do you call 'em bongs?"

"Ids da sownd dey make win day heet yor bool gawd." The attendant smiled, releasing pure hideousness.

"Ahhhhhh, it's the sound they make when they hit your bull guard." Greg faked a laugh. "Very funny."

"Ids true." The attendant pushed his glasses closer to his eyes and peered over at Petey.

"Well, we'll be leaving now." Greg started the car, but the attendant stayed pressed against his door. "Good talkin' to ya. We gotta get goin'." The attendant was staring at Petey like a child eyeing a lollipop. Greg took notice and stepped on the accelerator, forcing the weirdo to get jolted from the car.

Petey looked up at his father. "I didn't like that guy, Dad."

"Aw, he wasn't so bad." Greg smiled at Petey.

"So are we gonna live in Mildura, Dad?"

"That's the plan, buy a nice lil' ranch and start over. You, me and Benjamin."

"What about the other tigers?"

"We're gonna have to find a nice place to set them free."

"Can't we keep 'em, Dad?"

———

Mildura was a newly developing agricultural stronghold. Its system of rivers and lakes provided plenty of irrigation for both crops and cattle.

Many Aborigines made Mildura their home due to its fertile lands and abundance of food. Rolling green pastures coupled with many water sources made it a prime attraction to produce farmers and ranchers. Greg saw it as a perfect retreat from the tainted Tasmania.

They were a little more than midway to Mildura when they rolled up on the tail end of a caravan of Aborigines trekking along the dirt road. They were marching in single file; their faces were somber, perhaps from exhaustion, or maybe from bearing witness on their journey to the vanishing homeland the white men were so quick to claim as their own. Not too long ago they were free to roam, forage, hunt and live freely, but now their home was riddled with fences, borders, and racist white folk.

Petey studied each brown face as the Oldsmobile crept past. He had never seen so many natives. Nearly all of the Tasmanian Aborigines had been massacred in the mid eighteen's and those who surrendered died of new diseases which were unknowingly released upon them by the British settlers.

Nearly a quarter mile down the road, Greg saw another group of Aborigines stopped and huddled around something. As the Oldsmobile lurched closer he could see a pregnant woman sitting on the ground, surrounded by the others. Greg pulled the Oldsmobile just ahead of them and killed the engine. He drew a few glares from a couple of untrusting tribesmen.

"Stay here," he ordered Petey. Greg popped the door open and rushed toward the group.

"Howdy, mates. Can I help you guys out?" A few of the men gave him a quick untrusting glance but said nothing; they turned their attention back toward the young female sitting off the road, holding her belly.

"How far along is she?" Greg asked the growing crowd.

A young man spoke up. "Six months or so."

Greg darted back to his car, grabbed a plastic jug of water, and then ran back to the woman. He unscrewed the cap and handed it to her. Without hesitation she began chugging away at the cool, clear water.

"Are you guys headed to Mildura? This heats a lil' too much for a—" Greg said.

The young Aborigine interrupted. "Yeah, Mildura."

"Why don't you let her ride with me? I could squeeze another one a you guys in if you like? She really shouldn't be walking like this."

"Since when does one a you give a wallop bout one a us?" An older frizzy haired twenty something Aborigine spoke up.

"Look, I know there are some real scummies out there, but I'm not one of 'em."

"Then why ya got three coorina's locked up in the back a ya motorcar?" A few of the English-speaking Aborigines looked toward Greg's car and then looked back at Greg with disgust.

"It's not like it looks—"

"Stole 'em from the wild so you can put 'em on show?" the frizzy haired Aborigine snapped.

"Quite the opposite. I stole 'em from a zoo in Tasmania so I could set 'em free. They were starving to death." The frizzy haired Aborigine squinted at the tigers then looked at Greg knowing he spoke the truth.

The Aborigine dropped his tension. "You ain't like the lot of 'em. You don't mind giving her a ride to Mildura?"

"Not at all. I'd feel guilty if I didn't."

"She's toting mine in her belly."

"Well, that settles it. I'll take you both ahead."

The young Aborigine spoke in his native language to two of the elders. He pointed at the tigers and his voice escalated. The elders conversed in an undecipherable ancient language, and then the eldest laid his hands on the young father's shoulder. The eldest closed his eyes, stomped the end of his walking stick on the ground three times, and then placed his hand over Greg's heart.

Greg looked over at the young father who then gave a single nod. With his other hand, the elder started grinding his stick into the hardened dirt road; the heavy friction of wood on dirt echoed through Greg's ears, as if the energy was being transferred through the Aborigines hand and into Greg's body. One after another he twisted his staff until finally, his eyes sprung open. The elder kept his hand upon Greg's chest and peered toward the motorcar.

"Tungi ni gubbah undulak dobi pikano anuka deemo." While he spoke, the entire group of Aborigine's turned their attention to the motorcar, toward Petey. Petey looked behind himself to see what they were staring at, and then realized it was him. He felt uneasy but was enthralled by the mysticism.

"He says you're special people and that your son is a great spirit. A savior in the next life."

"Next life?" Greg looked back at Petey who was watching on with contentment.

"We'll take you up on that ride," the frizzy haired young man said.

A couple of Aborigines helped the girl up and walked her to the car. Petey climbed into the back and they placed her in the front seat. The eldest of elders looked through the window at Petey, spoke a few native words, and then bowed his head.

Greg looked at his son. "They really like you for some reason, Petey."

The eldest then turned his attention to the tigers and locked his gaze with Benjamin.

Petey climbed into the driver's seat and popped his head out the window to see what was going on.

The elder reached through the bars and placed his hand on top of Ben's head, raised his stick high into the air, paused, and then slammed it with force into the earth. He twisted the heavy wooden stick into the dirt and started emitting a series of tiger-like barks and chirps.

Greg and Petey were mesmerized; they watched on until the elder became silent and then bowed his head to Benjamin. The elder then spoke to the young father who had climbed atop the cage for the ride into town.

"He says you need to take the Coorinas to Nopango..." the frizzy haired man said.

"Take the tigers to Nopango? I've never heard of it. Where is it?" Greg asked. The young father spoke to the elder in their own language. The elder then turned to the other elders and spoke. One elder drew various lines in the dirt with his stick and pointed northwest, another motioned his hands high in the air then swung them to the ground. They carried on for a moment, until the eldest turned to Greg, spoke in his native tongue, and pointed northwest. The young father translated.

"He says you need to take the tigers to Nopangi. It's very important that you do so."

"Okay, but I don't know where it is."

"He says to follow the sun as it prepares to sleep."

"So head northwest."

"Nopangi is a hidden place, it's sacred, and he says his visions show you there."

"Is this a real place?"

"Oh, it's real, it's a protected place. He says it's very important for you to follow the sun. This is the only time of year when the sun will lead you to Nopangi. He says this is how he knows its fate. He wants to make sure you'll get your son and the tigers to Nopangi. Will you take 'em?"

"I…I reckon I haven't much of a choice."

The elder spoke a few words and then frizzy translated. "He says he knows you will. It's your destiny."

"Alright then, I guess it's settled. How the heck will I know when I get there?"

The young man spoke to the elder again, after a couple minutes of animated conversation, the young frizzy haired father-to-be translated. "He says you will travel for six days, you will come to a great canyon and beyond the canyon lies an ancient forest. He says the forest will welcome you."

"Okay, six days, a great canyon, and then an ancient forest that'll welcome us."

"He says that I should go with you. They will care for my woman."

The reality of it all started to settle on Greg. "Um…well…I really hadn't planned on all this, I was just trying to set these tigers free and buy a nice lil' place in Mildura."

The elder could sense Greg's reluctance and offered a reply.

The young man translated. "He says he is not worried. He has seen it and so it shall be." When the young father finished translating, the elder smiled, laughed and nodded his head at Greg.

How did I get myself into this? "Well, let's get the wheels turning," Greg said, and he climbed in and waved goodbye to the crowd of natives. He accelerated slowly and kept the speed to a minimum for the safety of the young Aborigine sitting on top of the wobbly make-shift cage.

The frizzy haired Aborigine leaned his head toward Greg's window. "My name's Jannali."

Greg spoke loud against the wind. "Nice to meet you, Jannali, I'm Greg and this is Petey."

"My woman's name is Warahtah, it means red flower."

Petey raised his voice a bit so Jannali could hear him over the rustling wind and engine. "What's your name mean?"

"Full moon, I was born on a full moon." Jannali pointed toward the sky.

Greg kept his eyes on the road ahead. "Does Warahtah speak English?"

"Not a lick. She's been with the Gomaki group her entire life. I was raised on a ranch with me mum, brotha and fatha. We were basically slaves until the old bastard croaked. After that we were free, so we met up with the Gomaki's. I love being with these guys, but the rest of me family didn't like the nomadic life. They moved on to another ranch to live a simple life. They got used to keepin' it simple. Not me though. I'm all for adventure."

"So you learned English on the ranch?"

"No way. Me and my brotha went to the public school."

"That explains your English. So where in Mildura am I taking you?"

"You're taking my wife to the Callandu outpost. I'm staying with you guys."

"The Callandu outpost? I'm not sure where that's at."

"You can't miss it. It's a big Aborigine settlement just before you get to Mildura."

Greg nodded. "So what is all this talk about my son being a great savior?"

Petey looked up at his dad. "Me?"

"Yeah, you. Mudalla is our eldest of elders. He's a great healer and shaman. Years ago, he was nearly killed by a brown snake. They say he slept for a more than three weeks and when he woke up he was changed. They say he always has one foot in the spirit world. That's where he gets his information."

"And so what was all that talk about my son?"

"He said your son is special. He also said that one of these tigers is special, and that the two of them will come back together in another life, as one great savior."

Greg smirked in disbelief. "Let me get this straight. He said my son and one of the tigers will come back in another life as some sort of great savior?"

"Yeah, he said their souls are joining as one. Sounds crazy, but he sees what he sees."

"Do any of his visions actually come true?"

"All of 'em."

CALLANDU OUTPOST

Mainland Australia - 1935

THE CALLANDU ABORIGINE CAMP WAS SITUATED ON THE WEST SIDE of the open dirt road, six miles before Mildura. It was a nice settlement by Aboriginal standards; initially built by early white settlers who relocated further north into the more fertile Mildura, they gave it to a group of local nomads in 1898, who then turned it into an open outpost for traveling Aborigines. The landscape was rugged, typical of the Australian outback; flat and sandy with a bit of rock, but littered with gum trees, the occasional palm and various low growing succulents.

There weren't many permanent residents at Callandu; it was more of a stopping point for Aborigines on walkabout. It became a well-known destination for the traveling nomadic tribes. Once there, they would rest, trade, and interact with the other tribes that gathered, and in return they would all partake in maintaining the outpost. There were eight cabins, various stick and mud shelters, a freshwater well, a sizeable emu ranch and a large produce garden maintained by the permanent residents.

A nightly fire, storytelling and a smoke ceremony took place whenever a group visited. The smoke ceremony consisted of burning piles of green leaves from various trees, the smoke was then fanned around an individual in an effort to relinquish spirits not needed in this life. The overall morale of the Aborigines across Australia was sinking due to the ever-increasing racism and constant confiscation of native land, however, the mood at Callandu was always friendly and inviting.

As the odd-looking motorcar pulled into Callandu, heads turned. A group of twelve Aboriginal travelers were sitting around a dry pile of wood gathered for the nightly fire. They couldn't help but stare at the oddity that had pulled up.

Greg gave an awkward wave to the group then popped the latch on his door. Jannali jumped from the mass of luggage and landed beside the passenger door. Petey exited through his dad's open door, unable to break his stare off the circle of motionless heads staring at them. Petey stood behind his father, peering out around him.

"G'day." Greg smiled to the group.

Jannali guided Warahtah out of the vehicle. "I doubt these guys speak English."

Warahtah spoke a few native words to Greg then smiled. Jannali translated. "She's very grateful for the ride and wishes you safety on your journey with the tigers."

Greg nodded in appreciation. "Thanks, we're probably gonna need it." He looked back at the tigers and thought about how much his life had changed within the course of a few days. "What's the plan, Jannali?"

"I reckon we get her introduced, should only take a few minutes. We can shove off tonight or in the morning, your choice."

"It's been a long day, how 'bout we leave at dawn."

Jannali introduced Warahtah to a couple of the permanent caretakers of Callandu. They showed great hospitality, placing her in one of the cabins with fresh bush tucker, two emu eggs, a few potato-like roots and a few oddly colored purple spotted fruits. The cabin was a single square room with a front door. The room had a square window at the front and another at the rear of the cabin, both wide open without any glass or coverings. Three wooden cots covered with identical green wool blankets were positioned on each wall except the front and a single four by four wooden table sat in the middle of the floor. The floor consisted of roughly aged wooden planks that were severely bowed; nearly every step forced a ghostly moan.

As the sun faded, Petey and Greg walked the three tigers around the outpost. The Aborigines watched on, enthused by the fact that white people cared so much for the welfare of the tigers. Jannali had explained to the locals how Greg and Petey helped his pregnant wife and told them about the vision his elder had about their upcoming journey. They accepted Greg and Petey as their own.

Greg placed the tigers back into their car mounted cage, poured them a large bowl of dry kibble, and then returned to the cabin.

Petey and Greg sat side by side on one of the cots while Warahtah stretched out on her own and fell fast asleep. Jannali sat in one of the wobbly wooden chairs at the table and rocked back. "She's out 'til tomorrow," Jannali said.

Greg studied the pregnant woman and found himself caught in a moment of déjà vu. For a few seconds he saw Millie lying there, pregnant with Petey and sleeping like an angel. He was brought out of the moment by the sound of chanting.

"Wanna join the group?" Jannali asked.

Greg looked at Petey whose eyes were growing heavy, teetering on the brink of sleep. He rolled up the wool blanket from the other cot, creating a pillow, and then gently laid Petey's head on it. Greg kissed his son's forehead. "Let's do it."

Greg was growing more curious of the Aboriginal culture. The roadside scene from earlier stuck with him; he was feeling drawn to their world.

Jannali and Greg squeezed into the circle, sitting on an unoccupied four-foot section of a log. The orange glow from the sinking sun transformed everything into a reddish bronze. The group of Aborigines had been joined by five of the permanent residents and they formed a complete circle around the fire.

A young Aborigine started blowing into the base of tinder stacked in the fire pit. After a few seconds smoke started billowing and then the bright glow of red fire danced around, awakening the native didgeridoo players. The eerie and haunting musical tones echoed through the hollowed out wooden instruments. The didgeridoos were adorned with earthy hieroglyphics and colored with white ash and berry dye. Each instrument produced a sound unique only to that individual piece of dead wood. And only through the death of a tree, its center having been eaten away by termites, can such a primal instrument come to be. The fire danced along, its flames rising, falling, swaying, and flickering while the didgeridoo unleashed its ancient song.

Greg was caught in the rhythm; he was unknowingly rocking back and forth, under the spell of the tribal ambiance. The drums began to pound, harder and harder until they captured and synchronized everyone within its pulse. Greg couldn't understand the words being chanted but they resonated within his being. He could feel every cell within his body vibrating, weightless and numbing, unexplainable. Time was gone; the entire group was lost in a trance.

Greg's senses returned when the didgeridoo next to him abruptly stopped playing. He turned his head to the right then focused on the native's face; he noticed a steady stream of dark liquid rolling down the man's forehead and into his lap. Greg shifted his eyes downward, looking at the ground below the native's legs. He saw the fluid puddle on top of the parched dirt. Greg watched on as the didgeridoo fell to the ground with a dull thud. The Aborigine then folded over onto his legs and crumpled to the ground, landing on top of his silenced instrument.

The music stopped, and everyone's eyes shifted to the young native who lay motionless atop his didgeridoo. Just as Greg leaned over to assess the young man, an all too familiar sound whizzed past his ear. In that sobering split second, Greg identified it as a rifle shot.

"Get down! Get down!" Greg yelled.

Across the fire sat a middle-aged Aborigine, he looked down at his chest, putting his index finger over a dime sized hole oozing blood. He stood up, looked around at the rest of the scattering group, his eyes squinted, confused, then he toppled forward into the fire. Orange embers exploded into the air as his face and torso impacted the fiery coals.

"Ruunn! They're shooting at you!" Greg yelled but the majority of the group just ducked and looked around. Then Jannali yelled a few words in his native language sending the group running away from the fire and into the cover of darkness.

Greg and Jannali scurried away from the fire and started making their way toward the cabin. "Racist murdering bloody bastards," Jannali raged as he crawled along the ground.

"My rifle's in the car," Greg whispered as he belly-crawled toward the cabin.

"I'll get it," Jannali said.

"The ammo box is underneath the driver's seat."

"I'll be right back." Jannali crouched and ran to the truck as fast as he could.

Greg crawled up the two steps of his cabin and cracked the door just enough to slide in. He shook Petey, waking him out of a deep sleep. "Get on the floor son, there's some bad men out there." Petey laid down on the floor, crawled underneath his bed and began to sniffle. "Everything will be fine, son, but you can't make a sound. Ok?"

Petey nodded and began to cry. He buried his face into his forearms and went silent.

Greg peeked through the window and saw Jannali belly crawling at record speed toward the cabin. He cracked the door and Jannali slid through. In the distance, Greg could see a motorcar approaching.

"Aw, for fucks sake," Greg cried. He recognized the vehicle; it was one of McPherson's personal ranch fleet.

A scenario played out in Greg's head; *McPherson was found alive, he swore revenge, put an absurd bounty on me and then released his goons. But how the hell did he find me?* He quickly realized it must have been relatively easy to track down a motorcar with a cage built into it.

Greg plucked the nine-round magazine from the rifle and loaded it within seconds. He was unscathed by the approaching danger. The loss of his beloved wife coupled with his recent excursions with Smitty, Tanner and McPherson had transformed him; no longer was he the simple and kind husband and father. He had become hardened. He knew what had to be done. Kill or be killed.

The rifle barrel rested on the windowsill, Greg squinted, held his breath, then squeezed. The rifle cracked, sending the lead bullet speeding toward its target. Greg chambered another round then squinted at the sights once again. As he lined up, the motor car swerved off the road, plowing through a dense thicket of scrub brush. His first bullet had found its target.

Greg kept his eye lined up on the rifle sights. "These guys are after me. We need to get the hell away from this camp," he said as he scanned the brush-line for movement.

"What in bloody hell did you do, mate?" Jannali said.

Greg heard the question but didn't answer, focused. "Let's get to the car." He was still scanning for movement when something caught his attention further down the road, another motorcar's headlights. "Shit, there's another car coming."

"Maybe it's just a traveler?" Jannali said.

"We're not sticking around to find out. Can you drive?"

Jannali grinned. "Does a Koala shit in a tree?"

"Bring the car up to the steps. I'll cover you."

"Alright." Jannali looked back at Warahtah who was still asleep—completely oblivious. "Typical."

"You wanna take her with us, Jannali?"

"If I wake her now those guys out there would be the least of our worries."

Greg scanned with his rifle while Jannali crept to the car. The moon provided just enough light to detect any movement above the brush-line. The Aborigines had all disappeared into the darkness, a skill of which they were masters.

Jannali reached the car and climbed in through the open window. The tigers were antsy, pacing and staring into the night from all the commotion. The car roared to life and within seconds was at the steps to the cabin. Jannali reached over and forced the passenger door open. Greg darted onto the porch and raised the rifle to his eye. "Okay, Petey, run!"

Petey crouched and ran, jumping from the porch into the front seat and then climbed into the backseat. Greg side-stepped, keeping the rifle aimed until he was against the car, then he dropped into the seat. The tires kicked bits of rock and dirt as it fish-tailed its way onto the dirt road. "Keep the lights off."

Greg leaned his head out the window, trying to locate the second motor car, but he couldn't see its headlights. *How many god-damned bounty hunters are gonna be after me?*

WESTWARD BOUND

Mainland Australia - 1935

THEY REACHED THE OUTSKIRTS OF MILDURA IN LESS THAN TWENTY minutes, sometime after midnight, stopping at a closed petrol station. The station was an isolated building directly on the main road just before entering the small township of Mildura. Petey watched on as his dad pried at the lock securing the fuel pump. It was an odd feeling for Petey to see his father breaking the law; it was so out of character.

After refueling and commandeering three extra fuel cans from the station, they were on their way.

"So much for leaving at first light," Greg mumbled. "Am I even headed in the right direction?"

"We'll need to drive north 'til about sunrise and then we'll start heading west. It's the afternoon and evening sun that will give us our bearing toward the *ancient forest*."

"Geez, this is so damned crazy."

"Ain't it though," Jannali said. He was raised with both the Aboriginal and white culture; he understood how insane the entire journey must have sounded to Greg.

After driving north for five hours the dirt road ended at a T-junction and two barely visible service roads took over, one east and one west. The service road was basically a path made by motorcars making long treks across the outback. The terrain was worn where each tire would tread, but the center was overgrown with grasses. The surrounding area was flat; the low-lying dry scrubs were scattered among taller clumps of healthy gum trees and palms. Greg stopped the car and killed the engine. Everyone, including the tigers, were able to take a quick pee break and stretch.

After pouring an entire can of gas into the nearly empty tank, Greg stood behind the car and stared long and hard at the road behind them, searching for any sign of a motorcar. He thought he may have spotted the slightest movement shimmering on the horizon but couldn't be sure; the unease was enough to end the break and fire the engine.

"I guess *this* is where we start heading west," Greg said. Jannali nodded in agreement as Greg spun the wheel to the left and headed west.

"Did you see something back there, Greg?"

"Not sure."

Petey wrestled with the back seat, trying to get comfortable. "How long 'til we get there, Dad?" Petey's voice was dragging from lack of sleep.

"Not sure, son, not sure."

———

Dawn arrived, and Greg kept driving; the fresh blanket of sunlight was a godsend. Now he could see if they were being followed. There was no sign of anyone behind them. He drove west until the car started sputtering and then came to a rolling stop. Greg wasn't concerned; he was too tired to be. He staggered out of the car, pulled another gas can from atop the cage and then poured its entire contents into the tank. He then threw it back on top of the cage, secured it, climbed back into the driver's seat and started driving. All while everyone slept in the cool morning air.

The terrain became void of nearly all trees as they approached noon. The grassy service road had turned into a sand and rock trail, barely visible in the desert-like terrain. Greg had pulled the car under the last small cluster of trees for as far as the eye could see. He felt a little more confident they weren't being followed, so much so that he sat down, leaned back against one of the tires and passed out. Jannali kept a constant eye on the trail behind them, allowing Greg to get some much-needed rest.

"Wake up, mate." Jannali shook Greg's shoulder. "Come on, man, wake up." He shook a little harder with more urgency in his voice.

Greg's eyes cracked open then focused on Jannali. His initial grogginess gave way to a moment of confusion. He looked up at the strangely familiar Aborigine, but Jannali hadn't been embedded into his long-term memory yet. He looked at him and waited while his mind pieced it all together; his scrambled thoughts started coming together, allowing him to finally recognize the young Aborigine and their dire situation.

Jannali pointed. "There're two cars heading this way." He offered his hand, pulling Greg from the ground.

Greg looked in the direction Jannali was pointing. "Shit." He saw two cars heading straight toward them. Greg scanned the landscape for any sort of cover, but it was flat and un-obscured; the desert-like terrain held no hideouts. "Did you refuel, Jannali?"

"Right on, mate."

"Tigers good to go?"

"Good to go, Greg. Petey and I just loaded 'em up."

Greg ran his fingers through his hair and exhaled deeply. "We've got no way of knowing if they're the bad guys. We've got to get moving."

"Agreed." Jannali shuffled to the passenger seat, climbed in and slammed the door.

The driver's door slammed shut and Greg cranked the engine. *Juh juh, juh juh, juh juh, juh, juh.*

"Shit! Not now!" Greg pleaded. He turned the key again. "*Juh, juh, juh, juh, juh, juh.*"

"Sounds like the battery's out on holiday," Jannali said.

"We've gotta push start it." Greg put the shifter in neutral, and then he and Jannali jumped out and ran behind the car. They noticed the two cars were getting closer. Greg and Jannali both leaned on the rear of the vehicle and pushed. It was like trying to push through wet concrete; the sand was unforgiving. They pushed harder and harder until finally the wheels started to turn. "Faster, Jannali, faster!"

Jannali pushed with everything he had. He glanced over at Greg just in time to see a bullet rip into the rear metal trunk panel, leaving a dime sized hole. Greg heard the dull thump and looked toward Jannali; their eyes met, then a barrage of three more bullets riddled into the trunk between the two men.

"Push, god-damn it!" Greg yelled. Sweat started rolling off the two men as they pushed with every ounce of strength they could muster. The Oldsmobile started gaining some momentum. Greg broke from his position, ran to his door, jumped in the driver's seat, and slammed the stick into gear.

The Oldsmobile jerked, then sputtered, it slowed drastically, jerking once more before coming to a deadening stop, sputtering, sputtering, and then a loud exploding backfire followed by a small smoke cloud, one last sputter, then the engine roared to life.

Greg pumped the gas and started to accelerate. Jannali dove into the passenger seat, dodging the barrage of whizzing bullets. Greg floored the Oldsmobile and sped off with the two cars less than a quarter mile behind them.

"I just topped off the tanks," Jannali said. "We can out drive 'em."

"Yeah, maybe. I wonder if they brought along extra fuel."

"So how do you know those guys, Greg?"

"I don't know them. I know their boss."

"I reckon he's the guy you done wrong."

"I didn't do anyone wrong."

"Well he's sure as hell got it out for you, sending his blokes all the way from Tasmania just to have a go at ya. Mind if I ask—"

Greg interrupted. "His men killed my wife." He paused. "So I killed those men, and I hurt *him*. I hurt him pretty good."

"Mate, I'm sorry."

"Don't be. I've accepted it." Greg didn't want sympathy, he had already dealt with the tragedy and was in survival mode; he wouldn't allow any other emotions to interfere with his newly focused world.

"Understood, sounds like they've stopped shootin' at us."

"We're obviously out-gunned, we're gonna have to out-run 'em."

"Or out-smart 'em," Jannali said. "If we could only disable their cars. They'd be done for out here."

Greg shook his head and threw his hands up. "And how do you suppose we *disable* their cars?"

"Don't really know."

"Well, if you figure something out let me know." Greg leaned out the window to get a look at how far back the pursuers were. "Looks like we're keeping the distance."

"What if we shot a hole in their radiator?" Jannali blurted.

Greg thought about it for a moment. "Crikey, that's a damned good idea. How are ya with a rifle?"

"Good enough to hit a bloody radiator."

Greg looked over at Jannali. "Do it, but be careful, they're gonna be shooting at ya."

"Jannali, No!" Petey cried from the backseat. The faithful Aborigine was sitting in the spot that his mother had taken for as long as Petey could remember. At first it was odd for him, but the oddness quickly transformed into comfort. The thought of Jannali removing himself from that special seat and putting himself in danger, frightened him.

Petey threw his arms around the Aborigine's neck and held tight.

"It's ok, Petey, I'll be right back." Jannali looked over at Greg. "I'm touched, Petey, but listen." Jannali broke from his grip and faced him. "I'll be right back." Petey let out a whimper. "I'm gonna go out there, shoot a hole into the front of their car and then I'll get right back in, alright?"

"He'll be right back," Greg said.

Petey lurched forward, threw his arms around Jannali's neck again, squeezed as tight as he could and then fell back into his seat, releasing him. "Be careful, Jannali."

Jannali rubbed the top of Petey's head, grabbed the rifle, then forced his torso through the window and seated himself on the ledge. He raised the sight to his eye but lowered the gun immediately. "I can't get a shot from here; the cage is in the way!" Jannali yelled against the wind.

Jannali climbed out the window and onto the wooden platform, placing himself behind the tigers' cage. The tigers, excited by Jannali's presence, stood up and sniffed at him through the bars. "Nice to see you guys too."

He squatted and leaned against the cage, resting the rifle upon it. He lined up the sights on the front end of the first vehicle. The bumpy terrain was more than challenging, the rifle bounced, sending the sights in and out of range, over and over. Jannali couldn't get a good bead on the radiator, but he had an idea. He leaned back toward the window and yelled in. "It's too bumpy! Stop the car for a second!"

Greg stuck his head out the window and looked back at the pursuing vehicles; after a quick glance he decided they were far enough away to make a quick stop. "Get ready!" Greg yelled out to Jannali who then braced himself against the cage. He hit the brakes and skidded to a complete stop. Jannali stood straight up, raised the rifle, lined up the sights, then squeezed.

Two seconds later, the front end of the first vehicle became engulfed in steam. Jannali made a direct hit. "Woo-Hoo!"

Greg looked back and saw the front end of the first car billowing in steam. "Son of bitch! You did it!" Greg yelled, stomping on the accelerator, and nearly throwing Jannali from the platform.

Three miles later and there was no sign of the second vehicle. Had they given up? Unlikely. McPherson would have put too high a bounty on his head for anyone to come this far and simply give up. Greg knew they'd be back.

They followed the sun's westerly bearing for another two hours until it disappeared below the horizon. As soon as darkness arrived they stopped to refuel and relieve themselves and the tigers. Jannali noticed the unfamiliar landscape was void of all plant life, with no cover, nowhere to hide and nothing to hide behind. The only obscurities in the sandy desert terrain were small boulders of various sizes littered across the background.

Greg was withdrawn, keeping to himself and speaking very few words; after relieving himself he climbed back into the driver's seat while Petey and Jannali walked the tigers. Everyone was tired, but Greg was exhausted, slumping over the steering wheel and closing his eyes. Jannali loaded the tigers back into the cage then walked over to Greg's door. "Y'all right, mate?"

Greg raised his head a bit then dropped it back onto the wheel.

"How 'bout I drive, and you sleep?"

Greg mumbled a few syllables of incoherent sounds then became silent.

"Let's get you into the other seat, I'm driving."

Greg didn't respond.

"Looks like your dad's tuckered out." Jannali grinned at Petey, who had already curled up under a blanket in the back seat.

Jannali grabbed Greg's shoulders and leaned him back against the seat noticing his shirt was oddly damp. Jannali leaned in to examine the wet shirt and caught a whiff of something familiar. He grabbed Greg's button-down shirt and ripped it open, exposing his bare chest. He leaned Greg out of the car and into the moonlight, scanning his torso until he saw a tiny hole just under the center of his left collar bone—trickling a slow steady stream of blood. Jannali realized Greg had been shot while they were pushing the car.

That can't be the entrance wound. His back was to the shooters, it must be the exit wound. Jannali leaned him against the wheel, pushed Greg's shirt down and examined his back. Sure enough, he found a small entrance wound in his left shoulder blade.

Jannali slapped Greg's face, causing him to open his eyes. "Damn it, mate. Why the hell didn't you tell me you were shot?" Jannali kept his voice low as not to alarm Petey. He pulled Greg's limp body to the ground and leaned him against the front tire. "You been bleeding out ever since we pushed the car?"

Jannali could see that Greg had lost a lot of blood and his first priority was to stop any further bleeding. The quick-thinking Aborigine leaned into the car and pulled one of Greg's shirts from the back seat; tearing it into several long strips. Jannali wrestled with the pieces of shirt, but due to the location of the wound, he couldn't get a bandage tight enough to stop the bleeding. He pressed a ball of torn shirt over the wound and held it tight. *Shit! Now what?*

He looked around at the rocky surroundings and then back behind the car, he listened for the sound of an approaching vehicle, but all he heard was the rhythmic breathing of a sleeping child.

Jannali felt helpless, but then it hit him. He let go of Greg's wound and leaned into the car, pulling his sack and the rifle from the passenger floorboard. He dropped the magazine from the rifle and removed a single round from it. Biting the soft lead end of the bullet, he twisted and pulled on the casing, separating it from the slug.

Jannali scrubbed at Greg's wound with the bandage. He removed all the dried blood and thick clumps of coagulation. He spread the wound open with his fingers and poured the entire round of gunpowder into it. Reaching into his sack, he felt around until his fingers clutched a matchbook. "This may hurt a bit." Jannali plucked a single match and placed the book in his mouth, and as if he had done it a thousand times before, he struck the match single handedly against the igniter strip. Jannali leaned in to Greg's ear and whispered, "Remember, your son's sleeping, so don't scream too loud." Then he touched the burning match to the hole in Greg's chest.

The powder ignited into a short burst of sparks. Greg grunted, pushing with his legs, writhing hard against the tire. His eyes opened and fired at Jannali. "Bloody fucking hell." The sizzling combustion of black powder and the searing of flesh jolted him from his lifeless stupor.

"I told you it'd hurt." Jannali smirked. "And why the hell didn't you tell us you were shot?"

"So that's what I smell like on the bar-b," Greg slurred. Weakened, he struggled to speak.

Jannali fanned the smoke and stench of gun powder and burnt flesh. "I really think you should tell me the next time you get shot."

"*Next time?*" Greg laughed a bit, then laid his head back against the wheel well and closed his eyes.

"You ok?"

"Tired," Greg whispered himself to sleep.

Jannali pondered his options; keep driving and continue running from the pursuers or stay and fight. Jannali had grown tired of running, always looking over his shoulder, in fear of the bounty hunters catching them. This could be the perfect time for an ambush; he had the cover of darkness and the element of surprise, but he was alone, tired and in need of sleep.

He scanned in all directions; then focused his eyes upon the silhouette of three large boulders nearly four feet high and approximately seventy-five yards southeast of their current position. It wasn't much for cover, but at least it was something. He reached into the car, heaved the ammo box onto the empty driver's seat and then opened it revealing a shiny pile of about a hundred rounds, maybe more.

AMBUSH

Mainland Australia - 1935

THE TATTERED OLD TRUCK RATTLED HYSTERICALLY WITH EVERY ripple of the sandy path. It sounded like its innards were breaking apart and falling off, but bump after bump after bump, it somehow continued on.

Two greasy men sat in the back on top of a legless and bloodied kangaroo carcass; dead for nearly two days, the gory corpse was beginning to stink. While the outermost parts of the roo were beginning to become rancid, the innermost meat was still edible; they would cut away the decaying meat and consume the flesh just underneath. Unphased by the gnarly carcass, both men scanned the darkness for any sign of McPherson's most wanted.

Within the small, cramped cab of the truck, the stench of body odor and rotted teeth were stagnating. For the past five years, the two men in the cab had made a living killing tigers, but now the tigers were few, leaving the unscrupulous killers scrounging for work. The tiger hunters couldn't refuse McPherson's irresistible offer; kill the father, son, and tigers, in exchange for their own motorcar, full time jobs at the ranch and five hundred shillings a piece. Five hundred shillings was a small fortune. It would allow the men to buy their own home, property, livestock and the finest of amenities; a prize with such an allure that it could turn good men bad in desperate times.

Mighty Joe McPherson, the victimizer, had been victimized; the untouchable and immortal McPherson had been touched and mortalized. No longer was he the invincible god of Tasmania, he bled like all men.

"Stop da truck," Frankie blurted from the passenger seat. Louie raised his foot off the gas, nearly toppling the two men in the back.

"What the fuck? You see somthin'?" Louie snapped.

"Stop da god-damned truck," Frankie snapped back.

Louie let the truck come to a rolling stop. Frankie stepped out and focused his eyes in one direction.

"Somnabitch. I see 'em!" Frankie whispered.

"I'll be damned, dem idiots dun went a made camp behind them rocks." Louie could barely see Greg's Oldsmobile silhouetted by the fire light a little less than half a mile southwest of them.

"Let's sneak up on 'em." Lenny jumped from the flatbed to the ground. "And shoot da shit out of 'em."

Louie cocked his rifle. "Stupid fuckers didn't think we'd see dat fire behind them rocks."

Louie assumed control of the group. "Alright, here's what we're gonna do. They're behind that cluster of rocks. We gonna make our way behind 'em, surround 'em, then open fire on my signal. They ain't never gonna know what hit 'em. Lenny, you and Bill make your way around 'em and move up good 'n close. Me 'n Frankie's gonna take 'em from this side. Don't shoot until you see me raise my rifle, then let 'em have it."

The four men crept off into the dark; Lenny and Bill went out and around, making their way to the opposite side of the camp. As the men surrounded the group, they could see three covered bodies sleeping beside the fire. The small fire crackled, drowning out any sound of the invading hunters.

Frankie and Louie inched closer to the sleeping bodies, placing themselves just forty feet away. Frankie raised his arm in the air and motioned to Bill and Lenny to get in closer. Soon all four hunters were touched by the dying fire's orange glow.

Louie raised the rifle to his eye and the other three men followed his lead. Crack! Louie's rifle released the first shot. Crack, crack, crack, crack.

All four rifles started unloading on the sleeping bodies; muzzle flashes flickered like lightning. One after another they cocked their rifles, unleashing a fury of lead into the sleeping targets. Crack, crack, crack, crack, crack.

The hunters were so focused they didn't notice that one of their rifles had stopped firing. Then another rifle stopped firing. Frankie unloaded his last round into the largest body, and then looked across the fire toward Lenny and Bill. They were both lying motionless on the ground. Startled and confused, he looked to his right. Frankie was lying on the ground clutching his chest. Louie knelt down just in time to hear the crack of a single rifle and a bullet whiz just over his head.

Frankie grabbed Louie behind his knee and clenched. "We…we…been…been…" Frankie gasped. "We…been ambushed." Frankie's grip loosened, his body relaxed, and eyes went blank.

Louie belly crawled away from his dead friend, making his way to the three lifeless bodies that had been sleeping by the fire. He reached out with his rifle barrel and forced off the blanket, revealing a pile of rocks.

"Rat bastards!" He grunted, realizing he had been setup. He knew he didn't have a chance; he was illuminated by the fire and had no idea where his attackers were. Louie raised the rifle with both arms over head and then stood up. "Ya got me!" he yelled out into the night. Louie threw the gun down and kept his arms above his head. "Ya can't shoot an unarmed man in cold blood."

The metallic sound of an unseen rifle chambering a bullet unnerved him. "I'm sorry for Christ's sake."

From out of the darkness a single body emerged into the orange glow of the dying fire. "I ain't gonna kill you in cold blood, not the way you just killed them sleeping rocks." Jannali couldn't help but crack a grin.

Louie's head jerked to the left toward the voice. "You gotta be kidding me. A fuckin' bong did us in?" Louie moaned in humiliating defeat.

"So how much they paying you to kill off a family?" Jannali spat in disgust, just missing Louie.

A tired voice emanated from the darkness. "Don't answer that. I don't want to know."

"Feeling better, mate?" Jannali asked. "Thought you were sleeping."

"How in bloody hell am I supposed to sleep with all the damned shooting?" Greg entered the dim circle of fire light, and visibly weakened, sat back on a three-foot boulder.

"Sorry, out of courtesy I guess I shoulda used me knife," Jannali quipped.

"So you come out here to kill me, huh?" Greg said. "You know you shouldn't have come out here. It's a very bad thing what you set out to do. There's consequences."

Louie interrupted, trembling. "Look, I'm sorry, just let me go on my way."

"There may be no law in Tasmania…"

Louie dropped to his knees, put his hands together and shook them at Greg. "I'll tell 'em I never seen ya."

"But there is law here." He pulled the hellish Bowie knife from behind his back, tilting the blade against the reflection of dying fire.

"Wha…wha…what ya gonna do wit' dat?" Louie twitched, resting his hands upon his head.

"You really wanna know? Ok, I'll tell you." Greg didn't give Louie a chance to answer. "I'm gonna push this blade through your belly, through your muscles, into your guts, and then I'm gonna force it up," Greg motioned the knife upwards. "Toward your heart, and hopefully, the tip will just barely pierce it, and you will slowly bleed to death on the inside."

"Aw, come on man, you can't do me like this, I have a wife. I'm bloody sorry!" Louie cried.

"Isn't it funny how all the evil and wicked men become sorry on their deathbeds?" Greg sighed. "By that time, it's just way too late for apologies." Greg stood, tucked the knife into the front of his pants and started walking toward Louie. "If he tries to run, shoot 'em in the back, I haven't got it in me to chase 'em down."

Jannali nodded, raised the rifle, and kept quiet, this was Greg's show.

Greg paced slowly back and forth in front of Louie. "Ya know, if I were the only one you were after, I probably would let you go." Greg looked into the nervous man's eyes. "But it's not just me." Greg kept his pace. "You crossed a line." Greg turned and passed in front of Louie again. "You're a bad, bad man."

Louie contemplated running but knew that he couldn't beat a bullet at such close range. "Look, mate, you don't have to do this. You can have my truck, our rifles, take everything, just leave me out here in the desert." Louie leaned back on his knees in fear that Greg would sling the blade and slice his throat.

"Sshh. It's too late. You're a dead man. You sealed the deal the second you became a threat to my son. There's no turning back now. Fair is fair, right? I mean, you *were* gonna kill me, my son and our tigers."

"Dad?" Petey's voice came from behind the boulders.

Greg turned toward his son's voice. "Didn't I tell you to stay with the tigers, Petey?"

"I got scared. Is that one of the guys that's been trying to kill us?" Petey stood still and stared at the grungy man.

Greg looked back at Louie then paused. "Yes, son, this is the man who was going to kill us."

"I'm sorry, kid. I ain't gonna ki—"

"Shut up! How dare you speak to my son." Greg's rage took over; hatred poured through his voice. Greg stopped his rage and spoke in an odd calm. "A few minutes ago, you were unloading bullets into what you thought was my sleeping son."

"I'm sorry," Louie cried. "I'm so sorry." Louie lost it, his cries destroyed the silence of night and resonated within little Petey's ears.

Greg was irritated by the sudden chaos. *I can't very well kill this bastard in front of my son.* "God-damn it, Jannali, get Petey out of here."

Petey started to whimper at the thought of the crying man being killed. "You gonna kill 'em, Dad?"

Petey cried as Jannali grabbed his arm and began pulling him into the darkness. "Don't do it, Dad." He wrestled against Jannali's grasp, looking back until he could only see the faintest bit of firelight. Greg looked into his son's eyes as they disappeared into the darkness.

———

That morning, Jannali was awakened by the sound of Greg's Oldsmobile coming to life. He and Petey slept together on the ground wrapped in wool blankets. The sun was just breaching the eastern horizon, bringing with it a blanket of warmth.

Greg called from the driver's seat. "You guys ready?"

Jannali opened his eyes and peered up at Greg.

"You don't quit, do ya?" Jannali yawned and shook Petey's shoulder. "Wakey, wakey."

Petey wiggled a bit then sat upright with a blanket wrapped around his shoulders. Petey's sleepy eyes went straight to his father. "Did you kill 'em, Dad?" He squinted as he plucked the dry crust from his eyes.

"He was a real bad man, son," Greg said.

"You killed 'em?" Petey asked.

"No," Greg paused. "I didn't kill 'em."

Caught off guard, Jannali paused as he was throwing the blankets into the back seat. "You didn't?"

"No."

"I knew you wouldn't kill 'em, Dad."

"What'd ya do wit' 'em?" Jannali asked.

"Tied his hands behind his back, and then tied 'em to a hundred kilo rock."

Jannali smiled. He knew the hunter's fate was now far worse than death; he would be forced to drag a boulder in the hot sun, damn near cooking in the heat, with no shelter, shade, or water.

"You give 'em any water?" Petey asked.

"I did indeed. I left him half a canteen."

Jannali was shocked once again. He thought for sure Greg wouldn't have afforded him that luxury. "You did?"

"All he has to do is get his hands untied." Greg winked at Jannali.

Once loaded into the car, Greg angled the wheel and made a wide left turn. They drove slowly toward the tethered man who clambered to his feet when the car approached. Jannali and Petey's necks stretched as the car passed him by, studying the pathetic man staring dumbfounded back at them.

"Why is he naked, Dad?"

Greg gave the man a grin and accelerated away.

ANCIENT FOREST

Australia - 1935

NINE HOURS LATER AND STILL FOLLOWING THE SUN, GREG FOUND himself navigating through nearly uncrossable terrain. There was no longer any sort of road or pathway and there hadn't been for more than five hours. What had been a flat, endless landscape was now a treacherous maze filled with erupted rock. Large sheets of flat rock were showing through the sand in places where the wind had swept them clean. The hard ground was cracked and broken, and the car was taking a beating from the constant jarring. Jannali had to exit the vehicle and guide Greg around some of the more treacherous terrain.

They decided to travel south, breaking away from the sun's bearing in an attempt to traverse the obstructions. They veered off course for more than thirty minutes until they maneuvered up to the ledge of a deep, hellacious canyon.

Greg sank back against his seat. "Let me guess. The forest is on the other side of *that*." Greg nodded toward the unwelcoming canyon of red rock before them.

"I reckon this is the canyon he spoke of." Jannali said, referring to his elder.

"Maybe we can let the tigers out here and just shoo 'em off in that direction," Greg joked.

"No way, Dad!" Petey blurted in the tigers' defense.

They exited the vehicle; Greg opened the tiger cage, while Jannali and Petey walked to the ledge. The tigers were more than able, but Greg helped each one down. He struggled as he lifted and lowered each one to the ground. "Go do your business." Greg leaned against the car, out of breath; he didn't understand why he had become so weak.

After a few minutes of scanning the ledge for vehicle access, they spotted a steep section of the ledge just south of their position that would allow them to drive their car to the bottom of the ravine. Jannali was reluctant, but Greg insisted the car would make it.

Greg grinned as the car leveled off on flat ground at the bottom of the ravine. "That wasn't so bad was it?"

Jannali popped the latch on the door and sprung out of the car. "I've done some stupid mucking in my day, but that was just reckless. I dunno if I'm ever gonna get back in after that. Poor tigers, they had no say in the matter."

"They're fine and we're all in one piece," Greg said.

"I wanna do it again!" Petey said.

Jannali rolled his eyes at Petey. "I knew you'd say that."

———

They set camp for the night at the bottom of the canyon. Petey bid goodnight to the tigers, reaching through the cage bars as they nuzzled at his hands, then he huddled down into his blankets.

Jannali took notice as Greg leaned against the car, struggling to keep upright. Jannali grabbed Greg's bedding and spread it out upon the ground. "You alright, mate?"

"Just exhausted." Greg slid down the side of his Oldsmobile and laid on top of the blankets. "Jannali," Greg whispered.

"Yeah…"

"You're a good man. If…if anything happens to me …"

"Oh, c'mon, mate, don't talk like that."

"I'm serious. Please, take care of Petey."

"Of course."

"There's enough money in the car to buy a small ranch and…"

"Enough, mate. Get some rest." Jannali pulled two extra blankets from the car and spread them out over Greg.

"Petey," Greg called out.

"Yeah, Dad?" Petey rolled over to face his father.

"I love you, son."

"I love you too, Dad."

They didn't bother with a fire even though it would have been concealed by the ravine's walls. They feared it would lead a bounty hunter directly to them, but Greg was confident no bounty hunter could make a successful trek across the desert without a large surplus of gas and food or any sort of road or path to follow.

Jannali and Petey were awakened around two a.m. by the sound of bark-like chirping. The three tigers stood in their cage staring into the darkness toward the source of the sound. Jannali thought it odd for the tigers not to growl or retaliate at the strange sounds, but rather they watched on, listening to the obscure ramblings of the unseen.

"What is that?" Petey nervously whispered to Jannali, sitting up with the blanket pulled over his head like a hood.

"I think they're tigers," Jannali whispered.

"Dad," Petey whispered. "Dad." Greg didn't respond so Petey leaned over and shook him. "Dad…" Still no response. "Dad, wake up."

Jannali crawled over to investigate. "Greg?" Jannali shook Greg's shoulder, fearing the worst until he heard a reassuring snore. "Let's not wake him up. He needs his rest."

One of the caged tigers started chirping back at the unseen tigers, seconds later the other tiger chimed in; within seconds they were barking and chirping together. Ben sat on his haunches and watched on, not participating. The ruckus went on for several minutes then stopped abruptly.

Jannali looked at Petey. "What the heck was all that about?"

"Sounded like they were talkin' to each other," Petey said.

"That's exactly what it sounded like, and I can't believe your dad slept through it. I guess the shows over."

Jannali was the first to wake at the crack of dawn. He went looking for tiger tracks but was unable to find more than just a few barely noticeable impressions left on the pebbly ground.

He then climbed up the steep slope and scanned the desert for any sign of potential followers. Confident there were no more hunters after them, he constructed a small fire from the remnants of long fallen trees that had gathered in the ravine. The smell of coffee permeated the cool air as Jannali pressed the grinds into the bottom of the old tin pot.

"Mornin', Jannali." Petey sniffed the air. "Eggs and bacon, too?"

"Sorry, mate, coffee is about the best I can do this morning. I could cook you up one of those potatoes if ya like." Petey leaned into the car and fumbled around in the backseat then reappeared with a massive three-pound potato.

Petey held up his enormous spud. "Me and my dad can eat this one."

"You could live off that thing for a week," Jannali said.

Petey grabbed a two-gallon tin pot, poured in three inches of water, and set it over the fire.

"Boilin' it up?" Jannali asked.

"Gonna boil it, mash it, then brown it up a bit."

"Aren't you the lil' chef?" Jannali sipped his coffee.

"My mom did all the cookin'."

"I bet she was a *great* cook, huh?"

"The best." Petey smiled.

"She'd be so proud if she could see you cookin' on your own like that."

"She *can* see me. She's right here with us."

"I'm sure she is," Jannali reassured.

"She talks to me," Petey said, poking at the boiling potato.

Jannali initially brushed Petey's claim off as a grief-stricken child's wishful thinking, but Petey was unflinching and over-confident.

"What does she tell you?"

"That soon me and my dad will be with her."

"Speaking of your dad, maybe we should wake him up."

"I'll do it." Petey pushed his pot into the coals and ran to his dad. "Time to wake up, Dad," Petey gently shook his father's shoulder. Greg didn't respond so Jannali pitched in.

"Come on, Greggie. Up and at 'em." Jannali shook Greg's shoulder a little harder. Greg finally grumbled something inaudible and tried to sit up but was unsuccessful.

"Ja…ja…Janalli…" Greg slurred.

"Come on, mate. It's time to get up."

"I can't ge…get up." Greg struggled to get the words out. "I feel…weak."

"Well, let's get some coffee in ya."

"Can…you sit…me…up?"

Jannali grabbed Greg's arm and pulled him up. His body was dead weight. Jannali pulled Greg over to the car and leaned him against the front wheel.

"What's gotten into you?"

"I dunno…sick," Greg mumbled as he closed his eyes and laid his head against the wheel.

"You ok, Dad?" Petey knelt beside him.

Jannali unbuttoned Greg's shirt then pulled it down, revealing his wounded shoulder. "Aw, Christ," Jannali said as he exposed the puss filled wound. "Found the problem. You're infected."

Greg's entire shoulder was red and streaky; pus was oozing from the swollen wound and the redness was starting to make its way up his neck and down his chest.

"Got any mumbo jumbo you can put on it?" Greg slowly grinned.

"You need antibiotics. Looks like its eating you from the inside out."

"Feels like it too."

"Well the good news is that we've found the tigers."

"Didn't know we lost 'em."

"Not our tigers, the ones from the forest. They paid us a visit last night."

"Great," Greg paused. "We can set 'em free now?"

"I don't see why not. The forest has got to be on the other side of that cliff." Jannali pointed to the opposite ledge. "I say we let 'em go now and start making our way outta this ravine, head west toward the coast."

"West?" Greg asked. "Your woman's back east."

"She'll be fine. You, on the other hand, need a doctor."

"I'll be fine." Greg grimaced.

"I'm calling the shots now. We're heading west as soon as we set the tigers loose."

"We gotta wait 'til tonight to set 'em free," Greg said.

"I dunno, you're in bad shape. I don't like the idea of just waitin' around while your infection gets worse."

"Jannali, I won't let you set the—" Greg inhaled, interrupted by the pulsing pain around his left torso. "...set the tigers free until tonight. We didn't come all this way for nothing."

Jannali noted the seriousness in Greg's painful tone. "Alright, alright, you win, but we're heading west as soon as we set 'em free."

"Fine."

———

After exploring the ravine for the better part of the day, Jannali came to the conclusion that their vehicle was stuck. Greg had driven down the slope without giving thought to an exit strategy. The ravine bottom was drivable for about a hundred yards in either direction, but any further past that and it began to fill with rocky obstructions making it impossible to pass via motorcar; Greg had driven the Oldsmobile into a point of no return. Jannali contemplated his options, but there was only one. He would have to leave Greg behind and go for help. Greg's condition was declining, and the futility of the situation was starting to trouble him.

Darkness arrived. Petey and Jannali waited, anticipating the tigers' return. Three hours later, Petey had fallen asleep and still no return. Jannali contemplated setting the tigers free without waking Greg or Petey, but his conscience got the better of him.

The waiting was too much; the sleepy Aborigine laid his head down and shut his eyes. Just as he did, whistle-like chirps started emanating from the darkness. *Soon as I lay down and shut me eyes they show up.*

"Okay, Greg, wake up, time to set 'em free." Jannali shook Greg's shoulder with no response. "Petey, wake up." Jannali shook him. "The tigers are back."

Petey sat up with weary eyes, snapping out of his sleep at the shrill sounds of the nearby tigers.

"Help me wake up your dad."

Petey leaned in and put his face an inch from his father's. "Wake up, Dad, the tigers are back."

Greg slowly opened his eyes, they were heavy and weak. "Okay, son," he whispered. Greg tried to sit up but struggled aimlessly until Jannali grabbed his arm and pulled him into a sitting position, then rotated his body against the wheel of the car.

"You ain't lookin' so hot," Jannali said.

"The tigers, are they here?" Greg whispered.

"Yeah, you ready?"

"Ben…Benjamin…" Greg's eyes closed.

"Ben's staying with us," Petey said.

"Look, mate, I'm letting 'em go. We can't wait any longer." Greg didn't respond. Jannali couldn't waste any more time; he rushed to the tiger's cage and opened the door.

"Not Ben," Petey said. "Ben's staying with us."

"I'm sorry, but if Ben wants to go, then you've got to let him go."

Ben sat at the back of the cage while the other two tigers leapt to the ground. The chirps from the darkness grew louder, triggering responses from both of the tigers. The first tiger emitted a short burst of whistles, looked back at Jannali then darted toward the sounds and out of sight. Petey knelt down and hugged the second tiger around its neck; it returned a few sniffs to the boy's face then trotted off, disappearing into the night. Ben leapt out of the cage and landed beside Petey.

"No, Ben, you're staying here." Petey wrapped his arms around Ben's neck, restraining him. Ben stood there, listening to the sounds of the other tigers.

"If he wants to go, Petey…"

"No!" Petey looked to his dad for help, but he was passed out against the car.

"He belongs out there."

Tears started falling from the boy's eyes as he felt Ben pulling gently away from him. "No, Ben," Petey cried. Ben started forward, pulling gently out of Petey's weakening grasp. "Ben, pleeeaaase," Petey cried. "You're all I've got."

A single tear formed then trailed down Jannali's face.

Ben turned his head toward Petey and released a soft melody of soothing whistles, then pressed his head against the boy's chest. Petey threw his arms around Ben's head and squeezed. "I love you, Ben." His grip loosened as Ben pulled away. Ben walked to Greg and sniffed his face and neck, but there was no response. Ben walked in the direction the other tigers had faded into. Just before Ben was completely out of sight he looked back at the crying boy, then vanished into the darkness.

Jannali embraced him, holding tight. "You're a good boy, Petey." Petey cried himself to sleep in Jannali's arms. It was a surreal moment for the Aborigine. *So this is what fatherhood is like?* He carried Petey to his blankets and covered him up, feeling as though he were covering his own.

As necessary as it was to leave immediately, Jannali allowed Petey to sleep 'til sunrise.

"Greg, wake up. Come on, mate, sun's coming up." Jannali shook Greg. "You too, Petey, wake up, we gotta get moving." Petey sat up and started scanning for Ben.

"Yeah, yeah…hi Millie," Greg blurted.

"It's Jannali, Greg, wake up."

"Lots of…lots of boats in the harbor this…this time of year," Greg mumbled.

"We have to leave now, Petey, get your things." Jannali knew the infection was reaching a point of no return, Greg's confused ramblings were a telltale sign.

Petey pushed the blankets aside and stood, then made a quick scan for Ben. "How's my dad gonna walk?"

"He ain't gonna walk, we're going to get help."

"You mean you're gonna leave him here?"

"We've got no choice, let's go."

Petey began shaking his head. "I'm not leaving my dad."

"You don't have a choice, Petey."

"I'm not leaving." Petey raised his voice.

"Yes, you are."

Petey ran to his father. "Dad, Dad, wake up, please!" Petey shook his father's shoulder. Greg opened his eyes and studied his son's face.

"Petey," Greg murmured.

"Jannali's trying to make me leave you," Petey cried. "Tell him I can stay with you. You need me to take care of you 'til he gets back."

"Jannali," Greg whispered.

"Right here,"

"Let him stay."

"I think it's a bad idea. He's just a boy, you can't even get up and a few minutes ago you were talking cuckcoo."

"I'm fine, and he's plenty capable."

"Alright, look, I'm leaving for help. Ration out the goods and you should have enough tucker for a week or so." Jannali gestured. "Come here, Petey."

Petey paused, then walked slowly toward Jannali.

"Take care of your dad, but more importantly take care of yourself." Jannali hugged the boy and kissed his head. "I'll be seeing you soon."

Petey watched Jannali walk south down the ravine and then disappear behind a cluster of yellow-orange boulders.

———

Petey poked at the fire out of boredom; the first few hours alone were spent listening to his father's unconscious ramblings until he had grown silent, leaning upon the car. When the darkness settled, Petey pulled his father to the ground, rolled a blanket for his head, and covered him up. He stoked the fire and added a few thick branches that Jannali had gathered, while listening to the faint sounds of distant tigers. He wondered where Ben was, what he was doing and how he was making out with his new pack.

Petey grew cold and snuggled in with his father, Greg managed to wrap his arm around him. He held tightly to his father's arm; always safe behind it.

Petey opened his eyes at first light, staring at the smoldering fire, fascinated by the thin line of wavy smoke rising from its lifeless gray ashes. "Morning, Dad," he whispered. "It's time to wake up." Petey pushed against his father's arm, but something didn't feel right.

Petey rolled over and faced his dad. "Dad." He gently tapped his dad's face. "Dad." Petey's voice grew louder. "Dad." Petey's voice cracked. "Dad!" Petey started crying. His father had died in his sleep; his arm still tightly wrapped around his son.

Petey couldn't leave the cold embrace of his father; he lay there, alone, clinging to his lifeless arms, staring into the smoking coals. He was alone and parentless in the unforgiving outback of Australia. The shock of losing both parents hadn't quite settled in. Maybe it never would. He knew that he was alone, and it didn't seem to bother him. Petey lay from sun-up to sundown in his father's lifeless arms.

The sun was dimming when Petey rubbed his eyes, still behind his father's final embrace. From across the fire-pit a figure approached and as it neared it started moving faster toward him. Alarmed, Petey sat up beside his father.

"Ben!" Petey yelled. Ben ran to Petey, slamming his flank against him, chirping and whistling. "I love you, Ben." Petey cried as he sank his face into Ben's furry neck. "I thought I'd lost you."

Ben and Petey curled up together under the same blanket for about an hour until Ben raised his head at full alert. Petey's heart raced as he heard distant voices. *Jannali's back?* He started walking in the direction of the voices with Ben at his heels, then stopped. Jannali's voice was absent. *Hunters?* "We gotta get outta here, Ben, that's not Jannali." Petey grabbed his backpack then started cramming it with food and a water jug. "Come on, Ben," he whispered.

Petey scanned the ravine and then realized the best escape would be to climb the slope they had driven down. Petey pointed to the top and signaled to Ben. *"Up",* and Ben started upwards, his heavily padded paws and nails gripping the terrain with ease. Petey held Ben's thick tail for stability until they reached the top. He looked down into the ravine and was able to make out three people heading toward his camp, none of which were Jannali. He could no longer see his father, who still lay beside the Oldsmobile.

"Let's go, Ben." Petey whispered as they set out into the desert.

They walked most of the cold night through the unending sand until Petey could go no further. He looked in all directions for any sort of cover but saw nothing. With no other choice, he laid down and pulled his chest, abdomen, face, and neck against Ben's soft back fur and tucked his hands under Ben's warm belly. He fell asleep shivering in the cold, open desert.

———

Petey was relieved when the first rays of sun hit his back, giving the slightest rise in temperature. Rather than get up and lose the warmth from Ben, he waited until the sun was completely over the horizon, and then sat up. Only then did Ben rise to his feet. Trembling from the cold, Petey rummaged through the backpack, pulled out a small bag of salt jerky then divided it between Ben and himself. Petey scanned the desert in all directions but couldn't determine which way they had come. Their tracks had already blown over and no sign of the canyon was visible.

Once the jerky was gone they started heading northeast, further away from the canyon. They walked all day, taking short breaks for water and nibbles of uncooked potatoes. The desert was barren. During the day it was an empty void of hot, flat sand. Even the lizards and snakes that were specially adapted had to bury themselves deep to escape death - only surfacing at night.

Petey had pulled his jacket off and tucked it into his pack. His tanned arms and neck had turned brick red from the unrelenting sun. An hour later, he instinctually draped the jacket over his head and shoulders for protection from the sun. They would stop for a few minutes at a time, but continued walking until night fell. Petey curled up with Ben once again until the sun arrived the next morning. They walked 'til noon then sat for water.

Petey noticed a cluster of large boulders in the distance. "We must be getting close to something, Ben," Petey said. He looked back at their tracks and noticed a large dark mass that covered the western horizon. "What's that?" he asked, curious.

Ben chirped at Petey and started running and bucking in the opposite direction of the darkness. Petey stood staring at the fast approaching black mass, captivated by its immensity. Ben released a series of louder, more aggressive chirps that caught Petey's attention. "Oh, I guess we should get moving. I think it's a storm."

Ben's innate survival instinct kicked in and he started toward the only cover available, a cluster of distant boulders, but within seconds the sun was drowned out and sand was being whipped in all directions.

Petey kept running, trying to shield his eyes with his forearms while following Ben's yelping. The storm was almost directly over them, the stinging sand sprayed the boy and tiger with skin piercing velocity.

Running blindly, Petey's feet collided with a six-inch boulder that sent him crashing to the sand. He held his arms tightly over his head and face, unable to stand and barely able to breathe with the wind and sand being forced into his eyes, ears, nose, and mouth. Petey could feel the dead weight of sand already covering his legs and could no longer hear Ben. Petey had given up against the storm; there was nothing more he could do. He started gasping for air but trying to breathe without inhaling sand was impossible. He then felt his shirt nearly yank over his head, then again, yank after yank. Ben was dragging him.

Ben managed to pull Petey behind the largest boulder and into the hollow entrance of a small cave. They were almost completely out of the storm's wrath. Petey brushed most of the sand from his eyes and blew it out of his nose, then took a few deep breaths. "Thanks, Ben."

Petey scooted a little farther into the cave as the sand started blowing in. Even though they had found cover, the sand was still whipping in through the entrance and stinging them. Petey kept pushing backwards until he felt another opening in the cave wall. They both crawled through the narrow hole that opened into a larger cave. Petey felt his way through the complete darkness, and then sat against the wall.

"Ben?" Petey reached out and felt Ben nuzzle his hand. "Good boy, Ben, good boy." Petey held Ben tight. "I love you, boy." Huddled together, they waited for the storm to pass.

The storm ravaged the desert and in less than an hour, transformed the landscape into an unrecognizable panorama of dunes and flats. Just as quickly as the tempest had formed, it had ended. From outside, there was no trace of the boulders; they had vanished, sealed, and buried under tons of sand. Gone…

AMONGST THE BONES

Present day

THE CREVICES AND MASSIVE BOULDERS WERE MORE THAN DIFFICULT to traverse. One by one they would push and pull one another atop the massive rocks, only to discover larger and more difficult ones ahead. Other than the occasional scrub lizard and pestering flies, there were no other signs of life, not even the kangaroo dared to enter this canyon. Once you made it in, it was next to impossible to get out. For nearly two miles, the group went up and down, in and around some of the most jagged and razor-edged rock in existence. Connor's leather gloves were shredded. His three inner fingertips were exposed and bloodied.

Kate looked down at her gloves, noting that her index fingers were starting to show through. "How the hell does rock get this sharp?"

Connor ran the palm of his glove over the dagger like protrusion emanating from the rock they were standing on. "Its weak mineral composition combined with millions of years of intense UV-rays allow the outer layers to degrade and slide apart, revealing this." Connor slid his glove along the shiny edge of the rocks outermost layer.

"This shit's unforgiving," George said, lifting his leg, showing off his torn jeans and bloodsoaked pant leg. Everyone was bleeding, but George had taken it to extremes.

"The tigers would've had to cross this canyon?" Kate asked.

"It's the only way to get to where we're going, that is unless you take a boat up the other coast, which I seriously doubt they did," Connor said. "I'm sure there are less treacherous areas."

Carl smirked, as though their efforts were pointless. "I don't see how any dog could make it across this crap."

Kate pointed at what appeared to be the opposite side of the canyon, a vertical wall of rock. "That's our destination, right?"

"That's it," Connor said. "Basically."

They continued to cross. One by one they heaved each other over broken pieces of crumbling rock until they finally reached the outer wall.

Mac leaned against a boulder and wiped his brow. "Beautiful! The only bad thing is we'll have to eventually go back."

Kate looked back at the ground she had just crossed. "Ugh, I don't wanna think about that."

The canyon wall looked much like the opposite wall they had rappelled into the ravine, just as high and stretching on for miles and miles in both directions.

Connor pointed toward the top of the cliff. "There *should* be a very old forest up there. I think that's where the tigers may be hiding."

"How do we get up there?" Kate asked.

Connor took a swig from his canteen. "Well, one of us has to climb to the top, secure a rope, and then we use a rope ratchet for everyone else to ascend."

"I take it you're the one climbing?" Kate insinuated.

"Yes, unless anyone else wants to do it." Connor grinned. "Let's walk south and see if there's an easier way up."

They walked for almost twenty minutes until they happened upon a sharp curve in the canyon. They ventured around the bend seeking a suitable area for climbing. The area around the bend was lightly shaded, however, the setting sun provided just enough light to explore without flashlights.

"What the?" Mac said as he noticed a large pile of something that just didn't fit with the surroundings.

"What is that?" Kate said, looking at the large pile of bright-white lying about thirty feet from the rear of the curve's innermost wall.

Connor started walking toward the pile. "Only one way to find out." As he stepped closer he recognized something familiar. "Bones," he said, continuing toward the heap.

It was a large, three-foot high pile of mostly articulated skeletons with various disassembled bones scattered around the bulk.

Mac stopped and scanned the area. "Looks like a slaughter."

Kate kneeled, and her mouth opened, pausing, "Oh, my God," she said, barely audible.

"I know," Connor said.

"They're all tigers," Kate said.

"Great God almighty," Mac whispered.

Connor didn't move. He stood still as his eyes took in the revulsion of it all. "I can't believe what I'm seeing. They were massacred."

Kate fought back tears. "Who would do such a thing?"

Connor kneeled and placed a hand on the skull of what he assumed to be a small female Thylacine. He rubbed it gently, a gesture of apology for whatever wrong was done to her. "We all know who does this sort of thing."

Mac put his hand on Kate's shoulder. "I've seen some gnarly in my day, but this is *off the Richter*."

Kate's eyes watered as she stood looking around at the countless number of Thylacines reduced to scattered bones.

George and Carl kept quiet, capturing the scene from two different viewpoints.

Mac placed his hands on a large skull and rubbed it slow. "There are bad people out there, but this is just too much. Gotta be hundreds of 'em."

Connor reached out grabbing a small rib from another skeleton. He rubbed it gently, then with a little more force, until it crumbled in his hand. "They've been here for quite a while." Connor knew it could take decades for bones to become so brittle in an environment like this.

He took a couple steps shuffling through the mound, then grabbed another bone, presumably from a front leg. He tried to crumble it like the other bone, but it wouldn't fall apart. He then tried to break it with firm pressure, but it was too strong. It puzzled him. This bone appeared more recent but how? So many questions ran through his mind, he was plagued because he had no answers.

"Let's set camp."

They shuffled back into the straight-away of the canyon and set camp. They decided against a fire and sat around a dimly lit battery-operated LED lantern, staring into the yellowed light.

"Were they thrown off the cliff?" Carl asked.

Connor shrugged his shoulders. "I don't know, kinda looks that way. I guess they were shot up top and then tossed off. We need to get a look at the clifftop tomorrow."

"Yeah, you're right, looks like they were shot and tossed," Mac said.

Connor shook his head. "That's all I can put together, but how? This is supposed to be untouched outback. That's a massive cull. There are hundreds of tigers back there."

"Why would anyone come all this way just to kill them?" Kate asked. "There's nothing out here, no ranches, no farms, nothing."

"For their bounties?" George suggested.

Connor shook his head. "Modern tigers weren't even known to exist here. Evidence shows they went extinct from Mainland Australia two thousand years ago, so it wasn't for the bounties. Even if it was, they all have their heads. To collect a bounty, they needed the tiger's actual head, but that was in Tasmania, not Australia."

Kate shook her head in disgust. "Ugh, that's just sickening."

"Yeah, why the hell would someone come all the way out to Timbuktu just to kill these guys?" Mac said.

"I highly doubt it was *someone.* This had coordination. It doesn't make any sense," Connor said. "What do *you* think, Mac?"

"I dunno what to think, makes no sense to me, no one ever thought Tazzie's existed way the hell out here, and to be completely honest, I didn't think we'd find a trace of 'em. So I really don't know what to think."

"I had my doubts, too," Connor said.

Kate laid her head against Connor's shoulder. "It makes me want to cry."

Connor wrapped his arm around Kate. "It doesn't mean we won't find any alive, if anything, it confirms they're here, or at least *were here.*"

"They sure took one hell of a beating though," Mac said.

Connor nodded in agreement. "Let's get some rest. I believe the cliff top may hold some clues."

ENTER THE FOREST

Present day

THROUGHOUT THE NIGHT, CONNOR TOSSED AND TURNED, wrestling with his thoughts, tormented by the hulking pile of tiger bones. He drifted off a couple hours before sunrise and was also the first to wake. He nudged Kate and together they emerged from their tent, anxious for what lay ahead. The sun was just rising, throwing a beautiful red hue. The sky was particularly brilliant with purple and orange swirled through elongated white easterly clouds. The air was considerably warmer than the normal morning chill.

"So, do we wait for everyone?" Kate asked as she ripped open a pack of instant coffee.

"I don't want to, but yeah, we need the cameras rolling," Connor said. "This sort of drama is what pulls viewers in."

Kate began clapping her hands. "Wakey, wakey guys, come on, up and at 'em."

Mac tripped stepping out of his tent. "Aye, you're worse than those damned jungle birds."

"Come on, guys, let's go!" Kate shook the springy fiberglass support poles on George and Carl's tents.

Carl's voice snapped from within his tent. "Is that really necessary?"

Kate kept shaking the poles. "Come on, George! Wakey, wakey!"

George's voice came from behind Kate as she shook his tent. "Good luck getting that guy up."

Kate spun around. George was already up and filming her. She smiled as she released the tent pole. "I guess you're not in there."

"Looks like we're just waiting on Carl," she said.

Carl blurted from inside his tent. "The stupid bones aren't going anywhere, relax!"

Kate shook her head at George and mouthed the words *I can't stand him.*

Carl's tent shuffled, and his head popped through the door. "I'm up, happy?"

Kate nodded big in astonished disbelief. "Wow, Carl, I'm impressed."

As anxious as they were, they still took time to scoff down their plastic pouches of corn beefed hash and scrambled eggs with ham. It looked like an eating contest as they raced to the bottom crease of their pouches. Coffee this morning consisted of instant pouches and room-temp water. Connor and Mac came in at a close second, just behind George who poured his meal rather than spork it. Kate gave up midway. She found the soggy, spongy eggs unappetizing. George then finished hers.

Kate tightened her backpack straps, put hands on her hips and started tapping her foot. "You guys ready?"

Connor threw on his hiking pack, containing all the climbing gear and looked back at Kate. "Let's go."

As Connor, Kate and Mac walked into the curve, they passed the massive pile of skeletons that haunted their thoughts. The ghostly whitish grey bones were illuminated by the early sun's diffused light bouncing off the cliff walls.

Kate sighed as she approached. "It's so overwhelming, look at them all."

Connor veered from the group, wanting to quell something specific that had been bugging him all night. He walked slow, taking careful steps toward the center of the pile, and kneeled. He examined the layers with his eyes, then reached in and tried to pull one of the bones from the very bottom only to have it shatter into dusty crumbles. He rolled the chalky white dust around in his hand and went deep in thought. He then pulled a rib from the top of the pile, tried to crush it, but it didn't give then he rubbed his fingers into its smoothness. He thought to himself for a few seconds. "Some of these are fresh, maybe six months to a year old."

"That recent?" Mac grabbed a femur from the top of the pile and held it close to his eyes, studying its surface.

"Looks like the ones on the bottom have been here the longest, they're frail and weak, and the ones on top are solid," Connor said. "Look closer at the ground. There are bits of hair and hide mixed in."

"So what does that mean?" Kate asked as she studied a lone skeleton, looking for any clue to its demise.

"I'm not sure, theories anyone?" Connor said.

"Maybe the people up there have been killing 'em for years, and when they get one they toss it down here," Mac said.

"That makes the most sense, but as far as I know there aren't any people up there," Connor nodded to the cliff top. "There shouldn't be any people for a few hundred miles."

Connor saw Kate examining the bones; he knew what she was looking for. "Causes of death, Kate?"

"All I see is a few broken bones here and there, ribs, legs, nothing to signify gunshots just yet."

Carl spoke from behind his viewfinder. "Where are all the hides?"

"Great question, Carl, nature ate them; bugs, birds, rodents and most of all, the weather," Connor said.

"Under the right conditions a fresh carcass can turn into a pile of bones in a month, maybe less," Kate added.

"Maybe we should—" Connor stopped mid-sentence, interrupted by the sound of pebbles and small rocks falling from the clifftop.

George swung his lens toward the movement. "Something's up there," he said as a blur disappeared from his viewfinder. Everyone looked up.

"You get it on camera?" Connor said.

George started rewinding the footage. "I think so." They all gathered around him and focused on the four-inch playback screen of his camera. The footage picked up with Kate's talking about a carcass turning to bone, then the sound of falling pebbles, the camera swung to the top of the cliff, zoomed in, and within a couple tenths of a second, a shadowy movement disappeared from view.

"Crap, that could have been anything," Connor said.

"Yup," Mac said. "Way too fast."

"Good job getting what you did, George, great reflexes," Connor said as he walked over to his hiking pack, unzipped, and pulled out a large length of rope and a few miscellaneous climbing tools.

"Going after it?" Mac asked.

Connor fastened his harness. "Sort of, but not really, just getting us to the top for starters."

Mac scanned the ninety-degree walls for an easier way of ascending. "Not much to grip."

Connor started clipping a heavy metal gadget to his harness with foot-long lengths of nylon cord attached to it. "Don't worry, I've got this."

"Wada those lil' pointy things do?" Mac asked.

"These are called tri-cams. They slide into cracks in the rock and open up creating anchored pull points. You've never used them?"

"I'm not big on heights. I'll do 'em if I gotta, but I prefer to keep my feet on the ground."

Connor tossed a heavy ratchet looking device to Mac.

"And this is?"

"Your elevator," Connor said. "Run the rope through this end, and push it up with your arms, then pull yourself up to it, reach and pull, reach and pull. It's a workout, but it'll get you to the top."

"Can't wait." Mac rolled his eyes.

"But first I've gotta go up and attach the rope," Connor said.

Kate leaned in and gave a quick cheek-peck. "Be careful."

Connor looked at George's camera lens and winked. "This could be dangerous."

He made the climb just shy of six minutes. Although it was vertical, his muscles were rested and fully enjoyed the vein popping work. One arm after another he heaved himself up the rope and secured his tri-cams to the small splits and cracks within the rock, creating leverage points to pull himself to the next crack or foot hold.

Connor's head breached the ledge and his eyes locked onto the incredible forest fifty yards from the cliff face. It was thick and mythically dark, laden with towering ancient and weathered Karri trees, Australian Pines and Eucalyptus. Its immenseness was incomparable to anything they had seen on their journey. The woodland was separated from the cliff by a mildly downward sloped rocky embankment, much less challenging than the vertical wall that separated it from the ravine.

"You guys gotta see this," Connor spoke down to the others and pulled himself atop. He secured the loose end of the rope to a boulder and gave the signal to climb.

Mac looked at Kate with a crooked face. "Why don't you go first? That way you love birds can have a few minutes of alone time."

"What's the matter, Mac? Scared of a little climb?" Kate taunted. She grabbed the ratchet from Mac and attached it to the rope and her harness as though she had done it a hundred times before. "Adios amigo." She pushed the ratchet as high as she could overhead—*click click click click click*, its heavy metal gears ticked away, producing a sound like that of an old wooden roller coaster, then as she pulled down, it's teeth bit into the rope, allowing her to pull herself up to it. The muscles in her arms and back glistened with sweat as she worked the ratchet. She hung for a few minutes about half way, allowing her muscles to recoup and then finished her way to the top.

Connor leaned over the cliff as Kate made her few final pulls. "Tired yet?"

"Not at all," she lied.

Connor reached down, and interlocked his forearm with hers, then pulled her atop the ledge.

She unlatched herself from the equipment and readjusted for a minute before she noticed the forest.

"Is that real?"

"It's something else, huh?"

"It looks dark, yet magical, like something out of either a Disney or horror movie."

Mac's climb up the rope was more of comedy routine than rock climbing. The higher he ascended the more unintentionally awkward he became.

Carl aced the climb. His lanky frame jetted to the top of the rope, easily surpassing Kate's ascension time. George on the other hand took his time and enjoyed the view.

Mac pointed at the gentle slope angled toward the forest. "Now that's more my kinda climbing."

"Well, guess what, Mac? We're done with the rock climbing, at least for now."

"No more climbing? Now that I'm warmed up I'm ready for Everest." Mac winked at Kate.

"*Sure* you are, Mac," Kate laughed.

Connor studied the ground around his feet. "Let's check this ledge out. There's gotta be some sort of evidence left behind by whomever slaughtered these guys. Look for bullet casings, cigarette butts, anything man-made. Also look for paw prints, feces, burrows or anything else that could suggest the tigers are still around."

"Are we staying together or going different directions?" Mac asked.

"Let's stay together, just spread out a bit and stay within earshot," Connor said.

The cliff top and the rocky slope leading to the forest was rather smooth. Large red broken boulders sat scattered along the ledge. The slope itself was a layer of smooth reddish rock riddled with cracks, some more than a foot wide. Some of the cracks were only a few inches deep, but others were greater than twenty.

The ledge produced no clues. Connor, Mac, and Kate methodically started searching the slope inward toward the forest. After an unproductive hour, they decided to make their way down to the forest. The slope was a gentle steepness and easily traversed. At the bottom, the rock ended, and forest began, with no visible gradient between the two.

The team walked into the shaded forest, in awe of the enormous Karri trees twisting into the clouds. When they stepped into the threshold, the atmosphere changed. A subtle shade covered them, and every sound became more clear and distinct due to the acoustics of a windless forest. The rustic Karri trees were massive. Their trunks were covered in furry velvet-green moss up to chest height, with scattered foot-step-like patches of enormous ingrown bark-eating fungi. The thickened trunks climbed skyward, tapering off beyond the lowest clouds.

Kate pointed to a narrow path about a foot wide leading from the very edge of the slope into the forest. "Looks like a game trail?"

Connor walked over to it and knelt. "Not sure why it would lead to or *from* the cliff."

Mac ran his hand across the dirt trail. "Most *game* trails lead to or from a watering hole back to its den."

"Man-made maybe?" Kate said.

Connor's eyes followed the trail into the forest. "I'd say highly unlikely, it can take months or even years of treading to wear a path. This place is so remote, I just don't see it being made by man. No footprints either, at least not here."

"Dingos maybe?" Kate said.

"Good possibility, but they're so dainty and nomadic, they don't usually wear a common path," Mac said.

"It's just an odd place for a game trail," Connor said. "I know it's early and I know we all wanna get exploring, but I think we should set camp here."

"Sounds good to me," Carl blurted from behind the camera.

"I bet it does, Carl," Connor said.

Connor set camp along the edge of the forest where it met the slope, about fifty yards south of the trail. The camp placement was strategic, if something was still using the trail they should be able to spot it without getting too close. They angled their chairs in a semi-circle facing toward the path. As the sun dipped below the horizon, the moon quickly followed. Its yellow green hues cast a haunting glow within the forest.

"What a great spot to camp," Kate said. "Too bad the others can't be here. Lisa'd really appreciate it."

"No fire tonight?" Carl asked as he zipped his weatherproof jacket all the way to the top.

Kate rolled her eyes. "Think about it, Carl."

Carl flipped his jacket collar up and settled his chin into it. "I guess we don't wanna frighten off the thyla-thingies."

Kate released an annoyed rapid sigh. "We've been on this expedition for how long? And you still don't even know the name of what we're searching for?"

"Okay, you two, let's keep our voices down. This is where we watch *s i l e n t l y*," Connor scolded.

Kate squinted at Carl. "Sorry, I knew that."

"Whatever," Carl bitched under his breath.

Mac couldn't stop smiling, reveling in Kate's sass. "Maybe we should split up a bit?" He laughed. "It seems like we'd have a better chance if we were scattered about."

"I'm down with that, but we need to be very quiet," Connor said. "Carl, why don't you tag along with Mac, and Kate, you stay with me."

"Maybe I'll hit the north side of the trail," Mac said.

Connor nodded. "Okay, I'm heading in to the forest about a hundred feet or so."

Connor, Kate, and George disappeared into the darkness of the woods. The moon was almost full, casting just enough light to dimly illuminate everything within about twenty feet, but in the distance, only the silhouettes of monster trees haunted the back drop. They moved as silently as possible until Connor felt they had reached a decent spotting area. They backed up to a Karrie tree at least thirty feet in diameter and nestled in among its enormous curvy exposed roots. The tree sat about fifteen yards from the path and even though they couldn't see the trail clearly, they could tell if something was on it by silhouettes.

"Get comfortable," Connor whispered. "Now we sit and wait."

———

Mac stepped, gently placing each foot onto the forest floor. *Why in the hell am I trying to be quiet when I've got Godzilla stomping around behind me?* He wanted to tell Carl to be a little quieter, but knew he'd get a smart-ass response, so he didn't waste his time. He decided to take cover in a well-established patch of large ferns. Carl squatted down just behind Mac, but not before prodding the ground with a stick to scare off any unwanted inhabitants.

———

Three hours later, Connor decided to call it quits for the night. As Connor, Kate and George made it back to camp, they saw Mac and Carl heading in their direction from the rocky side of the forest border.

"I guess they had an uneventful evening too," Connor mumbled.

"There's always tomorrow," Kate said.

Mac entered the camp shaking his head, then fell backwards into his chair. "Nothing, not even a possum on walk-about."

Connor shook his head. "Same here. No movement, nothing."

"What put you onto the tiger anyway?" Mac asked.

"That's a question I'm still trying to answer, I don't know exactly. I saw a short video clip of the last known Thylacine while I was in grad school, it was from the Hobart Zoo in Tasmania. Something about it captured me. I wish I could explain it, but I can't. I'm just drawn to it. I remember watching that grainy old video and thinking to myself that I was looking at the very last living tiger and that it was now dead. It was beyond surreal."

"It was a bad, bad thing, what we did to it," Mac said.

"Despicable," Connor said.

"Absolutely horrendous," Kate said. "It sickens me. Is mankind really stupid enough to persecute and force to extinction an entire species based on fear?"

"I hate to say it, but we are," Mac said. "And it's not the first time, probably won't be the last."

Carl's face went crooked. "Well, wasn't it killing all the livestock?"

Connor's dormant facial muscles came to life, producing an aggressive expression Kate had never seen on him. "So, you're inferring the extermination of the entire species was justified because some livestock may have been eaten?" Connor's voice elevated, slightly piercing the serenity of the conversation.

Carl's eye started twitching. "The livestock were the people's livelihood back then. If some wild animal was killing *your means* to make a living, you'd do whatever needed to be done."

Connor sprung out of his chair and kicked the mess kit that had been sitting where the fire would have been, sending the aluminum pots and pans airborne, scattering them out of the forest and onto the rocky slope. He looked at Mac and pointed at Carl. "That's the fucking mentality that eradicates an entire species."

Carl pressed his shoulders into the back of the chair, frightened.

Kate peered at Carl then tossed a wicked grin at him. "Calm down, sweetheart."

Mac was delighted to see Carl being dealt a handful of nasty aggression.

George powered his camera off and lowered it. With a single eyebrow raised to its limit he watched on. He had never seen this side of Connor, nor did he believe it could even exist in such a man.

Just as it seemed like Connor was going to relax, he fired off again. "You know what, Carl? You're a fucking coward. And you know what cowards are good for? Absolutely nothing. I have a theory. People like *you* wiped out the Thylacine, a big group of fucking cowards, running around with guns, killing every god-damned tiger you see. How about we turn the table?"

Carl stood and put his hands up, palms out. "Look Connor, all I was saying …"

Connor walked quickly toward Carl. "Shut the fuck up." He shoved Carl with both hands, full force, directly in the chest, sending him toppling backwards over his chair. "How's it feel to be outnumbered, alone and defenseless?"

Carl barked from the ground, feet still in the air. "I'll sue your ass." He grunted while wrestling himself over and then clambering to his feet. He stood brushing the dirt and leaves from his jacket. "You know—

fuck you, man," Carl blurted as he staggered off and into his tent.

Connor sat back down in his chair.

No one spoke for the next minute or so until Mac was brave enough to break the silence. "I reckon this pre-packaged army food is getting to ya?" Mac said as he ripped open a bag labeled *Beef Stroganoff*. "It's only so long that a man can eat this rubbish before he cracks."

As serious as Connor was he couldn't help but grin at Mac's feeble attempt to lighten the mood.

"I'm sorry, guys," Connor said.

Mac loaded his spork and shoveled it into his mouth. "Not accepted, that bastard had it coming."

"Seriously, don't apologize. He's a freaking asshole," Kate said. "And to be honest, I thought you were too easy on him."

"I was totally unprofessional, but I couldn't hold back. I thought about the massacred tigers and his arrogance. I wanted to smash his face in."

George's bold voice rumbled. "I wanted that too."

———

Thirty minutes before sunrise, Carl was the first out of his tent. The team would now have to approach him, rather than the opposite. He made his way to the circle of camp chairs, sat, and threw back a reconstituted pouch of *Grits with Cheese.* The sun was just kissing the horizon, pushing back the veil of night. Carl felt outnumbered, like an outsider; like one of the most unpopular kids in class, but not because he looked funny or had bad acne, but because he was a perverted asshole.

Connor woke up feeling hung-over and regretful, much like an excessively intoxicated one-night stand; waking the next morning to discover he had done something regrettable with something unidentifiable. He rolled over to find Kate wrapped in her sleeping bag with only her head exposed, already smiling and reminiscing.

Mac was the second to secure a spot at the semi-circle of chairs, marching himself right into position without speaking a word to Carl. That morning, Mac was little more adventurous with his choice of pouched meals, *Beef Enchilada.* He drowned it with his mini tobasco bottle (every meal came with one) and savored every slopping wet morsel.

"You really dig that crap, don't you?" George asked as he tapped the last bit of granulated instant coffee into his canteen.

Mac slurped the last tidbit from his plastic spork. "This stuff is delish, and look who's talkin', you're fixin' to drink powdered cigarette ash."

George extended the canteen toward Mac. "Wanna sip?"

"I'd rather drink stagnant pond water."

An odd tension surrounded the three men. Carl hadn't spoken and they didn't plan on speaking to him.

From inside the tent, Connor smiled back at Kate. "It's not funny."

"I'm not laughing, I'm smiling." Her grin grew larger.

"I was out of control last night. I have to apologize."

"I loved it, so did everybody else. Carl had it coming."

"It still doesn't give me the right to run off at the mouth like that. I shoved him for Christ's sake."

"You should have seen his face, Connor. I thought he was gonna mess himself."

"I can't ever let that happen again, I'm embarrassed and I'm so sorry for doing that in front of you."

"Don't apologize to me. I'm glad you did what you did."

The zipper on Connor's tent buzzed its way to the top, alerting Carl.

"Morning, guys," Connor said as he stepped out of the tent and walked toward the group. He could see Carl focused and fidgeting around with his camera, a nervous habit everyone was now aware of. Connor walked in front of the three men. "I'm sorry for last night."

"No worries here, mate," Mac winked.

George gave Connor a confused grimace that translated into *Why the hell are you apologizing?*

Connor looked directly at the skinny man pressing every button on his camera. "Carl, I'm sorry for my behavior last night, it was reckless and irresponsible of me. Can we bury the hatchet?"

I know where we can bury the hatchet, Kate thought.

"You scared the hell out of me, man," Carl whined. "I thought you were gonna kill me."

"I was heated over a sensitive issue. It's not your fault and I was wrong to attack you. The expedition is almost over, can we both be rational?"

Carl raised his voice to a higher pitch. "I've been rational the entire time."

Mac was irritated. "Were you rational when you were unbuttoning Sheila's—"

"That's bullshit Mac and you know it!" Carl snapped.

"Guys, can we just finish out the expedition professionally?" Connor asked as he fought back a sudden streak of hatred, it shot through his body, stemming from the very thought of Carl trying to molest his unconscious producer.

"I'll finish it out," Carl said.

Connor was about to extend his hand but stopped himself at the realization of whom Carl was. There were reasons why everyone had problems with him, and he finally put it all together in his mind.

Mac had enough of listening to Connor apologize. "So what's on the agenda for today?"

"Let's hit the forest. Trek in a few miles and trek back out this evening," Connor said.

While Connor and Kate ate breakfast, Mac decided to explore the rocky slope behind the camp for a few minutes with George filming. It was uneventful until George spotted something darting through the woods.

"Mac," George whispered, pointing, and trying to focus in on the swift shadowy movement. Mac looked, but the apparition disappeared as quickly as it emerged.

"Caught it on the cammie?" Mac said.

"Nope."

"It must have left some tracks." Mac started into the forest, making his way to where he saw the blur. He reached the spot and knelt down. "Holy guacamole."

"Tiger?" George asked.

"Yup," Mac whispered.

FROM THE DEAD

Present day

CONNOR WOLFED DOWN KATE'S EGGS THEN PUT THE EMPTY POUCH into the trash section of his pack. "Are you sure?"

"It darted through the woods and didn't make a sound. It was probably thirty or forty yards off. I couldn't identify it by sight, but its tracks are unmistakable."

"Maybe it was a wombat?" Connor asked.

"No way in hell. You shoulda seen this thing flying through the forest. Ain't no way a pudgy lil' wombat can move like that."

"I've seen some pretty fast wombats," Connor said.

"Not like this mate, this bloke was ghostly. I'm telling you it was a tiger."

Connor thought for a moment. "Okay, group, change of plans, we're going that way." Connor pointed in the direction of Mac's discovery. Mac was convinced, and Connor trusted him.

"Oh, my God, do you understand what this means?" Kate said. "If we can provide proof that a species thought to be extinct still exists."

"I know," Connor responded. "It's overwhelming."

"We can start breeding programs, ensure their survival," Kate said.

"We need to get going," Connor said. "Mac, ready to do some tracking?"

"That's what you hired me for."

The team set off, stopping at the initial track to give Connor a bit of physical proof. Mac knelt beside the tracks and Connor beside him. Connor traced the outline of a single track with his finger, taking caution not to disturb the soft earthy substrate. "I'll be damned," he said. He pulled the digital camera from his coat pocket and snapped a few images of the large print. "Mac, lead on."

Mac followed in the direction of the prints, using the skills his father had passed onto him; watching the soil, the bending of plants, smelling the air and so on. Mac kept finding solid prints from a single animal as well as an occasional scenting. The males of most territorial species are known for marking territory by spraying urine on select landmarks, creating a scent boundary, letting others within the species know the area is claimed. For more than six hours they tracked, only to find more prints and scent markers.

"How far is this thing gonna go?" Mac said.

"I hate to say it, but we should probably turn back," Connor said with regret.

Carl walked in front of the team. "I say we keep going."

"Since when do *you* wanna keep going?" Kate snapped.

"Bug off," Carl barked.

———

Connor led the way home at a much faster pace, trying to beat the setting sun. They were only a couple miles from camp when the forest went black, limiting visibility to distant silhouettes. Two hours after sunset and the tents seated in the clearing were finally visible. Everyone was ready to get off their feet and into bed. Connor stopped, crouched, and tried to peer through the moon lit trees.

"What's up?" Kate whispered as she nearly fell over him.

"Thought I saw some movement in the tree line on the other side of camp," Connor whispered. After a few seconds of nothing, he gave up. "Guess it was nothing."

They made their way out of the forest and walked toward camp via the slope, just along the border of the forest. Thirty yards from camp

Connor dropped, bending his knees, and patting the air with a rapidly waving arm, gesturing for everyone to get down.

Connor looked back at the group to confirm George and Carl were filming, which they were, and then he looked back toward the path almost fifty yards on the other side of camp. Kate and Mac were crouched behind Connor and locked into an unbreakable gaze. Connor tried to speak, but the words were lost; the culmination of the entire expedition was presenting itself in a way they never could have imagined. Mac snapped out of his dead man's gaze and crawled as silently as possible on his hands and knees to Connor's right side. "You wanted your proof?"

Kate took a few slow crouched steps, placing herself on Connor's left side.

Over a dozen Thylacines were at the beginning of the slope and more were entering by way of the path. One after another, the bold-striped and well-muscled beasts poured out of the forest and onto the beginning of the rocky angle. Tigers of all shapes and sizes were emerging from the forest and gathering at the base of the slope; some appeared to be huddled in groups. Packs of adults with young pups, others were unaccompanied, standing amongst the increasing numbers. The base of the slope became covered with at least a hundred Thylacines. A small female began to make melodic bark-like chirps which triggered a choir. The other tigers all began a symphony that escalated for about thirty seconds and then tapered down to silence.

The condensed gathering of the striped, wolf-like marsupials began to part at the foot of the path. The mass of tigers separated down the middle, until a clear path opened all the way from the forest trail to the top of the cliff.

George and Carl spread apart to film from slightly different vantage points. The team sat still, barely breathing. Not one word was spoken as they watched the bizarre forest drama play out.

A large male Thylacine emerged from the forest at the foot of the open path. With ribs showing through his thinning hide, he limped a bit but maintained a slow pace up the path lined by countless Thylacines. In his prime he would have been a remarkable animal, but now weakened by age, he was humbled by the universal law of time.

He stopped and looked back toward the forest trail; the tigers were falling in behind him. A single female made her way out of the crowded mass and onto the trail. She walked up the slope toward the fragile beast. Older, but still muscled and in good form, she approached with her head hung low. She neared the old tiger and raised her head, touching nose to nose, nuzzling for a few seconds until he turned away, toward the cliff. She stepped beside him and once more rubbed her elongated snout along his, pressing, this time holding. He caressed up and down along her jaw-line for but a brief moment, then once again looked toward the cliff and started toward it.

With her head hung low, she followed a few feet behind as he struggled to climb the rocky slope. He tripped and stumbled over the uneven edges and cracks. The old male reached with his front legs to cross a two-foot fissure, but his rear legs gave out, causing him to fall onto his side, bony ribs colliding with the jagged stone. The weakened beast struggled to get up. His aged legs shook as the strain tried to overtake his determination, but he stood once again.

He looked back at the gathered crowd, then his eyes locked with the following female, pausing. The old male broke from their gaze, raised his head to the sky and released an angelic burst of whistle-like chirps. He turned away from the female and broke into a perfect gallop up the steep slope. His padded feet and claws gripped the rock as though it were softened earth.

As he neared the top, he gained even more speed, running as though he were in his prime. When the final bit of ledge appeared before him, his rear legs reached far ahead for one last stride. His rear paws gripped the very last bit of rock and he thrust himself off the cliff.

He launched into the air with an unrivaled grace, soaring, almost taking flight. His body continued outward until it could no longer defy the natural laws that sent him smashing into the rocks, over one hundred and fifty feet below.

Just after his body thudded into the rocks below, nearly every Thylacine, lowered their heads and began barely audible chirping.

"What in God's name did we just witness?" Connor whispered as he looked over at Kate.

Kate's lower jaw was still dropped. She couldn't move. *This goes against everything we've been taught.*

Connor directed his attention back and forth to both cameramen who were on their knees in identical positions. "Please tell me you were both rolling."

They both nodded without taking their eyes off the viewfinders.

The congested slope of Thylacines started moving back into the forest.

"Shit, they're leaving," Connor whispered. "We need to follow 'em."

"Uh, I dunno, kinda feeling a bit outnumbered," Mac said, serious.

Connor turned his head toward Kate. "Pssst, Kate, you ready?"

Kate's eyes were still fixed on the tigers.

"Kate?" He spoke a little louder, still no response.

Kate's attention couldn't be broken from the mass breaking up and drifting off into the forest.

Connor grabbed Kate's arm and shook it. "Hey," his voice a tad too loud. It broke the surrounding threshold of silence; a few Thylacines on the outskirts of the mass turned their heads toward Connor's voice. They focused in until they discovered the hidden spies. They began chirping, fast and aggressively, starting a chain reaction of yelping that spread throughout the entire gathering; within moments the entire mass was gone, vanished in the safety of the forest.

INTO THE DEN

"Quick, grab everything you can," Connor said as he started stuffing his hiking pack.

"Are we breaking camp?" Mac asked.

"Yeah, we're going mobile. This is our last opportunity to…"

"We've got the footage, what more do you need?" Carl blurted.

Connor pulled at his tent poles, collapsing the tent. "We're here, we've found them. This is our only opportunity to do this."

Carl dropped into one of the chairs. "We've been footin' it all day, can't we just go after 'em in the morning?"

Connor's voice deepened. "Carl, I'm not paying you to whine."

Carl lunged out of his chair and started jerking the poles from his tent.

"Connor, we need to talk," Kate said as she stuffed her pack.

"I know," Connor rolled his tent as fast as possible. "Oh boy, do I know."

With Connor and Mac leading, they followed the heavy trail of four-toed prints. At first the tracks were thick and led straight into the forest, scattered all along the trail.

Fifteen minutes later, Mac knelt and scanned the ground with his flashlight. "Tracks are disappearing."

"Yeah, looks like maybe they split up, let's just follow what we can," Connor said.

"Um, they're gone," Mac said, still panning his light across the ground.

Connor shined his light across the ground trying to pick up the tracks.

"No more tracks?" Kate said, relieved and exhausted.

"Without any tracks we're tourists without a map," Mac said. "This forest is huge, and we can't see a darn thing."

"Let's go in the direction of the last set of prints," Connor said, unwavering.

"We've lost 'em. Why don't we just call it a night?" Carl said.

Connor walked off in the direction of the last set of tracks, paying no attention to Carl's whining or Mac's hint. After more than an hour of trekking with the team barely keeping up, he noticed light within the forest up ahead. He started walking faster, forcing the group to keep his pace.

Kate tripped over something but managed to keep from falling. "Slow down, Connor."

Connor kept his obsessed pace, oblivious to her plea. Mac looked back at Kate, her face illuminated by the scattered moonlight, shaking his head in disapproval. Connor was obsessed, and it was wearing on the team.

"Connor, slow down," Kate said a little louder than before.

He didn't respond, but instead sped up as the light was getting closer.

Mac looked back again at Kate who was now struggling to keep up. "Hey, mate," Mac whispered. "Mind if I take a breather with Kate?"

Connor kept his pace, unaware of anything other than his fixation on the light.

"God-damn it, Connor. Please!" Kate yelled. She felt something grab her arm, then it spun her around.

George pulled her arm downward. "Sit, sweetheart."

Carl joined her.

It took a moment for Connor to realize Kate had yelled. He stopped, looked back and saw George heading toward him.

"Snap out of it, man," George said.

"This is the chance of a lifetime, I'm sorry, George, but I'm not passing it up." Connor kept looking back and forth between the long-haired grizzly-bear of a man and the section of forest that appeared to be illuminated.

"I'm not telling you to pass up anything. Kate's exhausted. Give it a rest," George said.

"Tell ya what, go ahead and set camp here, I'll go investigate."

Kate shined her light directly in Connor's eyes. "So you're just gonna leave us here while you run off and do your thing? You don't think we're excited too? I want to find 'em just as bad as you, but I'm not willing to run everybody down in the process."

"I'm sorry, Kate. I was inconsiderate, and I should have stopped long ago. You're a biologist and you know how important this is. We saw things that I don't even think are possible, yet they happened. I need to know more."

Kate aimed the light away from his eyes. "Just give us a few minutes and we'll all go."

He stared back at Kate and it clicked. He realized how obsessed he had become.

He sat down and took a breather, no words, just the moonlight highlighting their swirling breath. Connor sat back against a tree and ran his fingers through his hair, sighing, trying to pass time. Five minutes later the wait was driving him mad.

Kate stood and threw the heavy pack over her shoulder. "You guys ready?" She walked over to Connor, leaned in close and whispered, "You did it. You found them." She offered her hand. "I need answers too."

They marched at a slower pace and approached the light. It became apparent as they neared, it was concentrated moonlight that shone in a fifty-yard circular clearing. They could see scattered mounds of red earth, some three feet high, other dunes nearly six; the area resembled a barren and desolate battlefield full of inverted trenches. The reddish clay was brilliant under the moon, almost blood-red.

Mac's eyes panned across the piles of compacted earth, noticing burrows at the foothill of every mound. "I think we've found the mother ship."

"By God," Connor paused, scanning. "This is the mother of all dens."

"You boys getting all this?" Kate smiled, referring to the cameramen.

"Yup," George said, grinning. "For a while I thought we were chasing ghosts, didn't think these guys were still around."

Carl walked away from the group and into the middle of the clearing with his eye to the viewfinder.

"Careful, Carl," Connor said.

"It's to the brink chockered with holes," Mac said. "Looks like every mounds got a couple of 'em. Wonder how far underground they go?"

"A mass communal den like this with a carnivorous species?" Kate said. "I didn't think it was possible, large dens alone have trouble finding enough food. How the hell can a den this size support itself?"

"They all looked pretty fit to me," Mac said, kneeling to the ground, and picking at the hardened clay. "You think they're home? I can't find any tracks. This stuff is like rock."

Connor eyed Carl as he walked alone among the mounds. "I'd imagine they've already retreated into their burrows."

"Should we look around?" Kate asked.

Connor inhaled deep then let the air inflate his cheeks as he exhaled, shaking his head. "This is their territory, I don't know if it's such a good idea. You know how aggressive wolves can be when an intruder gets close to their den."

Carl heard the warning. "Aw, come on, we're here and they're all scared shitless and hiding in their holes."

"Nice language for the video." Kate smirked, then she said under her breath, "Hopefully he gets ripped apart."

"It's probably not safe out there, Carl," Connor said from the tree line.

Mac watched on. "I say let him be a guinea pig."

Carl clicked on the camera's spotlight and shoved it into the entrance of a hole, ignorant of Connor's direction.

They watched on as Carl snooped around, forcing his camera into as many burrows as he could, hoping to get a close-up of what lay hidden, hellbent on outdoing George.

Carl was the chicken in a coop full of foxes, but after several minutes of nothing they decided it was relatively safe.

"You guys need to dig one of these up," Carl pointed to a mound.

"Are you nuts?" Mac asked.

Connor shook his head. "That's not what we do, Carl. We're not into destruction."

"Well, if you found some pups, we could bring 'em back. That'd be sensational."

Connor, Kate, and Mac hated the idea but knew sooner or later it would have to be done, to secure the species survival, captive breeding— behind bars. They, however, loathed Carl's reasoning, for media sensationalism.

Connor took a couple slow steps into the clearing. "It looks somewhat safe. Let's investigate a little but be careful."

"How 'bout I watch you guys from here?" Mac said. "I'll let you know if I see anything."

Connor looked at Mac and gestured his head toward Kate.

"I knew you'd say that," Mac said.

They all walked into the clearing. The cold, hard packed clay crunched under their boots as they spread about. George followed Connor.

Kate stepped slowly into the clearing, then stopped a few yards short of the center. She stood and panned the area. "I don't know guys, this doesn't feel right." The hair on her arms raised. "I really don't think we should be here."

"Agreed," Mac said standing beside her.

"I feel it too, something just doesn't feel right." Connor looked toward Kate and Mac from the opposite side of the center.

"Me too," George said. "It's weird, too quiet."

Carl looked away from his viewfinder and shifted his eyes to George, shaking his head in opposition.

Mac's expression froze. "Jesus, mate, at your twelve o'clock."

Connor looked up and saw a colossal tiger and its two piercing green eyes staring him down. It was walking slowly from the tree-line ahead of him into the clearing. The beast moved with its head low and shoulders fixed, eyes locked on Connor, stalking.

Connor froze. "Nobody run, act like prey and you *will* be prey." Connor recognized its slow walk. The same walk large predatory animals use to sneak up on prey before ambush. "Don't look it in the eyes," Connor said. "Line up beside me and stand your ground."

The tiger's head stayed low, looking through an un-obscured path straight to the helpless crew.

"I think he wants to eat *you*, mate," Mac whispered as he side-stepped toward Connor.

"I'm used to that," Connor said, confident. Everyone lined up with Connor; George and Kate to his right, Mac, and Carl to his left.

Kate's body was shivering, but not from the cold. "Connor, I'm scared."

He reached out and grabbed Kate's trembling hand. "Don't show it."

The tiger was still on its course, eyes locked on Connor.

George and Carl kept filming.

"Thirty yards and closing, got a plan?" George asked.

"Just stay together," Connor said. "If it jumps me, you guys take off."

"Fuck that," George said. "If *it* jumps *you*, *I'm* jumping *it*."

"Figured as much," Connor said.

"Twenty," George said.

Connor wouldn't look the creature in the eye; instead he used his peripheral vision. The beast's features were becoming clear, its broad head, shiny black nose, haunting green eyes, rounded erect ears, bulging shoulders and chest, fawn coat with jet black stripes; it was becoming all too vivid for his peripheral.

"Christ, he's gotta be a hundred kilos," Mac whispered, terrified.

"Fifteen," George said.

The tiger stopped at twelve yards, raising his head high into the air, sniffing in a semi-circular motion, sampling the strange scents.

"Shit, now he doesn't know who to eat first," Mac whispered.

The tiger then walked with a different gait, its head raised, toward George. He lowered his camera as a shield but dropped it. The tiger was unaffected by the sudden movement. It stepped in and took two sniffs of the black and grey object then raised its thick neck skyward, locking eyes with George.

"Don't make eye contact," Connor whispered.

George didn't respond nor breathe; his eyes were already locked into its emerald irises. After a few seconds he took a slow breath.

The tiger turned its gaze and moved to Kate.

"It's ok," George whispered.

The tiger looked back at George, trying to decipher the tall man's strange sound, and then it looked back at Kate, whose eyes were closed. The tiger sniffed the air and nudged her free hand with its cold nose. Kate's breathing became erratic as the fear took over, squeezing Connor's hand like a vice.

"Open your eyes," George whispered.

Kate fought to crack her eyelids, tremoring, forcing them open just enough to see. She looked down into the eyes of her fear and a calm entered her being. The beast's soft eyes told a story, one she couldn't comprehend, yet could undeniably feel. Her fear was gone.

Carl's camera whizzed as he loaded another cartridge, sending the tiger in his direction until it stopped in front of him. Carl peered through the viewfinder and focused in on the green eyes, terror shot through every sense of his being. He gasped then dropped the camera from chin level, sending it clattering upon the ground. Carl couldn't stop staring at the tiger; his arms crossed tightly, and his breathing was irregular and loud.

"Don't panic," Connor whispered.

The tiger looked toward Mac and a nostalgic sense of familiarity rattled his soul.

The tiger rubbed its snout along Mac's pant leg, up and down, taking in his scent.

The whizzing of a camera's gear mechanisms interrupted the silence of Mac's moment with the tiger. Carl had snatched the camera and was reloading a cartridge.

The tiger looked back at Carl calmly, but then snarled revealing elongated white teeth. It released a blood-curdling low rumble growl then lunged forward, snapping its jaws at Carl. Its huge teeth smacked together, startling everyone. Carl jumped backwards and fell, tripping over his own feet. The tiger watched with teeth bared as the skinny man scrambled into a better defensive position. He held the camera in front of his body like a shield. The tiger watched then settled its teeth, uninterested. It turned away and walked toward Connor.

Connor went against what he had been taught and looked down into the Thylacines green eyes. There was caution, but no fear.

The tiger sniffed his hand and nudged it. It waited a few seconds and then nudged it a little harder. "What do you want, old boy?" Connor whispered. The tiger placed its muzzle underneath Connor's hand and jerked its head back, sending Connor's hand on top of its head.

"You want me to pet ya?" Confused, Connor looked at Mac and then Kate. *This tiger has got to be domesticated. It's had human interaction.*

It nudged Connor's hand again, flinging it upward. Connor recognized the behavior; he had seen many dogs do the exact same thing whenever they wanted attention, but how could this tiger have adopted a similar behavior? He was baffled.

Connor looked at Kate and then back at the tiger. He showed a nervous reluctance as he placed one hand on top of its broad head. His hand ran over the tiger's thick, velvet-like coat, passing over the rounded heaps of muscled shoulders, then stopped out of caution.

The tiger raised its head in satisfaction then leaned in and nudged his hand again. It was unmistakable; the tiger wanted him to pet it. Connor placed one hand on the tiger's head and stroked slowly. The tiger stopped all movement and stared into his eyes. They locked in a gaze and Connor found himself elsewhere.

Connor's mind began a journey of fluttered visions, glimpses of their expedition flashed before him; bones in the cave, the rusted automobile, hieroglyphics, Sheila's vision, his near death experience, the cliff jumping tiger, the gathering of tigers; then he saw things he had not experienced, a young boy and a tiger together, a young tiger playing with a toy Koala, guns firing, heads of tigers being counted with a money exchange, a woman raped and murdered, a boy defending a tiger, sickly tigers behind bars, the zoo break in, a chase through the desert, jagged cliffs, and their new hidden sanctuary.

The visions stopped, and Connor dropped to his knees, out of breath, overwhelmed and speechless. He sat there, dazed.

The tiger started backing away from the group.

"Oh, my God. Look at them all." Kate's gaze was locked on the countless numbers of irradiant eyes, amongst the tree-line.

Connor still hadn't moved so Mac took charge, grabbed his arm, and pulled him to his feet. "I doubt they're all as friendly as this guy."

Connor, still confused, eyed the tigers standing along the tree-line. "We need to go."

The lone tiger raised its thick neck and gave an enchanting series of bird-like chirps. Dozens upon dozens of tigers emerged from the forest; males, females, pups, young and old, all advancing toward the group.

Connor looked back at the tree-line behind him. "It's time to go."

HUMAN NATURE

KATE OPENED A CAMP CHAIR THEN FELL INTO ITS CANVAS BACK stop. "What happened with you back there, Connor?"

Mac followed Kate's lead and plopped into his own chair. "Man, you really zoned out, looked like you were in some kinda trance with that tiger." Mac shook his canteen to dissolve any remaining orange flavored powder.

Connor opened his chair and sat. "I'm not sure how to explain it, but when I touched that tiger something happened." He shook his head. "Images, more like movie clips started playing in my head."

"Random thoughts?" Kate asked.

"Not at all. These weren't my thoughts, it was like I was... This is crazy, but it was like I was plugged into the tiger."

Kate grinned. "You're saying the tiger gave you these thoughts?"

Connor paused. "I think *so?*"

"And what does your rational mind think about that?" Kate asked.

"I *don't* know, all I know is they weren't my thoughts."

Mac was quiet, listening.

"Do you really believe they were from the tiger?" Kate asked.

"I know what you must be thinking, but trust me, I don't believe in hocus pocus, things that can't be proven, I'm not religious, I don't believe in the Sasquatch or any other nonsensical bullshit, but this was real."

"I believe you," Kate said. "And I'm still trying to figure out how a wild tiger could approach us like that."

"And then signals all his mates to come out," Mac said.

"I think we've made the discovery of the decade," Kate said.

"Decade? Millennium maybe? There's something big going on out here," Mac said.

"I think that's pretty clear," Connor said.

"Ben and Sheila are gonna flip when they see the footage. This is gonna be one hell of a final product," Kate bolstered.

"I know, it's astounding," Connor said, "which leads me back to the visions."

"What exactly did you see?" Kate said.

"Well, they were brief and so many of them, some were like little movie clips, but they painted a really big picture."

"Of what?" Kate said.

"Our entire trip flashed, but it wasn't of my doing. I'm telling you it came from that tiger, as crazy and insane as it sounds. I was shown everything, the bones in the cave, the stuffed Koala, the rusted car, then I saw other things, I saw a young boy playing with a tiger and the love between them, then I saw death, destruction, I saw misery, torment, cruelty. But the last thing, the last thing I saw was, was this, here, the tigers were here living in peace, unknown to the outside world."

"Do you believe what you saw?" Kate asked.

"I don't know what to believe anymore. It feels like everything I've learned—"

"I know," Kate interrupted. "None of this was in the textbooks."

"Textbooks?" Mac laughed. "We've got suicidal *Tasmanian* tigers leaping off cliffs, we've got intelligent tigers, we've got video of their freaking funeral congregation, and god knows—now there's some unseen telepathic communication going on between them and *you*."

Connor looked at Mac. "The elders at Fitzroy crossing were on to something."

"You mean you're believing the story that old abo told ya?" Mac said.

"How else can you explain any of this?" Connor said.

"Crazy thing is I'm starting to believe a wee bit of it too," Mac said.

"I can't even begin to understand what we've witnessed here," Connor said.

"How long have they been here?" Kate asked.

"Who the hell knows? That den is massive," Connor said.

"You did it, Connor, you really did it," Kate smiled. "They're gonna have to rewrite some of the textbooks. What's the world gonna say when they see this?"

Mac shook his head. "Even worse, what are they gonna do?"

Kate's smile dissipated.

Mac couldn't face the group; instead he stared at the ground, contemplating the evils mankind would unleash upon the tigers, for the second time.

Connor looked at Kate, her energy shifted from excitement to a depressed silence, their eyes met in an exchange of sadness.

"Great job, everyone," he said. "It's been one hell of a day. Thanks for everything. I don't know about you guys, but I think it's time to call it a night."

Within minutes, everyone disappeared into their tents. Connor and Kate didn't speak for more than an hour as both their minds tried to make sense of everything they witnessed.

"Did you hear that?" Kate asked.

"I thought it was you," he said. "That rustling?"

Kate sprung up. "There's something scratching at the tent."

"Probably a hungry possum." Connor grinned a bit.

Kate unzipped the door then panned her flashlight. "Oh, my God, Connor." Kate pushed the tent flap aside, revealing the cause.

"What the heck is he *doing* out there?" Connor sped to his knees.

Kate made a few mock kissing sounds with her lips and extended her hand to entice the small tiger pup. There he was, sitting on his bottom just outside the tent, staring at Kate with his head cocked sideways.

"Connor, he's adorable," she almost cried.

"Couldn't be more than three or four months old, post pouch," Connor said. "He must've wandered from the den."

Kate leaned out of the tent and scooped up the pup. She sat the tiger in her lap. "He's got no fear at all."

"It's like when Darwin visited San Cristobal Island. The animals had no fear of humans, they had never seen one before and didn't associate them as a threat." Connor ran his hand over the pup's brilliant stripes, stroking his velvety coat.

"These tigers have had total isolation," Kate said. "No pollution, no habitat destruction, no imprisonment, no hunting. It's like they're living on another world. They've never had to fear us."

"Until now." Connor looked deep into the pup's innocent blackened eyes.

"I guess we should get George. This is definitely film-worthy."

"I don't know." Connor inhaled slowly, until his lungs reached full capacity.

"What do you mean? You don't want to film this little guy? It's not every day we get this kind of opportunity."

"I feel sick, Kate."

"I'm falling in love with this lil' guy. Maybe we should take him back with us." The pup looked up at Kate and licked her chin. "Why do you feel sick?"

"For what you just said. Humans have now touched the tigers."

What did I say that could have made him feel sick? She pondered her last few words, then it clicked.

Connor caressed his stubble. "And we've only been here for a day. Imagine what's gonna happen when the world finds out."

"I should have known better."

"Once this footage goes public, people are gonna be lining up to see 'em. They'll pave the way and turn this place into a god-damned tourist attraction."

"But they'll be labeled an endangered species, they'd be protected."

"A label isn't what they need, Kate. This forest, everything we've seen here, the magic, the purity, it'll be stripped, reduced to an attraction for the enjoyment of the most destructive species on the planet. Sure, they'll be protected all right, by fences, rules, and government stipulations. How many pups will be taken in the name of science? How many will be put down for autopsy?"

A chattering of beautiful song-like chirps came from outside the tent.

The pup's ears sprung to attention and he darted from Kate's lap, straight out of the unzipped door.

"Mama's calling." Kate smiled.

Connor sat on his knees and peeled back the tent door. The pup was rolling on its back in front of the mother, kicking his feet wildly playful. The large female sniffed her pup, examining the strange human scents among its fur.

Connor and Kate watched the happy reunion until an abrupt thud and clank sent both animals sprinting off into the forest. Connor pushed Kate's flashlight toward the noise and saw Carl prying himself off the ground. He had been awakened by the chattering of the mother and in his failed attempt to film her; fell over on top of his camera.

Connor released the tent flap and zippered it back down. "That's what's in store for the tigers, and it's just the beginning."

THE TAPES

The morning arrived, and Kate tried to arouse Connor out of the tent. She rubbed his shoulder and called to him, but he grumbled, staying wrapped in the warmth of his sleeping bag.

Everyone was up, sitting in their chairs, waiting on Connor who was now more than two hours behind his usual schedule. The group finished breakfast and waited for him to rise.

Mac itched his scalp through the tangled mess of curly golden and black locks. "You sure he's even in there?"

"We had a late night." Kate rolled her eyes.

"There were some tigers scavenging around the tents last night," Carl said.

"Oh, no there was not." Kate sat up straight. "It was a mother looking for its lost pup."

The zipper on Connor's tent started a long slow ascent to the top. He stepped out, walked over to his chair, and sat down without speaking. He stared off into the forest, his face blank. Everyone could tell something was wrong; he was behaving way out of character.

They waited about four minutes as no one was brave enough to interrupt his uncharacteristic silence, but then he spoke. "I'm sorry, so, so sorry everyone."

"So you slept in a few hours, no big deal." Mac laughed.

Kate pulled her knees to her chest. She knew what was coming.

Connor stared into the smoldering fire, "Destroy the tapes," he muttered.

George stared into the fire, pondering Connor's words, deciphering, analyzing, and readjusting. George pressed the small grey eject button, which after a series of mechanical buzzing, jettisoned the latest cartridge of tiger material. George plucked it from the housing with gritty fingernails then tossed it into Connor's lap.

Carl's face went crooked. "Ha, ha, ha, he's joking of course."

Kate shifted focus to the smoldering embers. "It's the only way."

Carl's voice strained. "You're joking, tell 'em you're joking, it's not funny."

"He's not joking, mate," Mac said. "I've got your back on this Connor, I'm with ya."

"Come on, man, that's not even funny."

"I'm sorry, Carl," Connor said, still staring into the forest.

Carl clung tighter to his camera. "There's no way, no way you're serious, no way. I know you're joking."

"The tapes," Connor said shifting his gaze to Carl.

"Fuck that. You're not getting *my* footage. It's mine," Carl snapped.

"Give him your tapes, Carl," Kate said.

"You're all fucking crazy, you're not touching my footage."

Mac sighed. "Carl, just give it up."

Carl wrapped his arms around the camera. "I didn't hike my ass through all this shit and risk my life to just throw it all away, you're all fucking nuts."

"This is bigger than us, Carl." Connor's words were tired.

"I shot this video fair and square, its mine."

"It's not yours. Just give it to 'em," George said.

Carl looked at George in desperation. "How can *you* just give him your tapes? You shot that shit yourself and you worked hard for it. You know just as well as I do that its prize footage. How can you just hand it over?"

"It was easy, and you're gonna do it too."

"Fuck no I won't, this ain't right." Carl's voice cracked. "I'm keeping my tapes."

"They're not your tapes, Carl," Kate fired off. "They're the property of Natural Production's."

Carl began incessantly nodding his head in agreement. "That's right, they're the property of Natural Productions, and the last time I checked you weren't the owner. I'm bringing these back to Ben and Sheila."

"Just give 'em up, mate," Mac pleaded. "Do something right for once in your life."

"Go to hell," Carl snapped.

Connor kept his mild, tired tone. "Carl, listen to me. If we show the world what we've discovered here, we'll ruin everything. There's something special going on out here, and mankind isn't responsible enough to know about it…at least not yet."

"People have a god-damned right to know. You can't just cover it up. They're gonna find out one way or another." Carl stomped off to his tent with the camera held tight.

"Now what?" Mac asked.

"We'll *take* the tapes from him," Connor said.

"Good luck, I think he'll fight ya for 'em," Mac said.

"I'll handle it," George rumbled.

"No, George, I don't want you getting involved, you'll end up killing him," Connor said.

"And what's wrong with that?" Mac said.

"Even if we get the tapes, he's still gonna tell everyone back home," Kate said.

"What's he gonna say? That we went on an expedition to find the Thylacines, found them, tons of 'em, a massive den of 'em, and then destroyed all the evidence?" Connor said.

Kate stood and crossed her arms. "Good point. And if he says we witnessed an intentional suicide, by a cliff diving tiger in what looked to be a funeral congregation or some sort of mass mourning—"

Mac tapped on his noggin. "They'd reckon his think-tank sprung a leak."

"One last time, is everyone in agreement this is the right thing to do?" Kate turned to look at Connor.

"Yep," George said.

Mac nodded.

Connor looked away from the forest and into her eyes. "Without question."

A NIGHT TO REMEMBER

The homeward journey would begin in the morning, so everyone relaxed for the rest of the day. Connor, George, Mac, and Kate spent the day reminiscing over the trip and all its perils. Carl spent most of the day hidden within his tent. The sun was finally setting, signaling the last night before returning. A strong sense of wellbeing gave a renewed energy, fueled by the pact they had made to protect the secrecy of the tigers. The only problem would be with Carl, but who would believe the word of a less than honorable camera man, when paired against a respectable team of biologists? Their secret was safe if all the evidence was destroyed.

Kate sipped on her watered-down coffee; she was growing fond of its diluted nature. "I'm really gonna miss this. Just being together with you guys out here. It's been the most incredible adventure."

Connor carved away at a two-foot section of a stick, whittling the end to a point. "Indeed, it has. It feels good to look back on everything. We've been through a lot and I don't wanna get too sweet on ya, but Mac, I consider you my friend, not a paid guide."

"You're still paying me though. Right?"

"Seriously Mac, you've been such a pleasure to be around." Kate smiled. "Jesus, I'm gonna miss you."

"I love the flattery and all and I hate to change the subject, but what about the tapes?" Mac asked.

"Carl's been denned up in that damned tent with all the video," George said.

"Are we gonna destroy the entire expedition footage?" Kate asked.

"No, it'll still make for a great feature, we've had so much drama, and we just need the last few days of film," Connor said.

"Are you gonna show the bone pile?" Mac asked.

"I really haven't thought about it yet. How could we explain it?"

"Maybe you could show the bones as the last evidence of a massacre," Mac said.

"Sounds like it's settled, and that's how we'll portray it," Connor said.

"But we need to destroy the footage," Kate said.

Connor stood up and looked at Carl's tent. "We will. I'll talk to him again."

"Good luck, mate, that bloke ain't giving it up," Mac said.

The rest of the team watched as Connor walked over to Carl's tent and stood outside the door. "Carl?"

"What?" Carl snapped.

"Can I talk to you?"

"If you think you're gonna convince me to hand over the footage, it ain't gonna happen."

"Carl, we can't bring those tapes back, there's too much at stake here. The tigers are…" He paused.

"You're wasting your breath. You're not getting 'em."

"Carl, listen to me carefully. There are two ways we can do this—*the easy way*," Connor paused. "Or *the hard way*."

"Fuck you, Connor."

"I guess it's *the hard way* then," Connor looked over at the group and shook his head, smiling. He grinned as he walked back to the group.

"He's gotta come out sooner or later," Mac said.

"Or we just go in there and take the damned tapes," George said.

"I'd like to be as non-confrontational as possible, *if* possible."

"Oh, it's gonna get ugly," Mac said.

"Go ahead and start a fire, make it big," Connor said.

———

Forty-five minutes later the fire was roaring, four feet in diameter with flames well over four feet high. The chill was creeping in, colder than usual, and the night a little darker. They sat close to the fire, absorbing its dry toasty heat.

"You think he's pissin' in there?" Mac thumbed at Carl's tent.

"That sicko is probably drinking it," Kate quipped.

"Well, ladies and gentlemen." Connor stood. "It's time to take back what is ours."

"Got a plan?" Mac asked.

"Just follow my lead," Connor said. "Kate, you stay in the background, don't get involved."

Connor walked to Carl's tent with George on one side and Mac on the other.

"Alright, Carl, last chance to hand 'em over."

"Go to hell," Carl's voice fired from within the tent.

Connor grabbed the zipper, pulled it to its peak, then opened the flap.

"Give 'em to me." Connor peered into the tent.

"I don't have 'em, asshole."

Connor reached in, grabbed Carl's arm, and pulled him out of the tent. George grabbed and held him from behind by both arms. Carl tried to struggle free but was no match for George's brute strength.

"Let me go, you son of a bitch." He struggled. "I'll sue your fucking ass."

George squeezed a bit harder.

Connor rummaged through Carl's tent. Connor sprung out of the tent, enraged. He grabbed Carl's shirt collar with tight fists and pulled his face close. "Where are they, Carl?"

George released Carl to Connor.

"Where. Are. The. Tapes?"

"I told you I don't have 'em."

Connor tightened up on his collar, cutting off some of the blood flow to Carl's head. "So you sliced your tent apart at the seam, you snuck out and hid them in the woods huh?"

"That sneaky lil' devil," Mac said.

"You're...choking...ughhhh...me." Carl coughed.

"I'd tell him where the tapes are mate, he's not muckin' around," Mac said.

"Fu...uck...ugh...you," Carl choked.

Connor shoved Carl as hard as he could backwards, sending him toppling over, landing on his back.

"You're finished, you motherfucker," Carl screamed from his earthy landing pad. "I'm suing you for everything you've got."

"Ah, ah, ah," Mac shook his finger at Carl. "You'd better speak nicely to him. He's your only way out of the forest."

"Fuck you, asshole, I can get outta here myself."

"We've gotta find the footage," Connor said to the others.

"You'll never find it, and you can trust me on that, you son of a bitch." Carl stumbled to his feet, darted into the tent, grabbed his camera then ran into the woods via the back door.

"He's taking off with the camera!" Kate yelled.

"It's empty, I opened it when I was in the tent," Connor said.

"Maybe we should follow him?" Mac asked.

"Nah, he'll be back. He left his pack here." Connor opened it, and saw uneaten food, two water rations, clothes, med kit, miscellaneous hygiene supplies and stuffed deep inside an interior pocket, a single digital memory cartridge aka a tape. Connor pulled it from the bag and studied it, unlabeled.

"I wonder what's on that one?" Kate said.

George was walking back to his tent to retrieve the other camera. "Let's find out."

———

Carl ran through the forest, trying to trace his way back to the hidden cartridges. He stopped running, and then twisted his head in every direction, expecting to find the team chasing him. His hot breath puffed in the moonlight. He searched for any sign of where he may have left them. *Fuck, where are they?*

Carl ran further into the forest, panicked and looking for any familiar landmark. *God-damn it.* Carl spotted a large fern patch and ran to it, pushing and pulling the leafy green plants in a futile attempt to locate the footage. "Damn it! I've lost 'em," he cried. Carl twisted his head from side to side, his beady eyes squinted, his bounding heart forced his lungs to rapidly expel hot billowed swirls in and out of the cold night air. He cried; the thought of losing his precious footage was unbearable.

He paused for a moment then began rummaging through his pockets until he felt what he was after, deep within his jacket he could feel the rigidity of a hard-plastic cartridge still in its packaging. He plucked it out, ripped off the plastic wrapping, dropping it to the forest floor, then slid the cassette into his camera.

"I'll get the footage." Carl started toward the mounds.

————

George sat in a chair, holding the camera while everyone else gathered behind him.

"Probably blank," Mac said.

George pressed play.

The screen fluttered then went black, then it came back on. The footage started on the ground with the sound of footsteps. It panned up then went blank again. A few seconds later, the screen lit again, this time the footage was a total blur, only the sounds of footsteps could be heard, then a second later it became clear. It was the team, hiking single file, filmed from behind. The camera zoomed in on Lisa and it closed in on her ass, remaining there for more than thirty seconds as she hiked, then the footage went blank again.

"He had a woody for Lisa's ass," Mac said.

"God-damned pervert," Kate grunted.

The footage kicked in again, this time the green ambience of the night vision illuminated the screen followed by the sound of someone taking methodical slow steps coupled with the sound of slow crushing leaves and twigs. A few leafy branches passed in front of the screen.

The stepping stopped, and Carl's heavy breathing was the only sound audible. The camera zoomed in from afar, capturing Connor's backside as he held Kate against a tree in deep penetration. George's split-second reaction stopped the tape and at that very moment, Kate gasped.

"I'll fucking kill him!" she screamed. "That *god-damned* pervert was in the *god-damned* bushes filming us."

George pulled the cartridge from the camera and handed it to Connor. "I'm sure there's more on it."

"That guy has some serious mojo problems," Mac said. "He's a certified pervie."

Kate stomped her feet, screamed, and shook her entire body. "I feel so violated. I wonder what else is on that god-damned tape."

"He's reckless, and now he's gonna rat out the tigers," Mac said.

"No, he's not." Connor started walking in the direction Carl had fled. "I'll handle it."

The forest was cold. Connor's breath swirled as he moved with driven purpose, tracking every clumsy footstep. The clues were many; his scuffling feet and crumpled ferns, left a vivid trail of bread crumbs, all Connor had to do was follow them.

RETRIBUTION

Back at the camp site, Kate paced. "Guys, you gotta stop Connor."

"He's just gonna confront him, maybe give 'em a good wallop, and get the footage back. He's a smarty. I don't see 'em killing the bastard," Mac said.

"Did you see the look in his eye? Did you hear his voice?" Kate said. "Something was different."

"I did, but it doesn't mean he's gonna go kill 'em," Mac said. "George, you know him pretty well. What do you think?"

"Not sure."

"Does he deserve to die for what he did though?" Kate asked.

George studied Kate's face. "Probably," he mumbled.

Mac spoke up. "Look, Kate, don't assume Connor's gonna kill 'em. He's going out there to get the tapes back."

———

Carl could see the moonlit clearing just ahead. His greed for an Emmy forced his feet to speed up. He slowed as he reached the tree-line, panning his camera for tigers. He knelt in a bed of ferns, concealed in the darkness, sitting motionless, anxious.

Twenty minutes into his stakeout, the chirping of a tiger rang out from across the clearing. He jerked the camera, trying to find the source, squinting into the viewfinder. A heavy thud slammed into the middle of his back, tumbling him several feet into the clearing. He landed on his stomach while the camera landed fifteen feet away.

Carl was dazed for a couple seconds but recovered and spun over onto his ass. "What the fuck are you doing?"

"What should have been done long ago, Carl." Connor's voice left no room for negotiation.

"Look, I tried to find the cartridges, I searched, I can't find 'em," he pleaded as Connor approached. Carl put his hands over his head, but Connor had already grabbed a fistful of the reddish-brown hair. He jerked the man to his feet. "I'm not gonna fight you, Connor! I'm not fighting!"

"Good." Connor threw a vicious right cross that collided with Carl's left cheek bone, sending him backwards, tumbling over a four-foot mound.

Carl sat up on his ass and wiped the stinging blood from his left eye. He saw Connor walking around the mound with an unstoppable pace. "I'm sorry, I'm sorry. Look, I'm sorr—"

Connor's foot thudded into Carl's chest, knocking the wind from his lungs.

"Help me me meeee can't ba ba breeeeaatthhe," Carl gasped, trying to fill his lungs with air.

Connor grabbed Carl's hair and jerked him to his feet again.

"Please," Carl cried.

Connor sent a gut popping knee into his abdomen.

Carl barreled over. "Uuuugggghhhhhh."

Connor's focus was broken by the appearance of reflective green eyes watching from the opposite tree-line. Connor knew the footage was lost. Carl would never have taken a beating like that had he known where it was.

He looked down at the pathetic man, bloodied on the ground, condemning him with a wicked gaze.

Connor turned and started walking in the direction of the camp.

After a few steps he stopped, turned back toward Carl. "By the way, I found your little tape." Connor shook the small black cassette in the air, and then disappeared into the forest.

Carl trembled. He had been made. His squirrelly mind started working; *How can I explain the tape? I can come up with an explanation. Sex sells.*

Carl noticed the camera was a few feet away and the red record light was still on. He scrambled over to it, snatched it up and verified that it had been recording. *I've got that motherfucker, all the evidence I need is right here. I'll sue that fucker.* Carl grinned. "He's done."

Carl spotted some movement along the tree-line; three large tigers had emerged and were advancing, dozens more were appearing and entering the clearing. "Fuck, yeah! I've got that asshole assaulting me, and now I've got tiger footage."

Carl watched from the viewfinder as the tigers kept moving in his direction. The skinny man pulled the viewfinder away from his eye and glanced around, the tigers were everywhere, circling him, standing on the mounds, all watching while the largest three continued to advance. Carl started laughing. When all hope was lost, he unknowingly captured his beating, and was now filming hundreds of tigers in their den, all on his very last cartridge.

Carl backed away when the group of large tigers disappeared from his zoom, too close to view. They were within twenty feet of him and still advancing. An aggressive snarl from behind sent him spinning. He was surrounded by the largest tigers in the den.

Oblivious, Carl panned his camera over the mass of tigers. "Goddamn! Look at 'em all." He lowered his camera to hip level and walked toward the largest to get a close-up head shot. He neared the tiger with his camera extended. Without warning, the massive tiger snapped, smashing the camera between its oversized jaws, ripping it from Carl's hands. With a few vicious head shakes, the camera was reduced to a pile of mangled plastic and metal, tossed behind them.

Carl kicked at the tiger, but it didn't budge. "Fuck you," he snapped. *Fuck the camera, I just need the tape.* He tried to walk through the tigers but was snapped at by another large tiger. His heart raced, panicked. He looked around, twisting, and jerking in every direction. He was surrounded by tigers. He tried to walk but was met by smacking teeth in every direction.

Carl noticed a lone silhouetted figure along the tree-line; Connor was standing just in the shadows, watching.

"Could I get a little help here, please?" Carl advanced a little further into the barricade of Thylacines, triggering a smaller female to lash out, sinking its teeth into his right upper calf. The bite went deep, and with a simple shake of its head, it ripped through his pant leg, tearing most of the meaty-muscle from the bone.

"Ahhh, God!" Carl screamed as he fell to the ground. He looked down at what used to be his right calf. "Help me! Help me! Help me!"

He struggled to his feet, screaming in terror. "Connor! Do something!"

The silhouetted figure didn't move.

Carl tried to balance on one leg, while his other leg spurted blood. "For God's sake, man, help me!"

The Thylacines started moving in.

Carl dropped to his knees and looked the massive Thylacine in its eyes. "Fuck you," he spat at it.

The figure in the tree-line watched as a Thylacine grabbed Carl's shoulder from behind, pulling him over backwards into a writhing ball of snarling tigers. His screams were short lived.

———

Kate paced around the fire, circling then reversing, then repeating. "I can't take this," she blurted. "We should go find them."

"Connor's a big boy, he'll be fine," Mac said.

"Carl's a conniving bastard, Mac. I don't trust him."

"Trust me when I say there is *nothing* Carl could do to hurt Connor," George said.

"I'm just worried about him."

"Its outta your hands, sweetheart. Just put your feet up, relax and have faith in the greater good," Mac said. "He'll be back soon."

Kate dropped into her camp chair, pulled her knees to her chin, and stared into the dying fire.

The subtle crunch of approaching footsteps caught Kate's attention first. They all stood, watching as a lone figure emerged from the darkness.

"Oh, thank God!" Kate sprung to her feet and ran toward him but stopped mid-way. "You, your, your hands are bloody." Her stomach sank. As much as she hated Carl, the thought of Connor killing him, sickened her. "You killed him?"

"It's my blood." Connor looked down at his bloody hands. His knuckles were lacerated from connecting with Carl's cheekbone. His face was blank.

Kate rushed to Connor. "Oh, my God, are you ok?"

"I'm fine, it's just my hands." He spoke slowly and quietly while Kate and Mac hammered him with questions.

"You found him?" Mac asked, serious.

"Yeah."

"Get the tapes?"

"No."

"You guys have a tussle?" Mac peered at Connor's bloodied hands.

"Yeah."

"Split your knuckles on his face?"

"Yeah."

"Did you kill him, Connor?" Kate cried out.

Connor looked up from his hands and into Kate's eyes, pausing.

"No."

"Oh, thank God. I was so scared."

"The tapes?" George asked.

"They're lost." Connor mumbled.

"Forgot where he put 'em, didn't he? Not sure I'd believe him, mate," Mac said.

"The tapes are lost."

Kate took Connor's hands and studied the wounds. "He's lying, Connor. He knows where they are and as soon as he can, he'll come back to get them."

"He won't be doing that."

"How can you be sure?" Mac asked.

"He's dead."

Kate gasped and staggered backwards a few steps, distancing herself from Connor. She stared into Mac's eyes, unable to look at Connor. "He killed him," she murmured, barely audible.

"No, no, no," Mac said.

"Kate, I didn't kill Carl."

Kate looked Connor in the eyes, "Where is he?"

"He's back at the den, well, what's left of him."

"So he is dead?"

"He is."

"The tigers?" she whispered, barely audible.

"The tigers."

RETRIBUTION

Tasmania - 1935

HE TRIED TO SILENCE HIS FOOTSTEPS AS THE LOOSE DIRT AND gravel crunched beneath his feet. He never wore his service belt while on duty, but tonight it hung proudly around his waist. Shiny, polished steel handcuffs swung from the left and the wooden grip of a blue steel .38 revolver seated perfectly in its holster sat on the right. A shiny silver sheriff's star glistened on the front of his belt. The orchestra of nocturnal insects was overpowering, drowning the footsteps as he continued his slow but steady ascent up the driveway.

Earlier today it was business as usual, nothing out of the ordinary. Breakfast was great, lunch was better, but then he caught wind of the bounty. A good family he had known was broken. The wind whispered a father and son were on the run with an evil price on their heads.

He stepped upon the dimly-lit porch, as he had countless times before. This time it felt unrecognizable, its familiarity was gone. Reaching out, he grabbed the outer door and squeezed the latch. It was locked.

"Damn it," he sighed.

Earl pondered on his drive to the ranch. How many lives had been broken by the controlling arm of Tasmania? How many injustices had been done under his watch? How could it have become so out of control? Years ago, he took an oath, he swore to protect and serve the people of

Tasmania, but his integrity had been swept under the rug, pushed aside, and covered up by less than honorable men. The first few years of his own daughter's life were a blur, drowned in alcohol, numbing him to the disservice and treachery he provided as sheriff.

Earl knocked hard on the heavy outer metal door. It was louder than hell and there was no turning back.

He had never been more sure of himself. Day after day and year after year he had to look the other way while the controlling arm of Tasmania ran amuck. Good men were broken, families up-heaved and livelihoods stolen, time and time again, all while he looked the other way. Never again.

From the outside, he could see a body shuffling around behind the opaque glass of the inner door.

"Who the fucks out there?"

"It's me, Earl."

"God-damn it, what the fuck you want this time of night?" McPherson bitched, his voice still muffled from his prior tongue slashing.

Earl watched the shadowy figure fumble with an array of locks he had installed since his near fatal encounter with Greg McKinley. The inner door swung open to reveal McPherson. He was wearing white briefs with his fat gut hanging over the elastic band, a half-smoked cigar was clenched between his teeth and a rifle in his hands. A rush of spiced cologne and cigar smoke entered Earl's nostrils.

"What is it? Whaddya want?" McPherson unlocked the outer door and cracked it open.

Earl grabbed the partially open door and pulled it open, stepping in close to the fat man.

"It's over, Joe."

"What's over? You get that fucker that stuck me?"

"You're under arrest." Earl didn't blink, and his head was high.

"That's real god-damned funny, now why the hell you at my ranch this time a night?"

"I'm taking you in. Put the gun down." Earl rested his hand on the butt of his holstered revolver.

"Ha, ha, ha, listen, Mr. Sheriff, I own you. Now shut the fuck up and get outta here." McPherson tried to close the inner door, but Earl stopped it dead with his boot. Earl pulled the cuffs from his belt.

Earl's and McPherson's eyes became locked in a stalemate. Joe's grip tightened on his rifle and Earl noticed it.

"Don't even think about—" Earl cut himself off when Joe began to raise his rifle.

Earl kept his hand pressed on the grip of his revolver and grabbed the barrel of Joe's rifle with his left hand. He struggled to keep it down with one arm as McPherson tried to raise it with both. "Joe, don't do it."

Joe started to overpower Earl. The rifle barrel started making its way toward the sheriff's abdomen. "Drop it, Joe! God-damnit, this is your last warning!" Earl wrestled it with one arm.

Earl didn't come to McPherson's ranch to kill him. He was there to arrest him, to bring him in and to finally set an example. He wanted the people of Tasmania to witness the fall of a tyrant. He wanted the people to know that sooner or later, justice catches up with everyone, no matter who. Earl knew bringing in McPherson, placing him in jail and filtering him through the judicial system would be monumental for Tasmania. Earl was prepared to testify, condemning himself but saving his soul.

The rifle barrel started teetering within an inch or two of Earl's abdomen. He could no longer maintain control and without hesitation drew his pistol and cocked the hammer with lightning speed. In one quick motion, he placed the barrel against Joe's temple and squeezed.

The Mighty Joe McPherson was no more.

The End

Don't miss out on your next favorite book!

Join the Melange Books mailing list at
www.melange-books.com/mail.html

THANK YOU FOR READING

Did you enjoy this book?

We invite you to leave a review at the website of your choice, such as
Goodreads, Amazon, Barnes & Noble, etc.

DID YOU KNOW THAT LEAVING A REVIEW...

- Helps other readers find books they may enjoy.
- Gives you a chance to let your voice be heard.
- Gives authors recognition for their hard work.
- Doesn't have to be long. A sentence or two about why you
  liked the book will do.

ABOUT THE AUTHOR

Ever wanted to experience the thrill of danger from the comfort of your own reading space?

Thomas fuels his writing with true life experience – from being chased by frenzied sharks, to being bitten by eighteen-foot pythons, and having survived more than a few near-death experiences. He lives for adventure and spends his free time studying wildlife, reading, writing and pushing himself to extremes whether it's scuba-diving, free-diving, shark-diving, spearfishing, capturing feral species in the Everglades, fossil hunting in the alligator infested waters of Florida and more.

Thomas has a true love for the natural world and has studied wildlife biology and natural sciences.

His writing influences are the likes of Stephen King, Robert McCammon, Dean Koontz, James Rollins, Clive Cussler, J.R.R Tolkien and more. Action, adventure and horror are his genre favorites. In his writing you will find swashbuckling thrills, chills, adventure, horror, war, werewolves, historical fiction, Nazis, serial killers, paranormal, wildlife, conservation, twists and unexpected turns, and there is often a hero among the rubble - standing up to the various injustices of humanity.

Thomas understands writing can be mundane at times, but he yearns for the build up to the vivid action and gratuitous horror sequences, and the ability to convey a greater message to mankind. True life experience is key to the climactic intensity of his writing.

www.twpeltier.com
ThomasWPeltier@gmail.com
twitter.com/ThomasPeltier
https://www.facebook.com/TWPeltier
https://www.instagram.com/groundedspirit

Made in the USA
Columbia, SC
04 December 2018